At Their Mercy

Bennett Crime World Book 1

Mia Fury

TRIGGER WARNING

THIS BOOK ISN'T YOUR typical romance. The guys are mean, they do mean things, and these may offend some readers. If you have triggers, then sadly, this book may not be for you.

The book features stalking, violation of privacy, kidnapping, captivity, threats, violence, murder, dubcon/noncon, mind games, coercion, oh... and bad language.

I do not condone their behaviour, nor do I believe it has a place in the real world, but for the purposes of dark romance, I really hope you enjoy this book!

COPYRIGHT & DISCLAIMER

Names, characters, places and incidents within this book are either the product of the author's imagination or are used fictitiously, and any resemblance to actual persons, living or dead, business establishments, etc. is purely coincidental.

Copyright © Mia Fury 2021

All rights reserved. No part of this text may be reproduced, scanned, transmitted, or distributed in any printed or electronic form without permission.

Cover Artwork Copyright © Anya Kelleye Designs 2021

Website: anyakelleye.com

All rights reserved. No part of this image may be reproduced, scanned, transmitted, or distributed in any printed or electronic form without permission.

STALK ME

Join my mailing list to stay up to date and gain access to bonus materials:
https://mailchi.mp/1c8fb54b3542/newsletter-signup

If you want early access to everything, including bonus scenes, exclusive covers and more, come and join my Patreon group:
www.patreon.com/miafury

Want to be involved in discussions and have access to tons of giveaways? Join my reader group on Facebook:
www.facebook.com/groups/miasfuries

---

https://linktr.ee/MiaFury

CHAPTER ONE
HARVEY

I SAW THEM COMING to the door, and I knew. I just knew that I was in the shit, and nobody was going to be able to help me. *I owed them money.* A lot of it. You don't owe the Bennetts money, and get away with not being able to pay it back. I guess, when I borrowed it, I'd stupidly believed that I'd somehow find the money before this happened.

Samuel turned the sign on the door, showing anyone outside that my bookstore was suddenly closed, and he turned the lock. My stomach rolled, as I heard that ominous click. His brother, Seb, was watching me, clearly enjoying my panic. He grinned widely.

"Hello, Harv... long time no talk. Probably because you've been dodging our calls, bruv." He smirked as Samuel joined him, on the other side of my counter. It was nothing. It wouldn't save me. Nothing would.

"Seb, Samuel... look, I'm so sorry. I'm having a few cashflow problems right now. Books aren't the big business they used to be." I tried a smile, trying to appear as trustworthy, and willing to pay, as I really wished I could be.

Three months ago, the bank were trying to take this place away from me. A moment of weakness, some bad advice, and a whiskey or three, had sent me to their doorstep. They'd saved my business. But now... now... I owed these guys twenty-five grand, and they wanted it back.

"Harv... we're not being assholes here. You promised you'd have paid us back within two months, mate. We gave you an extra month. *A whole month*. That's because we're nice guys. Now, you're just taking the piss."

Samuel was shaking his head, playing along with his brother.

"Yeah, it's not nice, bruv. We did you a favour. We saved your business. This is how you repay our kindness?"

Fuck. I'm in so much shit. They're playing with me. They know I don't have their damn money. The question is... what are they going to do to me? Dead guys can't pay, right?

"Honest, guys. I'm trying. I have... Maybe three grand of it." I started rifling through papers on the counter, as if they would tell me a damn thing.

"*Three grand*. Wow... why didn't you say, Harv. That's so close to twenty-five fucking grand. I don't even know why we're hassling him, Seb, he's good for it." Samuel shrugged at his brother as he spoke.

Seb snorted. "Yeah... how many books do you even need to sell for that?" He picked up one of the books on the counter.

"'*In love with a demon*'? Who writes this shit? It's only a quid, bruv. How are you going to make back our money like this?" The book flew at my face, narrowly missing my eye.

"Fuck. Come on, please. You know I'm going to find your money. I didn't borrow from you, just so I could try screwing you over. I know better than that. I just need a little more time. Please." I was begging. I knew it. They knew it. Hell, anyone walking past the store would know it. Why the hell did I think that I could make enough money, in a few months, to pay them back? I'm a fucking idiot.

"I'll get a loan," I promised, holding my hands up.

"From who, bruv? You came to us, because nobody will loan you a fucking penny. We only loaned to you, because you put the store up as collateral. So I guess we own a bookstore now. Sammy, any idea how to run a bookstore? Apparently we start by stocking soft porn books... or are they hardcore, Harv? *Do they actually fuck the demons?* Big demon cocks, ramming into dainty little human girls? Is that what you like to read? You sick fuck."

They made their way to the end of the counter, striding slowly, and arrogantly. They had nothing to fear. They were the fucking Bennett brothers, and I'd fucked up, like never before. I should have let the bank take my business, declared bankruptcy, and walked away.

And why didn't I? *Her*. That's why. And what good had it done me? She still came here to buy her fucking books, but that was it. I just watch her, and want her, and jerk off in bed at nights, thinking of her. I don't speak to her. I'm a fucking pussy.

They'd reached my side of the counter. Seb grabbed my throat, and started dragging me to the back of the store, where nobody could see. They were going to kill me. *Fuck.* I prayed for someone, anyone, to save me.

CHAPTER TWO
HARVEY

They shoved me into the small flat that I live in, at the back of the store. I was thrown forcibly enough to crash into the opposite cupboard doors, which made them fall partially open, once I'd hit the floor. I shot a glance at the doors. Stay closed. Don't fucking open. *Don't let them see, please.*

I crawled away from the doors, my back and head hurting from the force of being slammed against them. One of the twins reached down and grabbed my hair, lifting my head just enough to slam a huge fist into my face. I fell back, wishing for fluttering cartoon birds, instead of the intense pain in my head and face.

"Please. I'll get your money, I swear," I whispered, as they both loomed over me. I'd seen the heavy boots on their feet, and I really didn't want them crashing into my face too.

"I'll do anything. Please," I begged.

They exchanged an amused look.

"They always end up saying that, don't they? *Okay*... what if we decided to run some other business through your little shop here?" One of them asked. Since they'd thrown and punched me, I honestly couldn't tell which was which. There were subtle differences between them, but right now, everything was strangely blurred.

"What kind of business?" I asked warily. I'd heard about their other businesses. I didn't want drugs being sold from my damn book shop. Mind you, wouldn't I prefer to be alive, to be pissed about it? What a fucking awful dilemma.

"Doesn't matter, Harv, old boy. It's our business. You just have to be open when we say, and pass packages to the people we tell you to. Simples," one of them said almost triumphantly.

"Is it drugs? I won't let you sell fucking drugs here," I muttered angrily, while being fully aware that they'd probably kill me instead. *Idiot.* Just sell the fucking drugs, and be alive.

A hand grabbed my hair again, and I was pulled to my feet. The hands went to my throat instead, gripping tightly.

"Doesn't look to me like you have much of a choice, bruv. You sell for us, or we kill you, and burn this place to the ground."

I gasped, pulling at his hands. "Those are the only fucking options? Come on. Give me something else. Anything else. *Please.* If you do that, you don't get your money." The other one had disappeared from my sight. Where had he gone? I didn't know the not knowing.

"Doesn't look like you're in much of a position to be making demands, Harv. You owe us a lot of money, and you signed the contract, you know that you forfeit your business to us by defaulting. We're being especially kind, by offering you a chance to keep it. All you gotta do is run some other business for us. The way I see it, we're offering you the best of both worlds."

He leaned close, glaring at me, his dark eyes boring into mine. I struggled to focus on them. There was madness there. That meant that it was likely Seb gripping me right now. He was known as the most dangerous of the two. *Fuck.*

"But drugs... come on! Kids buy their books here, man. And... if people find out, the business will be dead anyway." I was desperate to make them see sense.

Seb shrugged. "Then it'll just be a front for us. Either way we win, Harv. It's the nature of business. We're the big dogs, and you're the pathetic pussy who has no choice."

I frowned. Was he trying for a metaphor there? I suddenly realised why everything was so blurry. *My glasses.* Where the hell were my glasses? I'd heard a crunch earlier. Was that my fucking glasses? I was damn near blind without them. Unless something was right up close. Like Seb's ugly mug.

"Or we could just take his lady, bruv." My stomach rolled as Samuel said those words. I knew exactly where he was. At the cupboard doors. *Fuck.*

"NO!" I snapped, pulling at Seb's hands with renewed panic. *Not her.* He laughed.

"Yeah, I think we found it, bruv. The magic words. The one thing that'll really fuck him up, and make him do what we want. What's her name, Harv?"

I shoved at him. "Fuck you. I'm not telling you a fucking thing! You leave her alone, you hear me?" I was trying to punch *him* now, but I'm a pathetic, nerdy bookshop owner, and he's a fucking loan shark, crime lord type.

He threw me on the ground, slamming a foot into my stomach, leaving me curled up and gasping on the floor. Oh... and my head was pressing against something sharp. *I think I just found my glasses.*

"Who is she, bruv?" Seb was asking Samuel, as they pulled the cupboard doors wide, and looked at the hundreds of pictures of her. They were pinned all over the wall. **Her**. Her beautiful face. Her shiny, luscious black hair. That ass. All taken without her knowledge. Shopping. Drinking coffee with friends. Walking. *Sleeping.*

"You some kind of fucking stalker, mate? This is pretty fucked up," Samuel said, leaning closer to scrutinise the fragments of her life.

Seb laughed. "He stocks those demon porn things, mate. He gets off on this shit. You wank off, looking at these photos, Harv? I bet you do, you sad little prick. She's way out of your league. But not ours." He pulled a picture from the wall. And worse than that, I saw him grab my schedule. The planner that shows where she is, at various times of the week. At least as much as I've worked out, in five months and six days of knowing that she exists.

"No. Please. Don't hurt her. She's mine," I gasped out. A hand grabbed my hair again, pulling my head back. A photo blurred and moved in front of me, a bizarre mocking view of the woman I'd loved from afar for so long. "No!"

"She's fucking lovely, mate. I'm looking forward to fucking her. I think she'll be a nice sweetener for our little deal. You'll deal for us, and we'll fuck her brains out. At least until she's not so pretty anymore," Seb snarled, kicking me again.

"Please! Please don't hurt her. She doesn't deserve this. She's not a part of this!" I gasped out, desperate to save her from these monsters. I'd watched over her for so long. Protected her. *Loved her*. This couldn't be happening.

"Tell you what, mate. Because I'm feeling fucking kind... we'll take her. Then you'll have twenty-four hours to pay back everything you owe. And no calling the cops. You do that, and she goes free. *Unharmed*. After those twenty-four hours, if you're still hanging onto our money, she's ours. For whatever we want. I'm wondering if she's ever been fucked by twins before. At the same time. Each of us in a different fucking hole. Harv... don't beat yourself up, bruv. You couldn't have pulled a woman like her in a million years. Especially since you're just a pathetic fucking stalker. You did this to her. You brought her to us. I'll make sure she knows that, when I'm fucking her, and she's screaming for me to stop."

Then the kicking started, and the fists, and the agony.

CHAPTER THREE
Cassidy

I SAID GOODBYE TO Vanessa and Amy, my two besties, and headed back to work. I didn't even have time to stop by, and pick up those books I'd pre-ordered. Or did I? I glanced at my watch.

If I moved fast. If I went directly to the counter, and spoke to the cute guy, Harvey, and told him I was in a rush… he'd serve me quickly, and hurry me out of there. He was shy, but kind of sweet. Even if his eyes did seem to rest on me for just a little too long. Was it creepy, or cute? I hadn't decided yet. Time would tell.

I pushed my long black hair out of my eyes, wishing that my hair tie didn't snap earlier. Why do they do that? It had been all neatly pulled back, and smart for the office, and then I'd tried to tighten it, and damn… it hurts when the damn things snap like that, like an elastic band being flicked directly against my damn scalp.

And, of course, for some reason, I had no spares in my bloody handbag. Who doesn't have spares? I always carry spares! It was driving me nuts, hanging in my face, flicking into my eyes.

Shit. The door was closed, and the sign said closed. *Closed?* He's never closed for lunch. It was one of the things I loved about the place. Small enough that it was intimate, and actually smelled of books, and always open over lunch. A lot of small businesses couldn't usually manage that. People did need breaks, after all. I peered in the glass door, trying the handle, just in case.

"Hello?" I thought I heard someone call out in response, but it didn't happen again, when I shouted once more, so I sighed. Dammit. I'd have to find something to read on my e-reader for tonight. I much preferred the feel of actual books in my hands.

I turned to walk away, bumping straight into a big guy, bouncing back a few steps.

"Oh sorry, love," he said, with a charming London accent. Almost cockney, but not quite. More like they sound on *EastEnders*.

"No, it was my fault, I'm so sorry. I was... well, I guess I was distracted. He's not normally closed at lunch." I pointed at the bookshop, while I focused on the man's face. Dark hair, slightly scruffy. The stubbly start of a beard. Dark eyes. So dark, they were almost black. His lips quirked in a grin, but there was something unsettling about it. Knowing. *Dangerous*. I felt a little shiver down my spine, and backed up another step.

"Anyway, I'm sorry."

He shrugged. "I tend to enjoy it when sexy ladies brush up against me, love. It's all good." He smirked, and I shivered. There was something more than unsettling about him. Dark. *Threatening*. I cleared my throat.

"Anyway... Um... I need to get back to work." I turned and hurried away, just catching his words, as I rushed to put distance between us.

"I'm sure I'll be bumping into ya."

Crap, I really hope not. I practically ran back to the office, only slowing my pace when I stepped inside the building.

"Everything okay, Miss Cassidy? You look like you've seen a ghost," Bernie, the security guard said, stepping closer to the glass doors to peer outside. He clearly didn't see anything of concern, moving back to follow me, as I swiped my pass, and headed through the turnstile at reception.

I shrugged as I walked. "Just some guy creeping me out," I said, tossing my hair back because, damn, it just wouldn't stay back without help. Maybe Julie would have a spare tie, or something I could use. Or I might end up resorting to one of the elastic bands, from my ball of bands in my drawer.

I felt a chill down my spine, as I headed out of reception, turning to look back at the doors. I felt like I'd been followed from the bookshop, and I didn't like how vulnerable that made me feel.

HARVEY

LENORE FOUND ME. THANK God I gave her a key.

"H, what the hell happened?" She dragged me from the floor, depositing me onto the armchair across the room. I cast my eye away from the pool of blood on the floor. Everything hurt. Two of my fingers literally felt like they were twisted around, or bending completely backward. My ribs were screaming in pain. My head was bleeding, and so was my nose. My entire head was a throbbing mass of agony. My stomach felt like it had been dug out, and replaced with knives.

"Lenore," I murmured, unable to find any other words. I slumped in that chair, and passed out again.

CASSIDY

I'D DREADED THE END of the working day, so much. I knew that I'd have to go back outside, and there was this irrational fear inside me, that said that creepy guy would be out there waiting for me. Because he'd said so, hadn't he? That was a threat. A warning. A *promise*.

I'd debated working late, because I usually finish at three, and staying later would mean more people leaving at the same time. I prefer to start really early, purely so that I can finish earlier, on flexitime, but today that felt like a curse. Of course, staying later would mean walking home in the dark, since the clocks had changed just last week, and it's dark earlier now. There really wasn't a good solution to the problem.

I peered out from the upstairs windows, checking the street in both directions. No creepy dark-haired guys out there. It was just the normal flow of mothers, walking home with children from school, and the late shoppers. Why was I now trying to convince myself that that guy was stalking me?

Because I'd felt this way before, hadn't I? Not as overtly afraid as right now, but I'd often felt eyes on me. Often looked around, wondering if someone was out there, watching me. It was a creepy, skin crawling kind of feeling, and always made me feel relieved when I stepped into my home at last, and locked the door. And now, I was really afraid that I'd been right about someone watching me, and it was that scary guy from earlier.

Those eyes. They were full of something dark and dangerous. *Monstrous*.

"Aren't you off now, Cassidy? It's getting late. Don't you have your book group this afternoon?" Julie asked, glancing at the clock on the wall. Oh crap. She was right. Today's group was right across town, and we were meeting in twenty minutes.

I checked my bag, making sure my copy of this month's book was there. I'd finished it in one night, and hadn't even thought about it since. Some old school romance, which really didn't do it for me. The hero wasn't even a vampire, or a biker. Where was the 'treat 'em mean, keep 'em keen' part of the story? Honestly, I'd found it pretty dull.

I said my goodbyes, and hurried down the stairs, through reception, and out into the street. No longer did I worry about stalkers following me. I had to meet people, and I was never late.

To be honest, my preference of rather dark books was maybe what had made me wonder if I was being stalked. Did I want it? *No*. I was pretty sure that I didn't, but there was a romantic air about it in the books I read.

It was always some hot, damaged guy, who thought the woman was way out of his league, and loved her from afar, until circumstances put them together, and eventually led to that happy ever after moment. I really wanted one of those. To find my place with a man who loved and protected me, and was an animal in bed. I mean, who doesn't?

My mind was caught up in the wrong books as I ran to the meeting. My ability to participate in the book chat would be massively hampered, by the fact that I couldn't remember a single dull fact from that damn book they chose. Next time I wanted to choose. They'd probably be scandalised, as conservative as many of the members were.

That became the least of my worries though, when a hand snaked over my mouth, and I was pulled against a hard body, and dragged back into an alley.

"There you are, love. Been waiting for you."

Something sharp pinched at my neck, and then my consciousness started to fade, not even allowing me a second to try and fight.

CHAPTER FOUR
HARVEY

I struggled out of that chair, and shoved Lenore aside, as she tried to patch up the bleeding wound on my head.

"Do that one more time, and I'll kick you in the nuts," she snapped, shoving me back into the chair.

"I have to go! She's in danger," I said desperately. She quirked a brow at me, in that expert way she had.

"And you'll be one hell of a hero running to her rescue. Can you even make it two steps, before you pass out again? Jesus, Harvey."

I groaned and sat up again, just that small movement making me want to throw up again.

"You don't understand, Lenore. They'll hurt her. *Rape her*. I need to stop them," I gasped, holding onto my stomach, as it roiled dangerously.

"Who, H? Who did this?" Lenore asked, her anger spiking at the thought of a woman being in that kind of danger. I stared at her.

"Samuel and Seb Bennett."

Her eyes widened. "What the hell were those two psychos doing here? You know better than to let that kind of monster in here. They're practically mobsters!"

I glared at her. "Does it look like I *let* them do anything?"

She just smirked. "No... I'm sorry. I'm sure your face fought back really hard against their fists. The question is why they even know you exist, H."

She fixed me with a glare. "They want to run drugs through here," I said, thinking that maybe that would be enough for now, without the whole pathetic story.

She quirked that damn brow again.

"I know you would never allow that, H... still... how do they know of this place at all?"

I stood up, taking a moment to fight the nausea, before I could get my balance back.

"First we have to stop them getting her." I grabbed my phone, scrolling through and finding a number, and ringing it immediately. Thank God I'd found my spare glasses, or I wouldn't be able to see a damn thing.

"Harris and Associates," a woman's voice announced perkily. "Julie speaking."

I sighed. I'd hoped Cassidy herself would pick up.

"Hi Julie. Can I please speak with Cassidy Donovan?"

She paused for a second. "I'm afraid Cassidy left a few minutes ago. Can anyone else help you?"

I groaned. "Dammit. No, but thanks."

"Is everything okay?" She asked warily. I racked my brain trying to think about where she might be. They took my planner, and with my head throbbing as it is, I can't remember where she goes on a Monday.

"I just really need to speak to her. Any idea where she's gone?"

Julie fell silent. "Are you a friend of hers?" I stared at Lenore. *Fuck.*

"Uh... I have some books she ordered, but she didn't come by for them yet. I... uh... I'm closing soon," I half-lied.

"Oh, you're the bookshop guy?" She seemed to know of me. My heart soared for a moment. Does she notice me too? Does she talk about me?

"Yeah, I'm Harvey. She comes here pretty often." I shrugged at Lenore, biting back a wince of pain, because my back felt like it had been kicked too. Did they keep kicking me after I passed out?

"Oh. Okay, well, are you in her book club? That's where she's going now." Fuck. I should have remembered that. I nodded at Lenore.

"Dammit, of course she is. I'm not a member, but I know she goes there. She needs these books for that, I think," I lied.

"Sorry, Harvey. I don't know where she meets up with them. Maybe try the community hall."

Fuck. Of course. I'd seen her go there sometimes with the book club. They alternated between several places. I had them all written down. My head was awash with pain, and it was affecting my ability to remember her movements.

"Perfect, thanks Julie. I'll go find her."

She cleared her throat. "Is she safe, Harvey? You sound worried." Crap. I took a breath, trying to sound less like a creepy stalker, afraid for the life of my unknowing victim, and more like a normal person. I should be used to faking it by now.

"Uh... yeah, sure... why wouldn't she be? I just want to get these, uh... books to her. Thanks for your help, Julie."

I rang off before she could question me any further.

"Okay, so now you're going to tell me what the fuck is really going on. You're not really trying to deliver books to someone," Lenore stated sharply.

I frowned. "We need to get to the community centre, before they find her."

She glanced to the side of me, a frown on her face. "Is it her?"

I followed her eyes. *Jesus.*

"It's not what you think, Lenore." I strode over to the cupboard, slamming the doors closed on my Cassidy shrine.

"It looks to me like you're a fucking stalker, H. I thought I knew you better than that." She looked like she could barely hold back from kicking my ass. Lenore was tough, could absolutely kick my ass all the way around town, and looked like she really wanted to.

To be fair, she could probably take one of the Bennett brothers down too. She'd been training in various martial arts, and fighting techniques, for years. Ever since what happened to her, before we even met.

"If you've put this woman in danger because you're a creeper, I'm going to beat you down far worse than this. You're going to be pissing into a bag. You hear me?" She warned me.

I backed away from her, and the cupboard. "It's not like I wanted her hurt, Lenore. I was trying to reason with them, the twisted bastards, and they found... this... and they decided to go after her. I tried to stop them. I wouldn't hurt her!"

Lenore's fists clenched by her sides. "We save her first, and then I teach you the merits of not being a fucking perv." She pushed past me, and pulled the door open. My phone buzzed in my hand as I started to follow, and I glanced down. The number was unknown. I opened the text. *Fuck.*

UNKNOWN: *TWENTY-FOUR HOURS FROM NOW. NO FUCKING COPS OR YOU BOTH DIE.*

Holy shit, they've taken her already.

CHAPTER FIVE
CASSIDY

IT WAS DARK. I felt sick. My head was throbbing. I couldn't move. I tried to speak, and found that impossible too. There was something over my mouth.

The darkness suddenly disappeared, in a blaze of agonising light, that burned into my brain. I blinked, squeezing my eyes shut for a moment, although the brightness even seemed to seep through my eyelids. *A blindfold*. That was why it had appeared so dark.

"I'll still be here when you open them again, love." that voice said. That scary guy's voice. I shivered, trying to back away from him, but I really couldn't move. I was trapped. My eyes flew open.

He was grinning widely, like my intense terror were somehow a gift to him. He peeled the tape from my mouth, making me wince.

"Hello, love. Remember me?" I glared at him, trying to force anger in front of the fear.

"What did you do to me?" I struggled again, realising that I was tied to something. A chair. And he was straddling another chair, facing me. I glanced around the room. It was pretty plain. A sofa along one side of the room. Another guy sitting there, sipping a coffee. He looked almost exactly like the one in front of me. Twins?

"Wouldn't you rather know what we're going to do to you, love?" The man asked, casting his eyes down, letting them crawl over me, like something slimy and disgusting, but with way too many legs.

I gasped, looking at the other man.

"Help me, please."

The other guy just grinned. "I'm not your saviour, love. I'm just enjoying a cup of coffee." I looked back at the first guy.

"What do you want?" He lifted one eyebrow.

"Well, let's see... you're pretty enough as you are, but how much prettier will you look when you're naked, and crying, and tied down for me? Maybe begging me to stop?"

I felt tears slip from my eyes, as his words chilled my soul. "You want to hurt me?" Who the hell were these monsters?

He shrugged. "Doesn't every man? I'm just up front about it. I like it when they cry. Doesn't mean that you have to, just to please me. Struggling works too." I choked back a sob. I was in hell. And they were demons. Monsters. *Evil*.

"Please don't hurt me," I whispered. He grinned wider.

"Yeah, that works too. Keep begging, love, it's music to my ears."

I glanced at the other guy again, seeing him adjust his pants as he sat there. Oh god no. Both of them were sick raping monsters. I struggled against the bonds tying my hands back.

"Why me?" I asked finally, not knowing what else to ask that wouldn't turn them on, or make them put what they were saying into practice.

Monster number one smirked at me. "Let's just say someone owes us, and you're the payment, love."

I gasped, sobs pouring out of me, at my predicament. "Who? Who did this to me?" He shot a glance at the other guy, his mirror image of evil. They both laughed.

"Your boyfriend."

I stared at them, my chest heaving with panic.

"I don't have a boyfriend."

HARVEY

I HAD TAKEN PAINKILLERS and ibuprofen, and they were doing fuck all to help. My fingers were not broken, but I definitely had some cracked ribs. I'd never realised how much that alone could hurt. It was like someone had cracked my entire chest open. Every damn time I took a breath. Lenore had known how to wrap them, but it still hurt like a bitch.

I'd finally caved, and admitted to her that I owed money to those bastards, and this was the result of not paying, because if she didn't know everything, how could she help?

"Fuck. What do I do?" I moaned, staring at Lenore, who was putting her jacket on.

"First off, we try and find where she was when they took her. If we find where that happened, we might be able to follow their trail from there."

I stared at her. "How?" She shot me a withering look.

"By looking for clues, dumbass. Once I know where she was snatched from, I'll ring my friend Mikey. He owes me a favour. I'll get him to look for traffic cams in the area, and see if we can see what vehicle they used, and which way they went."

I frowned at her. "Mikey?" She smirked.

"He's a copper, H. He owes me a few favours, actually. Don't ask. He'll be discreet. I know they said no cops, but he can be trusted."

I grabbed my keys. I was beginning to think that I didn't really know her at all. I mean, I'd known her more than ten years, ever since university, but did I know her at all? Why would a police officer owe her favours?

We ran from the store, heading across town, to the community centre. Lenore popped into the building, while I stood outside, breathing hard, and wishing for death, every time my chest soared with pain.

She reappeared. "She never turned up for book club. That means she was snatched on her way here. Where does she work?" I pointed down the road.

"Big glass office building at the bottom of the hill."

She started walking in the direction I'd pointed. I didn't know what we were looking for, but she was scrutinising doorways, and alleyways, and suddenly stopped. I followed her as she stepped down an alley, about halfway between the community centre and Cassidy's office, and crouched down.

"Here," she said, pointing to scuff marks on the concrete.

"That's it? You're looking at some smudges, and telling me this is where they snatched her?" I stared at her, wondering if she'd gone mad. They could be from anything.

She shot me a glare. "They're shoe marks. Like someone grabbed someone else, and dragged them backward. But if that's not enough for you... there's that..." She pointed to a handbag on the ground, the contents partially spilling out.

I crouched down, grabbing the bag and rifling through it. *It was hers*. I recognised it from seeing it on her shoulder each day. I could smell her perfume too. I found the bottle inside, lifting it to my nose, breathing in her scent.

"Jesus, we don't have time for you to be a fucking perv! Shove it all in the bag, and get back to your place. I'm ringing Mikey now." She lifted her phone to her ear, and I hurried away, clutching my ribs, heading back to the bookshop, wondering what the fuck good that would even do.

Once I got inside, I emptied Cassidy's handbag onto the shop counter, catching a few items before they fell. Her phone. Her purse. A book she'd bought from me ten days ago; a lame sappy romance, and not her usual fare. The perfume bottle, and the lid, which had come loose in the bag. A notebook and pen. Some chewing gum. Some crumpled up receipts.

There was a zip up pocket inside, and I unzipped it, reaching in, and then grimacing as I withdrew several tampons, in brightly coloured wrappers. I shoved them back, and zipped it again.

I stood there, staring at the bag. It had been in her hands. Her hands had touched all of these items. Those... those tampons... they would go inside her. Where I wanted to be. Why the fuck didn't I just risk talking to her? What was the worst that could possibly happen? She laughed in my face, and called me a nerd? So what? I could have fallen back on stalking her, but at least I'd have tried. I mean, hell, she might have actually gone out with me!

"Tell me you didn't just stand there sniffing her stuff, and getting a hard on, H. We need to save the girl, not give you a fucking orgasm," Lenore snapped, marching past me. She grabbed Cassidy's phone, and pressed the button on the side. The screen lit up, and she swiped across it.

"No passcode. That's careless. Still, it'll help me right now." She messed with the phone, ringing someone on hers, and giving them some information, which they apparently had some purpose for. It didn't help me find her. What would? Her phone wasn't with her when she was taken, so what possible use would they have for her details? Her phone was here.

Lenore ended the call.

"Mikey is having someone triangulate her signal, so we can pick up any other numbers near hers at the time she was taken. Then we can ping those phones, and see if we can find her that way."

I stared at her. "I have no idea what any of that means."

She grinned. "It'll help us work out where the fuck she is. Listen dickless, you get in there and make some coffee. Until we hear back, we can't do much, but we're staying awake all night, if that's what it takes to save this girl. I mean... unless you have twenty-five fucking grand hidden somewhere?"

I glared at her. "Of course I fucking don't. None of this would have happened if I had the money, would it?"

She smirked. "It was worth a try. Now coffee. Hurry up. You're too much of a pussy to plan how to save her, so I'm doing it. You're going to do what I tell you, and after this, you're going to apologise to this poor girl, burn your fucking shrine, and get help. Got it? And you're staying away from her."

Fuck. If only that were possible.

CHAPTER SIX
CASSIDY

They sat and leered at me for maybe an hour, before they left the room, and left me alone. I was tied to a chair, after all. Where the hell could I go? I knew that I was in serious danger.

These guys weren't normal. They were big. Scary. *Unhinged*. The twin thing was unnerving, but I could see that one was slightly less crazy than the other. Wow, that's the only difference I'd noted? I needed to be more observant. Maybe that was what would keep me alive.

It freaked me out even more, not knowing why I was here, and who the hell had used me as a pawn in their business dealings. What kind of bastard does that? I had to find a way out of here, before they made good on their threats.

The door banged behind me, breaking the silence, and I jumped. A quiet chuckle followed my reaction.

"Just you and me now, love. My brother had to go do a thing. So... how shall we keep ourselves from getting bored? Eh?" A hand stroked the back of my head, and I flinched away.

"Don't touch me!" I snapped, and that hand returned, gripping a handful of my hair, trapping my head.

"Now why you gotta be unfriendly? Huh? I was just thinking how nice and soft your hair is, and now I'm wondering how much of it I can pull out in one go."

I gasped. "Please."

"Is that you begging again, love? What exactly are you begging me for? Rip your hair out? Or don't rip your hair out?" His face was close to mine, his breath against my ear as he spoke. I trembled in his hold, at his closeness.

"Please don't hurt me," I whimpered. He pressed his face against my neck, taking a deep breath. Then he nuzzled his face into my hair, and took another deep breath. It made my skin crawl.

"You smell good, love. Maybe I need to get access to more of your skin, and more of this smell. Makes me hard. How does that sound?"

I bit back a sob. "*Terrifying*. Please. Please don't. Just let me go. I won't tell anyone."

He moved around me, so his face was right in front of mine.

"Now, why would I let a pretty thing like you go? What's your name, love?" I blinked at the change of subject. He didn't even know my name? Or was he just screwing with my head?

I looked away, wishing he'd move back.

"M... Mary."

That hand tightened in my hair, and he tilted my head back.

"You think I took you, without knowing exactly who you are, love? *Don't lie to me.*"

I blinked. "Why did you ask then? Let me go, please."

He smirked. "I don't think so. See, we promised him we'd keep you here for twenty-four hours. Give him time to get the money together."

I felt a wave of relief. Twenty-four hours? And then I'd be free? Surely I could survive for twenty-four hours. Knowing that there was an end in sight was a blessing.

"Oh thank god," I murmured, hearing him laugh. I didn't like the sound of it. Or the look on his face.

"Sorry, love, I wasn't clear. I said we gave him twenty-four hours... during which we won't hurt you. Then either we get our money... or..." He winked at me. "We get to keep you."

Fuck. I felt a wave of something else at his words. Nausea. Panic. *Terror*.

"Why? Who is he? Surely I deserve to know who did this to me?" I begged him for some kind of information. Something to tell me why it was me trapped in this place, why my life was being destroyed for someone else.

He leaned back, releasing my hair at last, dragging that chair closer, so he could straddle it once more. Yeah, he was the crazy one from before. Would the other one be better? Kinder?

"I'm Seb," he said, nodding at me, telling me to be honest this time.

I sighed. "Cassidy. But you knew that, didn't you?" He shrugged.

"Maybe. Just let me tell you this. Every time I ask you a question, I expect the truth. No pissing around. No trying to delay anything. Just answer honestly, and maybe I'll be nicer than if you don't."

I shivered again. "I understand. Who gave me up for their debt?"

He smirked. "Someone who owes us a *lot* of money. Someone who promised it back a month ago. Stupid fucker, shouldn't get involved with people like us, if he doesn't plan on paying his debts."

I chewed my lip nervously.

"How much does he owe you?"

He focused on my mouth, on my lips.

"Twenty-five grand, love." I gasped. Who borrows such a huge amount of money? For what?

"What if..." I swallowed; my throat suddenly dry.

"What if he doesn't pay?" That wasn't what I'd been about to ask, but I nodded anyway. He shrugged.

"Well, we'll kill him. Burn down his bookshop. And then you'll pay his debt. Night after night. Until such time as we get tired of you."

I felt ill. I felt my head drop, my senses whirling, dizziness setting in. I'd never been more terrified in my life. *Wait*.

"Bookshop?" I asked suddenly, lifting my head again. His dark eyes showed amusement. He was enjoying this. *Bastard*. I felt a wave of anger, despite my terror. I'd get free, and when I did, I'd kick him in the nuts so fucking hard, he'd cry.

"You catching on now, love? Your boyfriend, the bookshop nerd." I frowned at him.

"Harvey?" He grinned.

"Right bastard that one. He offered you up to us. Said you're a good lay. Said we could do whatever we want to you."

What the fuck?! I glared at him, pulling at the rope around my wrists yet again. My skin was burning from all the struggling so far. I wouldn't stop though. I'd never stop trying.

"Yes, love. Little quiet Harvey. Pretends to be the good guy. Clearly he's more than happy selling out his girl, rather than paying us what he fucking owes. As I said, though… he's on borrowed time. He won't be able to pay, and when he runs out of time, I'm going to remove his fucking head, and send it to his mum."

I recoiled from him, nearly tipping the chair back. What kind of an animal was he? And he'd said… he said, 'won't be able to pay'. He didn't have the money!

"What if… what if *I* pay it?" I asked desperately, flinching when he lifted a hand to my face, tucking my hair behind my ear. I didn't want him touching me.

"You got that kind of money, love? You'd pay his debt? Doesn't seem fair, since he doesn't value you at all." He twisted a lock of my hair around his fingers, leaning closer to me, too close.

"No!" I gasped out. His eyes narrowed at me.

"No what, love?"

"I won't pay his debt. I'd be paying for my freedom. You'd still get to do whatever you wanted to him. But I'd be free." What was I saying? I didn't have that kind of money, any more than he did!

Seb pulled back, tilting his head.

"Problem with that offer, love, is that I'd rather get to keep you and ruin you. Letting you go leaves me with just him to torture. And he's really not my type. Get it?" I began trembling rather violently at the thought of what he was saying. Ruin me? Torture? God no.

"But you'd have your money. See? That's what this was about, right? *Money*. I can get you that money. More. You want more? I'll find more. I'll steal it if I have to." I was desperate. Beyond desperate. My words were coming faster and faster.

The door banged again, and the other brother came in, staring at his phone.

"Got a text from him. Stupid fucker," he muttered, holding a phone screen in front of Seb. His eyes widened, going from the screen to his brother.

"Really?"

HARVEY

I HAD TO DO whatever the fuck I could, to try and keep her safe. I don't know why I did it, but I did. I'd clearly lost my mind.

"You did what?" Lenore snapped, snatching my phone. She read the text on the screen. The one I'd sent to that unknown number.

"You told them you've got the money ready? Are you out of your fucking mind? You don't have any money to give them!" She thumped me in the shoulder, and I winced.

"Christ, Lenore. Don't punch me. I'm barely holding it together here."

She folded her arms, waiting for me to explain my stupid idea.

"What? You had something better than this?"

She smirked, tossing my phone back to me.

"Anything is better than bullshitting them, you idiot. You don't think they're going to call you on this?"

I groaned, running a hand over my hair.

"I was desperate, Lenore. They could be molesting her, or something."

She shot me a dark, angry look.

"Just remember, anything they do to her... that's on you. This is your fault. You put her in this position, because you're a fucking sicko."

That hurt. I frowned at her. "I love her, Lenore. I'm just... afraid..."

She snarled, lunging forward, and punching me in the face.

"You stupid, fucking, cowardly dick! You put an innocent girl in the hands of two monsters, because you're stalking her. Invading her privacy. Taking pictures of her, when she's living her life, and thinking she's safe. I saw those fucking pictures, H. Some of them were of her in bed. *Asleep*. You've been spying on her in her own fucking home!"

I cradled my face, blood flowing once more. Seriously, how much more blood could I afford to lose?

"I couldn't have foreseen this, Lenore. I was just working up my nerve. To talk to her. Get to know her. Maybe ask her out. They did this. Not me."

Lenore glared at me, like she'd never met me before.

"You're just as bad as they are, H. I thought you were a good man. Jesus, I've known you almost half my fucking life. You're pathetic. You're a little boy. Hiding in the body of a man who's nearly thirty. It's time you grew up, and took responsibility for your fuck ups."

CHAPTER SEVEN
Cassidy

WHAT HAD HE SENT? What had he said? I looked from one of them to the other, waiting for some sign of hope. It was agonising, waiting to find out, because they were completely ignoring me for a moment.

"Tell him you want proof," Seb said to his brother, who'd dropped onto that sofa again. He sent a text, and set the phone aside. He shot a look at me, then looked at his brother again.

"You didn't hurt her, right?" Oh god. Thank god. He's going to keep me safe. He's not like his brother at all.

Seb smirked. "Nah, bruv. We're just talking here."

The brother leaned forward.

"Twenty-four fucking hours, Seb. You keep it in your pants until then." I stared at him in horror. He wasn't saving me. He was just keeping to their bloody agreement.

"You're both sick bastards," I spat, glaring from one to the other, anger overtaking my fear for a moment. Seb laughed, standing up and throwing his chair back, crashing it against the wall.

He leaned down again, his fist snatching at my hair, so my head was tilted back again. He moved so close that I couldn't even focus on his face. I was back to terrified and trembling in an instant.

"You have no fucking idea, sweetheart. But I promise you, you're going to find out."

I screamed. *Right in his face*. Loud. Desperate. Petrified. He laughed. He actually laughed. In fact, they both did.

"Go right ahead, love. Scream your head off. Everyone around here knows to ignore any screaming they hear. Unless they want to be the next ones screaming in pain." I went from screaming to gasping sobs.

"Oh god… oh god… you're going to kill me. Fuck… you fucking monsters!"

He glanced at his brother. "I'm quite enjoying the insults from her, are you? I like a little fire in them."

The brother shrugged. "Whatever. No response from that dickhead yet. He's bluffing. I say we up the ante a bit."

"What have you got in mind, Sammy?" I glared from one of them to the other. The brother, Sammy apparently, stood up, aiming his phone in our direction.

"How about a nice selfie for him?" He suggested, and Seb snorted, moving around behind me. His fingers closed around my throat, choking off my air, making me gasp, and choke.

"Maybe don't kill her just for a photo, bruv," he said, and Seb laughed, fractionally releasing the tight grip, but leaving it tight enough to make me feel trapped, and afraid. He pressed his face against mine.

"Smile for the camera, love."

I cursed at him instead, and he chuckled.

"Perfect. Keep hitting me with those dirty words, love. Lucky for you, I know exactly how to live up to those." Shit. No.

Sammy held the phone up for a second, almost saluting his brother with it.

"All done."

HARVEY

MY PHONE PINGED AGAIN, and I lunged for it. They'd asked for proof of the money being ready. What the fuck was I supposed to do? The temptation to grab a picture from the internet had been strong, but they weren't the kind of people you lied to. I'd already learned that the hard way. Or at least I thought I had.

"Fuck." My reaction brought Lenore, who snatched the phone from me.

"Shit. They just sent this?"

I nodded dully. *Poor Cassidy.* She looked terrified, shaken up, and she'd been crying. A lot. And that bastard had his hand around her throat. His smirking face pressed to hers, like they were just taking a nice little selfie together. That sick fucker.

The phone pinged again, and Lenore groaned.

"It says 'we're just going to have some fun until you send us that proof'."

Fuck. "But they said they wouldn't hurt her for twenty-four hours."

Lenore stared at me. "Was that *exactly* what they said?"

I racked my brain. Was it? Or did they just say they wouldn't kill her? Did that mean they could do other things to her, and I wouldn't be able to save her from them?

"Let's call the police," I said to Lenore, even though they'd been clear that we shouldn't. She handed me the phone.

"You go right ahead, if you think that'll help. But think about it, H, you know why bastards like them aren't in jail? Because they have cops on their payroll. You report them to the wrong people, and you could get her killed."

FUCK! She was right, and I had no idea what to do next!

CASSIDY

THEY WERE LAUGHING.

"Yeah, he's gone silent on us now. So... what shall we do to keep busy, bruv?" Seb asked his brother. Sammy shrugged.

"Whatever. I don't care."

I stared at them both. "You said you wouldn't hurt me. You said twenty-four hours." It wasn't much, but it was something. They had to stick to that, right?

Seb shrugged at me. "We said we wouldn't hurt you... we didn't say we wouldn't play."

"Play? What the fuck does that even mean? *Wait*. No, you don't want to do anything horrible to me. Please." I was begging again. I didn't care. My entire world had shrunk to a chair in a room. With two sick bastards who wanted to hurt me. Because of another sick bastard. *Harvey*.

Had I ever suspected him of anything, besides being a little creepy when I visited his shop? No. I certainly hadn't imagined that he might be the kind of person who would offer a woman he barely knew, to monsters like them, to clear a debt. I felt another wave of anger, and hatred toward him. And them.

Seb glanced at Sammy. "How about we make it a game? Every few hours we'll take something from her."

Sammy quirked an eyebrow.

"Like what? She didn't bring anything with her."

My stomach was clenching with terror.

"Please don't."

Seb stepped closer. "I say we take an item of clothing. Or..."

I glanced at them, panic making me breathe fast.

"Or... Or what? What? Anything other than that, please!"

He grinned widely again. "Exactly. So, either an article of clothing, or you do something we ask."

WHAT?

I looked from one of them to the other. Was this really happening? What was wrong with him?

"Like what kind of things? What would you ask?"

He shrugged. "Could be anything, love. Make us a cuppa. Cook us dinner. *Suck my cock*. That kind of thing."

I closed my eyes, trying to slow my breathing. Please no.

"Choose one, love. Then you have two hours, and we'll go again." He leered closer, his hand stroking the front of his trousers.

"Clothing," I mumbled, and he leaned closer.

"What was that, love? Speak up."

"Fuck you, asshole!" I snarled, wanting to spit at him, but not wanting to make him angry.

"Wow... you went straight to that?" He shot a surprised look at his brother. "I thought we'd take longer to get into her pants."

What? I looked from one of them to the other.

"What? What? *No*. No, that's not what I meant. Stop it. Don't come so close."

He laughed. "Oh I'll *come close*, love. I'll be inside you when I do. Well... most of the time."

I gagged. I felt sick, and the room was spinning. I'd never been so terrified of anyone, or anything, in my entire life.

He suddenly waved a knife in front of me, and my terror went into overdrive.

"No! God no, please don't."

He sliced the front of my beautiful bright blue sweater, the one that I'd paid more for than I should have. Then he sliced the sleeves, and pulled it off, no longer a sweater, but ragged, fraying blue wool. He tossed it on the floor, while I trembled in my sleeveless shirt. Thank god he'd taken clothing, and thank god I'd layered up for the cool weather.

Sammy aimed the camera on his phone at the remains of my sweater, and I heard it click, then the tone that said he'd messaged it to someone.

Seb looked back at me, that knife in hand, his eyes crawling over me once more.

HARVEY

FUCK! THOSE BASTARDS!

I showed Lenore the photo I'd just received. The blue jumper, the one that Cassidy had been wearing in that first picture, was now shredded on the floor. What the hell were they doing to her? I felt sick.

This was all happening to her because of me. Because of my pathetic inability to just go up to her, and talk to her. Had I sentenced her to death?

"Get your head out of your ass, and help me! We need to find these bastards. I have three addresses to try. Mikey says the nearest phone to hers, around the time we think she was taken, has been at these three places for a period of time. That means she could be stashed at any one of them," Lenore said urgently, roughly nudging me with her elbow.

I nodded. "Your car here?" She just shoved me out through the door, and locked it behind me.

"Get in the bloody car. I've got the addresses on my phone, so check the texts, and tell me the nearest to here."

I looked through them. "Okay, one of them is a few miles down the road, so I say we try that one first. Head left out of here, and follow the road down to the roundabout."

CHAPTER EIGHT
CASSIDY

They'd left me alone again. I was so thirsty. I'd been trapped here for hours. And whatever they'd drugged me with, had left me with a nightmare of a headache, and a terrible thirst. All of my panicking, and gasping, had made both so much worse. By the time one of them returned, I was actually glad to see him, as bizarre as that was. He leaned down to look at me.

"You're looking a bit peaky, love." He frowned down at me. I was surprised. It was the brother, Sammy. He wasn't quite as mean as the other one.

"Thirsty," I croaked out. He nodded, disappearing, and returning with a glass of water. He tilted the glass to my lips, and let me take a few blessed mouthfuls. He kept it there, until I stopped, and nodded.

"Thank you." He shrugged.

"No sense in letting you get sick. He won't care either way, but I do. Don't go getting excited, love. I'm just not into making you suffer. Not like that."

He sat on the sofa, watching me as I tried to sit back, my arms stopping me from being able to settle back properly. Everything ached.

"Can I please be untied?"

He smirked. "Really? You think I'm the dumb one? Is that it? I'm the brains, love. He's the brawn. Well, he's also all kinds of fucked up. Enjoys hurting people. It's why people are so scared of us. He'll do anything to make a point. And he really likes it when they break."

I let out a moan, my head dropping onto my chest.

"He's going to kill me. I mean, he wants to hurt me and kill me, doesn't he?"

Sammy stood up, coming over and reaching out to lift my head, his fingers surprisingly gentle on my chin.

"Look, love, it's nothing personal. It's business. I'd rather we let you go, relatively unharmed, but we can't look weak, or people will walk all over us."

I stared back at him. "So you're saying that you guys have to hurt me, so that people stay afraid? How is that fair to me? I'm nothing to do with your business. Or the bookshop guy. Why do you have to hurt *me*?"

He frowned. "You're okay for a little while longer, love. Maybe he'll surprise us, and come through with the money. Just try not to wind Seb up. He's itching to do something nasty to you. He doesn't need a lot of encouragement."

I blinked back tears. "But you're not like him. You could let me go. You don't want him to hurt me. You don't want to hurt me. Do you?"

His face hardened, and his fingers tightened on my face.

"Don't mistake me for soft, love. I may not be into causing people pain, in the same way that he is, but I enjoy a good fuck. And you look like a good fuck. So I'm going to go with the flow, love. We'll get our money, or we'll get to break a few people. It's how this business works."

"But I have nothing to do with you, or him! I'm not a part of this. Why do I have to be broken, to prove that you're bad guys? This is ridiculous! People are going to realise I'm gone, you know!"

Sammy shrugged. "I don't make the rules, sweetheart. I just follow them. My advice would be to do exactly what he asks, and at least there's a chance he'll be gentle. You really don't want to piss him off."

I trembled as I stared at him, feeling a rush of anger at his words.

"Well, the joke's on you fucking idiots anyway. I'm diabetic, and you didn't bring my purse when you kidnapped me. I'll likely slip into a coma soon, and I'll be dead before your twenty-four hours are even up. I actually hope he doesn't pay, because then you guys get fucked. TWICE!"

Sammy's face dropped, and he backed up a step. "You're lying."

I glared up at him. "Am I? Then just keep waiting around, and see what happens. And starving me too. That just means it'll happen sooner. You didn't know diabetics need to eat regularly? Fucking amateurs."

He stormed from the room, while I sat there and hyperventilated. What the hell was I doing, winding them up? My anger would be the death of me!

HARVEY

THE FIRST TWO ADDRESSES were a bust. *Empty.* We were on our way to the third, and I was freaking out.

"What if they're hurting her, Lenore?"

She glared at me as she drove.

"This is all on you, Harvey. I'm so pissed at you right now. I want to kick your ass all the way out of town. How could you let this happen? That poor girl."

I slammed my hands on the dashboard.

"I didn't plan this! I didn't mean for it to go so wrong! All I wanted was to save my shop! Why would I ever imagine that some girl I'm in love with, would end up on their radar? They're the bad guys, not me! I never touched her!"

Lenore slammed the brakes on, as we reached the third address.

"You are just as bad as them, Harvey. You did this to her. And I'll make sure she knows that, when we save her. Get out of the car. We're here."

"Why are you calling me Harvey? You never call me that. You always call me H."

She glared as she marched toward the door.

"You don't deserve a nickname anymore. You're going to have to earn it back. And the only way you will manage that, is by saving this poor girl, before she suffers anything that you can't apologise for. Get a move on!"

She kicked the door open, and marched inside, while I prayed that we'd found the right place at last.

Chapter Nine
Cassidy

THEY WERE GOING TO figure me out soon enough. *Diabetic*. What the hell made me say that? I didn't know the first thing about that illness, or what would prove my lie to them. Eventually it would be pretty damn obvious. Idiot!

"*So*... where do I inject this stuff then?" Seb suddenly appeared with a syringe in his hand. Shit! If they injected me with insulin, they could kill me. I was pretty sure that it wasn't safe for non-diabetics to use! But then... that small part of me wondered if it would be better than the alternative. He leaned down to look at me, and I stared at the syringe warily.

"Come on, love, chop chop. Don't want you going into a coma now, do we?" I glared at him.

"Go to hell."

He laughed. "Well then, shall I just inject it wherever the fuck I want? Come on, girl. You say you'll die without it, so here I am, ready to save you. Best we get on with it, eh?" He held the needle at my throat, and I froze.

"No."

"Wrong place? Should I stick it here instead?" He aimed the needle at my heart. I was pretty sure a needle wouldn't go in easily, but my knowledge of anatomy is pretty shoddy, so again I froze.

"Stop!" I gasped out. He aimed lower with the needle, aiming too close to an intimate area that I hoped he'd never get closer to.

"Don't!"

He laughed. "*You stupid bitch*. Do we really look that dumb to you? Bear in mind, that your answer might cause you a lot of pain. You think we didn't look into you, when we took you? You don't snatch someone, and not check if they're on any life-preserving medications. You think you're so smart, eh? Maybe I *should* stick you with this, just for shits and giggles. I wonder what it would do to you." He brandished the syringe at me, taunting me.

I glared right back at him.

"Go ahead. Accidentally kill me now, and you don't get to torture me later. It's a win win, as far as I'm concerned!" Where was this coming from? I'm not this brave. I'm a quiet, play-it-safe kind of woman.

Of course, playing it safe got me here. Trapped in a room with twin twisted bastards. It was time to grow up, and act my age. I'm not a teenager anymore. I can do this. I can survive this. And then I'll find Harvey, and kill him.

He grabbed my chin, making me wince. I'd be bruised there, if they kept doing that, but it could be worse, I supposed.

"You think you're going to talk your way out of this?" He smirked at me. "I kinda like the sassiness, Cassidy, but I'm going to enjoy your pain, and despair, so much more."

I shuddered, pulling my face away from his grip.

"Stick yourself with that stuff. You could do with something to make you sweeter."

He threw his head back, laughing.

"Damn... you're just full of surprises, love. You've got a mouth on you. I look forward to getting to know it better."

I glared at him, letting anger fuel my words.

"I have teeth too."

He shrugged, looking completely unconcerned.

"Oh don't worry. I can fix that, love."

I frowned, pulling back as far from him as I could.

"What does that mean?"

He leaned close again, leaving me with nowhere to go.

"I'll leave that to your imagination."

The door popped open. "Nev's here, bruv. Shall we do this?" Sammy's voice said. Seb looked at me again, a grin creeping across his face.

"Bring him in here. I think Cassidy here should be part of this."

My heart thudded in my chest.

HARVEY

THE THIRD ADDRESS WAS fucking empty. We'd run out of ideas. I slid my phone from my pocket, staring at it. Did I really have the balls to ring the police? I mean, what had I done wrong really? Refused to run drugs? Borrowed from the wrong people? Okay... *stalking*... but that's not exactly a crime, right? It was harmless. And was it even really my fault that I'd fallen in love with her?

"Whatever you're planning, don't do it," Lenore warned, glaring at me.

"I need to call the police. I can't let this happen to her. It doesn't matter what they do to me." Because surely I won't be in that much trouble anyway, right? And it's worth it to save her. Anything would be. Even though they'd warned me not to. I stared at my phone, willing myself to do it.

"You don't know who they own, dickhead. If you speak to one of their guys, you'll be signing your own death warrant. Are you so stupid, that you think you'll talk your way out of that?"

I stared at her, my heart thudding heavily in my chest.

"I'll give up my business, my freedom, my life. Whatever. She shouldn't suffer, because I was an idiot."

She laughed, snatching the phone from me. *"And a stalker.* Don't forget that. If you'd just stayed away from her, they wouldn't even know she exists."

I snatched the phone back. "If that were the case, maybe it'd be you instead, trapped with them, at their mercy. You're the only other person who matters to me. You think they don't know about you?"

She shrugged. "If they had me instead, they'd already be getting fed pieces of their genitals. You get me? I'm not a victim. Not ever again. They take me, and I'll take them apart."

She'd jabbed a finger at me with that last statement, and you know what? I believed her. I wished I had her balls. It also made me wish that they *had* taken her instead, because then this would already be over.

"What do we do now?" I asked her, waiting for that machismo to solve my problems, as it always did.

"Call them. Tell them you'll give yourself up, and your business. Offer them the damn world. They free her, they get you." My stomach rolled.

"What?"

"That's what I thought. Too much of a pussy to do it, even while you stand here, and say all the things you think I want to hear. What I want to hear, is that you'd do *anything* to save a woman in need. Instead, you're leaving her in their grip. Every hour she's there, they could be doing anything to her. You know what men like them will do to a woman. *You know that*, and yet you keep stalling, when you could fix this all with one call." She was staring at me like she didn't know me at all. Maybe she didn't. But she was right, wasn't she?

I shoved her aside, striding out of the empty building, and walking past her car. Fuck her. I'll fix this myself. I called the cops.

CHAPTER TEN

CASSIDY

They threw a guy into the room, and he landed with a heavy thud on the floor in front of my chair. He took one look at me, and the two of them, and swore.

"I'm sorry, honestly. I'll get the money, I swear. I was on a streak. I was going to make it all back with one hand. They played me!" He just wouldn't shut up. Clearly he was a gambler, and he'd thrown good money after bad, and now he was at their lack of mercy, because he was in so far over his head that he had no way out. He was older than them, his dark hair showing some grey at the sides. He looked panicked, and he should be.

Seb raised an eyebrow, looking from him to me.

"Tell you what, Nev. Because I like you, I'll give you an easy out, how about that?" He glanced at Sammy, who stood opposite him, also looming over the prone gambler.

"Wh... what?" The man stammered, glancing at me again. I frowned, shaking my head. Whatever they were about to offer him was a trap. It had to be. They didn't play fair.

The man glanced back at Seb again.

"*Rape her*." Seb pointed at me, and I gasped, struggling with the ropes again.

"No! You bastards! You promised!"

Sammy laughed. "I wouldn't worry, love. He hasn't got the balls. He's nothing but a pathetic, dickless wonder. Aren't you, Nev?"

The man, Nev, groaned.

"Please. I'll do anything. Not that, please, not that."

Seb nodded. "Yeah... but see, it's *this*, or we beat you to death right now. *Slowly*. Is she really worth that? You could get your end away, and then walk away from this. A free man. Free sex, and your freedom? What the fuck could be wrong with that deal?"

"It's rape, you sick motherfucker!" I snapped at him, silenced when Sammy's hand suddenly covered my mouth. I struggled and bit him hard, making him pull his hand back, laughing quietly.

"Yeah... she won't go easily, Nev, but we can leave her tied for you, or hold her down. Strip her off, just for you, you lucky bastard. I can't see that anyone ever had a fairer deal than this. Only a complete moron would say no."

Seb was laughing. "See... we made a deal with someone else. Said we wouldn't touch her for twenty-four hours, but... *you're not us*. You could fuck her if you wanted. It wouldn't be a breach of our agreement with her fella. You could warm her up for us. Soften her up. Not that I want her to lose all that fight. I'm actually looking forward to that."

I stared at him in horror.

"You really are a sick monster, aren't you? What the fuck happened to you? Were you dropped on your head as a kid?" He shot an amused look in my direction.

"See? She thinks we're all talk right now, just because we're honouring an agreement. But you... *you don't have to*. You can have her, and do what you want with her. And we're still honouring that agreement, like the gentlemen we are."

The guy looked like he had started to waver, his eyes casting over me.

"And you'd write off my debt? All of it?"

Seb and Sammy looked at each other. "Yeah. Fifteen grand written off, mate. Just stick your dick in her, and fuck away your debt. You jammy bastard. Bet you thought you were going to die when they dragged you in here, being so behind with your payments. You haven't been a great investment opportunity, Nev."

The man pushed himself up, onto his knees, staring at me, his blue eyes gliding over me.

"Who is she?"

I glared at him. "Your worst fucking nightmare, you sick fucker!" I'd never said so many curse words in my entire life, but the situation I'd been forced into had changed me, maybe forever. I'd never known such fear and rage, which seemed to fight each other for dominance.

Sammy crouched beside me, his hand on my thigh, while I tried to flinch away.

"She's ours, mate. Or at least she will be, in about twenty odd hours, maybe sooner. She's never getting away, or telling anyone. You're safe. Take what you want. *She's right here.*"

The man pushed himself up to his feet, shooting each of them a glare.

"How about I just fuck her mouth? Wouldn't that count?"

Sammy laughed, holding up his other, somewhat bloody, hand. Yep, I'd drawn blood. I allowed myself a moment of pride, while wondering how the hell to get out of this situation. If I read the situation right, I was only moments away from being raped, just to help another guy settle his debt. *Another stranger.*

"She bites, Nev. You want to risk her teeth on your cock? She bites it off, and we won't give a fuck. We'll let you bleed to death."

Nev looked at me, sadness on his, otherwise almost fatherly, face.

"I'm sorry, love. I'm sure you're a perfectly nice lady. But I have a lady too, and we're about to lose everything. Our house, everything. This would fix that." He stepped closer.

"Raping me is a better alternative than losing your home?" I asked quietly, desperately. He glanced back at the other two, who'd stepped closer to each other to watch, gleeful grins on their faces.

"They'll kill me if I don't. I'm sorry. I don't want to die," he said sadly, reaching for his belt.

"Well, I don't want to be raped, you pathetic fucker. Man up, and fight your way out of this. I'm their captive. And I never even borrowed from them. I didn't even know who they were. I'm here because someone else like you fucked up." He slid the belt from his pants.

"Can we gag her? I can't listen to this shit," he asked, his face crumpling a little.

"Do what you want, mate. Just get on with it. You have five minutes to get started, or we start removing your limbs," Seb said, winking at me, like this was some cute little gag, or game.

I glared at him. "No matter what happens, I'll get free, and I'll fucking destroy you," I snarled at him. He made a mock scared face, and shrugged.

"Looking forward to it, baby. Make sure it hurts *so good*."

The man, Nev, approached me with his belt, aiming to gag me with it, and I panicked.

"You know why they're doing this, right? I'm a sex worker. I'm not afraid of being fucked, but they chose me because I'm dying. You've heard of HIV? Aids? They're tricking you into catching it." I glared at him, watching his face fall.

"What?"

I nodded. "That's not all I've got. Turns out I'm not that big on safe sex. Got me all kinds of diseases. You'll get them all. You go back to your wife with all that, and you'll infect her too. And then your pathetic dick will fall off. They're playing you."

I heard Seb laughing. "She's got balls, that one," he said to Sammy. The man leaning over me took a deep breath. He leaned closer, putting his lips near my ear, his stubble tickling me enough to make my skin crawl.

"I'm sorry about all of this. I don't know what will happen next, but I hope this helps. When they start on me, I want you to run. Get out." I felt him reaching behind me, pulling at the ropes tying me. He loosened them enough that I felt them give, but then he pulled back to give me a warning look.

He glanced back at them. "I'm going to untie her legs. I need her out of the chair to fuck her." My stomach rolled, but I could see what he was planning.

"You sick motherfucking asshole!" I snarled at him, and he grinned a little.

"You'll shut the fuck up, and take it like the bitch you are," he replied in a sharp tone, playing his part.

Seb and Sammy laughed. "I never saw him having the balls to do this." I worked my fingers free of the ropes holding my arms back. I kept my arms around the back of me, playing along.

As Nev untied one of my ankles, Seb suddenly leaned forward, stopping him.

"Leave the other one, and make it work. Get on with it. Your dick better be in her, in the next minute, or I'll gut you like a fucking fish." He shoved Nev, who crashed against me.

"Try and get the other one untied. Then RUN. Don't look back," he whispered to me, as he suddenly stood up, turning to glare at the brothers.

"I've changed my mind," he said in a clear voice.

"Grown a pair, have we? Don't want to rape a defenceless woman anymore?" Sammy asked, chuckling as Seb drew that knife from his belt.

"I'm glad, to be honest. I've really been looking forward to removing your face, and wearing it, when I visit your wife. I'm betting she'll be a good fuck, especially if she resists."

Nev roared at them, as he lunged at Seb.

"You leave my fucking wife alone!"

I desperately pulled at the one remaining rope on my ankle, my arms almost dead from being pulled behind me for so long. I fought against the pain, finally pulling the rope off, and shoving away from the chair.

I reached the door, just before a hard body slammed against me, trapping me between it and the door, that I could no longer even hope to open.

"Not so fast, love. We haven't finished with you yet," he whispered, as I gasped and screamed for help.

CHAPTER ELEVEN
HARVEY

THE POLICE CAME QUICKLY, and they met us at that warehouse, which hadn't even been the right place. Lenore kept staring at me, and mouthing things at me, calling me a fucking idiot, and various other nasty names. She was probably right, but I was desperate, and out of ideas.

PC Oliver, and his partner, PC Kent, questioned us aggressively, and after about half an hour of them checking out the building, that we'd already told them was empty, they cuffed us, forced us into the back of their car, and drove us to the station. *Fucking hell.* This wasn't why I'd called them.

"I wanted you stupid bastards to go and save *her*, not arrest us!" I snarled at them, from the back of the car.

PC Kent glanced at me in the rear-view mirror.

"Have we arrested them, Jacko?" PC Oliver shrugged.

"Don't remember reading them their rights. Did I miss you doing that?"

PC Kent snorted. "Nah, mate. Poor saps seem to think they've been arrested though. Do you want to tell them what's actually going on?"

PC Oliver, Jacko, turned to grin at us.

"We're just taking you to see our bosses. The real ones, that is." He looked away again, and Lenore elbowed me in the chest.

"I fucking told you."

I glanced down at my handcuffed hands, in front of me, and hers, in the same position. My heart sank, as I realised that we were completely in the shit. They'd said no cops. Lenore had said no cops. *And I called the fucking cops.* The ones they owned. Dammit.

"You work for them?" I asked the officers. They both just laughed. "You pathetic bastards! You're supposed to be the good guys. How can you wear those uniforms, and pretend to be decent, when you work for the fucking bad guys?" I slammed my fists against the mesh barrier between us and them.

"Settle down back there, or I'll tase you. Been wanting to try this fucking thing on someone," Jacko said, holding up a definitely non-police-issue taser.

I glanced at Lenore, and she just shrugged. That's helpful. I guessed I'd pissed her off enough, that she wasn't thinking about helping me anymore. Just herself. I didn't blame her.

I'd been so wrapped up in myself, and my problem, that I'd ignored the fact that I'd dragged her into this situation. A situation where she could get hurt. Maybe worse than me.

CASSIDY

SAMMY KEPT ME CRUSHED against that door with his body, his hand fisting in my hair.

"Please just let me go. I'm not a part of this," I whispered, as he pressed his face into my neck, breathing deep.

I could hear punching, and sounds of pain from behind us, so I knew that Seb was beating the hell out of Nev. The poor man that I'd cursed at, and thought was a bastard, had sacrificed himself for me. And I'd failed. *He'd given himself up for nothing.*

Sammy ran his tongue over my skin, making me shudder.

"Please stop. Don't do this," I whispered to him. I could feel he was aroused, his body pressed against mine as it was. The hand that didn't grip my hair was pressed against the door, so close to my face, that I knew biting him again was probably my only chance for escape.

"Don't even think about it, love. Not unless you want to have no teeth by this time tomorrow," he muttered darkly.

"I thought you were the nice one," I whispered desperately. He chuckled, tightening his fingers in my hair, his teeth sliding over my skin now.

"I warned you about that. I'm not your saviour, girl. I'm just less crazy than him. Doesn't mean I'm not still a monster. I know that what I do is wrong. It just doesn't stop me doing it." His teeth closed on my skin, biting into my neck, making me whimper with pain.

He pressed against me harder, rocking his hard cock against me. Just a reminder that he had everything he needed to destroy me, *right there*, so close to me.

"When he fucks you, it'll be because he's fucking nuts, and he thinks it's okay. When I do, I'll know it's wrong, and cruel, and still, I'll enjoy it. Not because I like hurting you, but because I want you." I trembled, tensing my body, to try and push him away. He groaned softly.

"Every movement you make feels fucking amazing. Keep pushing back against me, pressing yourself against my cock. It just gets me harder."

I dissolved into tears. My whole body sagged, as I gave up, pressing my face against that door that I'd never managed to escape through.

The room had fallen silent behind us, then Seb chuckled.

"Don't get started without me, bruv. I need to get rid of this thing first." Sammy dragged me away from the door, turning us both, so we faced a bloody Seb. And the still body of Nev. There was a lot of blood. He'd been beaten, and stabbed, and he wasn't moving. I gagged.

The smell of the blood was overwhelming, and horrifying. Seb grinned widely, his teeth bright against the dark red of Nev's blood, which had splattered across his face, his clothes, and dripped from his fists. His bloody knife lay on the floor beside him.

Sammy let go of me, just as I dropped to my knees, and threw up. I retched and gagged, and threw up, until there was nothing but bile coming up. It burned my throat, and my nose, and I couldn't breathe.

They were both looking at me with something more like disgust right now. That suited me just fine. I glared up at them, with bile dripping from my face.

"You're fucking evil. I'll make sure you both die horribly." They exchanged a look, matching grins on their faces.

"Yeah, whatever you say, love," one of them said. I couldn't see properly. My eyes were blurry. I felt a wave of dizziness, and tipped over, back against the wall.

"You're... evil..." I struggled to stay alert, while the room darkened around the edges of my vision, and then faded away altogether.

HARVEY

WHEN THEY PULLED UP on a dark road, out in the middle of nowhere, I knew we were about to die. I mean, who takes people out into the middle of nowhere, unless they're planning to kill them? And these were the police! We'd trusted them. Or at least, I had. Lenore had known that this was a risk we shouldn't take.

How had she known? She was glaring at the backs of their heads, and I really hoped she had a plan. When both coppers slammed their doors, and reached for ours, I knew it was the moment for action. Time for me to man up, and fight for our lives. As my door opened, I threw myself out, landing on the bastard, and knocking him onto his back.

I brought both fists up, and slammed them into his face, narrowly avoiding his hand, as it brandished the taser at me. I heard fighting from the other side of the car, and hoped that Lenore was faring well against her attacker. Every movement made my chest throb with pain, but I had no choice, or I'd die.

"Stupid little shit. You think you can fight back against us? You're nothing, you hear me?" The officer fighting me was snarling. I was thrown aside, and he dropped over me, that taser hitting me in the chest. As god knows how many volts poured into me, I felt my whole body tense, and I gasped as waves of pain ran through me.

He was knocked away from me, and there were fighting sounds beside me, while I tried to remember how the parts of my body worked, and tried to fight against the waves of trembling that ran through me. My heart was racing, and I felt like I could taste burnt toast. *Jesus.* I shuddered as I lay there, realising the night had fallen suddenly silent.

Lenore suddenly leaned over me; her wrists no longer cuffed. She reached for mine, and I tried to wrench them away from her. What if somehow they'd electrocute her, because I'd been tased?

She snorted, grabbing my wrist, and unlocking the cuffs. I trembled again, as my body started to come to life after the shock it had received.

"F...fuck," I gasped out. She shot me a look.

"Grab his keys," she snapped, going back to lock the cuffs on the bastard. I did my best to control my body, even though it twitched now and then.

As I moved, I realised something more embarrassing than being overwhelmed by that guy, or tased. *I'd pissed my fucking pants.* I guessed that it was probably a normal reaction to being tased, but it was mortifying. Lenore dragged me to my feet.

"Swap pants with him." She pointed to the cuffed officer on the ground by me. I didn't argue. My hands worked better now, so I fought to steal his trousers, having to remove his shoes too. I tossed them as far away as I could manage, then dropped my pants, and tossed my underwear.

I slipped into the stolen trousers, commando, and did them up. They were almost the right size. They stayed up, at least. He'd worn a belt, so that helped too. Lenore had grabbed the keys from me, before I focused on undressing the cop, so she started the car, and then sat there bitching and moaning, while I sorted myself out. I finally joined her in the passenger seat.

"So now we're stealing a police car?" I asked her, and she just glared at me.

"What choice do we have, fuckface? We're in the middle of nowhere. You want to try walking?"

I glanced out the window. "And we're just leaving them there?"

She steered the car away from them. "Well, if you want to have a fucking tea party, I could pull over so we can pick them up. Or shall we just stick them in the boot of the stolen police car, Harvey?"

"Jesus, will you stop being an asshole? I'm just trying to figure out what the hell we're doing."

She pointed to a phone in the central console.

"Check that. If they're in touch with the Bennetts, maybe we'll find out something, like where the fuck they are." I picked up the phone, trying to access the information.

"Crap. It needs fingerprint recognition." She slammed the brakes on, putting the car into reverse.

"Then go and fucking get it," she snapped, pulling the handbrake on, and waiting for me. Naturally, it wasn't the first guy I went to. The second one, who was luckily still out cold, was clearly the phone's owner. Pressing his finger to the screen made it open up.

"Thanks, mate," I muttered, running back to the car.

"Don't let it time out, we're not going back," she said, as I slid back into the passenger seat. I checked the phone's settings, switching off fingerprint recognition, and making sure there was no passcode either.

I started scrolling through the most recent text messages, as she pulled away again.

"Shit, we're screwed. They know we called the police on them."

CHAPTER TWELVE
CASSIDY

I WOKE UP ON a bed, and for a few blessed moments, I thought I'd been rescued, or maybe it had all been a horrific dream. Maybe I was safe. I moved to stretch, and realised that my hands were tied.

My eyes flew open, and I looked around me. I was alone, but on a bed. My hands were tied in front of me, but my legs were free. What was going on? I felt ill. Weak. Shaky. My breathing became shallow. *Panicked*. I'd gone from blissfully unaware of my situation, to terrified, in an instant.

I sat up, using my tied hands to help me up. The room was dimly lit. There was a window, but it had boards nailed over it, letting in no light. The room contained just this bed, and a bare lightbulb in one corner, which was on, and providing nowhere near enough light.

I checked myself. I was still dressed, thank god, but my clothes were damp. All of them. And my hair felt damp too. Had I sweated that much while I lay here? Why did my head hurt so much again?

"About time you woke up, love," a voice said, and I realised that the door had opened. One of the brothers stood there, and in that moment, I couldn't even tell which one. I shuffled back, against the headboard of the bed, curling myself into a ball. I wouldn't let him touch me.

He grinned. "We had to hose you down. You were covered in vomit, and you know... not very appealing to us like that." I glanced at my damp clothes again. Why didn't that wake me?

He closed the door, approaching the bed.

"We drugged you again, while you were passed out. It was easier than dealing with you, while we had a body to get rid of. That's probably why you don't remember."

I sucked in a breath. "What else did you do to me, while I was out of it?" He smirked.

"Unconscious isn't really my kink. Seb's either, not surprisingly." *Ah, so this was Sammy.*

"Why not just kill me?" I asked, wondering why I was putting ideas into the sick bastard's head, although I'd have to be an idiot not to figure that the idea was already in there.

He laughed, sitting on the bed a few feet from me. "Where's the fun in that, love? Now... I'm guessing you'll be hungry, after that all that upchuck. If I bring you food, will you eat it?"

I frowned at him. "What do you care?" Yes, I really wanted food, but could I trust them to supply it?

He huffed a sigh. "I keep telling you. We don't want you unconscious, or dead. That means we have to feed you, give you water, you know... let you breathe... *for now*..."

I closed my eyes, pressing my face against my knees.

"Just go away. I'd rather starve, thank you."

I felt the bed move, and then his hand grabbed my hair, forcing me to lift my head and look at him.

"Come on, love. You're only hurting yourself. Do you really think that being weak and helpless is the best way to survive being here? Don't you want the strength to fight him off?"

I blinked the tears away, really wishing I wouldn't keep wasting the moisture, because I was pretty sure I needed to conserve it.

"What's the point? I have no chance against either of you. You'll torture me, rape me, and kill me. Maybe I'd rather die of dehydration or starvation than that."

He reached up and brushed some of my tears away with his thumb. It was an unexpectedly gentle gesture, from someone who'd only shown me his mean side so far. I had been pretty sure it was his only side.

"Cassidy, you should care about survival. You should care what happens to you. You could still get out of here, without being touched by either of us in that way. It definitely won't happen, if you're too weak to move." I stared at him. This softer side was confusing. He'd told me that he wasn't my saviour. Told me he was evil. Now he made me doubt those words.

"Harvey doesn't have the money, does he?" I asked him, my voice low. He shook his head.

"Unlikely. He borrowed from us out of desperation. He needed fifteen grand fast. Agreed to our terms like an idiot. If he didn't have that much, he won't be able to afford the high level of interest. So now he owes us twenty-five, and he'll lose everything. It's how it works."

"So there's no way out for me. Why are you being nice? You're going to hurt me."

Sammy sighed. "Yeah... probably... doesn't mean that's the only way this will end. Keep fighting, you hear?"

He backed up again. "So I'm going to bring you some food, and a drink. Try not to throw it back in my face, yeah?"

I stared at him. "No promises."

He laughed. "Yeah... I can live with that." He left the room, and I stared at it, confused.

Why was he being nice? Did he care? Was he on my side? Or was he just playing me? Could I trust him? *No.* I was pretty sure that would be the biggest mistake I could make. Still... it had been nice to feel hope, even for a few moments.

HARVEY

IF YOU'D TOLD ME, even a day ago, that I'd be in a stolen police car, after being tased, and attacked by dirty cops, and the woman I love would be in the hands of vicious monsters, I'd laugh it off. Well, after I curled up and cried in the corner for a while.

I'm not a tough guy. I sell books, for fuck's sake. I stalk women, or at least, one woman, and I sit at home and jerk off, while I imagine her body, her naked body, and mine, skin to skin, while I fuck her.

The worst part of all of this was knowing that, while before it had been damn unlikely, now it was a certainty. She'd never want me. Even if we saved her before anyone hurt her, she'd always remember the fact that I'm the reason why she went through any of it. Everything was destroyed.

"Will you stop the fucking moping? I need you to find something in that phone that we can use."

I looked at the phone again.

"The last text just says, 'bring them'. Like they were meant to take us to the brothers. I don't know where though, or why they stopped off where they did instead. Does the car have GPS? Maybe we can look at where they've been?"

Lenore stared at me. "Seriously? You just expect everything to come easily, don't you? You don't even fucking try. Why the hell am I still hanging around with you, after ten fucking years of you being a pathetic loser, and me always having to bail you out?"

I frowned at her. "Because you like me. Now shut up. I need to think."

She pulled over when the radio made a crackling noise, and a voice asked for an update from the officers we'd left handcuffed in a ditch. I stared at her, panic written on her face, as it probably was on mine. What should we do? If we replied, they'd know it wasn't them. If we didn't reply, they might send someone to check on them. Police cars could be tracked, I was pretty sure.

"We need to ditch the car," Lenore said. She was right. It was the only sensible option.

We left it by the side of the road, and ran.

"Now what?" I asked her.

"Why do you keep asking me? I'm not an expert in this shit!" Lenore snapped at me.

"Well, what fucking use are you, then?" I snapped back, because honestly her PMT-esque moaning had started to get right on my nerves.

She strode ahead of me, and I did the only thing I could think of. I rang the number on my phone.

CHAPTER THIRTEEN
Cassidy

When Seb strode into the bedroom they were keeping me in, he was staring at his phone, which was ringing. He shot us both a wide grin as he answered it.

Sammy had just placed a tray in front of me, with a sandwich on it. And a cup of coffee. Coffee. *Really*. How was that going to be a smart move? I could throw the hot coffee in his face. But then, of course, it'd only slow him down for a moment, and then he'd be seriously pissed off at me.

"Harv, me old mucker. What do you want at this ungodly hour? You woke me up from a lovely dream!" Seb said into the phone, shooting a grin at me.

"Is that him? Is that him?" I started babbling at Sammy. He put a finger to his lips, shaking his head. I lifted my tied hands, showing him both middle fingers, watching him laugh at my response.

"Well, that doesn't sound like the deal we discussed, Harv. As I recall it, you owe us twenty-five fucking grand. How is it that you think that anything other than twenty-five grand is going to get your girl back?" Seb was saying.

"I'm not his fucking girl!" I hissed at him. Sammy held up a hand.

"Don't make me gag you again. Eat your food." I glared at him.

"With my hands tied?"

"That's why it's a sandwich, smart-arse. Eat."

I stared at it. "What's in it?"

He shook his head. "*Food*. Fucking eat." He turned to look at Seb, who'd fallen silent.

"You think they're the only two coppers we own? Get your head out of your ass, Harv. You think we're playing around? You think we don't mean what we say? You have twelve hours left. It's hardly the time to be fucking about with us."

I stared at Sammy. "Twelve? Already? I've been here that long?"

He snorted. *"Eat. The. Fucking. Sandwich."*

"Yeah, that's right, Harv. I've just changed the terms of our agreement, by shaving off six hours. That's what happens when you try to play games with us. Now find our fucking money, or we're going to fuck up this lovely girl here. And she seems really sweet. It'd be a shame to destroy her, mate. But we will."

I felt sick, setting down the half-eaten sandwich. I glared at Sammy, who smirked, shrugging his shoulders.

"You're just going along with this, like he's not a fucking psycho?"

He laughed again. "Oh baby, we're both fucking psychos. Just eat that, before I shove it in your gob, and gag you until you swallow it." I grabbed the coffee, staring at him. It was hot. It would burn.

"Cassidy, if you throw that at me, it'll be the last drink you get," he warned, glaring at me.

Fuck... was it worth the risk?

HARVEY

I STARED AT LENORE in horror.

"Twelve hours? What the fuck? That's not the agreement. We have eighteen hours."

Seb laughed. "Yeah, that's right, Harv. I just changed the terms of our agreement, by shaving off six hours. That's what happens when you try to play games. Now find our fucking money, or we're going to fuck up this lovely girl here. And she seems really sweet. It'd be a shame to destroy her, mate. But we will."

I gasped. "God no, please don't. I'll find the money, I swear. Just please, please don't hurt her."

Seb went quiet, but I could hear Sammy talking to her in the background. I couldn't make out words, but she sounded angry, and she definitely had a right to be royally pissed.

"Tell you what, Harv. I'm a reasonable guy. Give us that woman friend of yours. Lenore, is it? Give us her, and we'll let you have Cassidy back. Only slightly soiled."

What? I squeezed the phone in my hand, while Lenore looked at me with wide eyes. I had the phone on speaker, so she could hear what was happening, and I regretted it in that moment. She glared fiercely at me.

"Go to hell! I'm not giving you Lenore!" I yelled at him.

"Then we're both going to fuck Cassidy in twelve hours. I promise you, whatever you get back isn't going to even remotely resemble the woman you love."

Fuck.

Lenore grabbed the phone.

"If I come to you, you'll free her?"

Seb laughed. "Hello, Lenore. You'd give yourself up for this prick? Do you really think he's worth that?"

I flinched under the glare she aimed in my direction.

"No, he's definitely not. But she is. She's innocent. Don't hurt her, and you can have me instead."

Seb fell quiet. Had he hung up? Finally he spoke.

"How about this, Lenore, my lovely. You have one hour to find us, and actually show up right here, and I'll take your deal. But after an hour, the deal becomes six hours to find the money, and *then* we fuck her up."

There was an angry yell in the background, and the call ended suddenly.

I stared at Lenore. "What the fuck just happened?" She widened her eyes.

"I have no idea, but we need to find them now. If I can get in there, I'll beat both of those fuckers to a bloody pulp, and then I'll feed them their own nuts. But none of that matters if we don't find them fast."

I shrugged. "I've got nothing."

"You're a fucking stalker! How can you not know where to find them? How can you have no bloody idea where they hang out, or where they hide? They must have a base of operations here in town. Think, you stupid bastard!" She snapped at me, and I grabbed her shoulders.

"Will you stop yelling at me? I'm trying! What are you going to do?"

She pulled her arms from me. "I'm going to see if Mikey can trace that number."

Good. *Because I had nothing*. Not a damn thing. Did I know where they hide out? No, because I hadn't followed them. Only her. But wait. I know where I'd found them that night, when I needed the loan. They had an office in town. What the fuck was wrong with me, that I hadn't even thought of that?

"Lenore. I know where they might be." She glared at me, while she held her phone to her ear.

"Get a fucking car, Harvey."

CHAPTER FOURTEEN
CASSIDY

I WAS RIGHT. Sammy was really pissed off when I threw the coffee. Of course, I didn't throw it at him. *I threw it at Seb*. Am I insane? Yes, apparently so.

But Sammy was the one who had threatened me with no drinks, if I threw it at him, so I tried for a loophole. It had mostly missed Seb, but some had splashed on his face, and he'd roared with anger, throwing the phone at the wall, smashing it to pieces, in the middle of his call. Then he'd charged at me.

Sammy had jumped between us, trying to stop him.

"Seb, think about this. Calm down. It's just a bit of coffee."

"It went in my fucking eye, bruv. I'll teach her not to fucking throw things at me!" He snarled, shoving at Sammy, doing his best to get to me. Sammy held him off, eventually shoving him backward.

"Go and calm yourself down. Have a drink. Go fuck someone. *Whatever*, just do it. Go. I'll explain to Cassidy exactly how we feel about her rudeness."

"Fuck, bruv. Just let me hit her. She could have blinded me," Seb urged, moving in my direction again.

"She didn't. Now back off. Take a breather. Clear your head. Do it," Sammy snapped, practically shoving Seb through that door, slamming it after him.

"You are one crazy bitch. I mean, seriously. What did you think that would achieve?" He asked me. I stared at him, fear making me silent. Because what *did* I think would happen? Seb would die miraculously of severe coffee burns, and Sammy would be so distracted, that I could run away? Get to the police, and be saved? What the hell had possessed me?

"I..."

He turned the lock on the door, and left the key there, rather than pocketing it. Then he turned and stalked across the room, straight over to me. He picked up the plate, with the remains of the sandwich, and tossed it across the room, the plate shattering against the wall.

"I was going to eat that," I said quietly, and he chuckled.

"You know... I thought you'd be weaker than this. You seemed weak. I thought you'd just break, before we even did anything to you. But there's more to you than that. You're going to be a challenge, and I think I'm looking forward to it." He moved suddenly, his hand grabbing my throat, while my tied hands tried to pull his arm away.

"I'm going to enjoy testing your limits, working out what scares you the most. What'll break you down, make you give up. I thought you gave up before, but you're still ballsy. It's actually making me want you even more." I trembled, trying to pull his hand away, but his fingers just tightened, cutting off my air.

"The more you fight, the hotter I find you. The fact that you tried to attack Seb, of all people, that just turned me on most of all." He grabbed the rope tying my hands, and dragged my hands down, placing them against his groin.

"See how hard you made me? I wish Seb had cut the time down to nothing. Because, honestly, Cassidy? The very second that clock runs out? I'm going to fucking have you. I don't care whether you struggle, or beg, or cry. I'm going to fuck you. And then I'll let Seb have you."

I gasped back a sob.

"Please."

He tightened his fingers again, having allowed me just enough air to not pass out, then he pulled me closer, still trapping my hands against the bulge in his pants. His face was right up against mine, almost touching.

"Yeah... you can ask nicely, girl, but I'm still going to fuck you. You think I'm the nice one? I'm looking forward to showing you just how wrong you are."

HARVEY

I'D TRIED RINGING SEB back. It was crazy, I know, but I didn't like the way the call had ended. He'd offered us a deal, and disappeared before we could discuss it.

Plus, Lenore's friend Mikey had needed me to be on the phone to him, for the quickest trace. Otherwise it was all triangulation, and whatever the hell that leads to, and quite honestly, I zoned out on the details. I was desperate to find Cassidy. My obsession with her was the sole reason that she was stuck with those bastards. She should be with me, not them.

Seb's phone wasn't even ringing. My calls went straight to voicemail. What did that mean? Did it mean something had happened to him? Was his phone dead? Had he ditched it? He'd just thrown us a bone, and then he rang off before we could even agree to it. Arrogant bastard.

"That's the place up ahead, yeah?" Lenore asked quietly. I glanced down the street at the small office, where I'd gone and begged for a lifeline, which had since become the destruction of my entire life. And Cassidy's. And maybe even Lenore's now.

"Yeah. It looks closed though." The lights were all off, and the street was quiet, dark.

"Duh, really. Well, I'm not planning to ring the fucking bell," Lenore snapped, climbing out of the car we stole. Yeah. *Our second stolen car of the night.* Luckily for me, Lenore knows how to do all this stuff, because I don't have a clue. I mean, I've watched it on tv shows, just like everyone, but it's nowhere near as easy as they make it look. In fact, I think they don't even show the whole process on tv. Bastards.

We crept along the quiet street, edging up to the closed door, and I tried the handle. *Locked.*

"It's locked," I whispered, and Lenore groaned.

"Obviously it's locked, dipshit. Get out of my way." She shoved me aside, and crouched down in front of the door. Was she going to pick the lock? How did she know how to do all these things?

She fiddled around with the lock, then shrugged, and stood up. Backing up, she launched a kick at the door, and it crashed open.

"What the fuck!" I yelled, because there was the end of our opportunity to sneak up on them. They'd have heard that, for sure.

Lenore had already dashed through the door, and was out of sight. Dammit. I ran after her. The place was dark. Silent. Empty. No sign of the bastards here.

"FUCK!" I yelled, kicking a chair over.

"Stop having a paddy and check the desks, look for anything that points to another address. Jesus, Harvey, you're worse than fucking useless!" Lenore snapped, shoving me at one of the desks, while she started pulling open drawers, and dragging the contents out.

"Wait... here's something," she said suddenly, pulling a document from a file. "It's the deeds for that old nightclub on the high street. You know the one that got shut down, after like the twentieth drug bust?"

I looked up from the pile of papers I was flicking through.

"What about it?"

"Well, obviously it looks like they own that. Maybe they're there." I noticed something on the paper in my hand.

"Looks like they have a few places they've taken possession of, like they were going to do with my place."

We ended up with four more addresses. We were running dangerously low on time, and even if we found the place, and they accepted Lenore in place of Cassidy, they would just hurt her instead. I know she was pretty sure she could kick both of their asses, with her Krav Maga, or whatever the hell it was she'd been learning lately, but they were dangerous guys. I wondered if she realised just how dangerous.

"Lenore?"

She glared at me from her phone, which she was using to photograph addresses.

"What? You found another one?"

I shook my head. "You'd really give yourself up for Cassidy?"

She sighed, dropping the phone on the desk.

"I don't really have any choice. She's in danger, and I'm better equipped to deal with that than she is. I mean, I assume I am. Unless you know something about her that I don't?"

I smirked. "I know a lot about her. But she doesn't even go to a gym. She works, and she goes to book groups, out for drinks with her two friends, Vanessa, and Amy, and she watches trash TV on Sunday afternoons, usually while she drinks a glass of red wine."

Lenore looked disgusted. "It's vile that you know all of that about her, and yet you've never dated her, or spent time with her. You know you have a problem, right? Stalking is wrong. Ugly. *Depraved*."

I groaned, tossing the papers onto the floor. They were useless anyway.

"Look… I didn't plan any of this. It just happened. I got scared. I wanted to ask her out, but she was… so… I don't know… beautiful. And delicate. And she smells of flowers… Lily of the Valley, according to her perfume bottle. It's really sweet. Like her. Her hair is soft. I know that, because…" I stopped speaking suddenly, realising that finishing that sentence would make things much worse.

Lenore's eyes narrowed at me.

"Because?"

I shrugged. "It looks soft… doesn't it look soft?"

"When did you touch her fucking hair, Harvey?"

I grabbed her phone from the desk, as I marched past her.

"We need to get moving. We have thirty-eight minutes to find her."

Lenore slammed something on her way out from behind the desk.

"If you've been touching her in her sleep, Harvey, I'm going to kick you in the nuts so fucking hard… You'll be pissing blood for a week."

Jesus. I started to run to the car.

CHAPTER FIFTEEN
CASSIDY

SAMMY LEFT ME ALONE, after the coffee incident, leaving the sandwich and smashed plate on the floor. I glanced at the shards of broken plate. Would they cut through the rope?

I got up and tried the door, which was locked from the outside now, the key gone. I could see through the small window into an empty hallway, as far as the blank wall opposite the door.

I could hear them talking out there somewhere. I couldn't make out the words, but they were angry. Angry was bad. Angry could make them decide to breach their fucking agreement.

Of course, Seb had already breached it, by cutting it shorter. I was starting to think that he didn't care about getting the money back at all. I was starting to worry that he was keener on keeping me. And I couldn't let that happen.

I'd heard what they wanted to do to me. Break me. Ruin me. *Destroy me.* Those things all sounded like things I should avoid at all costs. I grabbed one of the shards of broken plate. It wasn't very sharp at all. None of them were. I tried using one to cut at the rope around my hands, but there were two reasons why that didn't work.

One, there just wasn't a sharp enough edge to cut with, and two, it's really hard to try and cut a rope tied tightly around your hands. I guessed I should be relieved that they'd tied them in front of me, rather than behind me.

I tucked the shard under the pillow. Maybe it would be more effective as a weapon, if I had the opportunity, and courage, to use it.

I set to trying to pull the rope apart with my teeth. They'd managed to tie the knot underneath my hands, kind of between my wrists, which made it really hard to get my teeth at. I glanced around the room, looking for anything I could try and cut the rope with. There was just nothing in the room.

It occurred to me then that there was something pretty vital missing. *A bathroom.* Hell. I'd been ignoring my bladder, which was starting to fill up, despite the shortage of drinks, and vomiting spell, because I'd kept thinking I'd be out of here soon, but now that I knew I was locked in... it was getting serious.

"I need to use the bathroom," I said loudly. There was no response. Crap. I went to the door and started kicking at it. "You hear me? I need to pee, dammit!"

Seb suddenly appeared at the door, his face filling the small square window, making me jump back with a yell. I heard the door being unlocked, and then he pushed it open, standing there, glowering at me. I knew it was him, because his left eye was red, like it had been rubbed raw. I did that. With the coffee. He shot me a glare.

"You were yelling something?" I nodded.

"I'm sorry, but I really need to go to the loo."

He shrugged. "What's your point?"

I glanced around the room nervously.

"There's no toilet."

"And?" Clearly he wanted to be a dick.

I sighed. "You just want me to piss in my pants? I mean, I could... it's disgusting, and it'll smell really bad, but if that's what you want, I will. I can't hold it back much longer. Does the smell of pee turn you on? Just checking before I let go."

"Fucking hell. Come here." I frowned at him.

"Why?"

"Seriously? You want a fucking toilet, right?" I nodded warily. "Then you'll have to leave the room, since you so artfully pointed out that there isn't one here."

I nodded. "Just point the way, and I'll go."

He reached in and grabbed my arm in a tight grip.

"Yeah, that's going to happen. Come on."

I struggled against his grip, feeling his fingers bruising my bare skin. I wished for my sweater back, for a layer between his skin and mine.

"Will you stop dragging your fucking feet? You wanted to go for a piss, right?"

"You're hurting me, Seb." He stopped moving, fixing his eyes on me.

"Say that again."

"What?" I stared at him, as he held me in place.

"Say it again," he said in a low voice.

"Which part?" Where was Sammy? He was evil too, but at least he seemed consistent in his behaviour. Sometimes. More than Seb, anyway.

"All of it. Right now."

I shivered, my bladder starting to ache.

"Why?"

He shoved me hard against the wall. "Hey!" I yelled in pain.

He grinned, leaning close, pressing his body against mine, his hips hard against me. Oh god, my bladder.

"You'll make me pee on you!" I snapped, trying to pull away from him, but with nowhere to go.

"Then fucking say it," he snarled, leaning closer.

I racked my brain. What was it he wanted me to say? I bit my lip.

"I can't remember what you want me to say. Please, Seb. I need to go now. I don't want to pee on you."

His lip curled a little. "Tell me I'm hurting you, and use my fucking name again." What the fuck is his damage?

"Does it... do you like it?" I asked warily, and he smirked.

"Baby, I want to hear the words. And if you urinate on me, I'll make you regret it. I still haven't forgotten the coffee incident. Do you really want me even more pissed at you?"

I groaned. "If it makes you horny, I'm not doing it." His hand wrapped around my throat.

"Do I have to hurt you, to get you to say it?"

I squirmed as he pressed more deliberately against my bladder, and I felt a wave of panic.

"Please, Seb. You're hurting me!" His face seemed to light up. *What a sick fucker.*

"See? That wasn't so hard, was it?"

"Please. Now. I can't hold it!" He shoved me at the nearest door.

"It stays open."

I'd just stepped inside the small cloakroom, and started to close the door.

"What? No. I need privacy."

He shrugged. "You're a prisoner, Cassidy, not a guest. Sit down and piss, but keep the door open. If you want it closed, I'll just have to come in with you."

I frowned at him. "You're sick."

He shrugged. "You'll be half naked. I might get all excited, when I see that naked pussy of yours."

"Ugh. You're a pig!" I snapped, pulling the door half closed, and hurriedly sitting down on the loo. I wanted to pee as fast as I could, so I could get my clothes back on, before he decided to try anything nasty.

Oh, the relief. It hurt because I'd waited too long, but it was a relief too.

"Hurry up," he snarled from just outside the door.

"Don't listen to me peeing!" I snapped at him, trying to pull the door further closed. The door was wrenched open instead, and he stood in the doorway, arms folded.

"Now you get no privacy."

I burst into tears. I was frustrated. I was afraid. And I really didn't want to pee in front of anyone, let alone a perverted stranger.

He groaned, and turned his back. "Jesus, just hurry up."

I finished, wiped, and awkwardly pulled my pants back up, doing up my trousers. Thank god I'd worn trousers to work. I washed my hands, and then leaned down to drink from the tap. His hands suddenly closed on my shoulders, and he pulled me away, turning off the tap.

"That's enough. It's not a fucking hotel."

I glared at him. "Yeah, don't I fucking know it!"

He stepped into the small room with me, getting closer than I liked. I was trapped between him and the sink. He crowded me, one arm reaching around me, to rest on the sink.

"I'm thinking it might be time to take another item of clothing from you, Cassidy, don't you?"

I shivered, trying to push him away with my tied hands, which, by the way, made going to the loo really bloody difficult, but not impossible, because they are in front of me, at least.

"No. Stop it."

He pressed even closer, with way too much of his body touching mine.

"It wasn't a request, bitch."

I stared at him. "It was a question. I answered."

His hands suddenly came up, and grabbed my hair. Both of them.

"You think this is a game? You think you can just keep mouthing off at us, and you'll get away with it? That's not how this is going to work. The more you sass me, the more I'm thinking that even if the bastard pays up, I'm still going to keep you."

"What? No... that's not the deal!" I said, trying to pull away, despite his fingers still being tightly wrapped in my hair.

He grinned, leaning close. "I make the deals around here, and I want you naked. But I'll settle for you removing the top for now."

I struggled against his grip. "No, please. Stop. Let me go. I won't argue anymore, I promise!"

He smirked. "Okay... *counteroffer*... your top off, or a kiss."

"What? Fuck off!" He laughed, tightening his grip in my hair.

"You didn't want to do what I said, so I gave you options. And now you're bitching about that. There's just no pleasing you, is there?"

I glared up at him. "I'm not kissing you, you sick bastard!"

He nodded. "Exactly. So we're taking your top off. You'll still have your bra. It's not like you'll be topless. Not yet." I felt a clenching in my stomach. *No.* Just a bra to protect me from them? They were barely keeping to the deal as it was. If I had just my bra on, they'd go further. It wasn't enough protection.

He was watching me. "One kiss, love. You'd get to keep the top on for a few more hours. You can't say I'm not being fair."

I sighed. "You're never fair. You're abusing me, because someone I barely know owes you money. Go abuse him instead. At least he deserves it."

"Yeah, but he doesn't get me hard. *You do*. I have no desire to fuck him, but I really want to fuck you. For now, I'll settle for a kiss, or you without the top. You have ten seconds to decide, but bear this in mind... I'm not talking about a peck. I'm talking about a real kiss. With tongues."

I shuddered, and struggled against his hold again.

"Go to hell!"

He shrugged, pulling back and reaching for my top, while I fought to keep my arms down, holding it against me. He pulled the knife from his belt, and hooked it into the neck of the top.

"Wait!" I gasped, trying to pull back from the knife. I desperately needed to buy some time.

"Changing your mind, love?"

"How long a kiss?" He grinned widely.

"Long enough for me to taste you."

I shuddered. No, I couldn't do that. Could I? I chewed at my lip, him watching closely.

"How many more hours will I get to keep my top on for?" He smirked.

"Four."

"Six," I countered, watching his eyebrows shoot up, before a sly look crossed his face.

"You *kiss me back*, and I won't take your top for six hours," he offered. Ugh. *Wait*. Hang on a minute.

"Neither can your brother," I pointed out.

"Ah, but then he'd want a kiss too... you planning to tongue both of us?"

Oh god. I closed my eyes. "You're a monster."

He shrugged, shooting me a little grin.

"You say the sweetest things, love. So... you keep the top, and you let me kiss you?"

I looked away. How do I agree to that? Was it really any better than being stuck in my bra? Fuck... if I lost my top now... in four hours or so, they might take the bra anyway. Then I'd be even more defenceless.

I nodded, biting at my lip again.

"Oh... and if you bite me while I'm kissing you, I'll take the top, and the bra. Right away."

Dammit! How did he know? "Fucker," I murmured.

He grabbed my hair again, pulling me close to him.

"Now ask me to kiss you, Cassidy."

"What? Hang on a minute." What was he playing at?

"I want you to ask me for this kiss. Tell me you want it." Fuck. I pulled against his grip on my hair.

"That wasn't the agreement." He shrugged.

"I need to feel wanted, love. I'm only human."

"*Barely human*," I muttered, and he laughed.

"Ask."

"I hate you."

He laughed again. "Not that fond of you myself, Cass. Ask me to kiss you, or the top gets cut off. Five, four, three, two-"

"Kiss me," I snapped at him.

"Ah ah ah... that sounds like a demand... ASK."

"Fucking asshole." He waved the knife, keeping a tight grip on my hair with the other hand.

"Please kiss me," I muttered angrily. He smirked.

"*Say my name.*"

"For fuck's sake! Please kiss me, Seb, you sick fucker." He snorted, and then slammed his lips against mine. His body crushed against me, and I found my arms trapped between my chest and his. I couldn't move him. He pulled harder on my hair, and I gasped at the pain. That was all it took for him to thrust his tongue into my mouth, and kiss me harder. I didn't want to kiss him. Definitely didn't want to kiss him back, but... maybe... no... what the hell is wrong with me?

He'd made it clear. I had to kiss him back, or he'd still take my clothes. I put all of my anger, and hate into that kiss, my tongue pushing at his, and the urge to bite it off, burning through me like a command.

He moaned, pushing my head back, his tongue delving deep, as mine fought with it. Finally he pulled back, his head resting against mine for a few seconds, as we both breathed hard.

"Yeah... that wasn't so bad, eh?" He whispered to me. I took note of how we were standing, how my leg was between his, and I took my chance. Slamming my knee upward, I hit him right in the nuts, causing him to cry out, with a higher voice than normal, and then he fell away from me, clutching at his groin.

"Fucking bitch! You fucking... *Jesus*... Fuck! Sammy!" I stepped over him, trying to run past, but one of his hands caught my ankle, tripping me over. I fell hard, landing on my arms, which not only took the brunt of my fall, but also slammed back into my ribs, and chest. I sobbed out a breath, as pain erupted.

Sammy appeared at the end of the hallway, took one look at us both and groaned.

"What the fuck happened here?"

CHAPTER SIXTEEN
HARVEY

We'd managed to hit three of the five addresses, and they were a bust. We had twelve minutes left. *Twelve.* And we had two addresses, and although they weren't the furthest from each other, they were too far apart for us to hit both in time. The chances of the one we chose being the right one were fifty fifty. For the first time ever, those odds seemed unbeatable.

"We need to split up," I said, glancing at the clock. Lenore stared at me.

"They said it has to be me."

"So? We're out of time!"

She slammed her foot on the accelerator, driving as fast as she could feasibly manage on the inner-city roads.

"So if you turn up alone at the right address, it won't fucking help her. You pointless dipshit."

"But if we both go to the wrong one right now, it doesn't help her anyway. Maybe I could stall them."

Lenore slammed on the brakes as she hit a corner, sliding around it at almost the wrong angle.

"You couldn't stall a fucking thing. You turn up there, and they'll kill you, and keep her. That's not going to fix things."

My phone rang then, scaring the crap out of me. An unknown number, but not the same one as before. I answered, shooting Lenore a worried look.

"Deal's off," the voice I assumed to be Seb's barked at me, sounding breathless, and seriously pissed off. What the hell?!

"What do you mean? We're nearly there," I lied, because we couldn't fail now. It was time to bring Cassidy home. To me.

"That bitch has just ruined her chances of ever getting out of here alive. So you no longer have any chance of stopping us from destroying her."

Fuck. Fuck. Fuck!

"Come on, Seb. We're so close. Lenore is ready to take her place. You wanted that, remember?" I shot Lenore an apologetic look, as she peeled around another corner.

Seb laughed. "She's hot, I'll give you that… but this bitch… *Cassidy*. She just fucked with me for the last time."

"What the hell could she even do? She's tied up in a fucking chair! Come on, Seb. She's scared, and she wants to go home. Please, let's fix this any other way than hurting her," I begged.

I heard Cassidy scream in the background. Then she yelled at someone to get his hands off her.

"Jesus, what are you bastards doing to her?"

Seb laughed, a dark, disturbing sound.

"What she fucking deserves. You have a week, Harv. Get our money together, or we're taking Lenore, and your shop, and we'll leave pieces of you all over the fucking street." He ended the call.

"FUCK!"

Lenore stared at me, pulling over outside the next address.

"What did he say?"

"I don't know what Cassidy did, but they won't give her up now. He says I have a week to get their money, or they'll take you too. And kill me. Jesus… she was screaming." I felt tears burning my eyes as I sat there, but Lenore didn't pause.

She jumped out of the car, and ran for that door. She slammed her hands against it, screaming at them to let her in. But nobody did. *It was the wrong fucking building.*

CASSIDY

SAMMY MANHANDLED ME BACK into that fucking bedroom, and threw me at the bed. I couldn't breathe. My chest was hurting so much that I couldn't get any air. I gasped and sobbed, and panicked, because I couldn't breathe. Eventually Sammy untied my hands, letting me have them back, while I fought to catch some air.

"Just let her fucking die," Seb muttered from the doorway, still cradling his groin. Sammy glanced back at him.

"What's the point in that? You might still have to give her back. For all we know, this Lenore chick is about to walk through the fucking door. I know you said she might be slightly damaged, but dead isn't part of the deal."

I lurched across the bed, grabbing Sammy's hand.

"Please... get... me... to... hosp..."

He stared at me. "Just try to slow down, and breathe. You didn't break anything. You're just winded."

I slapped at him with my hands, trying to tear at him with my nails, as anger joined the panic.

"Fuck... you... hate... you!" He easily grabbed my hands, and pulled them away from his face.

"Breathe, you stupid bitch," I tried, I really did. Eventually, he asked Seb to toss him his knife. What?

I backed away, my hands up in front of me.

"I'm... trying... please..."

He nodded, approaching me with the knife.

Seb dialled a number on his phone. I thought he'd smashed it, but I guess guys like him have spares.

"Deal's off," he barked at someone. I guessed it was Harvey. Were they going to let me go? He listened for a moment, and then fixed a dangerous glare on me.

"That bitch has just ruined her chances of ever getting out of here alive. So you no longer have any chance of stopping us from destroying her."

I struggled desperately, as Sammy grabbed the front of my top, and slashed the knife through it, opening it up like a proper shirt.

Seb laughed. "She's hot, I'll give you that… but this bitch. *Cassidy*. She just fucked with me for the last time."

Next, Sammy hooked the knife under the front of the bra, and snapped that open too. I screamed, and shoved at his arms.

"Get your fucking hands off me, you sick, sick bastard!"

He pulled back, laughing. "I see you're breathing okay again now." Fuck! I'd been so angry, that I hadn't realised that my breathing had eased suddenly. I glared at Sammy, my hands now pulling the tattered clothes across me.

"What did you do that for?" I whispered.

"So you could breathe," Sammy replied, smirking at me.

"But now I'm half naked, you prick."

He shrugged. *"Bonus."*

Seb suddenly laughed, and a chill ran through me at the sound.

"What she fucking deserves. You have a week. Get our money together, or we're taking Lenore, and your shop, and we'll leave pieces of you all over the fucking street." He ended the call, shoving the phone in his pocket. His eyes settled on the remains of my clothes, which I tried to cover up with.

"Nice. And to think if she'd only been a bit nicer, she could have kept them on for a while longer."

I glared at him. "You're a fucking animal. Forcing me to kiss you like that."

"What's this now?" Sammy asked, looking from me to Seb.

"What? She asked me nicely, so I kissed her. I'd never say no to a pretty woman, when she wants a kiss."

Sammy groaned. "So this is why she kicked you in the nads? Because you were messing with her? Seriously, Seb. You're a loose cannon. You only had to wait a few more hours, and you could do what you want to her."

"Hey!" I snapped. "Nobody is doing anything to me. You hear me? You sick fucking monsters need to let me go. This has gone far enough. You could have hurt me back there, and then you'd be in real trouble!"

They exchanged an amused look.

"With who?"

"Duh. The police! It's illegal to kidnap women, and tie them up, and keep them somewhere, and threaten to rape them." Hah! That told them.

They both started to laugh. "Love, do you have any idea who we are? The cops around here let us carry out our business, and they don't interfere."

My stomach churned again. "You're lying."

"I don't think she's ever heard of us before, bruv, and I don't know how I feel about that," Seb said, coming over to sit on the opposite side of the bed to where Sammy was. The door behind them was open, but there was no way I'd make it, if I tried to make a run for it.

"Cassidy... you've never heard of us? The Bennett brothers?" I stared at them.

"Who?"

They laughed again. "Ever heard of gangsters, or mobsters, love?" My hands trembled, as I looked from one of them to the other.

"No... you can't be..."

They both shrugged. "Call it what you want. We own half of this town. Maybe more. We have cops on our payroll. We loan desperate people money, and when they can't pay it back, which is often, what with all the interest we add on, we take what we want from them. We only kill as a last resort, but we do it when it's necessary."

Seb was smirking as he finished his statement.

"Honestly love, I'm starting to understand why you thought you could fight back. You didn't realise just how much danger you were in. We're the worst of the worst. The only people in this town that you have no chance of beating."

I shrank back against the headboard, pulling my knees tight against me, trying to put as much distance between me and those two sick bastards as I could.

"Please," I whispered.

"She wants a kiss again. I swear, I can't keep up with the way her mind works," Seb joked. I groaned, closing my eyes, and resting my forehead on my knees.

"I'm never getting out of here alive, am I?" I mumbled. They didn't speak. Jesus. I sat there, sobbing into my knees, and they just watched.

CHAPTER SEVENTEEN
HARVEY

WE WENT BACK TO my place, because we had no other ideas. We'd just lost our chance to save Cassidy from those bastards.

Evidently whatever she had done, while she was their captive, had pissed off Seb enough that he was breaking the deal. I'd never known them to do that. I'd heard of their deals, and their games, and their trickery, but they apparently always kept to a deal in the end.

I sipped a glass of vodka that Lenore had dumped in front of me, taking one for herself. Ugh, it was burning my throat.

"I don't know how to fix this," I muttered to her. She sighed, staring at her drink.

"Me either. They could be raping her right now, and we failed to save her. Jesus." She looked broken. The strongest woman I knew, looked like it was going to happen to her. Again. I'd never seen her so defeated.

And it was all my fault, wasn't it? My fuck up had led to all of this. And Lenore was taking it on, because that's what she did. She took on other people's problems, and she solved them.

"You didn't fail at anything, Lenore. I did. I fucked up. You were right. I'm fucked in the head. I've been following her around for five fucking months. I know her address. I know where she works. I have her fucking work number in my phone, for fuck's sake. I watched her sleep. Waited in the shadows while she showered, sitting there, with a fucking boner, wishing I could just go in there with her. Who does that? Huh? Fucking psychos do. I'm a disgrace!"

She shrugged. "Not arguing with you. But none of that is as bad as what's happening to her right now. We had a chance to prevent it. We could have got her out of there, and back home, before they did anything to her."

I stared at my phone; at the last texts I'd received from those bastards. Then I frowned. Hang on. I closed the messaging centre, and went to my phone book. Scrolling through, I tapped a name, then hit the speaker button.

"Yo!" A man's voice answered. Lenore raised an eyebrow.

"Is that Terrence?" I asked, because I'd only spoken to him a few times, and he sounded different.

"Yeah, mate. Who's this?" The guy was clearly in a bar or something, but he moved so that the noise reduced a little. That was better.

"Terrence, mate. It's Harvey. Remember? From the pub." He went quiet, then laughed.

"Oh yeah, mate. I remember, the nerdy guy." I groaned. Was that all anyone saw when they looked at me? Lenore smirked. She always knew what I was thinking. Damn her. Why hadn't I fallen for her? Not that she'd have had me anyway. Not really her type. Too damn nerdy.

"Yeah, yeah, that's me. Listen, you remember the advice you gave me?"

Terrence groaned. "Look, man. If you've gone and got yourself into some kind of trouble, it really isn't my-"

"Don't worry. It's not that. It's just that I have to go take their money to them, but the phone cut off, before I could get the address, and now I can't get through. I think it's a signal problem. You know what they're like though. They'll expect me to figure this shit out."

I crossed my fingers, staring at Lenore, who was starting to look monumentally pissed off with me. Great. What now?

"Uh... well, you tried their place on Walker Street?" He asked. I glanced at Lenore for confirmation, because we'd been everywhere tonight, and she shook her head. Okay, that was a start, but let's be smart here.

"Uh, yeah... anywhere else you can think of, buddy?" Terrence went quiet again.

"I need to scroll through my texts, hang on." He stayed quiet for so long that I was starting to lose my mind. My fingers tapped on the table, as I fought the urge to scream at him to hurry up.

Lenore's hand suddenly slammed down on top of mine, smashing my fingers hard against the surface. I wrenched my hand back, glaring at her, and she shrugged again. I was definitely on her shit list. Probably forever. Fuck this day.

"Uh... yeah, there's another place they had me meet them once. You know the old warehouse on the industrial estate down the hill?" I shrugged at Lenore, but she nodded.

"Yeah, they own that place?"

Terrence snorted. "No idea, but behind that, there's a house. Must have been like a caretaker's place or something, only it's pretty big, no idea why. It's mostly boarded up, but I've been in there. You could try that." I nodded vigorously at Lenore.

"Great stuff, mate, thanks so much. I'll let you get back to your partying."

Terrence laughed. "Yeah, thanks. And nice one mate, most people don't manage to pay them back. I think that's kind of how they like it, you know?" I knew. Bastards.

"Thanks, buddy."

"Later."

I ended the call, and waited for the fallout.

"You are such a pointless fucking prick," she said first. I nodded, accepting her words.

"I know."

"You could have done that when this first happened. Why the fuck did it get this far, before you suddenly remembered this guy?" She drank a big mouthful of her vodka, and clenched her fist around the glass.

"Look, I'm not proud of any of this, but my mind kind of went to shit when all this happened. Let's not forget that when you found me, I'd been beaten up. My head wasn't with it. And this guy? Seriously, I met him *once*. He suggested them to me when I was struggling, and we exchanged numbers. I forgot, okay? I've barely spoken to him, and since I ended up in a situation, where I knew I was in too deep with these bastards, I pretty much put him out of my mind, because that was all I could think about."

Lenore stood up, grabbing her car keys.

"We're going now. Grab anything you can use as a weapon. We're going to beat the shit out of these assholes, and pick up what's left of your girl. And then I never want anything to do with you again. You are a complete waste of oxygen. I can't believe I never realised that before today."

Jesus. I grabbed my phone, shoving it in my pocket, and looked around for a weapon. Finally, because I had no other options, I grabbed a knife from my kitchen, slipping it into my jacket pocket.

CHAPTER EIGHTEEN
CASSIDY

THEY LEFT ME TO wallow. I don't know why. Since Seb had declared that the deal was off, and I was theirs, I figured they'd probably just do what they wanted and break me. I fell asleep eventually. It sounds crazy that it was even possible, but I was exhausted.

Spending the day and night being terrified, and terrorised, and drugged, and sick... it takes a toll. Being in a constant state of fear uses up all of the body's reserves. I woke up curled against that headboard, my knees still cradling my head. Everything hurt, and I stretched my back, as I awkwardly pushed my legs away.

The room was dark. Darker than before. The light was off, so the only brightness was coming in through that little window in the door.

I picked up on the sound of breathing, before I noticed him. He was sitting on a chair, which he'd obviously brought into the room. He'd been watching me sleep. I felt unbelievably creeped out by that thought. *Vulnerable.* Sleep should be something we do safely, without some creepy bastard watching.

"Who's there?" I whispered, not wanting to incite anything, but desperate to know which brother I was trapped in here with. Not that either of them would be a safe option.

"Who do you want it to be, love?" He whispered back. It was impossible to tell from the voice. They sounded so similar.

"Neither of you," I finally answered, and he chuckled quietly.

"Still giving us shit, eh?" He whispered. The whispering was unbelievably creepy too.

"What do you want?" I asked, not wanting the answer, but figuring that keeping him talking might delay anything else from happening.

"My cock inside one of your holes. I'm easy on which one it is."

Yikes. "Seb?"

He snorted. "See how well you're getting to know us, baby? You're learning the subtle differences between twin brothers."

I stared at him in the darkness.

"There's nothing subtle about either of you."

He laughed again. "I do enjoy the verbal sparring, love. I think I'll enjoy it more when you're naked, and I'm on top of you. I'm betting you'll keep sassing me the whole damn time."

I pulled my legs up, and hugged them to me again. It was uncomfortable, because my legs really wanted to be straight right now. They ached from the way I'd slept curled up.

"You didn't want me to sass you," I replied, because I didn't want to address the other part of what he'd said.

He snorted, and then he moved. Oh god no.

He approached the bed, and I flinched, moving away as he moved closer.

"Stop it," he said quietly.

"I can't," I replied, almost at the opposite edge of the bed.

"Don't make me drag you back over here," he warned. I stopped moving, but I didn't move back to him.

"Cassidy, if I wanted to fuck you right now, you'd already be naked, and pinned down."

I frowned. "You don't want to?"

He laughed, throwing his head back.

"Are you now feeling all dejected, because you think I won't fuck you?"

I glared at him. "I hate you."

He shrugged. "Makes no odds, love. I just wanted to watch you sleeping. Maybe creep you out a bit. I have to go see someone, but when I get back, I'm going to take what's mine. That's you. Just in case you're wondering. Your body. Your fucking dignity."

I trembled, glaring at the bastard. "Why don't you fuck off and die, while you're at it."

He laughed again. "Just keep it in mind, love. Think about it. Wonder about it. Get yourself all moist, thinking about it."

"Never going to happen," I snapped as he stood up from the bed.

"Don't really care either way. Just making polite conversation." Ha! Like he could ever understand what that even was.

He slammed the door behind him, locking it. I glanced around the darkened room, spotting something on the floor beside the bed. A paper cup. I leaned closer, and saw that it seemed to be full of water. For me?

I picked it up, sniffed it. No smell. Should I risk it? I wanted to. I really did. But what if it was poisoned? No, they wanted me alive, so they could hurt me. Poison might even be a blessing at this point.

What if they'd drugged it though? What if I drank it, out of desperation, and then I couldn't fight them off, because they'd taken away my ability to do that?

"Fuck," I moaned, staring at the liquid, which quite honestly, looked like heaven. Go without liquids for most of a day, including throwing up what you did have, and then stare at a glass of water, and tell me it doesn't look like the most beautiful thing you've ever seen.

"*It's safe*," Sammy said, from the doorway. Why did I keep zoning out, and not realising when one of them came into the room. I needed to be more alert. It might be what keeps me alive. My hand tightened on the paper cup, warping it slightly.

"*Don't throw it*. I know I said no more drinks, but it turns out we're not complete bastards."

I glared at him. "I disagree."

He snorted. "Honestly, you just keep pushing, don't you? Most women in your place would be afraid, hiding, begging for their freedom, trying to be as inoffensive as possible. You know, trying to ingratiate themselves, so their captors feel for them. But not you. You just keep running your mouth."

I shrugged. "Seems to me that all I have left is my sparkling personality, so I need to make the most of it."

Sammy grinned, coming into the room, and taking up the chair Seb had left behind.

"Seriously, Cass, drink the water. It's honestly just water."

I stared at it. "You didn't put anything in it?" He frowned.

"Like what?"

I sniffed it again. "Drugs."

He started laughing, gesturing at me to drink up.

"If we want to drug you again, love, we'll do it openly. No need to sneak stuff into your food or drinks, because we have no reason to hide that from you."

"You're as much of a prick as Seb, do you realise that?" I sipped the water tentatively, and groaned. It was cool and delicious.

He shrugged. "Didn't promise to be a saint, in fact, I think I've constantly warned you that I'm the opposite. You just seem to keep wanting to paint me that way."

"What are you going to do to me?" He raised his eyebrows at the subject change.

"What do you think we're going to do?" I gulped the water, before he could threaten to take it away. It felt so good sliding down my throat. I hadn't realised how dry and sore it had started to feel, but now it felt soothed, and I sighed with relief.

"I'm glad the water was good. Maybe I'll make you earn the next one." I frowned at him, clenching my fist, and crushing the stupid paper cup.

"You didn't give me a glass this time."

He raised his hands, palms up. "Why would we arm you with a weapon? We also didn't risk a hot drink again. You lost your chance for those."

I threw the crumpled cup at him, seeing it fall embarrassingly short.

"Yeah, you'll definitely have to earn the next one. Need to make you respect us a bit more than you seem to right now."

I flipped him off. "I'll never respect either of you bastards."

He stood up suddenly, and I flinched. The door was wide open, and I flicked my eyes there for the briefest second.

"You can try, but I'll catch you, and then I'll make you do something that I'll enjoy, but you won't."

I stared at him again, wondering how someone so attractive can be so mean, because I'm not an idiot, I can see how appealing both brothers are. Both brothers looked really alike. Dark, scruffy hair, really dark eyes. Square jaws, fairly tidy short beards, lips that looked kissable, even though they were mostly twisted into evil grins most of the time.

And they were kissable, dammit. I would never admit it, but Seb's kiss had unnerved me. Because I knew if I'd met either of them out in a bar somewhere, they'd have charmed my pants off pretty fast. But instead I was their captive, and I hated them. *Right?*

I chewed my lip. "Why? Why not just let me go? You've had your fun. You've scared the hell out of me. You've obviously fucked with Harvey. And by the way, when I see him, I'm going to kick him so hard in the nuts, that he'll cry blood. Just an FYI."

Sammy laughed again, looking pleased.

"I'm half tempted to bring him here, just so you can do that, love."

I nodded. "Please. Do it." He shrugged.

"I daresay we'll be killing him soon anyway. But I'm sure we can let you have first crack at him. Assuming you're still capable of walking by then."

My stomach rolled again. "Why do you do that?"

He quirked an eyebrow at me, waiting for me to elaborate.

"You talk to me like I'm a person, and just as I start to relax, you say something evil again."

He shrugged again, pulling his phone from his pocket, glancing at something on the screen, smirking at it.

"I asked you a question," I prompted, and he glanced at me, suddenly more interested in his phone.

"Huh?"

"Go to hell," I snapped, suddenly running for the door.

It took him a beat to realise what had happened, but I barely made it out of the room, before a hand grabbed my arm, and yanked me back. I was pressed back against the wall, and trapped once more between Sammy and another hard place. He stared down at me, his breathing a little faster.

"Nice try, love. Taking advantage of my distraction. Pity it didn't do you any good."

I pushed at him, and tried hitting him, but it was like trying to move a wall away from me. Honestly, I'd probably have better luck moving the wall behind me. He stared down at me, just watching me struggling, and muttering swearwords at him, and then he started to smile.

"You know what all this wriggling is achieving, love?" I stopped moving, blinking up at him. I knew exactly what he was going to say, because I could fucking feel it, pressing against me.

"You're an asshole. Have I told you that before?" I mumbled. He nodded, lifting a hand to run it down my cheek. I didn't like the gentle gestures from him, because they were a lie. *An evil lie.*

"I know, baby. But I think you're starting to like me." I shoved at him again.

"Don't flatter yourself."

He grinned again, running his hand down my neck, making me shiver just a tiny bit.

"I think, before long, you'll be willingly opening those legs for me. I can feel how much you're starting to want me. All of this so far? It's like foreplay for you. You like the idea of being with bad guys. It gets you hot. I bet you even get wet for us." I tried to punch him. I mean, I seriously tried. I've never punched anyone before. My clumsy fist glanced across his chin, and barely grazed him. He laughed.

"Now that's just adorable. You really don't have to pretend to fight, love. We won't think any less of you."

"You're sicker than Seb. I really thought he was the worst of you two." Sammy pressed his hips closer to mine, rolling them slightly, and I gasped.

"Stop it."

He trapped my hands in his, pressing them against the wall.

"I don't think that's what you want, Cassidy. I think you're enjoying every moment of this. Can you feel how much I want you? Wouldn't take much for us to be fucking right here, against this wall. You want that, don't you?"

"No! Stop it!" I gasped out, struggling against his grip on my hands. He moved suddenly, pulling both hands above my head, and trapping them with one of his. I was defenceless, and he had a hand free. He pushed my hair out of my face, tracing his fingers down my cheek, while I wriggled, and tried to kick at him. He shook his head, grinning, because he'd made sure I couldn't knee him, like I did with his brother.

Those fingers trailed down my neck, so soft, the merest caress on my skin.

"Stop," I whispered, turning my face away, so I wasn't staring into those eyes. His hand trailed lower, pushing the torn halves of my shirt away, and the scraps of my bra. Fuck. I'd forgotten that I'd needed to hold it closed. I'd tried tying it, but it wouldn't stay like that. His fingers circled a nipple, and I squeezed my eyes shut, a tear slipping out.

"Please don't."

He leaned closer, his tongue sliding up my cheek, tasting my tear. Then his fingers slipped over my nipple, and I gasped, flinching against him. I turned my head to yell at him, and his lips closed over mine. His tongue traced over my lips, and he nipped at them, small pecks of kisses. I could feel the fight draining out of me, and I needed to keep fighting, dammit! I shook my head, trying to break away from his lips.

He pulled back just a touch. "Why don't you just give in, Cassidy? It doesn't have to be anything awful. Don't you want me to make you feel all the things you're craving? You liked my fingers tracing over your skin. And you like it when I do this." His fingers tweaked my nipple, lightly pulling at it, and my breath caught in my throat.

"No," I whispered.

"You just keep saying that, because you think you have to. But you want it, I can tell. It's in the way you're breathing, the way you keep biting at that lip, the way your body keeps arching into me. These aren't things you do with someone you're not attracted to. Imagine how it would feel to have me inside you. My cock stroking deep, my tongue fucking your mouth at the same time. I could make you feel things you've never felt before."

"Stop," I moaned, trying to pull free of his hands. He stopped teasing my nipple, leaving it peaked, and puckered, desperate for more of his attention.

His hand tucked under my chin, as I tried to lower my head, and he ran a thumb over my bottom lip.

"It doesn't have to be a fight. It doesn't have to be something forced on you. You could enjoy it. Enjoy *me*. Just give in, Cassidy. Let me in."

His lips came down on mine again, at the same time as his thumb pressed down on my lip, and I opened up for him. I didn't mean to. It was all so confusing. I knew he was a bad guy, and wanted to do things to me that I shouldn't permit, but he was overwhelming me, my senses. Making me feel things I never wanted to feel. Not for him. Not for anyone who looks like him.

My body was responding, even as my head was screaming that it wasn't right. His tongue swept into my mouth, and he fisted his hand in my hair, tilting my face up to his.

One of us moaned, and I really hoped it wasn't me. His hips were rocking against me, and that hard ridge of his cock rubbed against me, making me tremble. It wasn't right. It shouldn't be happening.

His phone buzzed, and it must have been in his pocket, because we both felt the vibration. He pulled back, an aggravated look on his face, while I giggled. And then I was mortified. I fucking giggled?

"Stop! Please. This isn't right." I shoved at him, once my hands were freed up, and he checked his phone.

"Bollocks. Right, back in your room. I need to deal with this." I grabbed the tattered remains of my top, and pulled it tight around me. Confusion and doubt washed over me, as I stared at him. What had I been thinking?

"We'll finish this later, love. Trust me on that." He backed me into the bedroom, and pulled the door closed, locking it. My legs shook, and I slumped to the floor, my back to that door, and sobbed.

Chapter Nineteen
HARVEY

They weren't at the first address, but as soon as we reached it, I knew it was a stupid choice. It was too out in the open. You don't capture people, and hold them hostage in a residential street. They'd see everything. They'd hear the screaming.

Lenore groaned. "This was so fucking stupid."

I nodded. "I'm sorry. We should have gone to the other one first."

She started the car again, without us even getting out. It was dark, and clearly wasn't the right place.

"I should have insisted. I just figured since it's between your place and the other address, it made sense to stop on the way."

I grabbed her arm, doing my best not to make her steer off course.

"Lenore, none of this is your fault. It's mine. All of this is on me. I'm just so fucking grateful that you're helping me try to fix it. We *will* fix it. Somehow we'll get her back from those bastards, and we'll get her whatever help she needs, to recover. And I'll stop. I promise. No more stalking. I'll burn it all. Jesus... it hurts to even say that, but I will."

She nodded, carefully pulling her arm away from me.

"I don't know if I can ever look at you as anything other than a creep. You need to be prepared for that. I always figured you were safe, and decent. I would have never trusted you, if I thought you were capable of doing this to someone."

I groaned, checking my phone for the millionth time, although there was nobody I was expecting to hear from. It was just a reflex. We all do it.

"I know, Lenore. Trust me. I didn't start out that way. I guess something went wrong in my head. And she's the one paying the price. *I know.* I'll let them kill me if it gets her away from them. I promise."

She slammed the brakes on, pulling up at the side of the road.

"You'll what?"

I tucked my phone in my pocket.

"It's what I deserve. Man, if there was ever a time for me to grow a pair, it's right now. I'll make this right, Lenore."

She sighed heavily. "I know. I just wish there were a way that didn't mean you had to die. I mean, I still hate you now, but it'd be a shame, you know?" Her lips quirked a little, and she turned away from me, putting the car in gear again.

I pulled the small knife from my other pocket, brushing my thumb against the blade. It would be sharp enough. If I had to stab someone with it, it would definitely do the trick.

"That's what you brought?" Lenore asked, her voice a little shrill. I stared up at her, watching her as she focused on the road again.

"What's wrong with it?" I asked defensively, shoving it back into my pocket, trying not to slice myself in the process.

"It's a stupid idea. It's so easy for someone to get a knife away from an idiot who doesn't know how to use it. It'll be so embarrassing if they stab you with your own bloody knife!" She snapped.

I reached for my phone again. Desperation making me check it repeatedly, like it held all the answers.

"I didn't have a lot of options, Lenore. I'm a bookshop owner. And a stalker, apparently. Neither occupation lends itself to stockpiling fucking weapons!"

She was nodding. "We should have gone to my place instead of yours. I'm such a fucking idiot."

It was then that I realised she didn't even have a weapon. At least, not one I could see.

"You didn't even bring anything, did you?" I asked her warily. She just quirked an eyebrow.

"I *am* the weapon, you moron. They'll expect me to be weak, and that's how I'll fucking destroy them."

I really hoped that she wasn't overselling those skills of hers. I knew she'd been training in various disciplines, for as long as I'd known her. I knew that she had belts for various things. I didn't listen to that stuff as much as I should have, but then it's not something she bragged about.

I knew she'd started Krav recently, just because she wanted to try it out. Did I even know when or where she went? No. *Because I was stalking someone else the whole fucking time.*

CASSIDY

I COULD HEAR TALKING. Two similar voices muttering in the hallway.

"... says Harv phoned him earlier, looking for addresses," one of them said, almost too quietly.

"And?"

"Well... he gave him this one. So we're about to get a visit," one of them snapped at the other.

There was a low laugh. "Well... someone we know wants to kick him so hard he cries blood... shall we let her?" More laughter.

"She said that? Brilliant."

I felt a sick wave of pride at their words. In fact, they almost sounded proud of me themselves.

"Reckon if he checked the other place first, then he's probably about ten minutes away."

Their voices dipped lower, or they moved further away, and then suddenly there was a key in the door, I scrambled to my feet, before the door crashed into me.

"Fuck's sake... what are you doing down there?" I glared at him.

"None of your business, asshole."

He laughed. "Okay... Sammy did a good job of winding you up, while I was out. He says you have plans for Harvey the twat. Well, guess what, you're about to get your chance."

"Stick it up your ass," I snapped, because I just had to keep arguing. I wasn't going to be the pushover they imagined I would be.

Seb snorted. "Maybe up yours later. For now, why don't you lose the rags." I backed away.

"They're all I have."

He nodded. Reaching up, he pulled his own t-shirt off, and tossed it at me.

"Wear this instead. He doesn't get to see your tits. They're ours." The door closed again, and I just stood there, staring at the space where he'd been standing.

What the fuck was their game? All that work to make me lose clothes, just to provide something to cover me up again?

I lifted the t-shirt to my face warily. *It'd smell of him.* It did. The faintest whiff of a cologne that I couldn't identify, and the hint of manliness. It wasn't sweat. It was just the smell of man. A real man. Jesus. *A real man?* I've gone insane. They're destroying me, starting with my mind. My good sense.

I turned my back to the door, just in case they peeked, and stripped off the torn shirt, and the scraps of my bra. The t-shirt felt soft against my skin when I slipped it on, with the slightest residual warmth to the fabric, which made me imagine it against Seb's bare skin.

The reality was that it was probably my own hands warming it, as I held it and procrastinated, but still... my mind went to the place that it shouldn't.

Just like my eyes didn't see his bare skin when he stripped it off. The tattoos on his chest and back, that I didn't get time to scrutinise. The jagged scar across his back. He was gone too fast for me to see it properly. And that was good. I didn't want to. Dammit. I really didn't. *Did I?*

HARVEY

"OKAY... YOU READY FOR this?" My phone buzzed in my pocket, and I groaned, finally getting a message at the worst of moments. The screen said that I had a text from an unknown number. I could see the first few words on the home screen. *'Did you really'*... what the hell?

I opened the text and groaned, pulling Lenore back, just as she reached for the door.

I read the text out to her. *"Did you really think that you'd catch us out? We know you're outside. It's called security, numbnuts."*

I glanced up at the building. There were a few blinking red lights up high. Fucking CCTV. Bastards. But at least it was the right place, at last.

"Text them back." I stared at her.

"And say what? Ooops? It's not me? Pizza delivery? Come on."

She snatched the phone, and tapped away at the screen, sending a message. I took the phone when she handed it back.

"Jesus, Lenore!" I was dead. They'd kill me for *that*.

"'*Kiss my ass, dickless*'?! You sent them that? They'll kill me!" She shrugged.

"You said you were prepared for that, remember? Now, let's go in there, and rescue the poor girl *you* subjected to these monsters."

She grabbed the door handle and pulled, and it opened. The hallway was dark. My phone buzzed again, and I glanced at the screen.

"LOL... *LOL*?? That's their answer? Fuck. I'm dead. I'm so fucking dead. Jesus, Lenore." She turned round and shoved me.

"If you're too much of a fucking pussy, then go and wait outside, but I'm here to save *her*. You get that? *Her*, not you."

The corridor had a few doors, but only one had light coming from underneath it. We headed for that room. I wrapped my hand around the blade of my knife, keeping it inside my pocket. My only protection against the pair of monsters in this room.

CHAPTER TWENTY
CASSIDY

When they came back for me, I was ready for them. I waited to the side of the door, and when it opened, I lunged at whoever it was, knocking him backward, so he crashed into the wall opposite.

"Fucking hell!" He snapped, grabbing me as I turned to try and run. He pulled me back against him, his arms trapping me.

"Get off me!" I hissed.

He chuckled, and I could feel it rumbling through him.

"You're a fucking spitfire. I love it. Yep, keep wriggling, love. It feels sooooo good." I slammed an elbow back at him, making him grunt.

"Jesus... don't lose this fight. I want this when I fuck you." *It was Seb.* I sighed, immediately stopping everything, sagging in his arms. "Oh, come on, Cass... it was just getting good."

"You're a prick," I whispered, and he chuckled again.

"Yeah, but I think you're warming to me. How does it feel to be wearing my clothes, eh? They were on my naked body, and now they're on yours. Pretty intimate, eh?"

"What insult will work on you? I don't even know anymore," I grumbled. One of his hands closed on my throat, pulling my head back, so he could whisper in my ear.

"Can't insult a man like me, love. But what you can do, is earn yourself some home comforts." I stilled in his arms.

"What?"

He pulled me closer, his lips pressing against my ear as he whispered.

"Do as we say, while he's here, and we'll treat you *so* good." His teeth traced my earlobe, and I shivered.

"You'll let me go?" I asked hopefully. His teeth bit down, just enough to make me gasp.

"Hardly, but we'll make things more comfortable for you. You don't have to be locked away like a dirty secret. You could be with us." I shuddered, shaking my head.

"That's the last thing I want." He laughed quietly.

"I'd believe you, if you weren't squirming back against my cock like that. And those nipples of yours?" His hand skimmed over my front, and found a hard peak.

"Yeah... you're turned on right now. *By me*. By the thought of being with me. Imagine if you grew to like it here? I can make that happen."

I shuddered. "I want to go home." He pinched my nipple, wrenching a gasp from me.

"*We are your home now*. Let us make it nice for you."

I felt a wave of despair. "What do you want me to do?" He laughed.

"Exactly what we tell you, love. No backchat, no trying to escape. We're going to royally fuck him in the head. And you're going to help us. If you don't... well, we can stop being so nice."

He leaned down, pressing his lips to my neck, trailing kisses up to my jaw. His grip suddenly tightened on me, and I felt his teeth, and he sucked hard on my skin. I winced, trying to pull away. He laughed, doing it again, and again, and again. He turned and pressed me back against the wall, going at the other side of my throat, leaving more painful hickeys on my skin. Eventually he pulled back, admiring his handiwork.

"There you go. That's beautiful, love. Now you look like we've had a bit of fun with you already." I stared up at him, tears dripping from my eyes, because *they hurt*. They feel nice when they're part of a pleasurable experience, right? Not so much when they're inflicted on you, at the whim of someone who doesn't care if it feels nice. In fact, I think he liked that it hurt. That I hissed with pain, and struggled, and cried.

"You're a monster," I whimpered, and he grinned.

"Sticks and stones, love. Unfortunately, we don't have time for me to leave any more marks on you... but... hmmm..." His hands went to the neck of the t-shirt, and he yanked at the fabric, tearing it, so it hung ragged at my throat.

"Pity that. Damn t-shirt cost me sixty quid."

I glared at him, trying to push him away from me.

"Then you're more of a fucking idiot than I thought you were!" He grinned widely.

"Now... should I leave a handprint or two on your face too? Just to sell it?" I shook my head rapidly, wincing at the burning skin on my neck.

He laughed, grabbing my face, and slamming his lips on mine, kissing me hard, roughly crushing me against him, as my hands fisted in the replacement t-shirt he'd put on, and I tried not to kiss him back. What was wrong with me?

He'd just deliberately caused me pain, and now I was kissing him. I tried to kick him again, but he was ready for me this time. Laughing as he pulled back, he ran a thumb over my lips, brushing it across them roughly.

"Yeah... now you look well used."

He adjusted himself in his pants, and grabbed me by the hair, propelling me forward.

"The better an act you put on, the better we treat you later, love. I think you'll prefer that to the alternative."

He pushed open a door, and shoved me inside. It was the room I'd been in before. There was a dark patch on the light floor, which hadn't been cleaned up well enough after he'd beaten Nev, probably to death. Those hands that I tried to hate, touching me... *they'd killed*. They liked to cause pain. I had to remember that.

Sammy walked in, and took one look at me and smirked.

"Nice work, bruv. Pity you didn't cover her in cum too." Seb glanced at me.

"Oh fuck... good point." I shook my head frantically, backing away from them both.

They sat on the sofa, and then they stared at me, clearly expecting me to do something. I frowned, looking around. Was I supposed to run?

"Kneel," Seb barked at me. *What?*

"Go fuck yourself," I snapped, and he laughed.

"Ain't she a little angel?" Sammy nodded, then glanced at the door.

"Any second now, he's going to walk through that door. The bastard who put you here. If you want to have an easier time here, you'll do as we say. I thought you guys already had this discussion?" He aimed that last question at his brother.

Seb nodded, and glared at me. "Kneel the fuck down, right now. Or I'll put you down." I gulped, moving to where he pointed, between his and Sammy's legs, and I knelt down.

"Facing us," he said quietly. I swivelled on my knees, finding the floor uncomfortably hard, and regretting doing as I was told.

A few seconds later, the door crashed open behind me.

CHAPTER TWENTY-ONE

HARVEY

WE LUNGED THROUGH THAT door like we were ready to attack, and what did we see? Both Bennett brothers sitting, no, *lounging*, on the sofa, and a dark-haired girl kneeling between them, facing away from us.

Her hair was tangled, and messy, but I knew it as well as I knew my own. *Cassidy*. Jesus. It stopped me in my tracks, just inside the door.

"What have you done to her?" I demanded, and they both chuckled, after exchanging a glance.

"Whatever we wanted to. I told you the deal was off. She was a very unruly guest." Cassidy moved her head up, and then quickly looked down again, at a harsh glare from Seb. Her shoulders shook, and I knew she was crying. *Fuck*. I did this to her. Her clothes were dirty, or at least her trousers were. Her t-shirt looked clean, but it was also too big for her. My stomach rolled over. *It wasn't hers.*

"Cassidy?" I stepped closer to her, and Samuel raised a hand, pointing at me.

"Back off, or you're going to really piss us off."

I stopped moving. Lenore had come into the room with me, but stayed silent, casting her eyes around, clearly taking note of what was in the room, and where the exits were, and all the defensive stuff that a person should do in this situation.

Seb stood up, glancing down at Cassidy as her head moved again.

"Stay," he said firmly, and her head dropped again. They were treating her like a fucking animal.

"Lenore, love, really nice to meet you. I'm Seb." He strode toward Lenore, his hand out, like he was at a fucking job interview, or she was. She stared at his hand, and quirked an eyebrow.

"Can't say the same. Let the girl go."

He snorted. "This here is my brother, Samuel. He would get up, but he doesn't really want to." Samuel snorted.

"Yeah, Seb's the one with the nice manners." He rolled his eyes. "Nah, I just want to stay close to our girl here. She's been quite the comfort, since we've been left so out of pocket."

Cassidy muttered something, and his lips quirked, before he shot her a firm look.

"Took quite a bit to break this one, Harv. You've got good taste in women. Pity you're too much of a pussy to actually ask them out." Samuel put a hand on her shoulder, and she flinched, but didn't move away. He squeezed it, and she shook her head.

"*No.*" She gasped out.

He laughed. "Still got a bit of a mouth on her, but we enjoy a challenge, don't we, bruv?"

Seb kept his eye on Lenore, as he laughed in agreement with his brother.

"Seems to me that this one here would be quite the challenge too. You still looking to swap yourself for her?" He asked Lenore, and she folded her arms, glaring at him, looking as fearless as ever. She'd never looked more beautiful to me than in that moment.

"Is that option still on the table?"

He laughed, nodding at Samuel.

"Well... I do enjoy breaking a strong woman... Tell me, Lenore... you ever been fucked by two men at the same time?" She blinked, and her face paled a little. He didn't miss the way her body tensed at his words.

"Yeah... I read up on you, Lenore. We don't go into business without checking things out properly. I've seen the police reports. See, I'm thinking you're all tough now, but you still have a weakness. And I'm more than happy to exploit it, really... but... the thing is..."

He trailed off, backing away from Lenore, but never taking his eyes off her, moving back to the sofa and sitting down.

"We've got this one how we like her, so we're not looking for any new pets right now."

Samuel snorted, leaning down to stroke Cassidy's head, like a pet dog at his feet.

"Fuck you," I heard her snap, making him laugh again.

"Yep, still bites, but we're working on that, aren't we, pet?" He leaned close, and she trembled.

Lenore had stayed quiet, Seb's words perhaps undoing all of the years of hard work she'd put in, to try and forget her assault from all those years ago. *That bastard.* I should have known they'd be prepared.

I glared at the two bastards, my fingers wrapping around the handle of the knife in my pocket.

"I'll do anything you want. Please let them both go. I'll stay." Holy crap. It was terrifying to say the words, but something in me seemed to gain strength from them too.

Seb laughed. "Sorry, mate, but I don't fuck men. So, you see... you have absolutely nothing to offer us. You're not our type, and she's too easily broken." He nodded at Lenore. "While lovely Cassidy here, has just enough fight left in her, for me to really enjoy her again later."

She shuddered and Samuel leaned close to her, whispering something I didn't catch. She shook her head, and he fisted a hand in her hair.

"Do as you're told. Remember what we said." Her shoulders slumped, and she nodded.

What the fuck was he doing to her? How dare his hands touch her? She was supposed to be mine. She slowly pushed herself to her feet, turning to face me. Her face was wet with tears, and blotchy enough that I could tell she'd clearly been crying a while. My hand left my pocket, as I prepared to reach for her.

What made me gasp was the torn shirt, and the angry red marks all over her neck, and the tops of her shoulders. They'd marked her beautiful pale skin. *Those bastards.* I felt my fists clench at my sides.

She glanced back at Samuel, who nodded, shooting her a small grin. She moved slowly in my direction. Then she faltered.

"Oh... Seb... did you mention to our sweet Cassidy just exactly why we thought she was his girl?" Samuel asked suddenly. My heart crashed to the floor.

CASSIDY

I GLANCED BACK AT Sammy as he spoke, and Seb snorted.

"Oh... you mean the stalker shrine in his house? The hundreds of pictures of her, that she never knew he took? The schedule with all of her daily movements on it? The photos of her sleeping, and showering? You mean, did I tell her that?"

My fists clenched at my sides, as he rattled off every crime this bastard had committed against me. I felt rage filling me up. Raw, red, fury. For everything. For the horror, and the fear, and the pain, and the degradation. For the loss of my future. *For the loss of me.*

I roared as I threw myself at Harvey.

"You pervert!" I screamed, slamming a fist into his face. He fell back, landing hard on the floor, looking stunned.

"Cassidy..."

"You don't get to say my name, you sick, sick fucker!" I kicked him hard, right between the legs, enjoying the high shriek of pain that burst out of him. I drew back my leg to do it again, even harder.

"You did this to me, you fucking-" Hands pulled me back.

"Okay, love, that's enough. Don't grind his nuts into the ground," Sammy said, holding onto me.

"I'll crush the fucking things," I snarled, while he laughed, and shot a mock concerned look at Harvey, as he lay on the floor, tears in his eyes, clutching his genitals.

"And I didn't even think he had any balls," Seb said, stepping up at my other side. He crouched over Harvey.

"I think we're done here, fuckface. She's not going anywhere, and you should be glad of that, because if she goes free, she'll hunt you down, and kill you, like the fucking piece of shit you are." Harvey gasped for breath, cringing as Seb leaned over him, his hand closing over Harvey's throat.

"You still owe us the money, and you still have a week. That's it. At the end of that, I'll do exactly what I promised I'd do. And Lenore, love? I can see you preparing to snatch our girl. Touch her, and *I'll touch you*. And I don't think you want my hands on you, love. You're not as fixed as you think you are. You know what I'd do to you."

The woman they all seemed to know backed away, her eyes wide, and her lips trembling, as much as she seemed to fight to control them.

Sammy had pulled me back to the sofa, dragging me down onto his lap, one hand in my hair, so I couldn't pull away.

"Good girl. You just stay quiet now." I tried to turn and glare at him, but he held firm.

"I hate you," I muttered, and he laughed.

"I know you want me to think that, baby."

Harvey eventually scrambled away from Seb, and Lenore helped him to his feet.

"Get gone, before I decide to be the asshole she thinks I am," Seb said, jerking a thumb back in my direction.

Lenore dragged Harvey to the door.

"I'll find a way to save you," he muttered in my direction, and I flipped my middle finger at him.

"Stay away from me."

Sammy laughed again. "Don't bother trying to come back here, for her. We'll be gone before you can even try. She's ours now. Thanks to you." Lenore dragged Harvey away, while he tried his best to lock eyes with me, and I ignored him. The door slammed behind them.

Seb instantly marched to the doorway, and checked that they were gone. Then he checked his phone.

"Yeah, they're getting in their car. What a fucking disgrace." He snorted, watching a little while longer, while Sammy kept me in his lap, one hand on my thigh, as the other continued to hold my hair.

"Please let me move," I asked him, and he let me turn to look at him.

"I like you being on my lap."

"Well, I fucking don't," I snapped, and he laughed again.

"Argue again, and I'll lay you on this sofa, and get on top of you," he muttered, glancing back at Seb. "They gone?"

He nodded. "I'll get the car."

CHAPTER TWENTY-TWO
HARVEY

Fuck. Fuck. FUCK! That went so badly. It couldn't have gone any more badly. Well... we could all be dead, but... the car was moving too slowly, so I glanced at Lenore. Her eyes were blinking fast, as tears poured out.

I was struck dumb. *I'd never seen her cry.* Not even in those early days when we met, and she'd been so much closer in time to what had happened to her. I didn't even know the details. Those bastards knew, though. Somehow they fucking knew, and they'd used it against her.

"Lenore."

She ignored me, so I tried again.

"Lenore, honey, pull over. I'll drive." She groaned, and kept trying to drive. "Please. Lenore, you don't have to do this right now." The car seemed to coast to a stop, and I glanced around us, to make sure we weren't going to get hit by another vehicle. The road was empty, and we were mostly to one side. I pressed the hazard lights switch, and pulled the handbrake on.

"I've got it. Lenore, look at me."

"Fuck you," she snapped, keeping her eyes facing forward. *Hell.* I'd destroyed her, the same night that I ruined Cassidy's life. I was a piece of shit. I knew it. Maybe I always had. I knew better than to touch her. In this state, she'd probably break my arm. I got out of the car and walked round, opening her door, and crouching beside her.

"Hey. Swap seats with me, please." She started to move, so I backed up, and she got out, moving around to the passenger side, and I took her place. Once we were both seated, I put the car back in gear and got us moving again. I drove her home, because quite honestly, I didn't know what else to do, but maybe a familiar place would help her feel more like herself.

She was on autopilot when she got out of the car at her house, and walked to the door. Her fingers trembled when she tried to unlock it, so I carefully took the keys from her hand, and unlocked her door.

Once I got her inside, I went straight for her drink cupboard, and poured her a generous glass of her favourite scotch. She slumped into a chair, and I lowered the glass into her hand.

She stared at it; her eyes focused on the amber liquid.

"I thought... He... that bastard..."

I nodded. "I know. He's a fucking animal. He shouldn't have said those things."

She sighed. "He was right, though. *I'm still weak*. No matter how many classes I take, and no matter how hard I think I've made myself, it only took a few minutes in a room with two guys like them, and I'm right back there."

I crouched in front of her, feeling tears of pure remorse burning my eyes.

"Lenore, I'm so fucking sorry. This is all my fault. I really thought that I could fix this, and all I've done is made it worse. Now you're both paying for my mistakes."

She stared at me. "I'm not broken, Harvey. I just need a little time to regroup, and then we're going to find them again. This time I'll kill them, I promise. They can't be allowed to do that to anyone else. I'll be ready for them this time."

I stared at the floor. "She was... I mean, she seemed pretty broken though, right? They've done god knows what to her, and she's... that was nothing like the woman I knew. Or you know... watched."

Lenore snorted suddenly. "She was seriously pissed at you. I mean, it wasn't undeserved, but still... there's still fire in her."

I grinned suddenly. "I've never seen that side of her. It's pretty amazing, right?" I was glad I hadn't even remembered the knife in my pocket. I'd never have used it on her.

She sipped at her drink.

"Don't go getting even more horny for her than you already were, Harvey. She's not yours. She never will be. Especially not now."

I stared at her. "She's not theirs either. We need to get her out of there."

CASSIDY

THEY LOADED ME INTO a car, strapped me in, and Seb sat beside me while Sammy drove. They didn't drug me at least, but they were making damn sure I didn't escape. I didn't understand why.

If they had made a new deal with Harvey, and I wasn't a part of that anymore, why couldn't they just let me go home. They'd had their fun, right?

"If you let me go, I promise, I'll never tell a soul," I said suddenly, glancing at Seb. He grinned, looking up from his phone.

"Oh really, love. You'll just go back to your normal, boring life, and forget about the two of us? I don't think so. You'd dream about us every night. You'd touch yourself, thinking about the two of us fucking you. And of course, no other man would ever get you wet. You'd only want to come back."

I tried to slap him, and he caught my hand, too easily. Why didn't I take some kind of classes or training, so I could defend myself? Because I thought what they all do. *It'll never happen to me.* But it did, and I'd left myself defenceless.

"Now now, love. You can put your hands on me soon enough. Let's not distract Sammy while he drives, eh? We might get in an accident."

I kicked the back of Sammy's seat, hard.

"Fuck you both. I hope we all die."

Sammy growled. "Don't let her do that again, bruv. I'm on the fucking motorway."

Seb snorted, unclipping his seatbelt, and sliding over to me. He'd left the middle seat empty before, but now he fastened himself in there, with the waist belt. He slid one arm across the back of the seat, his fingers playing with my hair. His other hand held his phone.

"Want to watch some porn, love? I've got all sorts on here." He waved it at me, and I glared in his general direction.

"You're disgusting." He laughed, leaning too close.

"We'll be on the road a while, love. Why not let me make it a more pleasurable drive? You ever had an orgasm at ninety miles an hour?"

I glared at him. "Don't touch me." He shrugged.

"Most women love orgasms, Cassidy. What's your problem?"

I stared out the window, looking for road signs, or anything that would tell me what junction we were heading for, or what town we were going to arrive in.

"I asked you a question, love. Do you not enjoy sex? Are orgasms just not for you? Or do you struggle to get there? Boyfriends lacking in the bedroom?" I hunched down in my seat, trying to ignore him, and his probing questions.

"Cassidy, the more you keep it zipped, the more I know I'm onto something. Nothing normally shuts you up. You do get yourself off, right?" I shot him a glare, and then looked away again.

"Maybe just give her one, bruv," Sammy said from the front of the car, and I flinched when Seb put his hand on my arm.

"Don't. Please don't touch me."

He shuffled closer, crowding me, so that I had to press against the locked car door in an attempt to escape him.

"Look, love, you did what we asked back there. You were a good girl. I'd like to reward you for your behaviour. I'd like to make you come." I shivered, trying to shrink away from him. No. I needed to keep them from being nice to me, because I was weakening. I could feel it.

Sammy snorted. "I think you're losing your charm, bruv."

Seb laughed, his lips moving closer to my ear.

"Cassidy, don't you want me to make you forget all your worries, for a few minutes, at least? I can make you scream. You want that, don't you?"

I shivered, and stayed silent. Speaking would be too dangerous. There was a part of me that wanted exactly what he was offering. A very wrong part of me. I couldn't give in to that illicit desire.

His hand moved, and closed around my knee, and I flinched.

"Stop."

He chuckled in my ear, and his hand slid higher, closer, further.

"Please."

"How about this... I make you come now, or I fuck you when we get home?" I gasped, shaking my head.

"If I make you come, you get your own bed tonight. *Alone*. And we won't do anything to you while you sleep," he whispered.

"Oh god. You were going to do things to me while I sleep?" I moaned, trying to pull away from him again.

"Who knows? But, you know how to make sure it doesn't happen tonight."

Fuck. "Please don't," I whispered.

"You'll like it, I promise."

HARVEY

WE FELL ASLEEP. *HOW sick is that?* We drank too much of Lenore's scotch, and we both fell asleep. Drowning our sorrows, and bitching and moaning about those two bastards, and what had happened tonight. I'm embarrassed to say we both cried. We didn't sleep long. Maybe a few hours. I woke up with a head that swam, telling me I was still kind of drunk.

"Fuck... Lenore..."

She sat up with a start. How could she look so alert, and with it, when we'd drunk half a bottle, and only slept a few hours? I grabbed my head, waiting for the room to stay still.

"Coffee," I mumbled, and she pointed to the kitchen. *Great, I'll make my own then.*

CHAPTER TWENTY-THREE
CASSIDY

SEB MOVED HIS ARM, threading his fingers through my hair, being gentle, which I didn't expect from the most monstrous of the twins. He lifted his other hand, to stroke my cheek, the soft gesture making me look at him with a frown.

"Why the long face, love?" I chewed my lip.

"Why are you being nice to me? Is it just so it'll hurt more later, when you're mean again?"

He smirked. "Don't worry about later, Cass. Just let me touch you now, like you want me to. You want to say yes, you're just afraid that you think you're supposed to say no."

His thumb brushed over my lips.

"Just relax, love."

I let out a breath, embarrassed by how shaky it sounded.

"I can't relax around you."

He laughed. "I'll take that as a compliment. Now, *just feel*." He tilted my head, brushing a kiss over my lips, before he tilted my head further, to run his lips down my throat. I shivered, remembering how it had hurt when he left his marks there earlier.

He was gentle this time, his lips brushing lightly over my skin. His hand left my face, moving down to my knee. I tensed, and he sighed.

"Relax."

I couldn't. His hand slipped up inside his t-shirt that I still wore, and caressed my stomach, before travelling up to my breast, smoothing over my skin, and then circling my nipple. I sucked in a breath as he trailed his fingers over it, and then circled again. I started to relax into his touch, and felt him chuckle almost silently against my neck.

His fingers pinched suddenly, and I flinched, and then they smoothed again. He alternated between smooth caresses, and sudden pinches, and I could feel my body starting to, not only enjoy his touch, but to crave each pinch, to wait for it, and yet I still jumped every damn time.

I trembled as he kept teasing, and I felt him use my hair to angle my face back down again. My eyes, which I didn't even know I'd closed, popped open, just in time to see his mouth lower to mine again.

It was no soft brush of the lips this time. It was brutal, commanding, and his tongue thrust into my mouth the second my lips moved. As my focus moved to the force of his kiss, his hand moved again, slipping down between my legs, pulling my closest leg toward him, over his, to open me up. Then his hand settled between my legs, over my trousers and underwear, cupping me, then pressing, and rubbing.

His lips left mine, and he pulled back enough to look at me, watching as my hips started to move against his hand.

"Good girl. See? When you relax, it can feel really fucking good."

I shook my head, even as my breathing came in short gasps, and my hips kept moving.

"This is wrong," I whispered.

He shot me a wicked grin. "Nothing that feels so good can ever be wrong, love. Let's make it even better." He freed his hands, and worked on unfastening my trousers, slipping the zip down, and then he slipped his fingers inside. I flinched, trying to pull away, and he tutted.

"Come on now, love. You know it'll only get better from here."

"She still playing coy, bruv?" Sammy asked from the front of the car.

"Yeah... but don't worry, I'm not giving up."

I shoved his hands away.

"Stop. That's enough."

Seb leaned close again. "So which one of us are you bedding with tonight? Either way, you get fucked hard." *Dammit.*

I pulled my hands back, but I didn't know what to do with them.

"Let me make this easier for you, love." Seb released my leg and tugged at my trousers, slipping them down my legs, and off one foot, before he pulled my leg back up, then with one hand, he grabbed both of mine in a tight grip, and slipped the other one inside my underwear. I gasped, struggling to free my hands, and he shot me a grin.

"See, love? I've got you trapped. You can't stop me, even if you want to. That feels better, right?" I closed my eyes, as his fingers started to circle my clit, teasing me, making me tremble.

"Oh god."

He leaned closer, his mouth by my ear again.

"That's it, baby. Ride my fingers. Let me make you come." I gasped in small breaths, the only air I could seem to get into my lungs, as his touch started to feel good. It shouldn't, but it did.

He moved his hand, and a finger slipped inside me. He groaned.

"Ah, she's so fucking wet, bruv. I knew it." He leaned closer to me again. "You're drenched, love. Feel how easily my finger slides inside you? *You want me.* You don't want to, but you do."

I shuddered, feeling my legs trembling as he removed his finger, then slammed two inside me, hard, sudden.

"Oh! Oh god." I gasped, and he chuckled, low and intimate, his mouth at my ear.

His grip on my hands meant that, no matter how much I struggled, I couldn't push him away, and that meant it wasn't my fault, right? I couldn't stop him, so I might as well enjoy it. That didn't sound right to me, but I couldn't fight it. It was building.

My hips moved with his fingers, the two that plunged inside me, over and over, and the pressure of his thumb against my clit. It built inside me, and I tried not to go with it. I tried to fight it.

"Come on, love. Just let it take you, it's okay to give in," he whispered against my ear. His fingers sped up their movements, and he pressed down hard on my clit, and I broke. Desperate pleasure crashed through me, and I let out a strangled yell, as my body flexed and fought against Seb's tight grip. His fingers only stopped moving once I'd settled back down, ceasing the teasing and sliding, and caressing.

He pulled them free, and sucked them into his mouth, while I fought to pull my hands away from him. His grip had been so tight near the end that it would bruise. He moaned as he sucked at his fingers.

"I fucking knew you'd taste sweet. Hey... what'cha doing now?" I'd pulled away from him, curling toward the door as best I could, while trapped by a seatbelt.

I closed my eyes, my head resting against the seat back, as the tears trickled from them. *That was wrong.* It was wrong to enjoy it. I shouldn't have let him touch me. What was wrong with me?

"What's going on?" Sammy asked from the front seat, the car starting to slow, as he moved onto the slip road from the motorway. I looked through the window, trying to catch sight of the signs, having seen various towns in Avon and Wiltshire on a previous sign, but I don't know what town we'd ended up in. Everything looked blurred right now anyway.

"Baby's feeling bad for feeling good," Seb said, his voice gruff. He sat back into his seat, and ignored me for the last part of the journey.

HARVEY

WHEN IT COMES DOWN to it, finding someone who's been kidnapped is pretty much impossible. We ignored what Samuel said, and we headed back to the place where we'd found them. Lenore kicked the door in, because I'm not ashamed to say that she's fucking amazing, and twice the man I am.

The place was empty, just as they'd promised, and we'd lost about four hours in total, with the wasted journey, and the sleeping. They could have gone anywhere. We searched the place, finding absolutely sod all. A torn women's top, and a bra, that had been cut open. A crumpled paper cup.

There was a patch on the floor in the room we were in before, that looked like blood. I knew it had been there before, so I didn't worry that they'd killed Cassidy. In fact, they'd seemed to quite like her, so I figured killing her probably wasn't part of their plan. They'd clearly hurt her though. Those bastards had touched her, molested her. Hurt her. Made her cry. And all because of me.

I tossed the bed, and found nothing, except a ceramic shard under the pillow. The bedding had been messed up enough that I think it had been used, but there was nothing there. There was hardly any furniture in the place, which limited the hiding places they could use for vital information.

No computers. No landlines. *Nothing*.

Lenore even pulled a vent off the wall, and climbed up to push the ceiling tiles up, to check for hidden things up there. I swear, without her, I'd have missed any clues that might have been up there. She was fucking amazing. She'd pushed past the upset from earlier, claiming to be fine now.

I worried about how she'd react if we came face to face with the Bennetts again. There was no hiding just how dangerous and depraved they were. She'd frozen when he challenged her, but then he'd done his homework, and knew exactly what to say to fuck her up. I really hoped I'd get a chance to make him pay for that.

It was strange. I knew that I'd been the one to get Cassidy into this, and it killed me to see her so beaten down and defeated like that, but I barely knew her. In reality, I knew that. My entire experience of her, boiled down to stolen photographs of her living her life, completely devoid of any involvement with me.

But Lenore... I knew her. I'd known her more than ten years. I'd seen her deal with all kinds of shit, and always bounced back. *This*. This was like a new level of agony. Seeing her hurting. My best friend. The one person I trusted, and confided in, and relied on.

They wouldn't get away with it.

CHAPTER TWENTY-FOUR

CASSIDY

THEY LED ME INTO a house, in the middle of nowhere. I'd been given the opportunity to get my trousers back on, and I'd slapped away any attempts by Seb to help me into them, making him chuckle.

I followed them inside. What other option did I have? We were god only knows where, and I hadn't seen any other property anywhere, within miles of this house. Not to mention the fact that the only road in was a dirt track, and looked barely travelled.

Once inside, I went where they directed, and curled up in the bedroom they'd given me. I pulled the blankets around me, and made myself a cocoon to keep me safe, then I drifted off into an uneasy sleep.

HARVEY

LENORE WAS ON WITH Mikey again, trying to find out what other tricks they could use, to try and find the Bennetts, and I was sitting there, being completely fucking useless, because that's all I know how to do now. Maybe it's all I ever knew.

The bookshop should have been open by now. It was after eight in the morning, and I'm normally open already. It was the last thing on my mind though. My mobile was on charge, and I was trying to whip up something for breakfast with Lenore. The least I could do was try and feed her.

She was making other calls, and so when my mobile rang, I grabbed it in a panic, expecting it to be the Bennetts. Maybe wanting to make a different deal. As if.

"Is this Harvey?" A woman asked. I frowned.

"Yeah, who's this?" I unplugged the charger, and straightened up.

"My name's Julie. I work with Cassidy. We spoke before." Oh fuck. I looked around for Lenore, but she was far too busy with her calls to bail me out of this shit.

"Oh... uh, hi. Did you mean to call me?" I asked, hoping she'd mis-dialled. But then she did mention my name, didn't she?

I could hear her tapping away at a keyboard.

"Sorry, I know it's random, but Cassidy hasn't come to work. She's always here before me. And she's not answering her mobile." Fuck. I glanced at Cassidy's handbag, and rummaged in it for her phone. It was dead, so I plugged it into my charger. Thank god it fit the same charger.

"Oh, that's strange. What about her home number?" Julie cleared her throat.

"Ringing non-stop. I'm worried, Harvey. Did you find her yesterday? With the books?"

That was what I'd told her... but of course, it had been too late. *I had been too late.*

"Uh, no... I got caught up at work, and didn't make it. She hasn't come by for them either." It's not like I could have told her the truth.

She groaned. "Bugger. I'm worried. I didn't know who else to call. Her best friends don't know where she is, and they weren't impressed at being woken so early. I don't know what else to try. Maybe I should call the police." FUCK!

I took a deep breath. "I'm not sure that's going to be wise, Julie. As far as we know, she's just running late to work. Does she drive? Maybe she has a flat tyre." What the fuck is this bullshit I'm spouting? I know she walks in to work. I know everything about her.

She sighed. "Damn. You're right. I'll cover for her as much as I can today. If you see her, can you get her to ring me?" I nearly laughed. As if that would happen. Christ, what a fucking mess.

"Yeah, of course. She might stop by for her books, I guess."

Julie thanked me and rang off. It was unnerving that she'd made a note of my number yesterday. I should have been more careful. I grabbed Cassidy's phone, and powered it on, now that there was a little juice in it.

It took a few moments to come to life, but then messages popped up, and a few missed calls. I scrolled through. Three calls from 'work', two from 'Julie', and one each from 'Vanessa' and 'Amy'.

The texts were from her friends, asking what the hell she got up to, and did she 'cop off' last night. I smirked. As if. She wasn't that kind of girl. She always went home alone from bars. I knew that much from watching her for so long.

Lenore suddenly made a whooping sound.

"Got something!"

CASSIDY

SOMEONE WAS STROKING MY face, and it was nice. I smiled as I woke, enjoying the caresses, until my eyes focused on the face of the person touching me. I gasped, and pulled back.

"Well, that's not very nice, love. I woke you so gently and all." I wasn't sure which twin it was. My eyes were too blurry from sleep.

"Leave me alone," I mumbled, shoving him away. He snorted, and whipped the covers away, or at least he tried. They were wrapped around me in such a way, that I'd have to roll to release them, and I so wasn't doing that.

"Don't touch me," I snapped at him.

"Fuck's sake, Cass. I've got food here, and a drink. Just sit the fuck up, will you." I still couldn't tell which one it was.

"I'd rather die," I muttered at him, turning over, so I couldn't see him. I heard him get up and leave the room, and smiled to myself. It felt good to beat them for once.

Footsteps returned, and two people snatched at the bedding, and wrenched it away from me, nearly tossing me onto the floor in the process.

I sat up and glared at them both.

"Fuck off!" I screamed at them.

"Well, that's just bloody charming, isn't it? You cook her breakfast, and bring her a drink, and I made her come all over my fingers last night, and she just throws it back in our faces. I think someone's forgetting to respect us, bruv."

I glared at Seb. "Well, you can go fuck yourself first, and then he can join you."

Sammy laughed, slapping his thigh.

"I swear, she just gets feistier."

I glared at them. "I'm not eating or drinking anything. So you can stop trying. You're keeping me here against my will, and I won't take part in it anymore. I'll die first."

Seb snorted, coming over to the bed, grinning at me when I shuffled across the bed, to keep distance between us.

"And here I thought we'd bonded a little last night, love. I mean, I can still taste you."

"You're a pig!"

He shrugged. "Here's the thing, though… think about what you're saying. We were taking it slow with you, but if you decide to starve yourself, you're just guaranteeing that we'll start playing with you straight away."

I frowned. "No. What? That doesn't make sense!"

He glanced at Sammy. "Do unconscious chicks do it for you, bruv? Or half-starved twiglets?" He shook his head.

"Yeah, me either. So think about it. Right now you're conscious, and curvy, and sexy. It would be monumentally stupid of us to wait until you're half dead, or scrawny, to start fucking you. So you'd just be speeding things up."

"FUCK!" I screamed. "I hate you both so much. Somehow, I don't know how, I'm going to fucking kill you both, and I'll smile when you die. I'll fucking *smile*!"

Seb nodded, looking mildly impressed.

"You're sexy when you're screeching at us, love. Keep it up. It gets me hard. Want to see?" He reached for his pants, and I screamed at him again.

I lunged, throwing my fists at his face, trying to claw him, hurt him, anything to shut him up, and make him go away. Strong hands pulled me away from him, while he just laughed at me.

"Calm down NOW, or I'll drug you again, and when you wake up, you'll be back to square one. Tied to a fucking chair, and helpless. Only this time you'll be naked, so we can at least enjoy the view. You did so well... you were free to roam. We were bringing you food and drinks. I mean, for a captive, that's a pretty fucking cushy life. Look at your room. It's lovely. It's actually decorated, with actual furniture. That's an improvement on the last one. See? We promised you an upgrade, and we delivered. The only person messing this up, Cass, is you." Sammy fell silent, waiting for my reaction.

The fight drained out of me. Because he was right, wasn't he? They hadn't hurt me. Not really. Threats. Some minor altercations. Nothing serious. And they'd promised to make me more comfortable, and they had. He was right, and I was wrong. They'd been honest with me. And I was being a brat.

Sammy released my arms, and I slumped on the bed. "I'm sorry," I whispered.

He shot a glance in Seb's direction.

"Did she really just apologise?" He asked quietly, and Seb nodded. "Interesting."

Sammy stood up, and placed a tray on the bed, that he'd kept out of the way until now.

"Breakfast. Orange juice. If you stop acting out, I might even let you have coffee later. You'd like that, wouldn't you? You like coffee?" I nodded, barely looking at him.

"Thank you."

He backed up, glancing at Seb again, his brow furrowed.

"Right... we'll leave you to it. There's a knife and fork there, and I expect them both to be on that tray when I return. Don't go screwing yourself out of an easy life, Cass. Eat up, there's a good girl." He left, and Seb followed, closing the door behind them.

It was interesting. As soon as I started to do as they told me, they seemed to lose confidence. Was that the answer? Play along, until they let their guard down completely, and then take them out? *How much would I have to endure though, before we reached that point?*

CHAPTER TWENTY-FIVE
HARVEY

"When we reached their place last night, there was a car, tucked around the side of the house. I made a note of the number plate, and since it was gone today, I asked Mikey to track it. It was picked up on several motorway cameras overnight."

I stood up. "Where are we going?" She grinned.

"Swindon." Shit.

At least she'd had a plan. I hadn't had a plan. She'd taken the time to get a number plate, while I was pissing around with my phone last night. She'd had her world shaken, and still remembered to get that checked out.

And thank god for all the cameras on the motorway right now. All those average speed cameras, as well as your basic traffic cameras. All in all, it's pretty hard to cross the country without something somewhere picking up something.

We loaded the car with supplies for the journey, filled up the tank, and got moving.

"Who was that girl who phoned you, Cassidy's friend?" Lenore asked, as we reached the motorway.

"Julie. The one she works with." She nodded.

"She gonna cause us any trouble?"

I shrugged. "Hell if I know. She's worried about her. But I think she's just going to cover for her for now. Hopefully she'll still have a job when we get her back."

Lenore nodded. "At the end of the day, we'll need to keep this bird in the loop, or she might decide to go rogue after all."

I stared at the road, watching as Lenore whizzed past cars, staying in the fast lane as long as she could. It was terrifying.

"If I tell her the wrong thing, she could do exactly that." She sighed.

"I get that, dipshit. But maybe ring her before the working day ends, tell her you've got an update. Tell her something."

"I have her phone. I could text Julie and her other friends, pretending to be her, and say she's ill?" Lenore shrugged.

"We'll think of something, but for now, let's find these bastards. Mikey is trying to pick up where they went, once they came off the motorway. He's also looking for addresses they might own there."

I nodded. "I could ring that guy again. Terrence."

Lenore paused. "Let's hold off on that. I don't know if we can trust anyone who actually knows them." Fair point.

CASSIDY

THE FOOD WAS GOOD. Bacon, eggs, toast. Normal breakfast foods. Orange juice. Again, normal. How could they pretend that everything was fucking normal, and feed me food like this?

Seb's words had freaked me out. They were still planning to rape me. If I gave up now, they'd just do it sooner. But the question remained, why hadn't they done that yet? They'd told Harvey the deal was off, and that they were keeping me.

They'd made it clear to me that they planned to keep me here. There was no longer a time limit protecting me from their depravity. So why were they still holding off? Did they truly just want to scare me, and didn't plan to do that at all? Or were they dragging it out, so I'd either start to hope it wouldn't happen, or lose my mind with terror.

As soon as the thought hit me, I knew exactly which one it was. Why just do what I fear most, and have it over and done with, when they can keep pushing me, and messing with me, and enjoying the build up to it? It was all about breaking me, right? *Sick bastards*.

I finished the food, and the juice, and put everything back on the tray, as per Sammy's command. I had to pick my moments, choose my battles. This wasn't one I could win.

I needed time to get an idea of the layout of the house, where the phone might be, stuff like that. I didn't imagine it'd be that easy, but maybe I could get hold of one of their mobiles, and phone for help. Not that I even knew what town I was in, but they can track phones, right?

"Good girl," Sammy muttered, walking into the room, seeing the tray. I was standing at the window, looking out at the rolling hills, and heavy rain outside. I turned when he came in, so he wouldn't be able to sneak up on me.

"It was nice, thanks," I finally said, because I had no more fire left in me right now. He shrugged, tilting his head at me.

"You can have a coffee later, if you keep behaving."

"I'm not a fucking child." Oh, there it was. *My fire*.

He snorted, running his eyes up and down my body. "Fucking right, you're not." He joined me at the window. "As you can see, there's nowhere to run to."

I stared outside again. "Where are we?"

He snorted. "Not in Kansas anymore, Dorothy." I groaned.

"If you're just going to be a prick, can you please go away?"

Sammy grabbed my arm, turning me to face him. "I know you think if you say 'please', that you won't get punished for mouthing off at us, but that's not how this works. We might enjoy your mouth, but you keep pushing me, and I'll enjoy your mouth in a way you might find less agreeable."

His fingers were digging into my arm, and it hurt, but his words were more terrifying. I stared at him, staying silent, waiting for him to let go, back away, anything but hurt me.

"Now, see... I'm not sure I like you so quiet, either. It's quite the dilemma." I sighed.

"You make me afraid to speak."

He jerked me closer to him. "Fear can be a hell of an aphrodisiac, love." I gasped, trying to pry his fingers away from my arm.

"No."

He snorted, letting go, and watching me stagger away from him.

"You keep saying that word, like you think it makes a difference to us. See, we both know, that when you say no, you really mean yes."

I shook my head. "That's absolutely what's wrong with men like you. You fucking sick monsters, who think that rape is okay, because no means yes. That's why so many fucking women out there get raped, and you know what it does to them? It destroys them!"

Sammy smiled, running his tongue over his lips.

"Now you're just turning me on, love. You want me to fuck you, I will. Trust me, I think it's long overdue." He stepped close again, trapping me against the window. The cold glass made me shiver through the thin t-shirt I wore.

"And when you think about it... we've been pretty fair to you. You even got off last night, and we both went to bed unsatisfied. Is that any way to treat the men who are feeding you? Looking after you? I mean... you're living here rent free. Not many people get a chance to do that. I feel like you should really be doing something to repay our kindness." I was trembling, trying to push him away from me, but his body was hard, solid, immovable. He smirked.

"See... you're barely trying to push me away. You don't want me to move, not really. You like me this close. You like me so close that you can smell me, feel me... *touch me*." He leaned back slightly, pulling off his t-shirt, tossing it behind him, then he grabbed my hands, which now faltered in the air between us, and pressed them against his bare skin. He had no tattoos on his chest, but his arms were heavily tattooed.

"No," I gasped, trying to pull back, and he laughed.

"There's that yes word again. I knew you'd like this." He kept hold of my hands, running them over his hard chest, his taut stomach. I tried to clench them, inadvertently scratching him with my nails as I moved my fingers.

He groaned, his eyes almost closing, as he stared down at me.

"Fuck... yeah, baby... claw me. That's good. We'd best keep those nails long, so you can use them to pleasure me."

My head dropped, as I felt that helplessness wash over me. I wasn't strong enough to push him away, or even pull my hands away from his bare skin. I could feel his warmth seeping into me, and I couldn't bear to see my hands on him. I could feel my whole body trembling, and my shallow breaths became sobs.

"Please, stop," I gasped out.

Sammy growled softly. "Look at me, Cass." I shook my head, and he tightened his grip on my hands, pushing them lower. The threat was there. *Look at him, or he'd put my hands in his pants.*

I looked at him through my tears.

"You're telling me to stop, but you're the one touching *me*, Cass. Shouldn't I be the one who decides if you touch me? Is it so awful? Does my skin not feel warm, and comforting?"

I shook my head fast. "Nothing about you is comforting. You terrify me. Maybe more than Seb." He grinned, never moving his grip on my hands.

"Wow... now you're just trying to compliment me. Why am I scarier than him? He's the crazy one."

I shook my head again. "You're worse. You're crueller than he is. He likes me scared, but you? You like it when I break. *I'm breaking, Sammy.* I can't take this. Please just let me go."

He released my hands, lifting his to my face, shaking his head when I flinched from his touch.

"I like it when you break, Cass, because it's fucking beautiful. If you could see how you look right now... desperate, trembling, and the tears... the fucking tears. They make me *feel*. And I'm not used to feeling." Oh god. I wanted to push him away, but to do that, I'd have to put my hands on him. *Willingly.* I glared at him.

"Enough, okay. This is enough. You did what you wanted. I'm terrified, and begging. You won. You can back off now." I could hear the desperation in my voice.

Sammy shook his head, leaning closer, bending his head to mine. His lips touched down on my cheek, his tongue flicking out to taste my tears.

"No."

He nodded. "I know, baby." He kissed his way over my cheeks, his tongue taking time to taste the salty wetness of my skin. Eventually I had to put my hand out to push him away, risking the skin-to-skin contact, to try and gain some space. He moaned softly when I touched him, and his hips rocked against me.

His lips moved to mine, and softly teased and tasted, while my fingers started to tense against his skin, and my nails started to dig in. He moaned again, and fisted my hair as he started thrusting his tongue into my mouth, kissing me hard.

I tried pushing him again, but he just accepted the pain of my nails digging into his skin, enjoying the small bites of pain, as he kissed me, trapping me between him and that window.

My trembles became almost full body shudders, and I felt my body starting to respond to his touch, to his forcefulness. It terrified me, because I should keep fighting. It shouldn't be making my skin heat this way, or making my nails dig in harder. And it sure as hell shouldn't be making me press my thighs together, as I felt myself heating up there. *No.*

"Fucking hell... you didn't wait for me?" Seb asked from the doorway, and Sammy started to laugh, his lips slipping from mine. He turned his head to look at his brother, without letting me move a millimetre. I tried pushing him away again, but he didn't budge at all.

"Sorry, bruv. We got... carried away, I guess. Ain't that right, Cass?" I shook my head, trying to push him.

"I didn't want that."

He snorted, backing away suddenly, nearly making me fall forward. He adjusted his hard cock in his pants.

"We were just getting acquainted; you know how it is." They watched me as I went to the bed, and pulled the bedding up around me.

"Yeah. I know exactly what you mean. Why didn't you just fuck her?"

Sammy turned to look at me. "We'll be doing that soon enough. Look at her. I bet she's fucking soaked."

Seb quirked an eyebrow.

"Prove it."

I stared from one of them to the other. I didn't like the looks on their faces. And I really didn't want any proving of anything. *Because I was going to lose.*

CHAPTER TWENTY-SIX
HARVEY

WHEN WE FINALLY REACHED Swindon, I felt a wave of fear. Not because I was afraid of facing the Bennetts again.

This time I'd be ready. I was fed up with being afraid of them. I needed to do what had to be done to rescue both women. It was time for me to step up, and be a man.

No, the fear was purely because we had no idea where to go next. We hadn't heard from Mikey yet, so we had no info on places they'd been seen, or any properties they owned. I don't know Swindon. It's not exactly a place I'd choose to go to.

We followed a dual carriageway towards the town, and I just groaned, staring at Lenore as she concentrated on the unfamiliar roads.

"Where next? We don't have a fucking clue! I don't even know how big this town is, or if we're heading for their centre, or just for rows of fucking houses that could be anyone's," I said, my frustration making me louder than normal.

Lenore shot me a glare. "It's not like I know any better than you do, dickhead. I'm just not as ready to give up as you are. Mikey will call. And when he does, we'll be in town and ready."

We found the town centre, and parked up, paying ridiculous parking fees, while we headed for the nearest fast-food place, and stuffed our faces, because we were starving.

"God only knows what they've done to her by now. Maybe she's dead," I muttered, sipping the coffee I'd ordered with my food.

"Either way, we're going to find them, and end them. They fucked up my head, and I can't forgive them for that, on top of everything else. And when this is over, H, you're going to explain to the police exactly what your part in all of this was. She'll get her justice, and you'll pay for what you did. Stalking is a crime. At least I think it is, and either way, you caused her to get dragged into this, so you're due to do some penance." I nodded, keeping my head down.

I wished I could go back three months, and never make the deal with the Bennetts. Then we'd all be fine. Living as normal.

Sure, I'd have no business, or a home. But nobody would be at the mercy of those bastards, and I could still see Cassidy. Smell her. Watch her sleep. *Fuck*. Lenore's right. I need help.

Her phone rang then, and she snatched it up. "Mikey," she said to me as she answered it.

"What do you have?" She listened, sighed, slammed her hand on the table. "Fucking hell. *You said Swindon*."

I stared at her. Dammit. Don't tell me we're in the wrong town.

"Okay, but you definitely mentioned Swindon. They were seen coming off the motorway here."

I started gathering up our food wrappers onto the tray, ready to dispose of them.

"Where the fuck is that? Back on the motorway?" She looked furious. Eventually she ended the call, and shoved her phone in her pocket.

"They're not here, are they?"

She glared at me. "Apparently they have no business or property in Swindon, but they do, in the villages off the motorway, in the other fucking direction." Damn! We dumped our rubbish, and ran back to the car.

We'd wasted valuable hours messing around in Swindon, when we were in the wrong damn place all along!

CASSIDY

I SAT AND STARED at the almost identical brothers, as they watched me with amusement. I pulled the blankets tighter around me.

"Leave me alone."

They exchanged a glance, both grinning. Even though they weren't completely identical, it was still like watching a person in the mirror, when they moved in sync like that.

"Maybe she only gets wet like that for me, bruv," Seb said, shooting a smug grin in his brother's direction. "There's no shame in that. I am the hot one."

Sammy laughed, leaning over and shoving his brother with one hand. "That's not what the girls normally say. You're the scary one."

He shrugged. "Either way, I'm happy. The girls like me just fine."

I stayed silent. I was in a dangerous situation right now. Both of them were in the room, and both of them had sex on their minds, and I was terrified that my time had run out. And even scarier was that part of me that felt some kind of attraction to both of them.

"She's never been this quiet before, bruv. What do you think is going through that mind of hers?" Seb asked Sammy, as they both approached the bed. I stared at them both, one either side of the bed, and the open door at the end of the room. I started loosening the covers.

"Maybe she's just getting ready for us," Sammy said, smirking at Seb. As soon as they were close enough, I bolted.

Dashing awkwardly across the bed, and out of the room. I didn't pause to see what was what, I just ran. There were stairs, so I ran down them, almost tripping over my own feet. At the bottom, I looked for a door to the outside. There!

I grabbed the handle and pulled it, and it opened. *It opened!* I ran outside, instantly regretting it, when the heavy rain soaked me in mere seconds. Still, I had to take my chances now. All I had on was the soaked t-shirt of Seb's, my work trousers, and the flat shoes I'd worn to work.

How I wished I'd worn boots. I hadn't taken the shoes off since I'd been trapped there, because I knew that if I had to run, I'd need shoes. Of course, flats were absolutely no good for running in. They kept slipping off the backs of my feet as I stumbled along.

It was so strange that neither of them had dived on me yet. They must be right behind me. Surely? I was too afraid to look back, as I stumbled away. I imagined them running behind me, ready to grab me at any moment. *It was terrifying.*

The rain was loud. It was impossible to hear if they were even out here. It was full on torrential rain, the kind we normally only get if we're due for a storm. I really hoped I wouldn't be stuck outside if we started to get thunder and lightning.

Once I'd made it out of the long garden, I ran for the hills behind it. Surely to god there had to be some kind of help out there somewhere.

My shoe got caught in the mud, and it was pulled from my foot. I gasped, falling to my knees, and turned to grab it, pulling hard to free it. I chanced a glance behind me, but there was nobody there. They hadn't followed me?

Maybe they'd slipped, and broken their evil necks. I hoped. I really hoped that was what had happened. My shoe finally came free, and I tipped it, to try and shake free any wet mud, before I could put it back on.

"Oh, Cass. I thought we had an understanding," a voice said from the side of me. One of the bastards had sneaked around me, while I was freeing my shoe. He'd crouched down to speak, and I turned, shoving him back, as I stood up to run for it.

The other twin was just feet away, smirking at his brother on his ass in the mud. I threw the shoe at him, and ran in the other direction. Fuck! Now I was running back toward the fucking house! I stopped, faltering as I looked around me, searching for an alternative.

An arm came around me, another across my throat, and I screamed. I couldn't breathe. The arm around my throat was choking me. I gasped, and desperately tried to pull it away, but he just kept pressing until I started to feel dizzy. He kept the pressure on, and my attempts to free myself stopped completely, when my arms no longer had any strength.

As I felt myself passing out, I heard him whispering.

"I can't wait to make you pay for this one, love."

CHAPTER TWENTY-SEVEN
HARVEY

WE WERE DRIVING ALONG bloody country lanes, and it had started to pour with rain again. It had rained on the motorway, but nothing like this. It was so heavy that we could barely see in front of the car. We probably should have pulled over to wait for it to pass, but Lenore was determined not to stop.

We had addresses again. Three of them. All remote, and far enough off the beaten path that nobody would ever know what happens there. Those sick bastards. How many times have they even done this?

Cassidy might be the hundredth woman they've kidnapped and tortured. And it was my fault she was there. They'd done a runner with the woman I wanted, and they'd probably done awful things to her. She'd never forgive me for that. I mean, I don't think she would. Should she? Could she?

"First one's coming up after this village. It's a few more miles down this road. Keep an eye out," Lenore said, sighing heavily as a tractor pulled out of a side road up ahead. "Shite. Another bloody tractor. Is that all they have around here?"

"What are we going to do when we get there?"

She sighed. "I have no fucking idea. They'll see us coming, unless we park up somewhere, and wait until it's dark. Of course, first we need to know which is the right fucking place, before we even plan what we're going to do, and while I'm doing everything, what the fuck are you bringing to the party? Huh? All you do is whine and moan, and ask me what to do next! Man up, Harvey, for fuck's sake!"

I stared at her, blinking against the burn of tears.

"What do you think I'm trying to do here, Lenore? I'm terrified of these guys, but I'll keep trying to find them, and I'll go in there, and I'll try and save her, because I'm trying to man up. I'm sorry I don't have people to ring for information, and all your skills, but I'm doing my best."

She nodded. "I know. I'm sorry. It's just, well, it was a long fucking night, and now we're driving around the country looking for a needle in a haystack, and I still don't know what we'll do if we find them. She was pretty messed up when we saw her last time, and they've had her for hours since then. I can't promise she's alive, or even anything like the girl you were stalking, but we're going to do our best."

The car hit a pothole, and skidded when she tried to correct it.

"Crap!"

A minute or so later, we realised the road wasn't suddenly at a funny angle, but the car was. *We had a flat tyre.*

CASSIDY

I WOKE UP IN bed. For a few moments, I couldn't remember what had happened before. My hair was wet. In fact... I felt damp, and so did the bed. Like I'd sweated buckets in the heat of summer. I lifted the covers to look for the culprit, and noticed something unexpected. I was naked. *I don't sleep naked.*

As my memory started to return, and added itself to the throbbing in my head, I realised what this meant. After one of the brothers had choked me out, one or both of them had stripped me naked, and put me in this bed. The question was, did they do anything to me, while I was out for the count?

I tried to inspect myself under the covers. Nothing looked marked or wounded. Was I sore anywhere? Yes, but mostly my head, and my throat. I didn't feel sore *down there*, so maybe they'd left me unharmed.

They did say, after all, that they preferred their women conscious when they rape them.

Jesus. I cast my eyes around the room. It was dark, curtains closed, slivers of light coming in under the door. I held my breath, listening for anyone in here with me. Nothing. It was silent. I sat up, pulling the bedding with me, to make sure I was covered up.

It was bizarre. I expected to find one or both of them doing something creepy, like watching me sleep. And they weren't even in the room. Why did it bother me? Because I didn't know where they were, or what they were up to? Or because some sick part of me wanted one or both of them in here with me.

I wanted to get out of the bed, but I also didn't want to leave the only protection I had. If I got out, I'd be naked. And if I took the bedding, I'd be tripping over it, if I tried to run from them again. But wait. I glanced at the door in the corner. The one that wasn't the door to the hallway. An ensuite. It had to be.

I kept my eye on the bedroom door, sliding out of the bed, and making my way for the door. I listened first, making sure one of them wasn't hiding in there, because at this point, I wouldn't put anything past them. It was silent.

I carefully opened the door, and found a small ensuite. Thank god. I rushed in there, closing the door, the muted light from the small high window lighting my way. I reached to lock it. Fuck. It needed a key, and of course there wasn't one. *Bastards*. But it was still a toilet I could get access to, when I needed it.

After I'd used the facilities and washed up, I grabbed the one big towel in there, and wrapped it around me. It was better than nothing. I looked in the mirror. A messy, bedraggled woman looked back. My hair was a ragged mess. My makeup from the day before had mostly disappeared, aside from some smudges of mascara around my eyes. I looked tired. Afraid. Was this me now?

I heard a noise in the bedroom and froze. Another noise. Nobody spoke. Footsteps approached the ensuite door. Nobody opened it. Nobody knocked, or spoke. The longer I was in there, and I knew someone was out there, even though they made no further sounds, the more terrified I became.

Time dragged on, sending me into a silent panic, and I backed away from the door, clutching the towel, and ended up sitting in the shower cubicle within the bath, curled up in a corner.

"Cass, you have ten seconds to come out. Or I come in," a voice declared from outside at last. I trembled as I sat there, wondering why my legs wouldn't work. I tried, I really did. But they wouldn't work. Fear had taken my ability to stand up. When the door crashed open, I cringed, hugging my legs to me.

"Come out of there," he barked, and I ignored him, staying curled up and trembling. The shower door was wrenched open next, and he towered over me. "Cass, I'm not kidding. Get out of there right now."

"What's going on?" The other one asked from the bedroom.

"Yeah, she won't move."

He appeared at the door, peering over his brother's shoulder.

"So make her."

I whimpered, trying to curl up smaller. Why couldn't they leave me alone?

"Cass, you're pissing me off now. Get up." That had to be Seb. He had zero patience.

One of them crouched in front of the shower cubicle.

"Cass, you need to come out of there now." I shook my head.

"Fuck's sake. This isn't a game. I'll drag you out of there."

I peeked at him over my knees. "I'm scared." He glanced behind him at his brother.

"What are you scared of?" *Really?*

"You."

He grinned. "Aw love, of course you are. That's pretty much the point. Now come here, and let me get you out of there."

"Which one are you?" He snorted. "You can't tell? I'm hurt, love. We *are* individuals, you know."

He reached out a hand, and I stared at it.

"You'll hurt me if I come out."

He glanced back at his brother again.

"We're more likely to hurt you if you stay in here."

"But why?" I whispered.

"Because we're bastards, love. Come on. *Now*." I stared at him, unsure if my legs would work now, any better than before.

"I can't."

He glared at me. "Stop fucking stalling, and get out of there." His brother leaned over and grabbed his shoulder.

"I'll sort it." They swapped places, and the result was a fist grabbing my hair, and pulling.

I screamed, trying to free my hair, as I awkwardly lurched to my feet. He dragged me out of the shower, and tossed me at the bed.

I barely managed to keep the towel around me.

"That hurt," I whispered, trying to smooth my hair back down.

He shrugged. "You were being a brat."

I stared at the two of them, standing there like almost identical monsters.

"It's not being a brat, when I'm so scared *my legs won't fucking work*!" I was screaming by the end of the sentence. Their only response was to share one of those amused looks of theirs.

"Does this mean you feel bad for making us run after you? Getting soaked in the rain? Having to carry you back?"

I glared at him.

"You were doing so well. You were opening up to us, letting us get to know you. And then you betrayed our trust, by running away." I think it was Seb, but I still couldn't tell. When they were pissed off, they were too alike.

"Which one of you choked me out?" I asked bitterly. They glanced at each other again.

"Who do *you* think did it?" One of them asked.

"Fuck it, I can't even decide which of you is which right now. How can I work that out?"

One of them smirked. "Okay, love... here's what we'll do. You'll kiss us both, and tell us which of us is which. You could tell from that, right?"

I glared at him. "I'm not kissing either of you."

One brother crouched beside the bed.

"Listen, love. You hurt our feelings. All this petulant shit isn't winning you any prizes. You need to make it up to us, so here's how it's going to go. Either you make us feel better, or we get to punish your bad behaviour. *Choose*."

"Dammit. You're Seb. And you're a sick bastard. I'm not doing anything to make you feel better. You're the bad guys! I'm the unwilling and terrified hostage! Why do you both seem to keep forgetting that I don't want to be here? I didn't choose to be here! *I was kidnapped*. Forced to be a part of your sick games, because of someone else's debt. And now I'm stuck here, naked, and you guys are being so creepy!"

My desperation didn't seem to soften their hearts even a little bit. Further proof that they probably didn't even have hearts.

They both laughed instead.

"At least she guessed the right name. I was getting pretty pissed off that she couldn't tell us apart. I'm nowhere near as fucked up as you," Sammy said to Seb, who flipped him off.

"Actually, you're worse," I said, and he quirked a brow.

"How's that then, love?"

"You pretend to be nice, but you like it when I cry."

He shrugged. "You're sexy when you cry."

I looked away from them both. "That's not normal, you know. Normal guys don't like stuff like that."

"I'm still waiting for your decision, love, regardless of how you're judging us right now."

That was Seb, obviously. I shook my head.

"You already punished me. You took my clothes away."

He snorted. "You ruined your clothes, Cass. They were soaked, and muddy, and if we'd left you with them, you'd have ended up ill. We did you a favour. Even though you hurt our feelings, we looked after you."

I frowned at him. "You really believe the shit you say, don't you?"

He grinned. "Actually, I'm getting fed up with the sound of all of our voices. I'd prefer to hear your screams. Pain or pleasure, I'm easy on which."

"Oh god... you're fucking insane," I whispered, pulling the towel tighter around me.

Sammy sat beside me. I knew it was him, because Seb hadn't moved.

"We're giving you the option of pleasure, Cass. I don't know why you keep complaining. Most women would love screaming orgasms, at the hands, or whatever, of two young studs."

I shifted away from him a little.

"I won't give you my pleasure. That's not something you can just make me do."

"We *can* make you give us your pleasure, you know. You liked it when Seb made you come, didn't you, love? It felt good. You keep wanting to hate us, but we're the only ones who really understand what you need. How long have you been denying yourself what you really want?" He leaned forward, stroking my hair from my eyes, and I flinched from the contact.

"You're evil. You want to rape me. How can you think I'll find pleasure in that? You're both fucked in the heads." His fingers stroked my hair next, teasing at the tangles I had hated to see there. He'd shuffled closer too, and I froze.

"Please don't." It was like a reflex at this point, to keep saying it, regardless of what they did. Because I should. Because none of this should cause that weird yearning inside me that said 'hey, maybe they're right', and 'nobody ever made you come like Seb did'. It was horrifying and confusing.

"Cass... think about your time with us so far. Have we done anything to hurt you? I mean, sure, you're afraid, but that's just because you don't want to admit to yourself that you're attracted to us. You can feel it though, can't you? *Deep inside*. That moistness between your legs, that shiver that runs down your spine, when we touch you. The way the sound of our voices makes you feel warm, and shaky. Be honest with yourself.

What you really want, deep inside, is to lay back, and spread your legs, and welcome us inside you."

"NO!" I pushed his hand away, trying to scoot across the bed, away from him. What I had forgotten though, when his words seemed to tie me in knots, was Seb. Seb, the bastard, who'd grabbed a fistful of the towel I wore, as my protection against them.

When I tried to move, it kept me from escaping. At the same time, it loosened the towel enough that the part I'd tucked in, to keep it in place, slipped free, and I had to clutch at it, to keep from flashing them.

"You forget, love. We've already seen it all," Seb said quietly. "You think we didn't look, when we stripped you off? You think we didn't spread your legs, and feast our eyes on that beautiful fucking pussy of yours? The only reason we didn't fuck you then, was because we want you awake, and aware of it, because you want that too. You want to feel every inch of me sliding deep inside you. You want to be staring into my eyes, when I fuck you deep and hard. Don't you, love? Don't lie now... we can tell when you do."

I pulled free of the towel, scooting across the bed, and pulling the blankets around me instead. I couldn't take it. Their words, the way they wormed their way into my head, my soul. They just made me want what they kept detailing, even though it would be wrong, and pathetic of me, to give in at all. Did I want pleasure? Who the fuck doesn't? But did I want it from two men who'd drugged me, and terrified me, and kept me tied up, and locked away?

They were watching me, like they could see the internal battle raging through me. They both started to smirk.

"Stop looking at me," I finally said, my voice low, shaky. "This isn't right."

Seb balled up the towel, and tossed it in the direction of the bathroom door.

"You need to stop lying to yourself. At some point, very very soon, you're going to be begging me to fuck you, because you can't even consider breathing without some part of me inside you. I'll be so much a part of you, that you won't be able to get through a day without thinking about me, and wanting me. You're halfway there already. It's just the bullshit you call 'normal' that's getting in the way. Bruv, I've got something to do, so I'll leave her with you. Enjoy."

He stood up, and strode from the room, and I watched him leave, with something like regret filling me. I covered my face. My hands were shaking, and I hated to admit it, but my body was definitely reacting to their words, and their presence. It was harder to hide without clothes. The bedding was my only protection.

"Cass, I'm going to bring you something to eat and drink. And you're going to thank me for my kindness, and you're going to finish them, like a good girl. Understand?" Sammy glared at me, and I nodded slowly, burying my face in my hands immediately again.

"So fucking repressed," he muttered as he left the room, closing the door.

CHAPTER TWENTY-EIGHT
HARVEY

A FLAT FUCKING TYRE! Perfect. We were in such a dangerous place, on such a narrow road, just after a bend. Anyone could whizz around the road at high speed, and not see us until it's too late. But what choice did we have? We had to change the fucking thing, and get moving again.

Lenore threw the boot open, and fiddled around with the contents, probably freeing the wheel from its mount.

"FUCK!" She screamed, suddenly kicking the back of the car, and slamming the boot closed.

"Jesus, don't tell me," I said, defeat sloping my shoulders.

"Punctured. I was sure I had that fixed," she muttered angrily. I couldn't believe it. To get this far, and be scuppered by her failure to get a flat tyre fixed, or replaced.

Looking at her angry face, I knew that mentioning how badly her fuck up was screwing us would likely get me killed, so I shrugged instead.

"Shit happens. We need to abandon the car, though. We'll get killed if we stay here." She glared at me.

"I'm not leaving my car here, Harvey. We'll have to push it."

I stared at her like the insane person she clearly was.

"Lenore, how the fuck are we going to push it anywhere? This road is narrow, and twisty, and the first bastard that races through here, at about ninety, is going to crush us to death!"

She glanced at the bend behind us.

"Then we'd better get moving. I want to leave it somewhere it won't get trashed. I'll call the breakdown service for it, then we can walk on like fucking morons."

I groaned, knowing that she wasn't going to budge on this.

"Fine. You'll have to steer, and I'll push from back here."

We started slowly pushing the car down the country lane, in the heavy rain, looking for anywhere the road widened enough to safely leave it.

CASSIDY

SAMMY BROUGHT ME ANOTHER sandwich, and coffee. *Actual coffee.* They talked about punishing me, and then he gave me hot coffee again.

He shot me a look as I reached for it.

"Last chance with coffee, Cass. If that goes anywhere other than down your throat, you'll never have a hot drink again."

I groaned at the heavenly smell from the mug, lifting it and staring at him.

"Cass," he warned, backing up a step. I grinned suddenly. It was unbelievably empowering, to see one of these bastards back away, because I was a threat to him, even for a few seconds.

"Aw don't be scared, Sammy. I'm not going to hurt you," I said, feeling cocky.

He raised an eyebrow. "I can't promise the same, Cass. Eat. Drink. I'll be back in a while, and that better be gone." He turned and headed for the door, while I contemplated throwing it anyway.

"Oh, and if you try anything stupid again, next time you wake up, you'll be tied to that bed, spread-eagled and open, for us to fuck any time we want."

My stomach clenched painfully, and every ounce of confidence I'd briefly felt disappeared again. The door closed soundly, and I stared miserably at the sandwich.

HARVEY

WE MANAGED TO GET the car a bit further down the road, at least away from the blind bend, but it was exhausting, and eventually even Lenore had to give in, and abandon the car. She left the hazard lights on, and called it in to her breakdown service, tucking the keys under the passenger side wheel arch.

"What if it gets nicked?" I asked her as we started walking. She frowned at me.

"Nobody better steal my fucking car. But if I don't leave them the keys, they can't sort it." She was right about that. But it was unnerving to have to leave the keys there. I'd reminded her to remove her house keys at least, so some creep couldn't sneak into her place, and... *fuck*... I'm that creep, aren't I?

I've finally realised just how fucking messed up that is. I'd been sneaking into Cassidy's house, because she had a broken window lock, in the laundry room of her house. She obviously hadn't known, so I'd kept making use of it, but now it was finally starting to dawn on me just how fucked up that was.

Had I taken any of her underwear from that laundry room? *Maybe*. Had I wished they hadn't been washed first? *Of course*. Because I'm a fucking animal. Jesus... I hung my head as I walked in the rain, finally starting to realise why Lenore had been so horrified with me.

CHAPTER TWENTY-NINE
CASSIDY

THE FOOD WAS TASTY. There wasn't enough of it, but it was good. I'd grown used to feeling hungry all the time. At least they were giving me some food, but it wouldn't keep me strong, and maybe that had been their plan this whole time.

I was definitely weakening, and it wasn't just a physical thing. I shouldn't find anything about them appealing, but they were worming their way into my head, and each time I pictured them, they looked less and less like monsters, and more like... *something else*...

I kept arguing with them, and saying no, and calling them evil, but... if I gave in, what would that make me? I had an awful feeling that I was about to find out very soon, because I no longer had my clothes as a barrier between us, nor for them to use as a game to taunt me.

What was left to take from me now? Just the things they'd threatened. The things that didn't sound quite as awful now, as they had yesterday.

Wow, was it only yesterday that they'd snatched me? Time had a funny way of disappearing into a vague nothingness, when life or death came into play. Suddenly all I knew was that it was getting darker outside, but did that mean it was almost night? Did that mean they'd had me for twenty-four hours now? Or was it dim outside because of the god-awful weather? Would it suddenly brighten again, and it'd turn out to be lunchtime?

Having no idea of the time was messing with my head too. I wouldn't have been surprised if they knew that too, and were using it as another tool to torment me.

And did Harvey and his friend Lenore just give up, and go on with their hunt for the money, while they left me with these bastards? I supposed

I hadn't exactly made an effort to make them want to keep trying. I wondered if he could even walk properly yet, after that kick I'd given him. It had been strangely satisfying, to cause him such pain because, wasn't it deserved? All of this was his fault, after all.

And what had the deal been with that woman he was with? She looked about his age, *our age*, and she seemed tough, but whatever Seb had said to her had screwed with her head pretty badly. Was it just some bizarre gift these two bastards had? To freak women out enough that we grew weaker around them?

Or had he referred to something that had actually happened. I tried to remember what he'd said to her. Something about police reports, and sex with two men... was that it? Oh god... were they the two men? Had they raped her?

I went from relatively calm, to horrified and afraid again. The more hours that passed, the more likely it became, that they'd come for me. And how many more times would I escape the same treatment from them, before they forcibly took what they'd threatened?

I went and retrieved the towel that Seb had tossed away, wrapping it around me once more like a really crappy toga, and then I inspected the window, behind those heavy curtains. Could I get out this way? They seemed to leave me alone for long periods of time, so would it give me time to climb out, and run for it, while they thought I sat here quietly like the good girl they kept calling me? Ugh... I wasn't their pet. I was a human fucking being. Anger pushed away a little of the fear, at least for a moment.

The window opened, and revealed an opening just large enough for a smaller person like me to climb through. But the drop outside was significant. One storey is a long way to fall if you're trying to squeeze out of a hole in the wall, and have no idea how to land properly. It even looked like the ground sloped down from the wall, and the fall might be even more extreme. And how far could I even get, without clothing, and potentially with two broken legs?

And then I had that mental facepalm moment. *We came here in a car.* A fucking car! If I could find the keys, and get out to the car, I could be driving away and, even better, they wouldn't be able to chase me, because I'd have their car, and they'd be on foot.

Perfect. I had a plan. Now I just had to find a way to get my hands on those keys. And that meant I'd have to play along for now. Stop acting up. Let them start to trust me again. As I heard footsteps approaching the bedroom door, and my hands started to tremble again, I wondered if I'd even have the guts to try.

HARVEY

THE SAD THING ABOUT people in my lifetime is that they don't trust anyone. I mean, it makes damn good sense not to, but when you're stranded in the middle of nowhere, and it's pissing down with rain, it's really fucking annoying.

Nobody stopped. Nobody cared that they drove past a broken-down car, and now two people hiking in the rain. Some of the bastards even managed to half drown us with puddles splashed over us, as they raced past. I'd never been so wet, miserable, and willing to give up, in my whole life.

How Lenore just kept powering on, I didn't know, but my respect for her just kept growing. This wasn't her problem, not personally, and she'd been more motivated than me this whole time. Maybe the hope of saving someone from going through the hell she did was keeping her going, but whatever it was, she was actually showing me up yet again.

"Is that a pub up ahead?" She suddenly yelled, and I glanced up from watching my feet, just before I crashed into her. There was definitely a building up ahead, and from the way it was painted, and the car park at the side of it, I really hoped that was what it was. What I wouldn't give for a pint. Or pretty much any drink…

"I'm buying," I said as we started walking again, suddenly energised by the fact that salvation possibly lay just ahead.

When we stepped inside, and the assault from the rain suddenly disappeared, I felt my spirits rise, just a little. There was a blazing fire to one side of the small open bar. I headed straight for the bar, nudging Lenore in the direction of the fire.

"Shit weather, eh?" The bartender said, nodding at the door. The place was pretty much empty.

I laughed, trying to wipe the water from the lenses of my glasses, making them worse instead.

"Yeah, something like that. Our car broke down about half a mile away."

He whistled. "That sucks. What can I get you?"

I glanced at Lenore, then back to him.

"How about two Irish coffees, with a side order of bath towels?"

He snorted. "I can do you the drinks, plus a couple of the towels I use for the glasses."

I shrugged. "Done. Got any food on?" He didn't. He did, however, have pre-packaged sandwiches, and other snacks, so I loaded up my arms with those, and joined Lenore, waiting for our coffees.

I handed her the tiny square towel, and she laughed.

"Well, that won't cover much."

I cast my eyes over her, suddenly really wanting to see her with just that tiny towel to cover her.

"Eyes, H," she said sharply, and I looked back into hers, a wave of guilt making me blush.

"Sorry. I uh…"

She shook her head. "Not gonna happen, stalker." Ugh. My shoulders dropped. She was just going to keep holding that over me, wasn't she? One mistake, and I'd never live it down.

CHAPTER THIRTY
Cassidy

SAMMY STEPPED INTO THE room rather cautiously, which I appreciated, because he clearly expected me to attack, and instead, I just stepped away from the window, straightening the curtains, and facing him.

He glanced at the tray, taking in the empty plate and mug sitting there.

"You just want me to call you a good girl again, don't you?" He asked, smirking as he approached the bed.

"I'm not your fucking pet!" I snapped, then mentally facepalmed, because I was supposed to be getting them onside. He laughed.

"You can just say yes, you know. You don't have to pretend that it bothers you." I shrugged, turning my back on him, before I argued again.

"Whatever. Don't let me keep you from whatever you're doing."

When he fell silent, and I couldn't pick up his movements, I froze. I knew he was probably doing it to freak me out, so I'd turn and look for him, but I fought to stay exactly where I was, as if he didn't terrify me just by existing.

The silence dragged on, making me start to freak out as much as it had when I'd hidden in the shower before. Everything in me was screaming at me to turn around. Figure out where he was, and what he was doing.

I tried to carelessly run my fingers through my hair, which was a big mistake, because it hadn't been brushed in a day, and it had been grabbed, and pulled, and rained on, and slept on, and it was snaggy as hell.

While I distracted myself, trying to smooth the knots out, my towel was suddenly whipped away from me, and I screamed, turning to try and wrap myself in the curtain, because it was the only thing near me that I could hide behind.

"Come away from there," he said quietly, and I shook my head.

"I'm naked."

He grinned. "Exactly. Let me see you. Let me run my eyes over every delicious inch of your naked body." I stared at him.

"Please don't."

He shrugged. "Let me look at you, and I'll let you have a nice shower. How does that sound?" I glanced at the closed door of the ensuite for a second, craving the hot water, and the chance to feel clean. To wash my hair. When I looked back at him, he'd moved closer.

"Maybe I'll even let you have a hairbrush. You'd like that, wouldn't you, love? Get that lovely hair back under control." I nearly moaned out loud at the prospect of being able to tidy myself up. I'd feel stronger if I did. *I'd feel more like me.*

"Would I get clothes to wear?" I asked softly. He tilted his head.

"You'd have to earn those." Oh god.

"What would I have to do, for clothes? I'm too vulnerable when I have none." I watched him run a hand through his hair.

"Well... we could come up with some ways of getting those... but first you have to stop hiding behind that curtain, and let me see you."

"For a shower, and a brush?" He grinned.

"Exactly."

I glanced around the room for a moment.

"What's to stop me just using the shower anyway? It's right there."

He snorted. "Gee, why didn't I see that coming? Oh wait... I did. It's an electric shower, love. You know what they do when the power isn't on?"

I frowned. "It's not on?"

He took a few steps closer to me and my curtain cape, which I clutched so tightly that my fingers looked pale.

"Do we look like we were born yesterday?"

I tried to pull more of the curtain around me. "How old are you?"

He leaned closer, his hand closing over the edge of the curtain.

"Thirty-four, love. Plenty old enough to know better, than to let you accidentally have anything we don't control." I frowned, tensing my hands on the curtain, because I could sense that he was about to try and tear that away too.

"Control?"

He didn't pull the curtain, instead stepping closer again, *too close*. I tried to step away, but if I did that, I'd have to let go of the damn curtain, and he damn well knew it. These game playing bastards were getting on my last fucking nerve.

"Do you think you've been in control of anything, since you were taken? Everything that's happened so far has been planned for, by us. You think you managed to run yesterday because we were dumb enough to leave you room to do so? You think you lasted out there so long, because we were standing here with our thumbs up our asses, wondering what to do next? There's nothing you can do, that we haven't already considered. You don't get to be what we are, without having some fucking common sense." I tried not to shrink from his gaze, as he practically pinned me with his eyes.

"I'll move if you back up," I said quietly. He shook his head.

"Not part of the deal."

I chewed my lip as I stared back at him, wondering how much longer his patience would last, while I desperately tried to think of a way out of this.

"Aren't you just exhausted, love? Tired of trying to be what you think you have to be? Wouldn't it be easier, just to relax, stop fighting what you're feeling, and just breathe?"

I let out a breath, embarrassed by how shaky it sounded.

"I'm afraid to."

He nodded. "Because you're worried you'll like it. Being free. Being out from under the weight of all those things you think you have to be. The rules you think you have to follow. Imagine just feeling weightless, unburdened... *at peace*."

My hands trembled on the curtain, and it moved the tiniest amount. His eyes caught the movement, and he smiled. It was almost a gentle look on his face.

"Who made you so ashamed of your body, Cass? Who made you want to hide it so much? Don't you just want to tell whoever it is to go fuck themselves, and just let go?" He was using that voice again. The one that seemed to echo inside my head, teasing me from the inside out.

Everything he said made sense. It made me want that. *To be free*. To stop worrying about what people might think. Stop worrying about what I'm supposed to be. Good girls don't stand naked in front of strange men. Especially ones who had wanted to hurt them, from the moment they met.

"I don't know... I... God, I don't know what to do," I choked out, feeling tears burn my eyes.

Sammy reached over, gently plucking the curtain from my loosened grip, dropping it, and baring me to his gaze. He took a deep breath, letting it out in a soft groan.

"Isn't that better? Don't you feel safer and calmer, knowing that you're choosing this?" I frowned at him. Had I made a choice? His eyes travelled over me, almost caressing me, without him even touching me. I felt a blush warm my cheeks, and my hands twitched to cover me up.

He shook his head, making a shushing sound.

"Beautiful, Cass. This is how you should always be. Naked. Visible. *Sexy*. Turn around. Show me everything."

I closed my eyes, my breathing shallow and nervous.

"Why?"

He chuckled quietly. "Because you're a fucking feast for my eyes, love. *Turn*." I huffed out a breath, and turned away from him, showing him my back once more.

"Stop," he said, while I was facing away from him. I could feel my whole body trembling, as I stood there, and he stayed silent. Was he looking at me? Was he imagining things he wanted to do to me? Had he left the room?

"Sammy?"

"Shhh..." His hands suddenly closed over my shoulders, and I jumped.

"Wha-"

"Shhh... just relax." The trembling was worse, now that he was touching me. His hands trailed over my shoulders, down my arms, and then his lips touched down on my shoulder. A whisper of a kiss.

Then he did the same on the other shoulder. His hands smoothed down, reaching my hands, and took hold of them. I felt him step up close, his body heat now warming me, while I shivered, and breathed fast. My heart was thundering in my chest, making me feel dizzy.

His lips continued to tease, sliding over my shoulders, my neck, his tongue drifting over my skin now and then. His body pressed closer, and I tried to pull my hands away from his.

"Cass, stay. Stop fighting how this makes you feel." His words were breathed against the side of my throat, while I started to gasp in small breaths, unable to fill my lungs.

His hands moved, from my hands, to wrap around me, trapping me against his warm body. I instantly tried to pry his arms away, and he tutted in my ear.

"Relax."

"How?" I practically sobbed at him.

"Let yourself feel. I'm not hurting you, Cass. I'm just showing you how your body pleases me. Don't you like pleasing me, love?" I didn't answer him, trying to focus on getting air into my lungs.

My fists clenched at my sides, as his hands started moving again, one coming up to cup a breast, his thumb grazing over the nipple, making me flinch. The other hand suddenly dipped lower, and I yelped, trying to pull away.

"Enough," he said sharply, and I froze again, because if I made him angry right now, I had nowhere to go. He'd hurt me.

His leg moved, nudging between mine, pushing me wider, and then his fingers slipped between my legs, one swirling over my clit, and then dipping inside me. Damn... I was so wet, that I could hear it, as he slid his finger back and forth. My cheeks were burning with shame.

"See, baby? Your body understands what it wants. You need to stop letting your head get in the way." I felt tears running down my cheeks, as his finger continued to tease, and slide through my wetness.

"No," I whispered.

He chuckled; his lips really close to my ear.

"Yes, Cass. *Your body says yes.* Would it be easier if I did this?" His hand left my breast, closing over my mouth, silencing any further protests, as his finger kept delving inside me, and then swirling over my clit again. My hands came up to clutch at his arm, holding on, but no longer fighting him.

My legs were shaking so hard, I knew I'd have fallen, if he hadn't practically braced my weight against his body. He was aroused. I could feel it pressing into my back. I felt another wave of shame, and gasped back another sob, as his finger slipped out, and two slipped back inside me.

"Switch off your brain, Cass. Focus on how good this feels. My fingers sliding in and out of you, my hand silencing you. I think you like the helplessness. I think it takes away that part of you that you think should keep fighting. Can you feel my cock pressing against you? Imagine how good it would feel, to just let me bend you over, and slam it deep inside you... I'd make sure you could feel every fucking inch of me, sliding into you, stretching you... have you ever been fucked so hard you could feel it the next day? Every time you move, you'd feel sore, and you'd think of me. You'd try not to, but you'd smile... thinking of how it felt when I was deep inside you, how every hard thrust felt, the sounds you'd make, every damn time I slammed in to the hilt. Tell me that doesn't sound like fucking heaven right now."

My legs almost gave out, as an orgasm washed over me so unexpectedly, that I couldn't even try to fight it back. The noise I made, with his hand pressed tightly over my lips, was like nothing I'd heard from myself before. I nearly buckled and fell, but he tightened his arms around me, his breathing fast.

A groan from behind us, made Sammy turn us both to face the doorway. Seb stood against the wall, his hand inside his pants, stroking up and down. My embarrassment turned to pure humiliation, and I started to cry again, trying to tear myself from Sammy's grip.

He wouldn't let go, and when Seb pushed away from the wall and moved toward us, his hand still in his pants, I started to struggle more. Sammy's hand left my mouth.

"No. Please."

Seb reached us, and watched me, as I tried to escape Sammy's tight hold. He chuckled, as he reached out to grip my chin, making me look at him.

"That was fucking hot, love. Damn nearly creamed my pants like a schoolboy. Now I know how Sammy felt when he was driving, and I was the one with my fingers deep inside you." I glared back at him, tears still spilling from my eyes.

He groaned, as his hand started moving inside his pants again.

"Trying to decide how you can help me get off right now."

"No," I whispered. Sammy chuckled, sliding his hand over my mouth again. His other arm was banded tightly around my waist, and I couldn't pull free. Seb's hand slipped to my chest, circling a nipple, pinching it a little.

With a grin, he leaned forward, taking it in his mouth, sucking it into his mouth, as I tried to fight against both of them, and sobbed into Sammy's hand. My hands were pushing at Seb, trying to move him away, but he was as unmovable as his brother.

He suddenly threw his head back, letting out a guttural groan, and I squeezed my eyes closed. I didn't want to watch him anymore. It was terrifying, and arousing, and that was even more terrifying.

He fell quiet, and I felt him move back, and then Sammy removed his hand from my mouth. I sagged in his hold, exhausted, and devastated, and so angry with myself for the way my body had reacted to them. Sammy manhandled me across the floor, and lowered me onto the bed, backing up a few steps.

"When you get your sea legs back, love, you can use the shower. I'll bring the hairbrush in a bit. Oh, and you earned yourself this." He pulled off his t-shirt, and tossed it at me. I grabbed it and held it in front of me, covering myself at last.

Why did they keep giving me clothes they had already worn? Was it some kind of macho bullshit? I curled up in a ball on the bed, waiting for my body to stop trembling, watching them leave.

The sound of the door closing was like a blessing. It didn't lock, I'd noticed, but at least they'd left me alone at last.

When the shuddering finally stopped, I took my chance to use the shower, noting the bodywash and shampoo waiting for me. The same ones I use. The exact ones, in fact. Fuck... the partially used ones, that I'd had in my own bathroom. *They'd been in my house.*

CHAPTER THIRTY-ONE
HARVEY

ONE DRINK AT THE pub became two, then three, and so on. Before we knew it, we were pretty far gone, and we'd forgotten about the person we were supposed to be saving. How does that even happen? We were soaked, exhausted, desperate, and we filled up on snacks, and drinks, and then we relaxed.

The heat from that fire warmed us, starting to dry our clothes, and we ended up sitting on the sofa together, chatting like we'd never chatted before.

Lenore had softened toward me again, no longer calling me nasty names, or glaring at me like I was a monster. We talked, we joked, we laughed, we got lost in our tiny pocket of reality, in a random pub somewhere we'd never been.

When it approached closing time, and the landlord offered us a room for the night, because it was one of those pubs with a few bedrooms for overnight stays, we agreed. We couldn't get home from here. We knew the car had eventually been collected, but we couldn't go and retrieve it until the next morning.

We paid for two rooms, and headed up the narrow stairs to the accommodation floor. I walked Lenore to her room, making sure she got in okay, and was settled, and when she pointed to the in-room bar, the whiskey and two glasses, which I figured was because this was a pub, and not a hotel, I agreed to stay for a drink.

As we sat together on Lenore's bed, drinking whiskey, and chatting about anything but the awful things that had happened to either of us, somehow we ended up kissing.

And from there, we ended up desperately stripping each other of clothing, until we were naked, and writhing about on her bed.

Considering I rarely get laid, I always have protection with me, so we went from drunk and naked, to fucking like rabbits, and then we fell asleep in her bed, wrapped around each other in blissful, drunken slumber.

CASSIDY

THE SHOWER MADE ME feel fresh, and clean, and after as long as possible under the too hot water, and after scrubbing at my skin until it glowed red, I finally felt like I'd washed myself clean of their hands, and their bodies, and their unnerving power over me.

I dried myself with the only towel they'd provided, and then I reluctantly slipped on the t-shirt Sammy had worn. I could smell his cologne on it. I didn't like the fact that it made me feel oddly comforted.

Nothing about either of them should feel comforting. They were monsters. I'd thought they would just throw me down and force themselves on me, but this was worse. What they were doing was even more evil.

They were breaking me down, burrowing their way into my mind, making me look at them differently. Not that I no longer saw them as monsters, but it was more like I was starting to hate that fact a little less. Maybe even appreciate it a little.

I'd tried my best to remove the knots from my hair in the shower, but I needed a brush or a comb, almost as much as I needed more clothing.

I finally had to brave it, and leave the bathroom. I carefully turned the door handle, trying to open the door as silently as possible, widening the gap just enough to put an eye to it, and check the bedroom. It was empty. The light was on. And on the bedside cabinet were two things, both making me smile, despite everything else.

A hairbrush, and a cup of coffee. The gesture shouldn't have made me as happy or grateful as it did. Was I becoming dependent on them? Well, duh. I had nothing here, unless they gave it to me. No contact with anyone. None of my own belongings, except for my toiletries. My toothbrush had also appeared in the bathroom, toothpaste, and some of my other products. Even a razor.

It had been bliss, to shave away the stubble on my legs, and other areas, which had driven me nuts, although, all the while, I'd hoped would make me less appealing to them. It wasn't a razor I could hurt them or me with, unfortunately. But then, as I even considered trying to slash them with it, I knew I wouldn't.

"Fuck," I moaned, sitting down to take a sip of the coffee, which they'd been making fairly strong, with milk and some sugar, so it was almost how I liked it. I picked up the brush. *Also mine.*

I started teasing it through my hair, starting at the tips, taking care to smooth away the lowest tangles, so I could then start further up. It took ages, but finally I could pull the brush through my hair from root to tip, without it snagging. I sighed with pleasure. The little things were all I had now.

"Better?" I glanced up, to see one of them at the door. He grinned at me, and I nodded.

"Thank you."

He shrugged. "You please us, and we treat you nicely. Piss us off, and... well, I think you can guess."

"Seb?" He nodded.

"What happens next?"

He raised an eyebrow. "In what way?"

I looked around me, then back at him.

"Me, you guys, everything. Do you just keep pushing me until I give in, then get bored, and let me go? Or will you kill me when you get bored? I want to understand. *I need to.*"

He nodded again, holding up a finger, and walked away. I groaned. What had I just done?

HARVEY

I WOKE WHILE LENORE still slept, and lay there watching her breathe. She looked so peaceful, so beautiful. How had I not noticed her this whole time? She had been right beside me for ten years, and I'd never really looked at her properly. Not in the right way.

Taking care not to wake her, I reached to the bedside table for my phone, sliding my finger across the screen to wake it up. Selecting the camera, I focused on her face. Her eyes closed, long lashes against her cheeks. Her lips parted just enough to breathe in quiet whispers. Her blonde hair was short, but there were strands touching her cheek, and I reached out, moving one of them gently behind her ear.

I switched the camera to video, catching the slight moan which came from her, as she moved closer to me. I moved the other wisp of hair aside, then stroked her cheek. She smiled in her sleep. Beautiful. *Breath-taking*.

She moved again, and I pressed stop on the video, setting my phone back on the bedside table, before she woke and saw me. Taking a deep breath, feeling more at peace than I had for a long time, I settled back beside her, and drifted back off to sleep.

CHAPTER THIRTY-TWO
CASSIDY

Seb was only gone a few minutes, but when he returned, Sammy was with him. They both held tumblers of something. Amber coloured liquid. I had no idea what it was, but there was a bottle with them too.

They came over to the bed, both sitting down on opposite sides of the end of the bed, facing me, while I was curled up against the headboard, my coffee cradled in my hands. I'd tucked the blanket over my lap, so I wouldn't risk flashing them, since I had no underwear.

They both stared at me, and I swallowed hard.

"Am I in trouble?"

Sammy laughed. "Whatever for, love? I'm actually pretty impressed with you." Seb nodded.

"For what? I'm weak. I break too easily. I should be able to withstand all this stuff, and I can't."

Sammy laughed, grabbing the bottle from the floor, and topping up his empty glass. He did the same for Seb, then looked at me.

"Irish coffee?" I glanced at the mug in my hands. There was enough room to add to it, so I nodded, holding it toward him. He tilted the bottle, adding a little to my drink, then set it aside again.

"You're not weak, love. We'd have lost interest if you were." I sighed, feeling my shoulders drop.

"So I could have been free already, if I'd just given up sooner?"

Seb snorted. "No, love. You'd be dead. We'd have had no reason to keep you alive." My heart thudded in my chest.

"My god... you're insane."

He burst out laughing. "Probably. It's much more fun than whatever the rest of you people do. I don't worry about stuff. I don't live with boundaries, and I don't respect anyone else's. It's incredibly easy living."

Sammy shook his head. "Nah, he lets me worry about that stuff. Bastard." Seb elbowed him, and they both laughed, and I just stared at them. What the fuck is going on? They're acting like two lads out for a beer or something. They're so relaxed, in this monumentally fucked up situation we have here. Why? Because of their lack of respect for my boundaries?

"How many girls have you done this to?" I asked quietly, after taking a gulp of my alcoholic coffee. Ugh... it was slightly bitter now.

Sammy glanced at Seb, and they both frowned.

"You mean this year?" Seb asked finally. My heart stuttered in my chest. *I was just one of many*. Why did that hurt so much? Why wasn't it anger that I felt, but despair.

"You okay, love?" Sammy asked. *Fuck*. I hadn't hidden my feelings as well as I thought. I cleared my throat.

"Uh... just wondering how you haven't been caught, if this is something you do so often. So many women. Must be lovely for you. You sick bastards."

He glanced at Seb. "Somebody's jealous." I glared at him.

"Go fuck yourself."

"Nah, that's your job." He shot back, and I flipped a middle finger in his direction.

"Charming. I think someone's getting spoiled."

Seb tapped a finger against his lips.

"I think you're right, bruv. Maybe we need to start taking things away again."

I gulped the rest of my drink.

"Well, you can't take that back now, so screw you."

"Don't make us take everything you could cover up with, love. We might be sitting here chatting like normal folks, but we aren't. *We own you*. You did figure that part out, right?" Seb finished his drink, and set the glass aside, and I frowned. I thought they'd keep drinking. Maybe even considered it my chance to get away.

"Now what's up?" He asked, leaning back on his elbow, watching me as I tried to look unconcerned.

"I think she hoped to get us drunk, and have her way with us, bruv," Sammy said, displaying that unnerving way they both had, of picking my brain, when I said nothing, even if they reached the wrong conclusions some of the time.

"As if," I muttered angrily, twisting the bedding in my hands, because now I had no reason to hold the mug.

"Got a better job for those hands of yours," Seb said, shooting me a wicked grin.

"In your dreams," I muttered, tucking them under the covers instead.

"And instead, she's going to play with herself. I definitely think we're giving her way too much freedom," Sammy commented, setting his own glass aside.

I felt a wave of panic, as they both eyed me. Maybe the alcohol was a bad thing. Maybe they'd lose whatever this control was, that they apparently had over their bodies. Maybe it would mean that they wouldn't stop, if they started messing with me.

"You never answered my question," I blurted desperately, watching as they glanced at each other again.

"Go on," Sammy said, sitting back again.

"What happens next? That's what I asked Seb before you guys came in here. Are you done with me yet? Will you let me go? I need to know."

He cleared his throat. "Uh... does it *feel* like we're done with you, Cass? We haven't even fucked you yet. You don't think that we're going to follow through with that promise? Or maybe you're just getting impatient, and want to speed things up? You want to fuck, I'll quite happily do you right now, because I'm up for that. But I'll tell you this much. You're not in control of what happens, or when. If I decide I want to fuck you, and it just happens to mesh with you begging me to do it, it doesn't mean you win. It just means that you stopped lying to yourself, in time to really enjoy it."

I pulled the blankets higher.

"That's not what I want."

Seb grabbed the bedding, and pulled at it, making me desperately hang on, to stop him uncovering me. His strength outdid mine, as he'd known it would, and the blankets slipped away, before I could grab them and pull them back, just enough to cover my legs.

"It will be. See, you think we're evil, or whatever, but you like it. You like our dark side. I think you have done ever since we first met. But you're too much of a fucking prissy little thing, to just go with it. We could hold you down right now, and force you. Of course we could. That's the easy way." He stood up, moving over to lean over me, his hand stroking my damp hair, while I fought the urge to flinch away.

"My preference is to have you so fucking confused, and conflicted, that you'll fight me, but at the same time, you'll be hating yourself for craving it too. You'll want my cock deep inside you, and you'll cry about it after, but the memory of me fucking you? That will be surrounded by the shame you feel for wanting it. *Wanting me*. And I won't stop, until I fucking own you. *In here*." He tapped a finger against my forehead. Then he turned and walked away. I pulled the covers back up to my chin, suddenly feeling chilled to the bone by Seb's words. *What. The. Fuck.*

Sammy snorted. "You will beg, Cass. You'll be so fucking wet for us, that you'll let us do anything to you, but you'll always cry after. And that's the way we like it." He gathered up the empty glasses, my mug, and the bottle, and walked to the door.

"Sweet dreams, love."

He switched the light off, and closed the door, while I curled up tight, and cried myself to sleep.

CHAPTER THIRTY-THREE
HARVEY

Waking up with Lenore was like nothing I'd experienced before. I mean, I've slept with a few women, but normally they left before we slept, so I had no idea what to expect.

She groaned, and opened her eyes, and then they fixed on me.

"H?"

I nodded, smiling at her, before she glanced around the room. "My head is throbbing," she moaned, and I laughed.

"Yeah... same. Don't suppose you have painkillers in that rucksack of yours?"

She nodded, and I sat up.

"Want me to get them?" She nodded again, so I hopped out of bed, and walked across to her pack. She hissed in a breath, and I turned to see her eyes fixed on my naked body.

"You okay?" I asked, as I retrieved them and handed them to her. I grabbed one of our whiskey glasses, and rinsed it in the tiny sink, filling it with water, which I brought back to her.

She ran her eyes all over me as I stood there.

"We... uh... we really did that, then?" I grinned.

"Hell yeah..." She groaned, focusing on sitting up and taking two painkillers, then handed them to me, so I cracked two from the blister pack for myself. I took the water when she was done, and washed them down.

She glanced at the wall. "Uh..."

I frowned. "You're not going to get weird now, are you?" I asked, going back to the side of the bed I'd slept in. I climbed back in, while she frowned, and watched me, like she couldn't believe what she was seeing.

"We were drunk, H. We shouldn't have done that. Jesus... were we even careful?"

I nodded. "I used a condom."

"Thank fuck for that," she breathed, holding the covers over her pert breasts, as she stared at me.

"Because I'm so disgusting, that you couldn't bear to have me inside you like that?" *Everything hurt.* How could she be dismissing the beauty of our time together?

She shook her head. "Don't put words in my mouth, H. We were drunk, and we crossed a line we've never even approached before. How did this even happen?"

I grinned slowly, remembering exactly how things started.

"You stuck your tongue in my mouth," I said, and she blushed, covering her eyes for a moment.

"Jesus. Yeah, I did... sorry, H." I laughed, glancing at her, then down at myself.

"Hey, I'm not complaining. Lenore... you don't regret it, do you? Because I don't. You're fucking amazing. It was... you know... really... uh... good."

She shook her head. "You're a loser, H. Pity that seems to be my type now." I reached out, stroking her hair behind her ear again.

"And you're beautiful, Lenore. Stunning."

She stared at me for a moment, biting her lip, and then she did *it* again. That thing she did last night, that led to all of this. Again, I welcomed her kiss, and pulled her on top of me, as I felt my cock go from a semi, to aching to be inside her again.

CASSIDY

I HAD A BAD headache when I woke up. It could have been for any number of reasons. As I glanced at the room, through eyes which made my head throb more, I realised that it could be fear, lack of food, or drinks, lack of proper sleep, crying, all of that hair pulling. I mean, there were just too many reasons for it.

I closed my eyes again, pressing my forehead against the pillow, aiming for that cool spot I hadn't already warmed.

The sound of quiet breathing made me freeze. Which one of those sick bastards was watching me sleep again? The breathing was too close. I glanced at the chair across the room, but it was empty.

I felt someone move, in the bed beside me, just as warm breath started to tickle the back of my neck. I was frozen with terror. I couldn't move. I couldn't breathe. *I wasn't alone in the bed.*

Gentle fingers swept my hair aside, before lips pressed against my bare skin, while the fingers trailed over my shoulder, and down my arm, under the covers. I knew he could feel my fear, my trembling. He moved closer, closing his lips over my shoulder, over those dark angry bruises Seb had left there.

Teeth grazed my skin and I whimpered, flinching away. The hand, which had been lazily trailing down my arm, wrapped around my elbow, and pulled me back. He moved again, and I felt his warm skin pressing against me, through my t-shirt. Something hard pressed into my back, and I knew exactly what it was. *No.*

"You done pretending to be asleep now, love?" He whispered.

"Please," I whimpered.

He laughed, his breath making me shiver, as it warmed my skin.

"I like it when you ask nicely, love." His teeth traced the arc of my shoulder, and nibbled teasingly, as his mouth moved back up the column of my throat. I could feel my entire body trembling, as I tensed, to try and pull away again.

"No, love. Stay," he whispered.

"I'm not a fucking animal!" I snapped, trying to pull away from his arm.

"Maybe not, *but I am.* So unless you want me to push you down on your stomach, and fuck your ass raw, you'll stay still, and do exactly as I tell you." Oh god. No.

"Seb, please."

He chuckled softly. "Well done, love. I mean, you'd really be in trouble if you called me by the wrong name in bed. Cardinal sin, that one."

"You need help," I whispered, putting my hand on his, to try and dislodge it. He moved, and suddenly my hand was trapped under his, so we were both holding me in place now.

"I do. You're going to help me, Cass. I'm in need, and you want to help me, don't you? To repay all the kindness I've shown you so far."

I moved my leg, trying to be stealthy about it. If I wanted to get him away from me, I had, maybe one chance to kick him in the right place, and it would be damn near impossible from the way we were pressed together, but I was going to try.

"Think about what you're planning, Cass. You hurt me, I hurt you. And we already know I'm going to be much more effective than you. I mean... I could break your fingers, or even your arm, before you even manage to get one kick in. Does that sound like something you'd like to experience?" He whispered, too close to my ear.

I shook my head, groaning when it throbbed more from the movement.

"Oh god. Please, Seb. I'm already in pain. *Please.*"

He used his grip on my arm to roll me toward him, so I lay on my back, and he leaned over me, to stare into my eyes.

"I've barely touched you yet, love." I squinted up at him, my head throbbing with my racing pulse. I squeezed my eyes shut for a second.

"Not all pain is physical, dipshit." I guess the headache was making me cranky, and maybe a little irrational, too.

He snorted. "You do love to push your luck, don't you? Tell me what's wrong."

I glared at him, again wishing I hadn't tried to focus my eyes.

"My head is killing me, okay? Does that make you happy? Is that what gets you off?"

He frowned. "I'm not a complete asshole, love. It's not a monthly thing, right?" He lifted the covers, trying to look at my body, and I fought to bring them back down, not missing the fact that I just caught a glimpse of his naked form in the bed with me. Hell. *He'd slept beside me, naked.*

"No, it's not a bloody monthly thing! You're such a pig." He stared at me, a calculating look in his eyes.

"Tell you what, love... I'll make you a deal. I'll get you painkillers, and leave you in peace..."

I sighed heavily. "What's the catch?"

He grinned widely. "You get me off, and then I'll do that for you." I closed my eyes.

"Dammit."

He moved suddenly, rolling on top of me, resting his hard cock between my legs.

"Or... I can just slide into you right now, and fuck you, until I fill you with my cum. How about that? You want to feel me spurting inside you? Maybe make a little Seb junior, in the process?"

I'd frozen like a startled animal when he moved on top of me, and squeezed my eyes closed even tighter. It hurt like a bitch, but if he decided to rape me, I didn't want to see that smug satisfied look on his face when he did.

CHAPTER THIRTY-FOUR

HARVEY

IF I THOUGHT DRUNKEN sex with Lenore was the best I'd had, imagine how great it felt, as she slipped a condom onto me, and then lowered her slick pussy over me. Her earlier surprise, and embarrassment, at accidentally sleeping with me, had disappeared.

She looked aroused, and wanton, and desperate for me. I took her hands, as she started to ride me, and pressed them down on my shoulders, before I took a heavenly warm breast in each of my hands, and rolled her nipples into peaks. Her gasps grew faster, as she rose and fell onto me, and I knew I wasn't going to last long, and it killed me, because this should go on *for-fucking-ever*.

I wanted to be inside her forever. Her eyes locked on mine, and the intensity in them, before she leaned down, and started to kiss me again, gave me that final push I'd tried so hard to hold back from, and I blew, hard.

"FUCK!" I practically yelled, as she shifted her body, rocking her hips against mine, to stimulate her clit.

I reached down, and helped her along, my thumb rubbing and pressing as she started to shudder, and then reached her own climax, as I started to feel him soften inside her. *Holy shit*.

Who knew, out of everything that had happened, that the right woman for me had been right there all along. Beside me. In my life already. For so fucking long.

CASSIDY

SEB WAS CHUCKLING, SLIDING his skin against mine, as he trapped me beneath him. He knew I was terrified. Knew I'd frozen up, and squeezed my eyes shut, to try and escape what he was about to do.

He leaned closer, and I felt his lips on mine. I started to struggle, trying to free my arms, and moving my body to try and shake him free of me. He groaned, as he tightened his grip on my wrists.

"Jesus, Cass... That's fucking perfect. Yeah... keep doing that, and I'm going to be coming all over you."

A sob burst from me, as I increased my efforts, to try and push him away.

"Get off me. Please. Don't do this, Seb!" I begged, and he snorted.

"The sooner I fuck you, Cass, the sooner you let go of the last of that fear, that you think you have to keep faking. You want me deep inside you, because you know it's going to scratch that itch you keep denying."

I was shaking my head rapidly.

"No. No. No. Stop. I don't want this."

He pressed his hips forward, his cock sliding against my pussy lips.

"NO!"

Seb lowered his face to my throat, chuckling softly.

"If I stop, you're going to make sure you get me off, aren't you, Cass?" He flicked his tongue over my earlobe, and then started to suck at my skin, pinching with his teeth. I winced.

"That hurts, Seb."

He grinned against my skin. "I know, baby. I'm still waiting for your answer, or I'm going to fuck you right now. I want to, so badly. One thrust, and I'll be inside you, Cass. Tell me you want it."

I shook my head, even as I felt my body warm at the thought of it. All I had to do was let him. He was right here. He was almost inside me. One word, and he'd plunge deep into me.

"See? That right there is what I'm looking for." He was staring at me now. "You want me, more than you realised. More than you'll admit to yourself. You're wet, your body is aching for me to slide inside... Cass, you want to feel my hard cock, stretching you wide, fucking you deep. All you have to do is say it, love. Just beg me to fuck you, and I'll give you what you want." He rocked his hips again, the soft head of his cock sliding against my embarrassingly wet flesh. Why, dammit... why was I so wet? Did they really know me better than I knew myself?

He arched his back, so he could seal his mouth around my left nipple, licking, swirling, and teasing. My body flexed, completely against my will. The sound that came from my mouth was a cross between a moan and a sob.

"Bastard," I muttered, feeling him chuckle against my skin. His teeth closed around my nipple, and I yelped, but even that somehow felt good. He was still sliding his cock along my pussy lips, each silken glide feeling blissful.

"*One thrust*, Cass. You're so desperate to feel me inside you, aren't you? You don't get that wet for someone you don't want. How much longer are you going to fight this, love?"

I thrashed my head on the pillow, tears flowing faster. He was right. In many ways, he was absolutely right. Didn't I want to just stop fighting, and give in? Didn't I want to feel him pressing deep inside me? Wouldn't it just feel right, to have him filling me, his body pressing me down?

The longer I lay there, and argued with myself, the more I worried that he'd grow bored, and just do it anyway, whether I said yes or not. And in some ways, maybe that would be better. If he forced me, rather than doing it with my agreement, then I hadn't become the same depraved creature they were. I shouldn't want him inside me. I should be fighting, and screaming, and hating him. So why didn't I?

Seb released my hands, which went to his shoulders, as if I could hold him away. His hands surrounded my face.

"Look at me, Cass."

I shook my head again, feeling the room tilt and sway.

"Now."

I opened my eyes, because I knew I had no bargaining power at all right now.

"There you go. Listen to me. The next time you call yourself weak, remember this moment. The moment where you could have had what you desperately wanted, but you held off, like the stubborn bitch you are, because you'd rather go unfulfilled, and unsatisfied. I mean, I could make you scream the walls down when you come. I could make you arch your back so hard, you'll be afraid it'll snap, and yet you won't give a fuck, because it'd be worth it, for the fucking orgasm that roars through you, setting every one of your nerve endings on fire."

I felt my nails digging into his shoulders, as I tried to fight off what his words were doing to me.

"Fucking hell." He moved suddenly, his weight disappearing, as he rolled back and lay next to me.

"Get some part of you around my cock, right now, and jack me off. If you don't make me come, I'm going to fuck you whether you give in or not. And I won't be gentle. It won't be pleasure that makes you scream. Not at first, at least." He grabbed the blankets, tossing them away from our bodies, and tucked his hands behind his head.

"Right fucking now, Cass. Before I decide to choose which part of you fucks me."

I sat up, wiping the tears from my eyes, and glaring at him, trying to only look at his face.

"Who fucked you up so badly, Seb? Were you ever a normal human being?"

He shrugged. "If you're not touching my cock, by the time I answer your question, all bets are off."

I reached out with trembling hands, and faltered, my eyes finally settling on him.

His body was toned, and muscular, in that dangerous way that said he'd probably built a lot of it through doing terrible things, rather than just a weekly gym membership.

The tattoos on his chest were many. Lots of different things written, or drawn. Some beautifully crafted, and others crude and clumsy.

"Cass," he growled, and I focused on his hard cock, which stood proud from his body, and looked like it'd need both hands.

"Shit," I whispered, and he snorted.

"Not really my kink, love... now grab it."

I shot him a glare, and then tentatively put my hands on him, wrapping them around his hot flesh. He hissed at my touch, his tight stomach muscles clenching slightly.

"Kneel up, put all of your focus into pleasuring him. If we're not both covered in my cum when you finish, I'm going to be seriously pissed off. Cass, you really don't want to piss me off."

I pulled my hands away, so I could move up onto my knees as he instructed. My only option right now was to play along. If I didn't, I was in too much danger of being raped by him. And I'd seen enough of his mean side to know that it would be brutal.

He groaned under his breath when I took hold of his length again, and started to stroke it, using both hands at first, to surround him, and slide up and down, then one hand, while the other rested on his thigh. He rocked his head back on his hands, letting out a low groan, and his hips started to move with my hand.

"Uh... what are the tattoos?" I asked, because I needed to distance myself from what was happening right now. It felt intimate, and intense, and was affecting me far more than I'd ever admit. Seb moved one of his hands from under his head, resting it on my thigh.

"Shhh... just fuck me with those hands." I heard his breathing speed up, as I increased the pace of my stroking, using jerking motions now, to simulate the friction he'd wanted so badly by fucking me.

I could feel my entire body responding to the experience, because whether I wanted to or not, I found him attractive, arousing... I'd been seconds away from giving in, and letting him fuck me, because he'd pretty much convinced me that I couldn't live another minute, without him inside me. I still wasn't sure he was wrong about that.

He sat up suddenly, moving me so I knelt closer to him, then leaned back again. That hand, which had been on my thigh, was now sliding up toward my centre.

"Spread your legs, while you keep jerking me. I want to touch you."

My heart was thudding so hard in my chest, I actually felt queasy. This was wrong. I shouldn't be doing it. I should be resisting at every opportunity, and fighting them, and eventually finding a way to escape them, and be free.

"Don't make me tell you again," Seb's voice warned harshly, followed by a soft curse, and a jerk of his hips.

I moved my knees apart, but kept my focus on his hard cock, which seemed to be responding to my attention, and was almost pulsing in my hands.

When Seb's fingers slipped between my legs, I flinched, and he groaned.

"Fucking hell, Cass. If you're so fucking wet for me, why did you not just let me fuck you? You know I'd fuck you right. Better than that little pussy Harv ever could."

"Fuck you, Seb."

He laughed. "My point, exactly." I fought the grin that appeared at his words, and then gasped, when he nudged a finger inside me, with a wet sound. We both groaned, as his finger started to fuck me, and his cock erupted in my hands.

His warm cum spurted onto my hands, and onto his stomach, and I trembled at the sight of him as he went over the edge. If I'd thought of him as attractive before, I'd just had my world rocked. That look on his face, as he came all over me, was animalistic, and devastating. He shot me a languid grin, his finger still sliding up into me.

"Very good, Cass. Well done. That was... not bad..."

I glared at him. "Looked better than 'not bad', asshole." He barked out a laugh, and sat up fast, pushing me, so I rolled and fell onto my side, then he pulled me back, straddling my legs, my t-shirt shoved up, baring me to him.

My hands were immediately pushing against his chest, and he took them, rubbing them over my breasts, smearing them with his cum. I groaned, protesting his degrading treatment of me.

He leaned close, still trapping my hands.

"You on birth control, love?" I glared at him.

"Did you see any pills when you ransacked my house, dickhead?"

He snorted. "No, and that's why I'm asking. If we get you up the duff, we're still going to fuck you, all the way through the pregnancy, and then we'll sell the baby. So I'll ask you again... are you?"

I glared at him. "I get the injection four times a year." He grinned widely.

"When did you have it last?"

I shrugged. "Just over two weeks ago."

He nodded. "Good." Then he moved again, pushing my legs apart, and kneeling between them.

"Wait!" He'd promised!

Instead of what I expected, he ran a hand over his stomach, smearing his cum over his fingers, and then he shoved them inside me. A squeak came out of me.

"Stop it!" I started shoving at him again, but he lowered himself, covering me, trapping one of my arms beneath him, and locked his fingers around my throat, squeezing lightly.

I gasped, and my free hand locked around his wrist, trying to pull it away from my throat.

His fingers moved inside me, and then he started to thrust them, jamming them roughly inside me. His other hand tightened around my throat, and I felt my breathing catch, and my temples started to throb, reminding me of my headache. I gasped out desperate noises, trying to get him to release me. He grinned, staring me in the face, as I tried to plead with my eyes, and the choked noises, for him to let me go.

He pulled his fingers out of me, thrusting them back inside, and then started rocking his thumb on my clit, as he roughly finger fucked me. Just as I started to feel faint, he loosened the grip on my throat, letting me gasp a few breaths, before he did it again, all the while, doing with his fingers what he'd wanted to do with his cock. If I'd let him, would he have been gentler?

Despite myself... Despite the throbbing in my temples, from the headache, and the loss of air, or blood flow, or whatever it was, I felt my body starting to flex in his direction, starting to writhe and crave each hard thrust.

My eyes started to roll back in my head, and then I erupted, an orgasm like none I'd had before, blasting through me, leaving me gasping, choking, sobbing. Seb pulled his hands away from me, pushing himself up off the bed. He stretched, smiling smugly, as he watched me shiver, and flinch, as smaller waves washed over me.

"Good morning, love," he said, stroking his hand down his body, which had mostly cleaned off, or rubbed off onto me. He cast his eyes over me, a satisfied look on his face.

"I'm going to get you those painkillers, love. You stay exactly as you are, covered in my fucking cum. If you've wiped any of it away when I come back, I'll jerk off and cover you with more, and tie you up, so you can't escape it."

My throat was hoarse as I glared up at him, and muttered at him to go fuck himself. With a laugh, he strode from the room.

CHAPTER THIRTY-FIVE
HARVEY

THAT SECOND FUCK ENERGISED us, and we finally climbed out of the bed, and showered, dressed, and went back down to the bar.

There was no breakfast service as such. A row of mini cereal boxes, and milk, some breakfast bars. The sort of offering you get at the thirty quid a night hotels. Pretty frustrating, considering we just spent sixty per room, and only used one of them.

I was tempted to go back for what was left of the booze up there. When the bartender asked if we'd drunk the whiskey, their version of a mini bar, we said no, because we already felt fleeced. Once we'd grabbed a fast breakfast, and coffee, we headed out of the pub in a rush.

"They say the car is at the local garage, but I can't see anything beyond this pub," Lenore said, glancing both ways down the street, grumbling to herself. The sun caught the lighter strands of her blonde hair, and they gleamed. It made me want to take pictures of her, to capture that beauty, and this moment.

"We came from that way, so I say we follow the road the opposite way," she finally said, not noticing that I wasn't participating in the conversation at all. I followed her, as I'd willingly do forever.

As we finally found buildings, and seemed to be walking into the tiniest village I could imagine, I realised something I hadn't thought about since we got up this morning. *Cassidy.*

I closed my eyes, realising that when I tried to picture her face, I saw Lenore instead. Fuck. I'd forgotten about the situation I'd put that woman in, because I'd lost myself in the beautiful woman beside me.

CASSIDY

WHEN SEB RETURNED, WITH painkillers and water, Sammy was right behind him. He shot a look at me, not having moved a muscle, because everything felt worn out, and my head was thrumming in sync with my heart, which had started racing again when they reappeared.

Seb hadn't even put clothes on. He was stark naked, and came to sit on the bed, once he'd placed the tablets and glass on the bedside table.

"Doesn't she look stunning, shagged out, and covered in my cum?" He asked his brother, running a hand over my thigh. I didn't even flinch. I just lay there, my eyes squeezing shut, so I didn't have to look at them.

"Did you hurt her?" Sammy asked, leaning over me. I knew only because a shadow blocked the small amount of light coming from the window.

"Nah. She's got a headache. That excuse just doesn't work on men like me." He snorted.

Sammy sighed. "Cass, let's sit you up, and get these pills down you. You'll feel much better." As soon as his hands touched me, I flinched, and moved, pulling free of both of their touch, trying to push the t-shirt back over me.

"Stop touching me!" I screamed at them, groaning and grabbing my head, which throbbed harder. Ugh.

"Take the fucking pills then," Sammy snapped at me.

"Why, am I ruining your fun, while I'm so rudely being ill?"

He glanced at Seb. "Has she been like this all morning?"

"I'm right here!" I yelled at him, clutching my head again. My stomach roiled, and I suddenly groaned. "Fuck."

They both glanced at me, the tone of my voice clueing them in to a problem.

"What?" Sammy asked, backing up a step.

"Sick," I muttered, staggering away from the bed, and running for the ensuite. I only just reached the toilet, before I started retching, and emptied my stomach of its meagre contents. It hurt. *Everything hurt.*

My head pounded heavily, aggravated by the vomiting, and the mere act of tilting my head forward to stay over the bowl. I groaned, once my body had stopped purging itself of bile, and left me quivering on the floor, my body temp dropping fast.

One of them peeked into the room.

"Jesus. What's wrong? Bruv, she looks half dead. What did you do?" Oh. Yes, he was dressed. It was Sammy. I curled up in a ball, and tried to breathe slowly.

"I didn't even fuck her, bruv. Just played with her a little. She woke up with the headache," Seb protested.

Sammy glanced back at him.

"Go get dressed, dickhead." He turned and crouched beside me. "Cass, let's get you back in the bed."

"I can't," I whispered hoarsely. He sighed, and pulled me up from the floor, lifting me and carrying me to the bedroom, where he lay me down. He removed the t-shirt I'd tried wiping my face with, then he disappeared and returned with a damp flannel, which he used to clean up my face, and then wiped the remains of Seb's pleasure from my skin.

Once I was clean, he tucked me into the bed, sitting me up, so he could offer the water.

"Stop," I whispered, and he frowned.

"What now?"

I reached out a shaking hand for the water, not able to take the weight of the glass, once he let me take it. He steadied it, and helped me bring it to my mouth.

I took a few sips, and thankfully nothing erupted from my stomach.

"You're being too nice," I finally whispered to him, and he laughed. Not the usual nasty, 'we're laughing at your pain' laugh, but a genuine one.

"Too nice? Make up your mind, Cass. I thought I was a bastard, an asshole, a monster... did I miss anything?"

I smiled a little. "Probably."

He helped me sip more water, then offered the pills. If I'd been more with it, I'd have wanted to inspect them. Make sure they truly were just paracetamol, and not something nasty, but truthfully, I just wanted the pain to go.

I managed to wash them down, after a few tries, because my throat was raw from Seb's throat grabbing, and the vomiting.

Seb returned, covered up at last, and he hovered in the background, while Sammy set the water aside.

"What do we do? Does she need a doctor?" Seb asked.

Sammy shrugged. "Been like this before?" He asked me, finally.

I stared at him. "Kidnapped and tormented?"

He smirked. "Be serious now, love."

I rubbed at my temples. "I get migraines."

"Fuck," Seb moaned.

"Oh, I'm sorry if my inability to stay healthy for your torture, is putting a crimp on your fucking day!" I snapped, and Sammy laughed out loud.

"Do you take special meds for it?" He asked me, instead of acknowledging my comment further. I shook my head, then groaned.

"Paracetamol, sleep, dark room. Oh, and it helps if I'm not dehy-*fucking*-drated."

He frowned. "Are you blaming us for this?"

"Of course I'm blaming you, you sick fuckers. If I'd been at home, I probably wouldn't have this, because I'd be eating regular meals, and drinking plenty of fluids, but you two with the one meal a day, and occasional glasses of water, you don't have a clue."

Seb glared at me, pointing at the bathroom. "There are fucking taps in there, you could be drinking as much as you want."

I groaned, slumping in the bed, and covering my eyes with my arm.

"Please just leave me here to die quietly."

Sammy laughed. "She's got a point. I'll get some breakfast on. You leave her alone for a while."

Seb snorted. "Nah... if she goes to sleep, I want to watch her."

"Psycho," I whispered grumpily.

"Ah, that's the one I forgot earlier," Sammy said, on his way out of the room. He stopped at the doorway. "Coffee good or bad?"

I shrugged. "It's yummy, but I need water too." He disappeared, and Seb dragged that chair over to the bed, straddling it, in the way he seemed to like so much.

"Would you have been so ill if you'd taken pills earlier?" He asked quietly.

I shrugged. "Maybe. No idea. If you guys insist on keeping me here, and alive for your games, you need to look after me better," I said just as quietly.

"I'm human. I need food. I need fluids. Occasionally I need pain relief. If you want to keep messing with me, you need to understand that."

He sighed. "Well, we'll know better with the next one, eh?"

I groaned. "I can't even muster up the strength to flip you off right now, but just pretend I did."

He laughed, but sobered suddenly. "You asked before, how many times we've done this..."

I moved my arm away from my eyes, groaning at the ambient light in the room, which felt like sunlight glaring into my eyes.

"Yeah, and you said I'm one of many."

He chuckled. "I'm pretty sure I didn't. But Cass... think what you like about us... but... believe it or not, none of this was planned. It was a spur of the moment thing, to mess with Harv. I don't think either of us expected to enjoy it so much. That's because you're a firecracker. If you'd been some pissy little thing, we'd have killed you both already."

I stared at him, wondering how it was so easy for him to say such things, right to my face.

"You know that normal people don't kill people who bore them, right?"

He shrugged. "Never promised to be normal. But I will give you some time to feel better, before I start playing again. Call it a reward for earlier."

I wasted some strength this time, showing him a middle finger, making him laugh as he stood up.

"So, what... like a few hours?"

I snorted. "Could be days, fucktard. Google it."

"Days? Jesus." He looked gutted.

I allowed myself a smirk. "Try being the one suffering it, dickhead."

CHAPTER THIRTY-SIX
HARVEY

THE CAR WAS READY. Another bill to pay, and we were back on the road. Instead of the angry tension we'd had building between us on the earlier part of the journey, we were relaxed, chatty... if not for where we were, and what we'd finally remembered we were meant to be doing, we'd be having a lovely time.

It pissed me off, to be honest, that we'd had to go through all this shit, to realise that there was something there between us. And now, even though it was my fault, I felt resentful for having to go looking for Cassidy and the Bennetts, when I just wanted to take Lenore home, and spend the day pleasuring her fucking gorgeous body.

All of that training, and working out, and all those classes, meant she was toned, and sinewy, and strong, and beautiful. I couldn't wait to watch her at her classes, see the sweat dripping over her skin, as she punched, and kicked, and moved, like a deadly dancer.

"H, hey, snap out of it," Lenore snapped, pulling me from my thoughts.

"Sorry, Lenore... uh, I was zoned out. What's up?" She pointed down the road.

"Is that the one we're looking for?" Fuck! I rummaged through my pockets for that knife I'd taken with me last time. I'd never used it, because... after all, the only person who came close enough for me to try attacking, was Cassidy. And even though she nearly castrated me, I hadn't even thought of using it on her. I needed it now though.

"Fuck."

"What's up?" Lenore asked, tucking the car down a side road, a little way down the road from the house.

"I've lost that knife," I said, opening the glove compartment, and checking around in the car.

She laughed. "No you haven't. I got rid of it."

I glared at her. "That was from my kitchen, Lenore." That wasn't even the point, but it was still annoying as hell.

"I don't give a crap, H. You know the second you tried to use it, one of those bastards would have snatched it, and gutted you with it. I don't need you arming them with weapons to use on us."

I stared over at the house we'd tracked down. To be honest, it was nice. I could see me settling somewhere like that. With Lenore. Maybe a few kids. Impregnating her would be fun.

"You know this might not even be the right place, right, H?" Lenore asked quietly. I reached for her hand.

"All we can do is try, right? If it's wrong, we keep going."

She sighed. "We're both missing work for this. If we keep not showing up, or in your case, keep the shop closed, we'll both be unemployed pretty soon. I work for a charity, dammit, I can't keep messing them around."

I stared at her, knowing how important her work was to her.

"I think the shop's gone already, either way we look at it, babe. But I don't want you to lose your job. If this isn't the right place, we'll head back home. I'll try again tomorrow, on my own."

I hated that idea. Hated it for so many reasons. Not least because she wouldn't be beside me, where I wanted her to be. And I'd have to face those fuckers alone again. And that thought in the back of my mind made itself known. How could I watch over her all day, if I had to be out looking for Cassidy?

CASSIDY

WHEN SAMMY RETURNED, HE brought food, and coffee, and more painkillers. Just another two. Like I couldn't be trusted with the whole damn pack. He even tossed another of his t-shirts at me, which I slipped into immediately, grateful for the chance to cover up again.

I ate the food. Chicken soup, and toast, because he figured a fry up would probably make me ill again, and although I hated to admit it, he was probably right. He sat with me while I ate, trying to look like he didn't care, but I felt it anyway. I mean, you don't cook for someone, and tend to them like this, unless you care about them a bit, right? And even Seb had sounded worried.

I realised that my plan had changed. *Evolved*. It was no longer about running, the second their backs were turned. It was now about messing with their heads, just as much as they'd messed with mine. Worming my way into their heads, and their hearts. Making them care, and maybe even love me. Because then, when I escaped them, I could make sure it hurt them too.

"Was that enough for now?" Sammy asked, as he lifted the tray away from me.

"Yes, thank you. It was really nice too."

He quirked an eyebrow.

"Watch it, love. You almost sounded like you were grateful then."

I stared at him, realising that my headache was starting to intensify again. That's the frustrating thing about painkillers. Generally they only ease pain for about half of the time they're supposed to be effective for. I couldn't take any more for another two or three hours, but they were already bloody useless.

"I *am* grateful. When you do something like this for me, I appreciate it. Maybe... maybe I could cook for you some time," I said quietly, testing his reaction.

That eyebrow quirked again. "Gonna wine and dine me, love? Put on a little apron, and prance around the kitchen like Nigella?"

I frowned. "Why do you have to be mean about it? I'm offering to do something nice for you. Even though I'm your prisoner, and I really don't have to even try. All I have to do is keep fighting, but I'm tired, Sammy. I'm so tired."

He grinned. "I keep telling you how to solve that, Cass. All you have to do is stop."

I sipped some of the coffee he'd brought me, and set it aside.

"What happens if I stop?" I pulled the blankets high, even though I was feeling too warm, rather than cold.

"Well, let me see." Sammy leaned his arms on the back of the chair, since he clearly preferred straddling chairs, just like his brother.

"We all get lots of orgasms, and you don't have to worry about a thing."

I frowned. "How is that even possible?"

That smirk reappeared.

"Orgasms? We're both really good in bed, love. Plus, you seem to be pretty good yourself, from what I hear. You're also way ahead on the orgasm scale, so really we're the ones being hard-done-by here."

"You're too much of an ass to have a normal conversation, aren't you? I don't know why I thought you'd talk to me properly, unlike your brother."

Sammy rested his chin on his fist.

"What exactly do you have to worry about right now?"

I frowned, staring around the room.

"Um... *everything*."

He followed my gaze. "Like?"

"I'm a fucking prisoner, you stupid dick," I snapped.

He looked at me, almost affectionately.

"And? You're safe. You're warm. You have a bed. You have food and drinks. You have two very able men looking after you, protecting you, paying for everything. So I'll ask you again, Cass... what the fuck do you have to worry about?"

It was scary, how he truly believed that they'd become my caregivers, or something. Looking after my needs, so that I didn't have a care in the damn world.

"What about my job? My house? My loved ones?" He tilted his head.

"I notice you didn't say *family*. You said loved ones. You don't have any family, do you?"

"Do you know that this whole 'know it all' thing is really annoying? No. I have no living family that I know of, because I was an abandoned baby. Thank you so much for bringing that up. Foster homes and stuff were the best I had. And yeah, they were okay, but basically I'm alone, except for a few close friends. So you have a pretty small chance, of any desperate people hunting you down, to find me. Not that you seem worried in the least. Must be nice to be you. Living your best life, taking advantage of desperate people, and kidnapping defenceless women, just so you can subject them to constant fear, and sexual assaults."

He just watched me ranting, that grin on his face.

"Are they really 'sexual assaults' if you enjoyed them? *If you came?* If you were so wet, we could actually hear our fingers sliding inside you? I think you want to call them that, so you don't feel guilty about how much you liked what we did to you. And how much you want us to do it again." And yes, he made sarcastic quote marks with his fingers when he spoke.

I sat up, jabbing a finger in his direction.

"Listen asshole, it's sexual assault if I said NO! I asked you to stop. I asked *him* to stop. I fucking begged. I said I didn't want it. Neither of you listen. That makes you rapists. That makes you animals. And that means that nothing you think you're doing to 'protect me', or 'look after me', matters a damn, because I shouldn't be here. And you should be in jail!"

He grinned. "Okay. Gotcha. *You keep lying to yourself.* Take those pills in two hours." He got up and refilled the water glass. "And drink everything."

He took away the breakfast dishes, and left the room.

CHAPTER THIRTY-SEVEN
HARVEY

WE SNEAKED UP TO the house, and checked in the windows, but saw no signs of anyone inside. A dog barked somewhere in the house. Would the Bennetts even have a dog? Or if they did, surely they would be big nasty ones, outside the house, on long chains, waiting to savage anyone who happens by.

Just as we were checking out the lock on the front door, to decide where to force our way in, we heard a shout.

"Oi! What do you think you're doing?" The man strode toward us as he yelled. He had a shotgun over his arm. Holy crap!

I held my hands up, hoping to calm him down, before he decided to load and use the bastard.

"Sorry, mate. Just looking for some friends of ours. Must not be in."

Lenore nodded, but looked ready to pounce if he attacked. Is there anything sexier than a powerful woman?

"Well, I'm home now, and I have no idea who you are," the man said, reaching the middle of the path and standing to glare at us. I frowned at Lenore.

"You selling something?" The man asked, looking at us both suspiciously. Lenore laughed, trying to look more relaxed than either of us were.

"We're just looking for a couple of friends. They said they live out here somewhere, but I'm starting to wonder if we've got the wrong house," she said. "I'm Lenore, this here's Harvey. You happen to know the Bennetts?"

The guy looked from one of us to the other.

"Don't know any Bennetts, love. There are less than fifty people living in this village, and I know every last one of them. I'm afraid you're on the wrong track here."

I stepped forward. "You don't know a pair of fraternal twin guys? Samuel and Seb? Mid-thirties, dark hair, dark eyes, mean as fuck?"

The man snorted. "Sure sounds like nice people you're friends with. Look, I've seen nobody like that around here, but they wouldn't have any reason to come to a village like this. We're not that kind of place. We don't get people like that around here."

I groaned, looking at Lenore. "Fuck. We're never going to find them."

She nodded at the man with the shotgun.

"Sorry to have bothered you. We'll get moving." She turned to walk away, and I saw him check out her ass as she walked. He saw that I caught him, and made an apologetic face.

"Word to the wise, mate." I stepped up close to him. "It's not me you need to worry about. If she catches you staring at her ass, she'll gut you like a fish."

The man blinked. "Understood. I didn't mean anything by it." He hurried into his house, keeping an eye on us as he did so.

"So we're back to square one?" I asked Lenore, as we reached the car again.

She groaned. "I have no fucking idea."

I stepped closer, pulling her into my arms, relieved when she didn't resist.

"Don't beat yourself up. You've done so much more than anyone else could, or would. You've been her best chance this whole time. Maybe they're just more prepared to disappear, than we are to find bad guys."

She pressed her face into my chest, her warm breaths against my t-shirt making me bite back a groan. How is it that I want to fuck her again already? She's been my best friend for ten years, and now suddenly, all I want to do is spend my time thrusting my cock into her, and watching her come.

And just as much... I want to build my biggest shrine ever, to celebrate every beautiful feature on her face, every expression I've seen on it. I want to watch her sleeping, on the biggest fucking TV I can get my hands on. I want to fuck her with a video camera running, so I can replay it later, and jerk off to it. She thinks that stuff isn't normal, but it turns out that it's normal to me. *And I won't stop.*

CASSIDY

THEY ACTUALLY LEFT ME alone for a long part of the day. It almost felt like a reprieve... but I couldn't help fearing the moment when they returned, and decided to start playing their games with me again.

The only time any of them returned, was while I was sleeping, and I awoke to find a fresh glass of water, and more painkillers. Never more than two at a time. They weren't giving me the tools to find a way out. Just helping me recover, so they could use me again.

"Awake at last?" A voice asked, and I realised that one of them stood in the doorway. The light behind him made it hard to pick out the details of his face. I was making an assumption that it was Sammy, because I was pretty sure he was the one who'd been looking after me.

It was so confusing. He kept giving me reason to think that he's the better of the two. That he cared. And then he'd be mean, or cruel, and it would break me that little bit more, because I'd let my guard down with him.

"Maybe," I said finally, because he just stood there staring at me.

He snorted, stepping into the room, and pulling the door half closed.

"How's the head?" He asked, almost sounding like he cared.

I groaned. "Still not great. Like I said before, it could be days."

He grinned. "I think the chances of that are pretty low."

I frowned at him, pulling the blankets up to my chin, because I'd obviously pushed them back in my sleep.

"You don't know that. What are you, a migraine expert now?"

He shrugged. "Looked into it. What type do you get?" I glanced around me.

"I don't know. My head throbs, and I get sick. Which type is that?"

He laughed, moving closer, and sitting on the bed.

"Chances are, if you do get them for days, you'd probably have seen a doctor about them. You haven't." I took a breath.

"You don't know if I have or not."

He leaned his arm on the bed, too close to my legs, making me shift away.

"Don't I, Cass? Don't I know every fucking thing about you? You don't know what we're able to look into, or find out. You don't know who does favours for us, and what businesses... or local surgeries... they work for." I scooted further away, sitting up against the headboard, trying and failing, to take the blankets with me, because the bastard had sat down on them.

"You didn't."

He smiled, showing lots of teeth.

"Didn't I, love? Do I not want to make sure we're looking after our little pet properly? I know the exact date of your last contraceptive injection, and when the next is due. I've entered it on my calendar," he said that in a creepy conversational tone, as if he'd just said something so normal, that he didn't understand my reaction.

"You crazy bastard. That's so fucking messed up! How dare you look into my personal information like that! I'll find out who looked it up for you, and I'll get them fired!"

He stood up, leaning over me, while I tugged the blankets closer.

"And just when do you think you're going to do that, love? You're never leaving here."

"You're insane," I snapped at him, as he towered over me.

"You're still ours, regardless of that fact, and whether it's accurate or not. Maybe you're the one who's insane. You're the one falling in lust with both of us. You think I can't tell when you're aroused? You get wet every time one of us is near you, and pretty soon, you'll be begging to suck our dicks, or have us in every fucking hole you have."

I gasped, reaching out and slapping his face hard, relishing the way his head moved a little with the force. His eyes fixed angrily on me, and a strange grin crept across his face. *Oh shit.*

"Oh god... I'm sorry. I... oh god, please don't hurt me!" I shrieked, trying to scramble away, while he moved fast, catching my hair with one of his hands, and stopping me in my tracks.

CHAPTER THIRTY-EIGHT
HARVEY

WE WENT HOME. I mean, what other course of action was there? We had no idea where else to go. The last address we thought we had, turned out to be an abandoned building we'd passed on the way back, and it was clearly empty. We had nothing. Nowhere to look. Nowhere to turn to. Nobody to ask. We had spent way more money than we could afford, to be out there looking for her.

It was ironic really. This had all started, because I'd run out of money, and needed a bailout. I went to the wrong people, and that led to a kidnap, and some frantic running around the streets trying to find her. We'd spent money we didn't have, trying to locate a perfect stranger.

We went to Lenore's place. When we got there, she went for a shower, and I offered to make us a snack. Before I did that, I checked around the place, even though I knew it fairly well, trying to work out where I could hide a camera or two. Just like she had a key to my place, I had one for hers, so I figured I'd pop back around tomorrow when she's at work, and start planning.

She poked her head out of the bathroom, calling me. When I reached her, she just looked at me.

"Are you joining me or what?" Hell yes. I shed my clothes as I followed her back in. Sometimes life could suddenly become perfect, without you ever realising how close it had been, the entire time.

CASSIDY

SAMMY DIDN'T DRAG ME by my hair, thankfully, because although my headache had almost dissipated, it wouldn't take much to bring it back. Of course, I hadn't told them I felt better. I'd keep popping the pills, and lying to them, for as long as I could.

"Just what made you think that you could slap me, and get away with it, Cass?" His voice was quiet, dark, dangerous. I trembled in his hold.

"Please, Sammy. I was upset."

He froze, quirking a brow at me.

"Sammy?" *FUCK!*

He shook his head. "Oh, Cass... first you slap me, and now you insult me..." He made a tutting sound, as I struggled to free myself.

"Seb, I'm sorry. I didn't... I mean... my head..."

He laughed, moving to whip the covers from the bed, baring me to him. Using his grip in my hair, he 'encouraged' me to move into the middle of the bed.

"Please."

He tilted my head back, getting really close to me.

"Seems like it's about time you pleased *me*. Especially after you just hurt my feelings."

I tried shaking my head, but it hurt to move.

"I'm sorry. Seb, I... you're scaring me."

He smiled. "Yeah, that helps a little, love. But you're going to need to do more than that, to make up for the insult."

Oh god no. I tried to pull away from him, and he smirked.

"The question is, love, what are you going to do, to make it up to me?"

I stared up at him. "I said I was sorry."

He shrugged. "That means fuck all to me. Actions speak louder than words, Cass." I tried shoving him back, but his grip never released from my hair.

"I don't know what you want," I said quietly. He loosened his grip on my hair then, moving his hand to stroke my face, the change from brutal to gentle shocking me enough, that I stayed still.

"Take off the t-shirt, Cass." I glanced down at the shirt of Sammy's that I wore.

"It's all I have, Seb."

He nodded. "And now you're going to willingly give it up, because you hurt me."

I wrapped my arms around myself.

"But then I'll have nothing to hide behind."

He shrugged. "You can try earning it back."

I stared at him, feeling like I had nowhere to go.

"If you take it away, you'll want more."

He grinned. "I'd want more if you were wearing a suit of fucking armour, love. I know how gorgeous that body of yours is, and I want to see it. It'd make me feel better, right now, after you physically attacked me, and insulted my individuality. Don't you think I deserve a proper apology?"

I stared at the bed. His words made a bizarre form of sense. I hadn't been fair to him, had I? I took a breath. *Hang on.* What the fuck is wrong with me? He's getting inside my head again.

"You can go fuck yourself, how about that? Fuck your apology. You don't deserve one. You're a monster, who is trying to completely brain fuck me into feeling sorry for you. Well, guess what? I don't. I hate you. I hate the sight of you. The smell of you. The sound of your fucking voice. I hate the fact that there are two of you. Yes. *You're the same.* You're both fucking psychopathic monsters. You have no idea how a human being feels, because you're both nothing like the rest of us!" I was screaming by the end of my tirade, and he just watched me, that unnerving grin on his face.

"Okay, love. I'm hearing you. What you're saying is... we're treating you a little too kindly, and you're getting ideas above your station. Good point. *Very well made.*"

He pulled the knife from his belt, and I shrank back.

"Wait." I held my hands up, and he laughed.

"My turn to make my point, love." He grabbed the front of the t-shirt, slashing the knife across it, almost opening it like a shirt. Then he tore it away from me, while I clutched my arms around me. Then he stood up.

Gathering up the covers from the bed, he walked to the window, and tossed them outside. From there, he took the pillows, slashing them with the knife, tossing the shredded pieces onto the floor, feathers and stuffing littering the carpet. Then he took the knife to the mattress, slicing the sheet and the mattress surface in wild slashes.

By this time, I was on my feet, my back to the corner of the room, watching in terror, as he destroyed the room I'd been sleeping in. He shot me a fierce glare, as he finished with the bed, breathing fast.

I followed his gaze to the curtains, my heart sinking, as he slashed the knife down them from above his head, to the floor. By the time he'd finished, they resembled those hippie bead curtains, and blocked very little of the light from outside. He shot me a triumphant grin, then tilted his head, glancing at the bathroom. *No.*

He pointed at me with the knife. "Don't fucking move." I shook my head fast, knowing that pushing him further right now, could be the last thing I ever did.

He returned from the bathroom with the one towel I'd been given, showing me the shredded remains, which he also tossed on the floor. He disappeared back in there, and a crashing sound came from inside.

My curiosity, at what the hell he was doing in there, was satisfied, when the remains of the shower door crashed out of the room, hitting the floor. It had been made of a frosted material, that clearly hadn't been glass, but was still breakable.

He stopped outside the bathroom door, staring at me, then casting his eyes around the room.

"Did I miss anything, love?" His voice was flat, almost disinterested. It was terrifying. He seemed like he had at the start, when they'd first snatched me.

I shook my head, keeping my eyes away from him, hoping that I wouldn't incite anything more. I had nothing left. Nowhere to hide, or cover up. Nowhere to sleep. *Nothing*.

I couldn't even shower safely, if they switched it back on, because I couldn't hide myself while I did. In a tantrum, which had probably only lasted ten minutes, he'd decimated everything that had made this room bearable.

He shot me a slow grin. "Bet you wish you'd just taken off the t-shirt, like I suggested. Maybe given me a blowie. Now instead, you have *nothing*."

He marched out of the room, like he'd just won some battle, and I think he had. I curled up in the corner of the destroyed bedroom, and hugged my knees, crying softly to myself.

CHAPTER THIRTY-NINE
HARVEY

WHEN MY PHONE RANG, as I sat with Lenore in her place, that evening, curled up together, with tumblers of scotch, feeling at peace, and loved up, I almost ignored it.

Lenore glanced at it. "Unknown number," she said warily. Oh hell. I grabbed it, because what if, even though we'd forgotten all about Cassidy, there was still a chance to do something to help her?

"Yeah?" I said, pulling Lenore back against me, so I could feel her warm skin against mine.

"Harvey?" A woman's voice.

"Yeah, who's this?"

"Julie. Cassidy's friend. She still hasn't shown up anywhere, and I'm really starting to panic. I don't know what to do. You still haven't seen her?" I covered the phone.

"Cassidy's friend, asking if I've seen her," I said quietly to Lenore, and she groaned.

"You can't tell her. She'll freak out."

"She is already," I said, and she sighed.

"Maybe it's time to let her call the police after all."

I lifted the phone back to my ear, hearing her calling my name, then I stopped.

"But I thought you said that would be dangerous."

Lenore snorted. "For us, yeah. We know too much. But not for her. All she can tell them is that her friend's missing, right?"

She was a smart lady...

"Hey, Julie? Sorry, I was just... uh... look... I haven't seen her since before we first spoke. I think, if she's still missing, that you should probably call the police."

She went quiet. "You're the one who told me not to before!" Oh she was pissed. Dammit, why did these women keep messing with my happiness?

"I just didn't want you to call them too soon, Julie. They expect you to wait a day or so. That's what they say on TV anyway."

She made a growling noise.

"You're a prick, Harvey, do you know that? I don't even know what contact you have from her, except from when she places book orders, but I had nobody else to turn to. Her best friends haven't seen her. She hasn't been to her place that we've seen, but her friends say some of her stuff is gone. What am I supposed to think? She wouldn't just do a runner."

Huh... "Some of her stuff is gone? Could she have been called away by a family emergency?" I asked, dumbly, because I knew that she had no family. I was pretty good at research, after all. But she couldn't know that.

"She doesn't have anyone. Harvey, I'm scared." Her voice had grown soft. She sounded cute. I wondered idly if she were cute. I'd never seen her, or met her, and there were no selfies with anyone called 'Julie', or any variation of that name, on Cassidy's social media. The only selfies on her phone were with her two besties. I'd flipped through them before, while she slept. I made a mental note to 'happen by' the office tomorrow, and find a way to meet Julie.

"Call the police, Julie. It's time for them to look for her. Maybe they can find something at her flat that tells them where she went. Will you keep me posted?"

She swore at me and hung up the phone. Something about it made me want to ring her back, just to hear her pissed off tone again.

"She calling them?" Lenore asked, shaking me from my thoughts.

"Yeah. I think she's pissed at me though."

Lenore laughed quietly. "I think that's just normal for women around you, H."

I chuckled, tickling her side, and making her laugh, and squirm about in my lap. Oh yeah... I needed to make her do that again.

CASSIDY

I COULD HEAR THEM in the hallway.

"... the fuck did you do that for?"

"Trust me, bruv. She was getting it too easy here."

"She was sick, you dickhead. It wasn't like she was playing us." That had to be Sammy.

"She might have been, but that doesn't mean she can mouth off at us. She needs to know her place." Seb really is a total prick.

"Well, I'm not cleaning that shit up. It's your mess," Sammy snapped, and Seb laughed.

"It stays that way until she tidies it. I mean... you know, if she wants to earn any privacy back."

The both chuckled quietly, and I groaned. I guess Sammy wasn't on my side after all. Just pissed at the mess. I realised that my entire life had shrunk to one room, and now that it had been trashed, it was like the whole horrible mess of being kidnapped had just happened again. I was back to square one. Afraid, naked, trapped, and with no option but to try and win them over, to get some of these 'comforts' back.

I got up and carefully picked my way through the mess. The sheet that Seb had shredded, along with the mattress, had some large pieces left, so I pulled at one, trying to fashion a makeshift cover for myself. It would have been large enough, but wouldn't go around me, so wouldn't stay on. Fuck. I checked the towel, which was worse. The curtains were a loss. No piece was wide enough to cover me. That bastard.

I crept to the door, hearing them muttering and laughing as they moved away from the room. I tested the door handle, opening it carefully, because although it had seemed crazy that they'd left me in an unlocked room, I'd stayed put, because my one foray out of the house had proved two things. I wasn't strong enough to get away, and they would always find me.

I tiptoed across the hallway, carefully opening the next door. An empty bedroom. A quick check through the wardrobe and drawers proved to me that it was literally an unoccupied bedroom. Dammit.

I made my way back to the door, carefully checking the hallway before I stepped back out, and pulled the door closed. I picked my way carefully across the hall to the opposite door, cringing when the floorboard directly in front of that door creaked lightly. I waited, but nobody came.

The room was definitely usually occupied. It smelled like one or other of the twins. Masculine, and dangerous. Being found here would be deadly. It would be like laying down and saying rape me.

I tiptoed around as carefully as I could. I put on the first t-shirt I found, then grabbed a pair of sweats, and put them on too. I could almost breathe with relief, because I suddenly felt ten times safer.

I rummaged around the room, finding and putting on a pair of socks. Shoes were out of the question; they were all huge. In the wardrobe, there were shirts. Suits. Long coats. These guys knew how to dress. I'd only ever seen them in jeans and t-shirts. Either wearing heavy boots, or trainers.

The ensuite bathroom revealed very little of who lived in this room. They wore similar colognes, maybe even the same one. They both could use any of the products in the room. I checked the cupboards, looking for anything of use, but it was mostly typical things you would find in a man's bathroom.

A few condoms sat in their packets, and I took two. It wasn't that I wanted sex, but if one of them decided to do it, I could try and encourage them to wear one. Maybe lie to them about having something they wouldn't want to catch. I groaned, as I left the bathroom. That would be pointless if Seb really had had someone access my medical records, of course.

I moved from this bedroom to the next, again, smelling of man. I had no idea which room belonged to which brother. Both were relatively tidy, and organised, beds made. It was strange. I expected one room to be messier than the other, more chaotic. That would have been my sign that it probably belonged to Seb, who definitely embraced chaos more than his brother seemed to.

This room also yielded very little in the way of anything I could use to protect myself, or hurt one of them. I had a suspicion that they'd made sure of that, since my room couldn't be locked. It did occur to me, however, that while they slept at night, I might have my best chance to either try to take one of them out, or... and let's be honest, more sensibly, I could look for the car keys, and head out of here to the police.

A noise made me panic, as I reached for the bedroom door. What if they were outside right now? What if I'd taken too long, and they'd figured out where I'd gone? They could be standing there waiting to jump out and attack me, as soon as I opened the door. My heart raced in my chest, and the residual headache, which maybe hadn't been a migraine at all, but a bitch of a headache, caused by the situation I was in, caused my temples to throb at the same horrific pace.

Finally, I carefully pulled the door handle, and moved the door as slowly as possible toward me. Peeking outside, I couldn't see anyone in either direction, so I quickly stepped outside, and made my way back to the room I'd been staying in. As I reached the door, I stood there for a few seconds, my hand on the handle, while everything in me screamed at me to run.

This was my chance. They were distracted, doing whatever it is they do while I'm up here. I could just run. Maybe sneak out of a window, so they don't know I've gone straight away. It'd give me time to hide out somewhere, and maybe they'd think I'd run further than I had.

Footsteps on the stairs suddenly lit a fire under me, and I let myself into the room in a hurry, going back to my corner to huddle, and wait for their next game, or trick, or assault.

CHAPTER FORTY
HARVEY

Dinner with Lenore was beautiful. We ordered a takeaway, which sounds so frivolous, when we've spent so much money trying to hunt for Cassidy, but we felt we deserved it, after all of the hard work we'd put in, even though it had been fruitless.

"I'm thinking I'll call Mikey again tomorrow, see if he has any other ideas about how to find the Bennetts. Surely they're going to be back at their place here soon, otherwise nobody else can make stupid deals with them."

I stared at her. How wonderful was she? Still trying to save Cassidy. I felt a bit guilty for how I kept forgetting about Cassidy, because now all I could see was Lenore. Her beauty. Her strength. Her courage. Her feisty nature.

"I added both numbers they called from on my phone. I could try them, and see if we can make a new deal for Cassidy. I know you'll feel better when she's free," I said, taking the dishes to the kitchen, and loading them into her dishwasher.

"Wait a minute, H." She followed me, turning me away from the dishes.

"Don't you mean *we* will feel better? You're the one who got her into this mess. This isn't about me, and what I want. This is about you doing the right thing, and fixing your fuck up, before something happens to her, that we can't ever make up for. We're going to keep trying, because it's the right thing to do."

I nodded. "I'm sorry, babe. I'm just… I guess, I didn't expect this. *Us*. And it's occupying my every thought right now."

She frowned. "I like you, H. I think I've always liked you, and not in the way it seemed for so long, but I can't... this can't be the reason that we leave a young woman to be raped, and murdered. You get that, right? The only way this becomes okay, is if we win, and save her."

I pulled her into my arms, trying to tuck her against my chest, but she pulled back, reminding me of her strength.

"H, I'm serious. *This* is tainted by what you did. If you don't help me fix it, then this can't continue."

"Jesus, Lenore. Don't say that. I'm not always great with words. If I led you to think that I'll just leave her there, because we're together now, that's not what I meant." It had been, I knew it. I just hoped she didn't realise. I couldn't lose her now. *She was mine.*

CASSIDY

WHICHEVER BROTHER OPENED THE door took one look at me in the corner, said 'hmmm', and disappeared again. What? I stayed still, not trusting that he'd stay away.

When the door opened again a few moments later, it was like seeing double. Both brothers came into the room, closing the door behind them. They both just stood there, arms folded, staring at me.

"Someone went walkabout, it seems," one of them finally said, looking annoyed.

"Been helping yourself to our stuff, Cass?" The other said.

I shrugged. "Seb ruined my clothes, so I went looking for more."

They exchanged a look. "Oh I did, did I?" The first one said, and dammit, I'd been half sure that one was Sammy.

I pointed to the mess across the room from me.

"I didn't do all that. That was you."

He glanced at Sammy. "She makes me trash the room, then blames *me* for being emotional. And then she ransacks *my* fucking room, and steals my clothes." Oh, so the first room was Seb's. I glanced down at the t-shirt and sweats. I guess he'd recognised the top, because the trousers were just generic grey.

"I didn't make him do anything, Sammy. He went mad at me."

Sammy snorted, glancing at Seb.

"You went mad at her, eh?"

Seb widened his eyes.

"She was physically and mentally abusive to me, bruv. I did what I had to, so I wouldn't attack *her* with the knife." Yikes! That thought actually hadn't occurred to me.

"Clean this shit up, Cass. Then you get food and water. Not before," Sammy said sharply, turning and leaving the room, and leaving me alone with Seb. He glanced around.

"Once you've done that, we can deal with the issue of sneaking around, and stealing." He winked at me, then turned and left the room too, closing the door. Jesus, what the fuck was wrong with these two monsters? I wasn't cleaning it up. I wasn't a bloody slave. They could go to hell.

I eventually went into the bathroom, kicking the remains of the broken door from in there, and then I pushed the door closed. The pull cord by the door worked the light, so I made sure that was on before I closed the door, and then I glanced around for some way to block the door. No furniture in the room that wasn't connected to the walls. No lock on the door, of course, or no key, at least.

Opening it again, I glanced at the bedside cabinet. It was small enough for me to move, and fairly close to the door, so I removed the lamp, and started dragging it across the carpet. It moved way too slowly for my liking, but I persevered. Eventually it slid onto the tiled floor of the bathroom, suddenly moving more easily. Bugger. I hadn't thought of that.

Still... if I laid it on its side, it would only be able move a few inches when the door was pushed, before it was stopped by the bathtub, so it wouldn't let them get in. The mat on the tiled floor had that rubber stuff on the reverse, which stopped it sliding across the floor easily, so I lay that across the floor in front of the door, before I dragged the bedside table on top, and pushed it against the door. The two would slow them down, at the very least. I wasn't dumb enough to think it would keep them out indefinitely.

Of course, what also occurred to me, was that this would serve one definite purpose, and probably not one I wanted to serve. It would royally piss them off. Not only didn't I do what they'd ordered me to do, but I'd locked myself in the bathroom, something they thought they'd prevented. I could survive in here for a while, safe from their abuse. No food, but I had water.

I had the bath, so I could sit in that, to hide from them. I should have brought in one of the trashed pillows, to make it more comfortable. I used the toilet, and washed up, brushed my teeth, and drank a few mouthfuls from the tap, then I huddled in the bath, and waited for hell to break loose.

CHAPTER FORTY-ONE
HARVEY

Lenore called Mikey, and while she did, I called the numbers I'd saved for the Bennetts. The first one just rang until it rang out. The second one rang for a few rings, before one of them answered it.

"Yeah." No idea which one answered. It was impossible to tell on the phone, but it was normally Seb who did the calling.

I cleared my throat. "It's Harvey," I said, trying to sound as much of a man as I could.

There was a chuckle.

"Well, hello, Harv. How are you doing, mate? Got our money yet?"

I took a breath. "I wanted to see what I can do to help Cassidy."

He chuckled again.

"Help her do what? She's perfectly fine. She has her own room, and we feed her now and then."

I clenched my fist, and held it in front of me, staring at the way my knuckles turned white, the tighter I clenched it.

"Listen, you sick bastard. I want to make a deal. I want her out. What do I need to do, to make that happen? You want the shop? It's yours. I'll move out of the flat, and you can take the whole place over. I don't care anymore."

He fell silent for a long moment.

"You been there lately, mate?" I frowned.

"Why do you ask?"

He chuckled again. "No reason. So... what can you possibly offer me, that will be sufficient for us to release our lovely young woman? She's very pleasing, you know. Gave me one hell of an orgasm this morning. Tell me what could possibly be better than that."

I slammed my hand down on the table.

"You bastard! Did you rape her?"

He took a moment to answer.

"Is it rape if she comes too?"

Jesus Christ! "You keep your fucking hands off her, you sick fuck!"

"Well... I don't think that's going to happen, mate. She's got one hell of a sexy body, and I love having my body all over hers. Did you ever try her out? Fucking hot, mate. Amazing pair of tits. And that mouth..." He made a groaning noise.

"Please! Stop hurting her! I'll give you anything," I said, because guilt suddenly returned with a vengeance, and I felt like as much of a monster as the bastard I was talking to.

"Anything, bruv? Hmmm... Tell you what, why don't I take a little time, and have a think. What could I want in place of the lovely Cassidy? With that sassy mouth, and very intuitive hands..."

"Fucking hell! Just tell me. Anything. Come on. The business, and anything else you want!" I said, suddenly feeling like he was about to end the call, and somehow knowing that he wouldn't answer if I called back.

I could hear him talking to his brother in the background, but I couldn't make out any words apart from my own name once, and Cassidy's name, although he called her Cass.

They had a nickname for her? I'd never reached that point. *Cass.* It sounded too abrupt for someone as beautiful as her. She needed all of the syllables she'd been blessed with. *Cassidy.*

"Okay, bruv. Here's the only offer we're going to make. Listen up, because you won't reach me on this number again after this. You listening, Harv?"

I took a breath. "Yes. Please. *Anything.*"

He laughed. "Okay. Set up a video call with us right now, and *kill Lenore.* Right in front of us. And when you're done... kill yourself."

I fell back into the dining chair, my heart thudding almost painfully. What the fuck?

"Are you serious?"

He laughed. "Yeah, mate. The only way we'll let Cass go... or what's left of her, anyway... is if you kill your bestie, and then yourself, and *do it right now*. On camera. No delays. No planning ways to fake it. You do it right now, or you fuck off and live your life, stalking some other poor bitch. Maybe your friend Lenore. She's fucking hot."

I looked at my hand again, seeing how it shook.

"Please, Seb. Anything but that."

He laughed. "Riiiight... so you'll do *anything*... but you won't do that. I guess *Meatloaf* was right all along. Either you call me right back on a video call, and do what I ask, or expect to see me in five days, when you'll hand me all of our money, or I'll gut you both like fucking fish."

The call ended, and I stared at the phone in horror.

"Lenore!" I yelled, running across her flat to find her.

CASSIDY

WHEN THEY CAME, I had to sit and wait in the bathroom, for them to work out what was going on. They chatted among themselves, did a little calling out to me, like a pet that had gone astray, and then a hand slammed against the bathroom door. It moved a few inches and stopped dead, as the barricade stopped it.

"Oh brilliant. That's what she's been up to. Built herself a fucking nest in there," one of them, I'm guessing Seb, said.

"Well, move it. If she can move something, then so can we," Sammy replied. I watched the door as they tried to push it open. The mat hadn't slowed the cabinet as much as I'd hoped, but it had now wedged one corner against the bath, once they'd pushed the door enough. An arm could reach in now, but that was as much as either of them could get in.

"Fucking hell, Cass, come out of there, right now!" One of them snapped, and I stayed silent.

"Can you see in there? Is she even in there?"

"Where the fuck else would she be? It's barricaded from the inside." I snorted, then covered my mouth with both hands, because I'd just made a sound.

"You think this is funny, do you? Cassidy, I'm going to lose my rag if you don't move that fucking thing right now," he yelled, and I cowered in that bath.

"Go away. I'm not moving it!" I called out, and they fell silent for a few seconds.

"So you're planning to starve to death in a bathroom? That's pathetic," was their response.

I looked around me, at what might be my final resting place, and realised it was better than many of the alternatives.

"Better dead than your prisoner," I said quietly, and they muttered among themselves again. It went quiet for a while, and then I heard a noise at the door again. A phone appeared through the gap, on a damn selfie stick, and they used that to snap some pictures of the room, or me, or both. It retracted just as carefully. More quiet muttering, and more silence.

Then suddenly, the light went off. Not just in this room, but in the bedroom too. I was suddenly trapped in pitch darkness, because it had grown so dark outside, and the tiny window let nothing in. I felt my breaths turn into little gasps, panicked, and desperate. *No.*

I hate the dark. Normal dark is fine, but pitch black? Where the walls disappear into the darkness, and you could be in a tiny box, rather than a room... that terrifies me. When it's pitch dark, nothing else exists. I folded myself into the furthest end of the bath, and curled up, trying to control my breathing, before I had a full-on panic attack.

It was only when I started to slow my breathing, that I realised I could hear something. A bump at the door, or where the door must be, in the pitch-dark nothingness of my new life.

Another bump, a slight sliding noise, and then another bump. What the hell were they doing? They didn't speak. They were just doing something by the door. The sliding noise... was it the bedside cabinet being shunted across the floor? How? Were the removing the door? I had no idea. Not knowing was beyond terrifying.

I could practically feel the menace coming from them both, as they did whatever the hell it was they were doing, to try and make their way into the room. I couldn't even get up and try to stop them moving the cabinet, if they even were, because I couldn't remember where it was in relation to where I was in the bath. And terror had taken my ability to even move my legs. I was frozen in absolute fear.

CHAPTER FORTY-TWO

HARVEY

"THEY SAID WHAT?" Lenore screeched at me, and I just stared at her.

"They're insane," I said finally.

She glanced at the time on her phone, having ended her call with Mikey, when I started yelling out for her.

"How long ago was this?" I dropped onto the sofa.

"A few minutes, I think. I don't know. I can't get my head around this." She frowned. "Did they say how?"

"Fuck, Lenore, really? That's your question?" I stared up at her in disbelief. What was she thinking?

"Maybe we can fake it somehow?" She said slowly. "I could... I don't know... you could make it look like you stabbed me, and we could use ketchup, and..." She looked around us. "Maybe you could stab me for real, if we make sure it's nowhere near an organ."

"Fucking hell! You are out of your mind! I'm not stabbing you. I'm not even pretending to. We've lost, Lenore. We can't beat these monsters, because we're not like them. I won't kill you. I won't even pretend to kill you, just to please them. And even if we faked your death, I'd have to fake mine too."

She glared at me suddenly. "Is that the bit that's really freaking you out?" She asked, her tone low, and somewhat dangerous.

"Think about it... we start a video call with them. We supposedly both kill ourselves, and lay there, pretending to be dead..."

She nodded. "And?"

"And how do we end the call? We can't. Which means those bastards could keep it open at their end for ages, to watch to see if we move. We would have to lay there indefinitely, not moving, hiding our breathing, and not knowing when the call ends. Because we won't be able to see the phone screen." I had probably put way too much thought into that side of it, but it was a valid point.

"Damn it, that's actually quite logical," she said finally, while I shot her a look.

"Thanks!"

She glanced at her phone again. "How quickly did he say we had to do this?"

I sighed, pushing my hair back, taking my glasses off, and rubbing them on my t-shirt.

"Immediately."

"Fucking hell, H! We're too late already!" I nodded.

"It would never have worked though."

CASSIDY

I'D THOUGHT THE DARKNESS was terrifying. The darkness, combined with those sounds of them moving, was a new level of fear. They were coming for me, and I couldn't see them to try and resist, or fight.

When there was suddenly a blinding flash of light, which made me screech, and cover my face, I realised they'd used a camera flash, or one of their phones. The result was that I couldn't see anything, except a weird flash of lines in my eyes, every time I blinked, which bore no resemblance to the room as I remembered it.

I felt a rush of movement, just before someone grabbed me, and threw me over their shoulder. I screamed, fighting against the hold on me, but he was solid and unmovable, as they both always were, every other time I'd fought them.

I was carried from the room, and expected to be dumped in the bedroom, on the bed, or even the floor, but he kept moving. The entire house was pitch dark, and terrifying, because if I couldn't see, how the hell could he? I was suddenly flying, and landed on something soft.

A second later, as I came to realise it was a bed, I felt someone leaning over me, and my arms flashed out, to try and fight them away. They hit something hard, and sharp, where his face should be, catching a nerve in the side of my wrist, and making me cry out with pain. My wrist and hand felt slightly numb, and I changed my tactic, to try and turn and crawl away from the person hovering over me. Hands stopped me.

"Nice try, love. But understand this... just because you can't see with the lights out, doesn't mean we can't," he whispered, too close to me.

"You know, I could do anything to you right now, and not only would you struggle to stop me, because you don't know where you are, or where I am, unless I'm touching you... but you also don't know which one of us I am. In fact... if you tried to tell anyone, you'd have nothing, because you can't see me. I could be anyone. I could be that pervert Harvey, fed up with watching you while you sleep, and deciding to force himself on you. Into you. Holding you down, while he forces his pathetic little cock into you."

I struggled against him, my arms trying to push him away from me.

"Stop, please. I'm sorry. I was scared."

He laughed. "You *were* scared? You mean you're not now? Maybe we need to up our game, bruv. It's getting old and jaded for her." I heard a murmur of agreement from somewhere on my left side.

"Oh god. Please just kill me," I finally said, losing all fight and resistance, and just laying still. He chuckled, and I felt his hand reach my throat, closing around it lightly.

"You sure you're ready to die, love? I'd hoped to spend much more time fucking you up first."

I trembled as I lay there, fighting the instincts inside me that told me to fight, struggle, kick, punch, *live*. I just sighed.

"Maybe you don't even have the balls to kill me. Is that why you keep threatening it, and never doing it?"

He growled under his breath. "You think you're going to play me? Trick me into losing my temper, so I kill you? You think it'll be over that easily?

There are so many things I want to do to you, Cass. So many things my brother here wants to do. Every time you challenge us, or attempt something like this, it just reinforces the fact that you're the one for us. We don't want easy. We don't want someone who just lays there and takes it, because she doesn't care. We want someone who fights us, and argues, and pushes her luck."

I took a breath, trying to push back my silent sobs. "I won't do any of that. I'll just go somewhere in my mind, and hide from you until it's over, and you kill me at last."

He chuckled, and I felt him move, placing something on the bed beside me, maybe whatever he'd worn so he could see me in the dark. His lips came down on mine, and then he squeezed my throat tightly, making me gasp and jerk, making him laugh against my mouth. I felt hands reach for the sweats I was wearing, pulling them down, and baring me to him.

"No!" I gasped.

"But I thought you were just going to hide in your mind, Cass? I don't think it's as easy as you think, but you can try that."

I felt him pulling at his own clothes, and heard a belt unbuckling. Fuck! No!

I started to fight him, slapping at him, and he laughed.

"Just as I thought, love. You can say you'll lay here like the dead, and pretend, but we both know, as soon as I start to get down to business, you'll either join in, or panic, and you'll move either way. Either to touch me, or to fight me. You physically can't just pretend it's not happening."

I could feel the hands of his brother, sliding up my side, edging under my stolen t-shirt.

"Let's just fuck her now," his brother whispered. "She's already mostly naked, and we're both gagging to fuck her."

Shit. That must be Seb. Which meant that this was Sammy holding me down, and threatening me. He did keep warning me that he was no better than his brother. Why did I keep expecting more of him?

"Please don't. Not like this," I whispered, and they both stilled.

"Like what, then?" Sammy asked, leaning close to me, finding my lips with his, running his tongue over them, before tightening his hand on my throat again. My mouth opened to gasp for air, and he took advantage, sliding his tongue into my mouth, as he kissed me relentlessly.

The other hands found my breasts under the t-shirt, and started rubbing and pulling at my nipples. I struggled to pull away from the kiss, but the hand on my throat tightened whenever I tried. I tried slapping away the hands sliding about under my top, but with Sammy in the way, leaning over me as he was, I couldn't even reach them.

My silent sobs had become real, and as fingers slipped between my legs, and started to slide over my clit, I felt that confusing switch inside me again, when suddenly their touches started to feel like teasing, like something other than the horror they should be.

My struggles faded away, as my mind was consumed with confusion, and frustration, and anger. I didn't know who to be angrier with. Them for what they were doing to me, or me for, even now, even after all that had happened, finding myself responding to their touches, even when I didn't choose them, or agree to them.

I tried doing what I'd said. I tried retreating into my mind, to try and distance myself from what they were doing to me, but every touch, every nip, every breath against my skin, brought me right back. I was sobbing, because I was breaking.

How could I be so afraid, and tormented, and yet somehow, my body was responding to them? And it wasn't alone. *My mind.* My traitorous mind was getting on the Bennett Brothers train, and enjoying the ride.

CHAPTER FORTY-THREE
HARVEY

I COULD SEE THAT Lenore was struggling with our most recent failure, to try and save Cassidy. She'd gone to sleep eventually, but she slept fitfully, her head moving now and then, and her breath catching. It was unbelievably sexy.

I recorded her for a few minutes, enjoying these unguarded moments, when nothing was measured, or planned. People are never more vulnerable, and real, than they are when they sleep. If anything happened in the room, there would be that gap between realising and acting, because the mind and body both needed to wake up, and realise what was going on.

It made me feel incredibly powerful, to watch over her, while she showed me that vulnerability. That trust. That she felt safe sleeping beside me, told me just how much she'd started to feel for me. Just a few days ago, she tossed around hurtful terms, like stalker, or pervert. And yet, now she slept naked beside me.

I lowered the bedding a little, revealing the soft curve of her breast, as she lay twisted and tensed in her dream. I filmed some more, lifting the bedding further, to aim the camera down the length of her, under the covers.

She moved, and groaned, so I stopped filming and slipped the phone under my pillow, just as her eyes sleepily opened, and she saw me.

"Harvey? You okay?" I nodded.

"Just needed the bathroom, babe. I'm sorry if I woke you." She shook her head.

"I was having a weird dream. I guess that's to be expected lately, right?"

I nodded. "Want to talk about it?" She closed her eyes for a second, then shook her head.

"Really just want to forget it."

I leaned down to kiss her lips.

"If you change your mind, I'll be here to listen. After the loo, of course." I faked a chuckle, and slipped out of bed, heading for the bathroom.

As I made my way back to the bed, expecting to find her flat out again, I was horrified to see her holding my phone in her hand, and staring at me accusingly.

Fuck.

CASSIDY

WHEN A SOFT MOAN came out of my mouth, I was horrified. Sammy's lips had moved to my throat, replacing his hand, as he kissed, and nipped, and his fingers started to thrust into me. Seb was still tormenting my nipples, pinching them, then rubbing them, and he'd moved close enough that he could whisper in my ear as he did so.

"Feel how that pussy is fucking drenched for us, love? You can keep pretending to fight us if you want, but we all know exactly what you want. You want to be our fucking toy, that we play with whenever we fucking want."

"No," I whispered, because at least I could stop the wrong word coming out... for now.

Sammy chuckled against my collarbone.

"Honestly, she's fucking choking my fingers with that pussy of hers. She's wishing I'd replace them with my cock."

Seb snorted. "So do it. What's she going to do to stop you, bruv?"

I tried pushing him away again, and then wondered why I'd chosen him to push away, and not Sammy. Sammy who posed the larger threat right now. Sammy who'd undone his pants, and could be about to rape me. Why? Why didn't I push him away? I slapped at Seb instead, who laughed, and backed up.

"I think that t-shirt needs to go, bruv."

"No!" I started to fight to keep it, but they easily manhandled me out of it, and it was thrown somewhere out of sight. Everything was, after all, out of sight, in the pitch dark of this damn house. They'd cut the power, hadn't they? It was the only way they could steal all the light at once. And they could see. That meant they had night vision kit. Only creepy stalking bastards have those.

"You're as bad as he is!" I gasped, trying to push them both away. They froze in place.

"As bad as who?" Sammy asked, his voice low and dangerous.

"Yeah... Cass... just who are you lumping us in with? Come on, don't keep us in suspense. Must be someone really awful, bruv."

I took the opportunity to slide my hands over my breasts, protecting them from Seb's touch, while he had been distracted.

"*Him*. The reason that all of this is fucking happening!"

They both fell silent for a few seconds, then laughed.

"You think Harv can measure up to us? And I don't just mean physically, because I'm pretty sure he's got a tiny dick..." Seb said.

Sammy leaned close again, trapping my hands against my chest.

"You think he could bend a woman to his will like we can? You think he can find his way into your mind, and make you desperate for him? He's a fucking oxygen thief, love. He couldn't even hope to have the power over a woman that we do."

I stared into the darkness, where I knew he hovered, staring down at me, whether he could see me or not.

"The more you people say stuff like that, the more I realise that the only way any woman will be safe is when you're both dead," I whispered, wishing I had the strength to make that happen.

He laughed, lowering his mouth to my throat once more, his teeth biting in, before he began sucking hard at my skin. Another fucking hickey.

"Stop that," I groaned, because while he went back to teasing me between my legs, the hickey actually felt good, the pinching suction making me gasp.

"You know what, bruv?" Seb said quietly beside us.

"Yeah?" His voice came gruffly from so close to my ear.

"She looks so naked. She wanted something to cover up with, didn't she?"

Sammy placed another hickey before he answered.

"Good point. Let's cover her."

I sighed with relief. Finally, they'd stop, and leave me alone. Give me back some dignity.

Seb groaned beside me, and I became aware of a jerking motion. *Oh god no.*

Sammy closed a hand around my throat, and sat up further, and I could feel him moving, as he started masturbating too.

"No! Stop. Get away from me!" Sammy squeezed tightly on my throat, choking off my words.

"Shut up, unless you want us both to come in your mouth," he hissed, his movements speeding up.

Seb grabbed my hand and pulled it away from my breast, his mouth lowering over it, sucking my nipple hard, before his teeth pinched it tight. I let out a yelp, and he followed that with a sudden move, and long groan, as spurts of warm liquid splatted on my chest, and nipple.

A few moments later, I felt Sammy jerking forward, and once more I felt warm splats of semen landing on me. Again on my chest and stomach. *Bastards.* I felt his fingers swipe over the mess on my skin, and then they were shoved into my mouth, making me splutter and try to pull away.

"Suck them," Sammy demanded, while I tried to punch him.

CHAPTER FORTY-FOUR
HARVEY

I APPROACHED HER SLOWLY, trying to prepare myself for the argument I was about to face. What reason could I give for videoing her sleeping? For photographing her, when she doesn't know I'm watching. Shit. I thought I'd have more time than this.

"Lenore?" I reached the bed. "You okay?"

She handed me the phone.

"It buzzed, and scared me, because I didn't know it was under your pillow. It said 'unknown'. I'm sorry. I opened it." Her face was sad.

I stared at the screen. It was a strange photo of Cassidy, cowering in a bathtub, terrified, and exhausted looking. It looked like she hadn't been prepared for it. What the hell were they doing to her?

I looked at Lenore, seeing my horror reflected on her face.

"What the hell are they doing to her, H? I thought when we failed, that they'd just never tell us. But instead, they're going to make sure we suffer with her."

I felt the phone buzz in my hand again, and opened the next photo message, practically on autopilot.

Cassidy. Naked. Crying. Terrified. I focused on the glossy skin of her stomach and chest... her perky nipples... trying to fight the twitch of my cock as I did.

"Fuck."

Lenore looked at me worriedly.

"What is it now?"

I handed her the phone, sliding into the bed with her, so she couldn't see how turned on I'd been, when I saw Cassidy like that.

"What is that all over her?" Lenore asked quietly, then she groaned. "They... that's..."

"Yeah." I took the phone, and closed the picture, setting the phone aside. "It is."

"Bastards."

CASSIDY

I SAW MORE FLASHES of light in that unbearable darkness. They were photographing me. Covered in their semen. Naked. *Broken*. Those monsters were taking such delight in the state they'd reduced me to.

I lay there, because what else could I do? It was so dark that I felt like moving at all would be dangerous, with unseen obstacles everywhere.

When the lights suddenly came on, blinding me with their normally comfortable brightness, I gasped, and clasped my hands over my eyes.

I heard chuckling in the room with me, but I didn't even look to see who, or where. I couldn't look at them after what they'd done to me.

My hands were lifted from my face, and something metal locked around my wrists. Handcuffs? I gasped, and struggled against them, and the bastard still clutching the chain between them.

"What the fuck are you doing?" I hissed at him. He had these strange goggle things pushed up onto his head. I guessed they were what he'd used to see me in the dark.

He grinned. "Anything I fucking want, love." He used something on the headboard to attach to the chain on the handcuffs, and just like that, I was tied to the bed, and unable to escape.

I just squeezed my eyes closed, tensing up for the next assault on my body. When nothing happened, and he moved from the bed, I opened them again, frowning at the two bastards as they stood beside the bed, staring at me.

"Sorry, love... not really feeling like a fuck right now, but thanks for offering," Seb said to me, smirking at his brother. I could tell it was him, because they were both shirtless, jeans hanging open at their waists, and I could see the familiar tattoos on his chest.

"Go to hell," I muttered at him, and he shrugged.

"Just been pretty close to heaven, love... not looking to leave just yet."

I glared at Sammy. "I thought you were less evil than him, but you're just as sick." He grinned at me, like I'd just complimented him.

"Nice of you to say so, love, thanks. Now, you're going to sleep here in Seb's bed, like a good girl."

I gasped, looking from one brother to the other.

"No!"

Sammy shook his head, patting his brother on the back, as he turned and headed for the door.

"Nighty night, kids." He pulled the door closed behind him, leaving me alone with Seb.

Seb disappeared into his ensuite bathroom, and was gone long enough that he'd showered, and brushed his teeth before he returned. I wanted the same. When he returned, smelling amazing, and looking sexy, with just a smallish towel around his waist, and his muscles and tattoos glistening ever so slightly, with drops of water, I stared at the bathroom, then back at him.

"Can I shower too?"

He laughed, removing the towel, and rubbing it over his wet hair, before he tossed it back through the doorway.

"No."

"Can I brush my teeth, you sick asshole?" He tilted his head.

"I'll brush them for you, but only if I use our cum as your toothpaste."

I swallowed, feeling a wave of horror.

"Jesus, why?"

He frowned, as he pushed the ensuite door closed.

"Why what?"

"Why can't you just let me freshen up?" I wanted to be clean. I could feel the stickiness of their fluids all over me, and I wanted to be clean, and I wanted rid of their taste.

"Freshen up from what?" He asked, coming around to the other side of the bed, straightening the pillows at what I now realised would be his side of the bed.

"Are you dumb as well as evil?" I snapped, glaring at him, as he grabbed the bedding which had been thrown from the bed, and neatly folded it in half.

"Well, that's not very nice of you, Cass. I thought we were becoming friends, but you hurt me with your words. You're going to sleep right there, covered in everything we did to you. Because you deserve it. You earned it. You don't get to wash it away. You don't get to remove the taste of us from your mouth, because we belong all over you, and inside you. In every fucking orifice. Just be thankful you didn't have to take both of us in your mouth, and swallow down both loads. I think we were pretty kind to you, actually."

He switched the light off, and returned to the bed, while my eyes adjusted to the almost pitch darkness of the room. There was a little light coming in around the curtains, and a little from under the door. It gave me just enough light to see his shadowy form returning to the bed, and then he adjusted the bedding, sliding under it, and making himself comfy. He fell quiet, while I stared at the dark figure beside me.

"Are you fucking serious?" I asked him suddenly, breaking the silence. He sighed.

"Can you keep it down, love? I'm trying to sleep here."

"Go fuck yourself," I muttered, kicking at him, because they'd left my legs free, and dammit I'd use them.

"Do that again, and I'll tie your fucking legs too," he snarled at me.

"Are you seriously going to leave me uncovered all night? You selfish prick!"

He laughed quietly beside me. "I'm sorry, love, are you cold?"

I glared at him even though he couldn't see it.

"What do you think, asshole?"

He rolled over, I'm guessing, so he could stare at me in the dark.

"I think that I don't want you getting that mess all over my bedding."

I fidgeted against the damn cuffs holding my arms up. "I fucking hate you."

He stayed silent, but I could feel his amusement, coming at me in waves.

"You're going to let me freeze here, because you don't want your own damn body fluids in your own bed. Where's the logic in that?"

He leaned closer, making me shrink back a little.

"Cass, love, I'm all clean from the shower. I don't want to get all messy again. Now get some fucking sleep, because you've got a lot of cleaning up to do tomorrow."

I wriggled on the bed, trying to turn over, to brush against the sheet, and remove some of their taint from my skin.

"If you dare think of doing that, or rubbing it on me, I'll spend the entire night fucking you. Your choice," he warned, and I groaned, rolling back again.

"I hate sleeping on my back, dammit," I said, because I just had to argue, somehow, while also fearing inciting what he'd just threatened.

"Do you know why we haven't fucked you yet, Cass?" He whispered, reaching out and cupping the side of my face, his touch gentle, which felt like the biggest lie of all.

I shook my head, trying to pull away from him.

He brushed his thumb over my lips, and then pulled his hand back.

"*Good.*"

He rolled over, and ignored me, while I cursed him under my breath.

HARVEY

LENORE WENT TO WORK when she woke, at the charity for abused women, that she had devoted herself to, and I stayed in her bed. I spent some time lounging in her bed, laying in her place, my face pressed into her pillow, as I breathed in her scent.

"Fuck. All this time, and you were right here." I rolled onto my back against her pillow, and pushed the covers away, palming my cock, which had started to rise, at the scent of her. My phone, which had been on my pillow, was in reach, so I grabbed it, and scrolled through the many photos I'd taken of Lenore.

As I stroked my cock, I pored over those pictures, at every detail of her face, and her body. Once my cock was rock hard, and aching, I opened the first video of her, listening to her as she slept.

I had the volume as high as it would go, and when that video finished, I switched to the next, focusing on her soft sighs, and the way her lips parted as she breathed.

My hand started to jerk at my cock, and when I switched to the latest video, the one of her moving restlessly in her sleep, and then the camera moving to take in her naked body under the covers, I erupted, spurting all over my hand, almost dropping the phone, as I relaxed and breathed deeply, relishing the moment.

CHAPTER FORTY-FIVE

CASSIDY

I woke up to aching shoulders, and numb arms, and a finger trailing over my skin. I flinched, and then moaned with pain, when my arms suddenly flared back to life.

"Good morning, love, did we sleep well?" Seb practically cooed at me, as his finger circled my nipple.

"I'm only sorry you didn't die in your sleep," I grumbled at him, making him laugh with surprise.

"Ouch! Someone woke up on the wrong side of the bed," he commented, tweaking my nipple. I didn't react. I couldn't. My arms and shoulders were so painful, that my focus was entirely there.

"Wrong bed. Wrong fucking life," I said, glaring at him.

"Wow... maybe I should try and put a smile on that face of yours, love. Want me to tongue fuck you?" He licked at his lips, wagging his tongue at me.

"You really can't read the room, can you? This is me in fucking agony, you sick, sadistic bastard."

He frowned. "We barely touched you last night, love. If we'd had our way, you'd be sore alright. In all the best places."

I tried to move, and tears blurred my eyes.

"Oh god."

He stared at me for a moment, then his eyes shifted to my hands.

"Jesus."

Sitting up on the bed, he released the link between the headboard and my hands, and I felt him start to lift them. I screamed, and he stopped.

"Okay... okay... hang on, love." He moved from the bed, returning a few seconds later, and unlocked the cuffs, releasing both of my wrists.

He rubbed at the raw flesh, almost soothingly, except for the fact that it was him touching me.

"I'm going to kill you, first chance I get," I snapped at him, watching his eyes widen a little.

"Damn... you're a scary bitch in the mornings." He moved slowly, easing my arms gradually down from above my head, watching as the tears rolled down my cheeks. I felt like they'd been dislocated, even though I didn't know how that felt.

"God, it hurts... please stop," I moaned, and he stopped moving.

"Steady, love." He turned to the door, and yelled for his brother. Footsteps approached, and the door was thrown open. Sammy was dressed, and looked like he'd been up for hours.

"What the fuck is all the noise? Did you start without me?" He grinned, and then took in what was happening.

"You left her arms up there all night?" He looked surprised, and Seb shrugged.

"Fell asleep, innit."

Sammy groaned, and came over to the bed, grabbing me, and rolling me onto my side, so that the pressure on my arms wasn't so bad, as Seb moved them back toward me.

He pulled away. "I'll get something." He disappeared, and Seb kept ruthlessly moving my arms back down. I was sobbing by the time he had them in front of my chest. My hands were numb, and my shoulders were screaming with pain.

Sammy returned, and ordered Seb to sit me up, which he did, even as I hissed curse words at him, and wished him dead a few more times. He just laughed, like nothing could penetrate that bloody thick skin of his.

"Here, take these." Sammy held up two pills, and I just opened my mouth, and let him poke them inside, before he tilted a glass and let me drink a few mouthfuls of water to wash them down. I nodded when they'd gone down, and hoped to hell they were powerful.

He held the glass up again, and I drank about half of the remaining liquid, before I pulled away.

He set the glass by the bed, and shot Seb a frustrated look.

"That was a rookie mistake, dipshit. What if she'd dislocated one of them in her sleep?" I'd almost think he cared, if I didn't know it was just because it would put a crimp in their torture plans.

"Sammy?" He glanced at me.

"Yeah, love?"

"I wish you were dead too, just so you know." He snorted, chuckling as he left the room.

"Yeah, you're welcome, Cass."

Seb stared at me, as I sat back against that horrible wrought iron bedstead, and couldn't move away from the uncomfortable bars against my back, with my arms still feeling so weak.

"I'm sorry I didn't undo them last night," he said quietly, and I frowned at him.

"Careful, Seb. You might actually start to sound like a human."

He shrugged. "Look, I wanted you to suffer, but not like this. I could have just left them cuffed."

I wriggled, trying to move away from the rigid bar digging into the soft tissue to the left of my spine.

"One day you'll accidentally kill me, Seb. Believe me, when I say that I'm actually looking forward to that day." He groaned, easing me away from the bedhead, and shoving a few pillows behind me, before he released me.

"Just let the pills kick in, and then we'll figure out what we're going to do to you today."

He smirked at me, and disappeared into his bathroom.

HARVEY

I SPENT A FEW hours assessing Lenore's place, working out which cameras and equipment I'd need, and then I left, heading home to gather up my kit.

It was a fair walk from Lenore's flat to my shop, but I lost myself in thoughts of her, her smell, her taste, the noises she made, when I fucked her, and made her come. Before I realised it, I was down the street from my shop, and the pervasive scent in the air finally permeated my senses. *Smoke.*

Something was burning. I glanced around for smoke, and there was none. Maybe there had been something burning, and it had been extinguished.

As I crossed the road, to head to the shop, I realised that I could see barriers, or cordons down toward the end, where my shop was. And then I realised what I'd smelled. What I had seen, but not absorbed. *A burned-out shell, where my shop used to be.* FUCK!

CHAPTER FORTY-SIX
CASSIDY

*T*HOSE PILLS WERE POWERFUL. Not normal paracetamol. I felt woozy. The pain had eased beautifully, now just a dull ache, but my head wasn't working right. I swayed when I sat up, and I felt my stomach clench a little. Fucking hell.

What had Sammy given me? I hadn't checked, had I? I just took them, because the pain was bad enough that I didn't care. Had he drugged me with something dodgy? If they were into criminal activities, why would I believe that they wouldn't have all kinds of illegal drugs here that they could use on me?

I pushed myself up from the bed, and stood on shaky legs. When I started to walk, the room spun, and my legs weakened. I had to stop at the end of the bed, leaning on the metal frame to get my balance back.

Once I felt like my legs would hold out, I pushed away from the bedframe, and made my way to the door. That was a mistake. My balance failed, as the room seemed to shift to one side, and I staggered sideways, crashing into the wardrobe, and landing hard against it.

"What the fuck?" Seb burst out of the bathroom, wiping toothpaste from his lips, and I glared at him.

"Fuckers..." I moaned quietly. Sammy appeared at the bedroom door.

"What now?"

I turned my head to look at him.

"What did you give me, you bastard?"

He glanced at his brother, a grin quirking at his lips.

"Painkillers."

"Bullshit!" I spat, trying to push myself up from the floor, stopping when the room kept moving in the wrong direction.

I clutched my head and groaned. "This isn't normal."

Sammy came over to crouch in front of me.

"It's just strong stuff, Cass. You were in a lot of pain. The doc prescribed them for me when I broke my wrist."

I stared at him, wondering why I couldn't focus on him properly.

"Which one?"

He laughed. "Yeah, like I'm telling you. Let me help you up, love, and we'll get some food in you. Probably should have eaten first, but you were in no state to do that."

He leaned down and hooked an arm around me, pulling me up with very little effort. It was terrifying, because these men were *strong*. Scary strong. And I had no hope of fighting them, even at my strongest, and I hadn't been that in a while.

Seb, who had thrown on some clothes now, because he was lucky and actually had clothes, pointed at the bed.

"Want to put her back there, until we feed her?"

"Stop talking about me like I'm a pet!" I snapped, trying to pull away from Sammy's arm.

"You'll fall if you keep doing that," he said, showing a little of the frustration I knew he felt.

"You'd like that, wouldn't you?" I moaned, giving in and pressing my face against his chest, because the room wouldn't stay still, and it made me feel sick. I could feel his laugh, as it rumbled through his body.

"Just shut up, and do as you're told, for once."

HARVEY

IT WAS DESTROYED. THE shop had burned to the ground. The flat I'd lived in was gone. All of my possessions. My life. *Everything I'd owned was gone*. What the fuck? There was a police officer there, with a guy who looked like he worked for the fire service.

I approached them, feeling like I was walking on a floor that moved beneath my feet. I was losing my shit.

"What the fuck happened?" I snapped at them, watching them both turn and glare at me. Probably not the best way to get what I wanted from them, but I was distraught.

"Move on, mate. None of your business," the officer said, turning back to the fireman.

"It's my fucking home. *And my business*," I said, staring at the blackened ruins. My hands pulled at my hair, as I tried to absorb the loss of everything.

"And you are?" The officer asked, clearly doubting my word.

"Harvey Clarke," I said, stepping closer to the ruins of my life. "Jesus... did nothing survive?"

He checked the paperwork in his hand, and looked at me, guilt on his face.

"Hell... sorry, Mr Clarke. We've had so many bloody rubberneckers coming by."

I shrugged. "When did it happen?"

The officer frowned. "Yesterday evening. Where were you?"

I stared at him, feeling numb, and confused.

"My girlfriend's place. I had no idea. Jesus."

The fireman guy was making notes on a tablet screen.

"She gonna alibi you?" He asked bluntly.

I rubbed a hand over my face, hating the burning smell that had settled in my nostrils, and clearly wasn't going any time soon.

"Fuck... hang on, what? You saying it's arson?" He glanced at the officer, then back at me.

"Are you?"

I dug my phone out of my pocket. No messages or missed calls. Surely they'd want to gloat. Those bastards!

"Screw you," I muttered at the fire guy, scrolling through my last calls, and finding Lenore's mobile number. It rang a few times before she finally answered.

"Hey, what's up?" Her voice was calm, relaxed. I hated to be the one to ruin that.

"Can you talk?" I'd moved a few steps away from the two bastards overseeing my ruin.

"Yeah. You okay?" She sounded hushed, like she was worried people would hear her.

"Uh... I've got news. Those bastards have upped the stakes." I glanced at the two men who looked like they weren't trying to listen, even though I knew they probably were. I didn't care anymore. I'd just lost everything.

"Oh no... is she okay?" I blinked, because I'd forgotten about everything except the fire.

"Oh... no, it's not about her, Lenore. The bastards burned down the shop. And my flat. It's all gone." My voice hitched, as a sob caught in my throat. "I've got nothing left." I fell back against the lamp post I'd been standing beside.

"Oh shit! Those assholes! I'm so sorry, H. Do you need me to come and get you?" I stared blankly at the road, barely seeing each car which drove slowly past, as they feasted their eyes on the destruction of my life.

"Uh... no... I probably need to be here for the police or something. I have no idea what happens next. Fuck, Lenore. I'm homeless." I tried to fight back tears, because this tiny corner of the world had been all I'd had. Hence why I'd put myself in the hands of those assholes, to try and keep it. And it had all been for nothing. It was gone.

"Shut up, H, you'll stay with me. We need to sort you out some stuff though. Clothes. I don't know what else. I'll pick you up from there after work, and we'll sort things out." She eased some of my panic, but I turned to look back at the shop, and felt all of that weight drop right back on my shoulders.

The officer was glaring at me, and waved at me to join them. I ended the call with Lenore, and wandered over to see what would happen next. Did I have anything left to lose at this point?

CASSIDY

SOUP FOR BREAKFAST WAS a strange idea, but it was easy to drink, from the large mug I'd been handed, and the few slices of bread I dipped in it, helped to soak up some of the strong painkillers. While I still felt queasy as hell, I didn't throw up, and the room stopped spinning so much. I fell asleep after I'd had the soup, because the pills had made me drowsy too. They left me there. In peace. Unmolested.

When they came for me a few hours later, they were gentle. Almost kind. I was taken to the bathroom in Seb's room, where they let me use the toilet, shower, and brush my teeth, with my own toothbrush and actual toothpaste, and not what Seb had threatened the night before.

Once I'd freshened up, and dressed in the t-shirt and sweats they actually provided, I felt more like the human I'd been, before all of this shit. So when they said they'd take me back to my room, I shrugged, and went with them, because suddenly, all of the crazy things they did last night seemed further from reality. They couldn't have happened, right?

When they opened my door, I took in the mess, and glared back at them.

"Seriously?"

"You think I'm going to clean up after you, Cass? Have I ever?" Seb asked, as he shot me a smirk, and shoved me into the room, making me stagger a few steps.

They both stood in the doorway, as I cast my eyes over the mess that Seb had made. The trashed bed, the smashed shower room door. The bathroom door... *wait*...

"You took my door?" Sammy shrugged.

"You abused the right to have a door on your bathroom, love. You could try earning it back at some point though."

I realised then that the bedside tables were both also gone.

"And the furniture?"

"Listen, love, this isn't a hotel. You don't get to live it up for free. You want nice things; you'll do as you're told."

I flipped a middle finger at them both.

"I don't want nice things, damn you. I want to go home!"

Seb laughed. "But you *are* home, love. So suck it up, and start behaving."

They weren't leaving. Why weren't they leaving?

"You guys fucked up my arms, and now you want to stand there, and watch me tidy up *his* mess?" I folded my arms, fighting back a groan at how sore they were, even with the strong pills.

They just stared back at me, in silence. It was creepy. I turned away to look across the room, at the wall opposite the bed, because out of the corner of my eye, I'd noticed something that wasn't there before.

"What the fuck is that?"

CHAPTER FORTY-SEVEN
HARVEY

THE POLICE OFFICER QUESTIONED me for ages, and then they finally let me look at the place, although the fire bastard wouldn't let me in, because parts were still smouldering.

It was all destroyed. No furniture, no possessions, barely any walls left. Everything I'd worked for was gone. Why would they do this, when they wanted their money back? I had even less chance of finding the money, now that I had literally nothing left.

"You got somewhere to stay?" The officer finally asked, looking like he almost cared. I nodded.

"That's all I've got now. Fuck me... how could they do this?"

He tilted his head at me.

"You got an idea of who did this?"

I turned to look at him, my arms folded over my chest.

"Be honest with me. There are people that you guys won't touch, no matter what shit they've done. Am I right?"

The officer frowned at me.

"If you know who did this, you have to tell me. *This was a crime.* And it could have endangered lives. There are flats on either side of this shop. Someone could have been killed."

I nodded. "Yeah... and they probably hoped it would be me. Look... there are bad people in this area, who do things they should be in jail for, but we both know that they're untouchable. So what's the point of me telling you? For all I know, you're one of the ones on their payroll."

He scowled, stepping forward, and jabbing a finger against my chest.

"You calling me dirty, you son of a bitch?"

I shrugged. "I'm saying that some of your boys are, and I can't tell the good from the bad, so I can't help you. I know I didn't do it, but that's all I can tell you."

The officer mused on that for a moment.

"In that case, get the hell out of my sight. You can sort this with your insurance company. Assuming you even had insurance."

I saw Lenore's car pull up, and waved.

"Yeah... I'll do that. Hope you find the bastards who did this. *Whoever they may be.*"

CASSIDY

WHAT THE HELL? THE wall had been decorated, and I couldn't believe what I was seeing. There were pictures all over it. Pinned up haphazardly, different sized images, all of one person. *Me.*

"Fuck," I breathed, walking over to look at them. Me walking to work, and back. Me at the bar with the girls. Me having my lunch. Me going into the community centre. From the locations of some of these pictures, I could tell they went back at least a few weeks. And there were more. Scarier ones. Ones that made that dizzy feeling return, as if the pills were affecting me again.

Pictures of the inside of my house. My pinboard in the kitchen, with my calendar and book club dates... from last month. They'd been watching me for that long? I stared at them for a moment, watching creepy matching grins appear on their faces. Every time I thought I was starting to understand them, they did something like this, and I felt like I'd been violated all over again.

When I looked back at the pictures, I noticed more than a few of me sleeping. *In my bed.* When I thought I was alone, safe...

"What the actual fuck? How long have you bastards been watching me? This is sick! This is absolutely vile! How dare you follow me, and...

you watched me sleep? In my own bed? What the fuck!" I started tearing pictures down, anger and fear making me gasp for air, until one of them grabbed me.

"Take it easy, love. That took us ages. And look... you're blaming the wrong guys. We didn't do this." I think it was Seb, but it was a guess. I pulled away from him, backing up a few steps.

"You just said it took you ages."

Sammy pushed the door closed, leaning against it, grinning at me.

"Yeah, but we nicked all of this from Harv's place. *He's* your stalker, remember? He's been watching you for months. Sick little bastard. You know... if he's been in your place, he'll have stolen your underwear, sniffed it, probably jerked himself off with it. There's no telling, really. He probably even set up cameras. Maybe one in your shower, so he could watch you soaping those lovely tits."

Jesus... I covered my face, feeling my hands shaking as I did.

"You're all insane. You're all damaged, or... or... I don't know... what the fuck! Who does things like this?"

Seb shrugged. "If it makes you feel any better, love... When our boys collected all of this for us... they torched his place. Burned it to the ground."

I lowered my hands, staring at him in horror.

"You... they... oh my god, the shop? They burned down the book shop? All those books!"

He practically roared with laughter.

"The books?! The books are the bit you're worried about?"

Sammy was shaking his head, looking up at the ceiling.

"Of course I'm upset about the books! You shouldn't burn books!" I was losing my mind. Nothing made sense to me.

Seb grabbed my arms, making me look at him.

"We punished Harv. *For you*. To punish his stalking *of you*. He has nothing now. He's homeless. He has no business left. Hell... he doesn't even have a scrap of clothing, short of whatever is on his back right now."

My knees felt weak, as I stared back at him.

"Was he... does he know?"

Seb shrugged. "I'm sure he knows by now. See... he had another chance last night, to save you, but he put himself first. *Again*. You have to ask yourself, love. Who are the bad guys really? Maybe it's just him. Maybe we're the good guys, looking out for you."

I pulled free of him again. "Are you out of your fucking minds?! Burning down a person's entire life doesn't make you a good guy. It doesn't make you a hero! It makes you a fucking animal!"

He glanced at Sammy, who had also lost his grin. He stepped up next to us.

"So this..." he pointed at the stalker shrine. "*This* is fine, but avenging this shit makes us bad guys?"

I backed away from them. "Everything you both do, is what makes you bad guys. It's just that Harvey is one too."

I looked back at the wall of pictures depicting my pathetic life. It was devastating. Was this really all I'd had? Work, two friends, and various lame clubs full of strangers, which didn't fulfil me... What was I really missing by being here? Who really would even notice that I was gone?

Sammy moved closer to the wall, pointing at one picture.

"You look happy in this one... but none of the others. Why?" I glanced at the picture. When was it from? Was I in a bar? I had no idea.

"Maybe I was drunk. I don't know. It's so strange, looking at my life from the outside like this. I feel like... I mean, what did I have really? A lame admin job? A few friends, who probably haven't even noticed I'm gone? Is this all I was? You're right. I don't look happy in most of them. I don't even look like I'm living!"

I started tearing the pictures down again, and this time, I gave in to the roaring pain that flowed through me. The horror, and the shame. The agonising loneliness. I'd been fighting to escape from the brothers, but for what? I barely existed. *I was nothing*.

Eventually, I just dropped down onto the floor, one of the photos in my hand, blurred through tear-filled eyes. He'd been right. I was smiling in this one. *Only this one*.

CHAPTER FORTY-EIGHT
HARVEY

I'D BARELY NOTICED THE journey back to Lenore's. She'd tried talking to me, but I was numb. Frozen. Lost. I had nothing left. *Nothing*. I didn't even know how to fix this, or try to rebuild my life. How does a person restart, when they have to start from scratch?

"H, come on. Drink that, it'll help." Lenore looked worried, her hand squeezing my knee lightly.

"Jesus, Lenore... I... fuck..." I couldn't even put words together. I sipped the drink, wincing at the burn, as it worked its way down my throat. The alcohol seemed to kick my senses into touch, just enough that I could focus my thoughts. I wasn't entirely sure that was even a good thing.

"They destroyed everything," I said numbly, staring at the glass.

Lenore sighed. "This wasn't anything we could have been prepared for, H. How were we to know that they'd attack you right now? They gave you time to put your money together, and now they've made sure you can't get it. Twisted bastards."

I stared at her. "They're going to kill me. It's probably best if I stay away from you. It doesn't make sense to drag you into this shit, any further than I already have."

She picked up her own glass, and emptied it in a few large gulps.

"I'm not going to leave you to sort this out alone, H. We'll figure something out."

I chewed at my lip, my brain trying to work. "We could run."

She snorted. "Seriously? That's your answer? Run away? And what do I do about my job, the women who rely on me? And my flat? I have roots here, H."

I groaned, removing my glasses, and rubbing at my face.

"You're right. That's dumb. I should run though. I can't pay them, and I have nothing left."

Her hand came back to my knee and squeezed, a little tighter than was comfortable.

"Am I nothing then?"

Fuck. "You know that's not what I mean. But this is too much. We're just starting to get going, and this is going to break us. You know it will. How long will you tolerate me leaching off you, while I try to find my way again? Those bastards." I drank the rest of the scotch, or whiskey, or whatever the hell it was.

My phone buzzed beside me, and I stared blankly at it. It was all I had left. My only possession, aside from the clothes I wore. I didn't even have a charger for it. I'd borrowed Lenore's, and now I had none of my own.

"Aren't you going to check that? Maybe it's your insurance company," she said, getting up to refill our glasses.

I stared at it. They wouldn't send a text message, and not at this time of the evening. It had said 'Bennettbastards' on the screen, before it went black again. I'd used that name for the last number I actually spoke to them on. I was afraid to look, and at the same time, I was so angry that I wanted to ring them and scream at them. But then, that would only make them happy, wouldn't it?

Finally I picked it up, using my thumb to work the phone, and open the message. It was another picture. *Oh shit.*

CASSIDY

I THINK MY RESPONSE to the wall had surprised the brothers. It was like they hadn't expected this reaction to it. Maybe they'd expected anger, and some kind of outburst, something they could manipulate. I actually felt that that was something they even enjoyed.

Instead, it did what they'd failed to do so far. *It broke me.* Because, instead of showing me what I was missing, or showing me how I'd had my privacy invaded, it had served only one purpose. Proving to me that I didn't matter. Nobody would care that I'd disappeared, because I'd made no impact on anyone's life. I had nothing to go back for. I tore that smiling photo into tiny pieces, sprinkling them on the floor in front of me, watching the shreds of me dissipate.

"Uh, bruv... what do we do with her now?" I heard one of them ask quietly.

"I thought she'd go on the attack," the other one whispered. "I have no idea what this is."

I moved to sit against the wall.

"I want you to kill me," I whispered to them, seeing identical frowns on their almost-identical faces.

"You want what now?"

CHAPTER FORTY-NINE
HARVEY

THE PICTURE WAS OF Cassidy, sitting on a floor, holding one of my photos. A second one came through of my shrine to her. On a new wall. *They'd taken it.* They'd taken my fucking pictures, before they burned my life down. And they'd used it to torment Cassidy. It had never been for her eyes. Or theirs. It was for mine only.

"What the hell is that?" Lenore had leaned over my shoulder.

"They're still hurting Cassidy," was my response, but I handed her the phone, because she'd seen it at my flat. She knew what I'd done.

"Jesus, H. That poor girl. You see what stalking does? What it can lead to? I know this is an extreme situation, but taking a few seemingly harmless photos of a woman, can lead to her life being completely destroyed." I nodded, snatching the phone back.

"Thank you for the advice, Lenore. I'll do my best to not be a fucking stalker again, okay? It's not like I made a habit of that shit. It was... I just had to know her. And now I can see it's fucked up. I get that. I wouldn't do it again. Not to anyone."

She was staring at me.

"You *are* done with that stuff, right? I mean... I'm not going to find you with a new shrine to some other girl, right?" She looked wary, nothing like her usual confident self, so it stopped me snapping at her, even though, hadn't I just said that?

I stood up, and pulled her against me, wrapping my arms tight around her, using her warmth to comfort the chill inside.

"I swear that I don't need anyone but you, babe. I don't even know how I've been around you for years, and not realised how you outshine every other woman out there."

She sighed. "That's corny as fuck, H, but I'll allow it for now." She hugged me back.

CASSIDY

SAMMY CROUCHED IN FRONT of me.

"You're not thinking right, love." I kept my eyes on his.

"I've never been clearer about anything in my... apparently fucking pathetic... non-life. There's literally no point in my existence. What do I have? *Nothing.* Thank you. Both of you. For proving to me that there's literally nothing about me that matters. At all." He glanced back at Seb, who shrugged slightly, looking confused.

"What? You tell me you're such bad guys, and threaten to kill me, and then when it comes down to it, you suddenly have a conscience? That's okay. Just give me a knife, and leave me alone for a while. I'll even do it in the bath, so you don't have a mess." I no longer had any fear, because I had absolutely nothing to lose. And what's the point of living if that's the case?

"Fuck that," Seb snapped. He glanced around the room.

"You're not going anywhere. You hear me? You belong to us. And we're not done with you yet!" He stormed out of the room, and Sammy stared at the door he'd just slammed.

"Huh..." he said quietly, glancing back at me. "So, this isn't what we thought would happen."

I shrugged, staring at my knees, which I'd hugged to me.

"I guess you thought you'd break me by raping me. I'm sorry to have disappointed you both so much."

Sammy moved, sitting against the wall beside me, one knee pulled up, with his arm draped over it.

"Truth be told, we never knew what to expect. We took you to hurt Harv... but..."

He trailed off, and I knew that something had happened. Something that would make all of this worse.

"He moved on," I said quietly. I guess I couldn't blame him. We were never really anything to each other, were we? And if his life had just fallen apart around him, what would I matter to him anyway? I was nobody's priority. It didn't even hurt to realise that now. I was defeated. *Numb.*

Sammy stared at me. "He's a sick fuck. He's moved on to that friend of his. *Lenore.*"

I shrugged. "I hope they'll be happy together."

"You don't mean that." I shrugged again.

"Does it matter? He gets to have a life. I don't. That's the price I paid for going into the wrong book shop. Or for... I don't know... having fuck all in my life, to make it worth it."

"He's shagging her," Sammy said, and I stared at him.

"Yes, I got that point, thank you. Not that I'd have slept with the slimy bastard anyway."

He snorted. "Yeah... but what I'm saying is... he's already doing the same thing to her."

I frowned at him. "Doing what?"

He picked up one of the crumpled photos of me.

"*This.* He videos her sleeping. I bet he jerks off to them, when she's not around."

I snatched the photo, not wanting him touching these pathetic fragments of my life. Of the person I had been. Because I'm not her now. I'm not even sure who I am anymore.

"And you know this how?"

He shot me a wicked grin.

"We cloned his phone, Cass. We know everything, because we're monitoring his calls, texts, emails, everything he has connected to his phone account. We saw the photos he's been taking of her, and the videos. Sick fucker just doesn't learn."

I turned to face him a little more, my legs tucked to my side. I felt a sick urge to hurt Harvey. Why should he get to be happy?

"So what are we going to do about that?"

He looked at me, a small grin twitching at his lips.

"What are you up to, woman?"

I shrugged, as I felt a small tremor of excitement.

"Time to turn the tables on him, maybe? He can't do this to her too. We should stop him."

Sammy reached for his phone, and dangled it in front of me.

"Want to do the honours, love?"

I took it from him, staring at the screen with a determined grin.

"Yeah. It's Harvey's turn to know how it feels to have your life fucked up beyond belief."

CHAPTER FIFTY
HARVEY

Lenore went for a shower before dinner, while I sat there nursing another glass of that alcoholic bliss that she'd poured for me. Everything in me was telling me to follow her into the shower. Shove her up against the wall, fuck her hard, and lose myself in the beauty of that damn body of hers. There was a louder voice, and I was trying really hard to ignore it.

It was berating me, for not having a camera up in her shower yet. I could be watching her shower. I could be watching her soaping up those tits, thinking that nobody could see her. I could watch as she touched herself between her legs. *Fuck.* I'd gone home today specifically for my spare equipment, so I could set up here, and that fire had destroyed everything.

My phone buzzed again, and I picked it up, idly thinking that I should really order some new kit anyway. Not that I could afford it. *Not now.*

It was another message from the number I had for those Bennett bastards.

BENNETTBASTARDS: *Does she know that you're up to your old tricks, Harv?*

I frowned, glancing around the room, suddenly wondering if those bastards had beaten me to it, and had cameras set up in her flat. But that's crazy, right? I messaged back.

ME: *You'll pay for what you did.*

It was a risk, to threaten them, but they'd taken everything from me. It took a minute or so for another message to arrive.

It was a picture of Lenore. *Sleeping.* What the fuck!

ME: *Where the fuck did you get that? You watching her?*

BENNETTBASTARDS: *Are you?*

Fuck. What did they do? I flicked through my photos on my phone. There. It was one of my photos. I felt a wave of relief, because that meant that they weren't watching her.

And then the reality kicked in. They could see my photos. They'd hacked my phone. It was all I had left, and they were inside it, snooping around.

No part of my life had been left untouched by them. I had no privacy. No freedom. And isn't that the biggest irony of all? Because I understood now. *I was feeling what Cassidy must have felt.*

CASSIDY

IT HAD FELT REALLY good, turning the tables on Harvey. I hoped that he was sitting there, freaking out, wondering what the hell was happening. I might have realised that I had no life, but for Harvey, he had just lost everything. His home. His failing business. His possessions. Me.

And now he was at risk of losing Lenore. Not that he deserved to have her in his life anyway. Why should he get to keep anything, or anyone, when I had been reduced to nothing?

Seb had come back, and he wasn't empty handed. He held a carrier bag, and an amazing smell came from it. Sitting down with us, he handed us tightly wrapped paper parcels of deliciousness. He'd been out for a takeaway.

I didn't even know that there was one near here, because I didn't even know where *here* was. I stared at him as he handed me food, like I was a person, rather than their possession. He just shrugged, and started unwrapping his.

We each had a steaming bag of chips, with plenty of salt and vinegar, and he put a fourth parcel on the carrier bag on the floor, unwrapping that to reveal two pies, some battered sausages, and a few large pieces of chicken. Along with that were several cups of curry sauce.

He stared at me. "Eat up, love. No idea what you like, but fill your boots. Who knows when we'll bother to feed you again." He quirked a small grin, and started tucking into his food.

I eagerly reached for a piece of the chicken, tearing off the skin, and stuffing it in my mouth with a moan of pleasure.

"Ah man… she makes sexy noises when she eats too. Wish I'd known that sooner," Seb muttered, shooting me a sidelong look.

I snorted. "Thank you for the food, Seb. I love chips."

He shrugged. "Was hungry." He almost looked embarrassed by his kind gesture.

Sammy ate for a few minutes, then pointed at the phone on the floor beside him.

"Cass wanted to mess with Harv."

Seb glanced at the phone, then looked at us.

"Tell me."

Sammy nodded at me, and I chewed fast, relishing every delicious mouthful of this unexpected dinner.

"Sammy told me you guys cloned his phone, so we showed him that we know what he's doing to Lenore."

Seb smirked. "Shitting his pants yet?"

Sammy snorted. "He will be."

I grinned. "We took Lenore's number from his phone, and sent her one of his videos of her sleeping. She'll probably kill him."

Seb laughed. "Excellent! Fuck it. I need a drink for this." He got up, and left, returning with a bottle of something brown, and three glasses clenched between his fingers. He poured a measure in each and passed them to us. "Here's to fucking up Harv's life."

I joined in the toast with them, but the whole time I was wondering what was actually going on. I mean, were they just trying to make me feel comfortable again, or at least not want to die, so they could destroy me anyway? I couldn't trust them. I could never trust anyone.

"What's that look?" Seb asked, looking warily at me. Fuck my lack of control over my facial expressions.

I shrugged, thinking fast.

"I was just wishing we had a camera in their place, so we could see the fallout." Sammy grinned, and nodded at Seb.

Seb pulled his phone from his pocket, and rang someone, grinning at us as he waited for them to answer.

"Oi Marco, where's our boy at?" He listened for a moment, and smirked. "You outside?... Good... Get up close, and let us see what's happening. I suspect the shit's hitting the fan right about now. Should be fun."

He ended the call, and nodded at us. A minute or so later, his phone buzzed, and he accepted the video call. We all leaned closer to see his screen.

CHAPTER FIFTY-ONE

HARVEY

I DON'T KNOW WHAT the hell happened. One minute Lenore was cooking dinner, after her shower, looking sexy in nothing but that silky robe, and the next, she was looking at something on her phone, and then she turned to stare at me, like I was the devil.

"You okay?" I asked, still reeling from the revelation that those bastards had hacked my phone. The truth was, that I couldn't see a way to fix it right now, either. I certainly couldn't tell Lenore why I needed a new phone, because then she'd want to know what I was so afraid of them seeing.

"You sick fuck," she muttered, as she looked at her phone again. I frowned, and walked around the breakfast bar to see what she could be talking about, although I was starting to feel a sickening suspicion that I knew what it might be.

"Lenore?"

"How could you do this? You fucking pervert. I trusted you. I let you in, and this is what you do?" She showed me her phone screen. Fuck. FUCK FUCK FUCK. It was one of the videos of her asleep. In fact... it was the worst of them. The one where I'd slipped the camera under the covers, to video her naked body. I couldn't be more screwed.

"Lenore..."

"And who the fuck even sent this to me, Harvey? It's an unknown number. Who did you share this with? Have you been laughing about me this whole time? How stupid was I to trust you?" She dropped the phone and turned, shoving me hard, making me fall back against the counter.

"Jesus, Lenore!"

She folded her arms. "Explain. Right the fuck now."

I stayed back against the counter, because I could see how pissed she was, and I didn't want to provoke her. Getting out of this, and getting her to trust me again was going to be difficult. Probably impossible. What a mess.

"It's the Bennetts," I said finally, and she shot me a withering look.

"Funny that, because I've never been in bed with either of them, but I'm starting to think that even one of them would be a safer prospect than you. You videoed me?"

I looked down.

"I'm sorry, babe. You looked so beautiful. So peaceful. I... I guess I just wanted... I wanted to capture that side of you, that you never let anyone see." I could be poetic when I wanted to. I watched her for a reaction.

"Capture? What you mean is, you like your women vulnerable, and unaware of your attention. Christ, Harvey. You need help. *Real help*. This isn't what normal people do. You do understand that, right?" She looked devastated.

"Babe, I swear. It was just a one off. I was blown away by the fact that you were there beside me. I guess I was worried it'd never happen again. I wanted to remember it." I tried approaching her, but a fierce glare stopped me in my tracks.

"The video you made shows that we were here. In my bedroom. That argument doesn't make sense, H." Her phone buzzed again, and my heart sank. No.

She glanced up at me, then down again, as it buzzed several more times, sounding ominously loud as it vibrated against the kitchen counter.

"Fucking hell... one video, eh? You fucking asshole!" She lifted her phone, scrolling through the pictures and videos, that those bastards had somehow known to send at that exact moment.

I glanced around the room, looking for how they were spying on us.

"I think they're watching us, Lenore."

She slammed the phone on the counter. "No. *You're watching me!* I can't believe I trusted you. I'm such an idiot. How many of these damn things are there? Do you have cameras in my home? Watching me when I think I'm alone? How long have you been doing this?"

I groaned, pushing my luck and grabbing hold of her.

"Lenore, don't let them do this. Don't let them break us."

She tried to shake me free, but I held on tight.

"Let go, Harvey. I don't want you touching me right now."

I had to fix this. I had to make her understand that I loved her! And she loved me! She shoved me back, and walked away from me, putting the counter between us.

"I trusted you, Harvey. How could you do this to me?" She sounded broken, defeated. She'd put her trust in me, when she didn't trust any men. And I'd betrayed her... I had. There was no other word for it.

CASSIDY

IT WAS BIZARRE, WATCHING the whole thing unfold. The guy who worked for the brothers had obviously found an open window, or even sneaked into their place, because he was close enough that we could hear every word. I felt so sick for Lenore.

It hadn't hit me when I decided to do this, that I'd be hurting her too. But then... wasn't she safer away from him? Wasn't it the whole point, to make sure he couldn't do this to someone else?

"I reckon she's going to kick his ass, bruv," Seb whispered, still holding the phone up. We'd moved either side of him, so it was easier to watch. It felt wrong. Especially since I had to almost lean up against him to be able to see. Thank god his phone was one of the larger ones, so the screen wasn't too tiny.

"Sending the other stuff was perfect," Sammy muttered, shooting me a grin. I didn't feel good for it. I felt evil. Playing with their lives like this... but didn't he deserve it?

They carried on arguing, moving across the room, and he grabbed her again.

"That's a bad move, right there," Seb whispered. "You don't manhandle a rape victim. Especially not one who could tear your nads off with one hand."

Rape victim? Oh Jesus... nobody had told me that, or had they? I was sure they hadn't. I wouldn't have messed with her if I'd known. Would I?

HARVEY

I WAS LOSING HER. I could feel it. She'd stopped trusting me. If only I could remind her of what she would lose, if she pushed me away.

"Lenore, please. Think about what you're saying. They're playing with us. I took a few pictures of the woman I love. What's so wrong with that?"

She took a deep breath, pulling her robe tighter around her, in the most defensive move I'd seen from her. I held my hands up.

"Babe, please. Just listen to what I'm saying. I'm a good guy, really. I just want to be with you. Nobody else. Is taking a few pictures of you really that bad? You can take pictures of me too. It's what people do."

She didn't like that I'd followed her around the breakfast bar, so she went back to the kitchen side, moving things around on the counter, like she was going back to preparing dinner.

"Just leave me alone, Harvey. I need to think." No. I knew what would happen. I'd leave her to think, and she'd decide that she didn't want me. Realise that she didn't need me. She'd kick me out.

I had nowhere else to go, but it wasn't even about that. I didn't want to go back to living off the vicarious thrills of wanking off to pictures, of someone living a life that didn't include me.

"Lenore, please. I'm not the bad guy here. I'm not the guy who kidnapped someone, and raped her. That's them. That's what they did."

She turned to glare at me, putting down the vegetable knife she'd been using to cut vegetables into jagged, angry little pieces.

"They kidnapped her because of you. I can't believe I started seeing you as anything other than the monster you are." She turned away from me, leaning against the counter, as she sobbed into her hands.

Jesus. *Look what I did to her.* I moved around the counter, and pulled her into my arms, waiting while she tensed, and shushing her, until she softened in my arms.

"I'm sorry, babe. I really didn't mean to scare you, or upset you. I guess old habits die hard, but I never meant anything bad by it. I just want to worship you." She shook her head against my chest.

"I don't want that, H. I just want to be safe, and loved. Why do men always make it into something bad?"

I pulled back to look at her. "I'm not. I'm trying to fix what I messed up. I love you, Lenore. I think I always have."

I slid my hand into her hair, pulling her lips to mine, and kissed her, teasing her lips, trying to get her to open up to me. Her hands pushed against my chest, but there was no strength behind them. *Good.* I pressed into her, feeling her mouth open to mine. *Yes.*

I kissed her deeply, trying to show her every ounce of love I had for her. As she started kissing me back, I let one hand slide down her side, and tugged on the belt of her robe, pulling it untied. She pushed against my chest once more.

"No, Harvey," she whispered the words, as she pulled back from my lips. *Fuck.*

"It's okay, Lenore. It's just me." I started kissing her again, and slipped my hand against her bare skin, gliding my fingers up her side, toward her breast. She shook her head, trying to pull away again, but I tightened my grip on her hair, keeping her mouth against mine.

Her arms started to push harder against me. I couldn't let her give in to the fear. She was all I had left. They'd taken everything else, but they wouldn't take her. I palmed her breast, rubbing at her nipple, as she started shaking her head again. She pulled free of my mouth.

"Harvey, I said no. Stop." I couldn't stop now. If I backed off, she'd make me leave. If I could just remind her of how good I could make her feel, she'd stop being so afraid.

I tightened my grip on her hair, and pressed her harder against the counter.

"Shhh babe… just let me show you how much I love you." I tried to kiss her again, but she squirmed, trying to avoid my mouth.

"Harvey, stop it. I need you to stop!"

I shook my head. "No, Lenore. That's not what you want. You love me. I know you do. Just let me remind you. You got scared, and that's okay. That's my fault, but you know I'd never hurt you. I love you."

I slipped my hand down to between her legs, while she started pushing me with more strength than she'd shown so far. I had gravity on my side, because I was practically pressing her back against the counter, but she was strong. Stronger than I'd realised. Even though I knew her so well, I never thought she'd fight *me*.

"Dammit, Lenore. Stop struggling. Just let me make love to you. You'll remember. You'll enjoy it."

CHAPTER FIFTY-TWO
CASSIDY

I STARED AT THE brothers, who both actually looked appalled at Harvey's behaviour. The guy holding the phone, videoing them, was cursing Harvey under his breath. He sounded like he wanted to get in there and save her.

"We need to stop him," I whispered urgently to them. Sammy leaned close to the speaker on the phone.

"Marco, get in there before the bastard rapes her."

The phone instantly started moving, then Marco set it down somewhere, and we could hear noise, like he was trying to get in. He'd been outside after all. Shit!

"He won't get to her in time!" I panicked. This was all my fault! I'd wanted to mess with Harvey, and now Lenore was the one paying the price. I was no better than he was. Than any of them were.

Sammy looked at Seb. "I have no idea how else to stop this." I started ringing Lenore's phone from Sammy's, hoping the sound would distract Harvey, before he raped his best friend. The woman who'd been there before.

What happened next made us all stare at the phone in shock.

HARVEY

I COULDN'T BELIEVE SHE was fighting me so much! It was me! I'd never hurt her!

I held her still, while I started undoing my pants. I just needed to get inside her, and start loving her, and she'd remember. She'd remember that she loved me. She just needed to feel me inside her again.

"Harvey, STOP!" She screamed. My pants fell to the floor, and I freed my hard cock, tearing her robe aside.

"NO!" She yelled, and then I felt it. Agonising pain, like a flash of white fire. *I started to choke, as blood filled my throat.*

CHAPTER FIFTY-THREE
CASSIDY

"OH GOD, OH GOD!" I gasped, dropping Sammy's phone in my horror, my attempt at calling Lenore aborted.

"What the fuck!" I screamed at the brothers, as they just stared at the screen. Then Seb grinned.

"Well, I think that's the end of old Harv…"

"It's not a joke! My god, we have to phone the police! She killed him!" I grabbed Sammy's phone again, and dialled the emergency number. The phone was snatched from me, before I could connect the call.

"Are you out of your fucking mind?" Sammy snapped, clearing the screen and shoving the phone in his pocket.

I pointed at the screen in Seb's hand, where we could see a man, presumably Marco, carefully approaching a distraught Lenore, as she gazed down at Harvey's still body, and the blood pooling around him.

"He's dead!" I screamed at them.

Sammy looked at me, frowning deeply.

"He tried to rape her, Cass."

I glanced at him. "And that's the correct behaviour when faced with a rapist. You'd do well to remember that." I'd noticed Seb's knife, which had been tucked into a holster thing at his waist. On my side of him. I'd already checked it, to make sure it would be easy to remove.

See, all the time that they thought they were lulling me into a false sense of security, I'd been assessing my situation, and planning my escape. And it was almost time.

LENORE

OH GOD OH GOD oh god... he was dead. I'd killed him. *I killed Harvey!* The knife crashed to the floor, splashing blood everywhere, just as I realised that there was a strange man in my flat, making a stealthy approach. How the hell did he even get in?

"Stop!" I screamed at him, my legs shaking so badly that I thought I'd fall. I was losing my mind. Fucking H. What a sick bastard. *He tried to rape me.* The police will understand that. They'll realise that I had to do it. I had the pictures to prove what he'd been doing. They'd believe me, right?

"Listen, love. I just want to help you," the strange man said, who'd stopped immediately when I'd yelled at him. His hands were up. He looked dangerous. Italian, perhaps. Dark hair, and olive skin, a slight accent.

"Stay back. Please! I just... I... Oh god." I dropped to my knees, only realising then that my robe wasn't only hanging open, but torn. When did it get torn? Did Harvey do that? Oh god, Harvey. How could he try to do that to me? Me?

I stared at his face, as he lay there, his eyes open, but empty. *Because he was dead.* Blood had poured from the wound in his throat, but had slowed. I'd jammed the vegetable knife into his throat, because he wasn't going to stop.

After finding out that he'd been doing to me what he did to that other poor girl, he tried to force himself on me. ME. He knew what had happened to me before we met. *He knew.* Well, he didn't know the details, but he knew I'd been raped. He knew that two men had forced me into sex.

I'd never talked about the things they did to me, but that bastard, that Bennett asshole... he'd known, or guessed, or even just assumed. It had shaken me enough that I forgot everything I'd learned. In those minutes, in that room with the two of them, I'd lost all of my confidence, because

I knew they could do the same. I'd never thought Harvey would be the one I should fear.

"Lenore?" The Italian man said gently, and I stared at him, a frown on my face.

"Do I know you?" I finally asked, brushing at the tears that just wouldn't stop falling, with hands that shook so much I couldn't control them. Red. *My hand was red*. I stared at it, numb.

"Lenore, let's get you away from there," the man said urgently. I couldn't stop looking at my hand.

"It's so red," I finally whispered through numb lips. I felt a mile away from myself, but also right there. In my trembling body. Beside the cooling corpse of my friend of ten years. The man I'd always had feelings for. The man I'd finally let myself trust. Let him touch me. His hands had been on me.

I glanced down at my torn robe, at the splashes of blood, and then my stomach clenched hard, and I turned, throwing up on the tiled floor.

The man approached me, carefully stepping over Harvey's corpse, avoiding the blood.

"Look, love. I want to help you. I want to get you away from him. But I don't want to scare you. Will you let me help you get up, and into the bathroom?" I stared at him again, wiping my mouth.

"I don't even know who you are. Why are you here?" He shot me a sad look.

"The Bennetts sent me."

I glanced around the room, feeling a new wave of panic.

"Oh god. You work for *them*."

He nodded. "They don't want any harm to come to you, Lenore. Please let me help you."

I focused on the blood on my hand again.

"*I killed him*."

He nodded again, crouching in front of me. "Yes. Because he was trying to hurt you. He deserved to die."

I shook my head. "Maybe I over-reacted. Maybe I... did I make a mistake?" He groaned.

"Jesus... I don't know what to say. *He tried to rape you.* You stopped him. I don't see any other way it could have played out, without you being raped. Do you get that?" I stared at my hand.

"It's so red. It's his blood." My mind was failing me. He heaved a sigh, and stood up again.

"I'm going to lift you, Lenore. Please don't stab me." He suddenly pulled me up onto my feet, and then he swung me up into his arms. I didn't fight him. How was it that I could be so terrified of a trusted friend, and yet not of this stranger?

He carried me to my bathroom, switching on the shower, and testing the temperature.

"Okay, Lenore. Listen up. You're going to shower, wash every trace of that fucker from your skin, and get yourself together. I'm going to work on fixing that mess out there. Okay?"

I stared at him. "Who are you?"

He grinned suddenly, lighting up his face.

"Marco. Now get in that shower, while I go sort out that bastard. Okay?" I nodded, waiting for him to leave, before I closed and locked the door.

Once I felt safe to lose the robe, I couldn't wait to get it away from my skin. I tossed the bloody pale peach satin robe straight into the bin, and stepped under the water, turning up the heat, to really burn everything from my skin.

CHAPTER FIFTY-FOUR
CASSIDY

SAMMY ANSWERED HIS PHONE when it rang, and I heard him say the name 'Marco', so it was obviously their guy who was still there with Lenore. He'd switched the camera off earlier, so the video call was over. I stared at Seb, as Sammy walked off to talk in private.

I hoped they were going to let Marco help Lenore. She was in that situation because of them, and me. *Especially me.* It was my fault, because I'd pushed things to happen.

I busied myself wrapping up all the mess from dinner, and stuffing it back into the carrier bag, and then I stepped over all of the mess in the bedroom, from Seb's destructive tantrum the day before, and went to wash my hands, and face.

I leaned over the sink, staring at the water as it swirled away, down the plug, feeling hollow. I'd caused Lenore to kill Harvey. I was no better than any of them. Maybe they were right to lock me away like this.

"Still beating yourself up, love?" Seb asked, leaning on the doorframe. I shrugged, not bothering to look at him.

"Shouldn't I?" I whispered, leaning forward to rest my head against the mirror.

He walked up behind me, his body against my back, his hands on the sink, on top of mine.

"Why do you care? He hurt you. And he was about to hurt her. She did what she had to."

"She shouldn't have had to." I lifted my head to meet his eyes in the mirror. He shrugged lightly.

"You didn't make him a stalker, or the kind of guy who'd rape his girlfriend, to win an argument." I shivered at the thought, and he pressed closer.

"When will you kill me, Seb?" I asked softly. His face showed no reaction to my words, but he finally grinned a little.

"Oh, not for ages yet, love. Too much left that I still want to do to you."

I sighed, leaning my head back against his shoulder. It wasn't because it was him, of course it wasn't. It was because he just happened to be the only one standing there to stop me falling. His hands curved over mine, so that he held them.

"Do you realise that he'd have ended up doing that to you? And maybe you wouldn't have been strong enough, or lucky enough, to have a weapon there to defend yourself? You wouldn't have even known how dangerous he was," Seb whispered these words close to my ear, his warm breath on my skin making a chill run down my spine.

"At least with you guys, I know you're monsters, right?" I whispered back, and he chuckled.

"Something like that. But I actually think that you like a bit of monster in your men."

I groaned. "I think it's more like there's a small bit of human, in the two monsters I'm stuck here with."

Seb snorted. "I can live with that... can you?" I shrugged, because words right now were too much effort.

"Want me to fuck you, love? You need to feel something right now, other than what just happened."

I met his eyes again in the mirror.

"What?"

He leaned closer, pressing his face into my neck, his lips teasing my skin. It sent a shiver down my spine again. He was so good at that.

"I can make you feel so fucking good, Cass... let me fuck you right now." He ran his tongue over my skin.

"I... I... this is wrong, Seb." He chuckled softly.

"That's part of the fun, love. For me, at least."

I closed my eyes, because looking at him, when he touched me like that, felt even more wrong.

They popped open again, when he lifted his hands from mine, and ran them up my arms. I moved my hands, meaning to stop him, and he grabbed them, lowering them back down to the sink.

"Keep them there, love."

I opened my mouth to argue, and he clamped a hand over my lips.

"Shhh... just do as I tell you, Cass."

He stared at me in the mirror, and waited like that, until I nodded. Why was I nodding? Because his closeness was overwhelming me, and he was right. I needed to feel something other than horror, and shock. Of course, that's how I'd normally react to him touching me. It was all very confusing.

He lowered his hands to the bottom of the t-shirt I wore.

"You'll lift your arms, so I can remove this, then you'll put them back on the sink. Understood?"

I took a breath and shook my head. *"Cass."* He used a low, warning tone, and it almost made me grin, because infuriating him might just be the only way I could let myself be touched by him.

I nodded, and he removed my t-shirt, baring my upper body to him. I put my hands back on the sink and tightened them, wondering what the hell I was doing.

"Seb."

"No."

I stared at him in the mirror. "No?"

He nodded, a small grin on his face.

"That's right. Now shut up."

I glared at him in the mirror, and that grin widened. When his hands cupped my breasts, I flinched, intending to push away from the sink, and get the hell out of this situation, but he crowded me against the sink, and started to roll my nipples in his fingers.

He watched me in the mirror as he touched me, and I tried not to appreciate just how good it felt. It shouldn't feel good. I shouldn't want this. But had anything in my dismal other life ever even felt like this?

He pinched my nipples, and I gasped, my knees weakening. His grin was wicked.

"Yeah, you like it a bit rough, don't you, love? Probably never had a guy give it to you as good as I'm about to." His words made my stomach quake. I was getting in too deep, and if I didn't stop him right now, this was going to go further than I wanted it to.

"Seb-"

"Shut your mouth, love. You know, unless I put you on your knees, because then I'm going to want it open wide." I gasped, and he laughed, curling his hand around my throat.

"Are you wet for me yet, Cass? Are you soaking those pants, because you want my cock deep inside you?" I closed my eyes, because I couldn't look at him.

"Cass, you're going to have your eyes open when I slide inside you, because I want to see in your eyes how it makes you feel." He moved suddenly, grabbing the waist of my sweats, and pushed them down my legs.

I squeaked, surprised, and tried to move, *to escape*.

Seb forced my hands back onto the sink.

"Don't fucking move them again. You hear me?"

He reached behind me, and I could feel his hands moving, as he undid his jeans, and pushed them down, his hard cock suddenly rubbing against me.

"Oh god."

Seb slapped his hand over my mouth again. "Remember to shut the fuck up, Cass. I'll allow you to make other noises while I fuck you, but no speaking."

I stared at him with wide eyes, as he rubbed his cock against my ass. I tried to shake my head, but he just tightened his grip on my face, so I couldn't move.

"Keep your hands there," he growled at me, as he grabbed my hips and angled me for his cock.

"Stop."

He ignored me, gripping my hips in a biting grip, as he thrust deep inside me, stretching me with his cock.

"No!" I yelped, as his hips crashed against mine.

He let out a long groan. "Fucking hell, Cass. Doesn't that feel better already?"

I shook my head. "I don't want this."

He grabbed a handful of my hair, and pulled, so my head was angled back.

"I know you think that, love. I just don't care." He moved back, slowly sliding his cock back out, and I breathed a sigh of relief. He'd listened after all.

He thrust hard, and filled me again, and I let out a ragged gasp.

"Stop."

"No."

He kept a tight grip on me, on my hip and my hair, as he kept shoving his cock into me, almost painfully hard.

"Please stop," I gasped out, my voice catching in my throat.

He snorted. "Not happening."

"So this is how it's going to be? I turn my back for one second, and you guys fuck without me?" Sammy asked from the doorway. I tried to pull away from Seb yet again, because now I was mortified, as well as conflicted, and freaked out.

"Join in by all means, bruv, but I'm not stopping," Seb grunted, pulling me back to him, as he kept thrusting hard into me.

Sammy laughed, walking into the room and pulling my face to his, thrusting his tongue into my mouth and kissing me hard, while his brother kept fucking me. It was confusing, and overwhelming. They were everywhere, and I was trapped between them.

Sammy's tongue stroked against mine, while his hands cupped my face, and Seb held me firmly in place, as he kept powering into me.

It was like sensory overload, my mind was already frazzled by the murder I'd caused, and when Sammy's fingers suddenly slipped down, and started to circle my clit, I felt pleasure starting to override the conflict inside. It shouldn't be happening, but it was, and it could be good, if I just stopped fighting them, and let myself enjoy it.

Seb put his lips to my ear, as he sped up his pace, and seemed to fuck me even harder still. His hand left my hair, and wrapped around my throat.

"Next time, Sammy will be in your pussy, and I'll be in your ass, baby. You're going to let us both fuck you at the same time, because you're our little slut, and we'll use you whenever we fucking want to."

It shouldn't have made me come. *It shouldn't have made me come.* I don't know why his awful words pushed me over that edge, but they did, and I wrenched my mouth away from Sammy's, as I screamed.

"Oh yeah... we love your screams, Cass. I want to hear that all fucking day long," Sammy muttered, lowering his mouth to one of my breasts, latching his lips around my nipple. I felt teeth, and shuddered, as aftershocks ran through me, and Seb suddenly came hard, spurting inside me, because of course, there was no condom. *Bastard*. He nipped at my neck, as he held me against him, forcing me to take every last drop from him.

"Told you I belonged inside you, Cass. I'm all over your insides now. Can you feel me inside you? When I pull out, it'll trickle down your legs." He pulled out suddenly, and backed away from me, and if Sammy hadn't held on, I'd have fallen, because my legs weren't holding me anymore, and I felt faint. Sick. Horrified. Tears spilled down my cheeks, as Sammy focused his attention on my other nipple.

"Stop... please..." I gasped out, sobbing and trying to push him away. He lifted his head to look at me, something like concern on his face.

"Why are you doing this to yourself, Cass? Why the guilt? The shame? You wanted to be fucked, and you were. And you came. Remember that part. *You came hard*. While he was inside you." I shoved Sammy away from me, and dropped onto the floor, shifting into the corner, holding my legs close to me.

"Leave me alone," I whispered, giving in to the tears, and the sorrow. I shouldn't have enjoyed that.

CHAPTER FIFTY-FIVE
LENORE

I FELL APART IN that shower. The terror and the heartbreak of what Harvey tried to do to me, and what I'd done in retaliation, made me crumble, like I'd only done once before in my life. I curled up in a ball, and sobbed, the hot water raining down onto me.

I kept seeing him, every time I tried to close my eyes. Dead, staring blankly at the ceiling, blood pouring from the wound in his neck. A wound I caused. I'd trained to kill. I'd learned so many methods for preventing exactly what he tried to do to me. I even taught other women how to defend themselves from rapists, and attackers. I prayed I'd never need to use those skills.

And now I felt shattered into pieces, because even my best friend hadn't been trustworthy in the end. Even he had been a monster. Even he had tried to force himself on me.

I stared at the wall. I had no idea what to do next. As sad as it was, Harvey had been my only friend. And if my only friend could do that, then what hope did I have of ever finding another person I could trust in this life? What was even left for me now? Living in fear? Jail?

I picked up my razor, staring at the blades, which would be damn near impossible to cut myself with. Why did they make the damn things so safe? Tossing it back at the edge of the bath, I stood up, and leaned over to open my bathroom cabinet. From there I picked up the pack of loose razor blades. The ones I'd bought *just in case*.

Because I always knew this day would come. Not that I'd murder my only friend, but that I'd need a way out, if things got really bad again. The paper wrapped blades were deadly, and would do the job nicely. I slipped one from its packet, and sat back down in the bath.

CASSIDY

I STAYED CURLED UP in the bathroom for so long, that my legs cramped up, and I felt ice cold. I glanced at the clothes Seb had peeled from me, before he fucked me, and didn't want them back. Didn't want them touching me. I also didn't want to stay here. I pushed myself up from the corner, pausing for a few seconds, to make sure my legs wouldn't give out, and then I left the bathroom.

The bedroom, still trashed, was not the safe haven I needed. I walked to the bedroom door, which they'd left open, and stood in the hallway. The house was quiet, with just the hall light still on. There was no sound from downstairs. Were they sleeping? What time was it? I had no idea. It was dark, so it was night, at least.

I walked past Seb's room, as silently as I could, not ready to face him again yet. I glanced at the room that I knew had been empty before, but I didn't go there. I stopped at the door to Sammy's room instead. What was I doing? Was I insane? I quietly turned the handle, and pushed the door open, stepping into the dim room.

LENORE

THE CUTS BURNED, AND then the flow of red began. I sat back in the bath, watching the red being washed away by the water raining down from the shower. It was hypnotic to watch... the washing away of my life. The pain, the fear, the degradation. I'd be free at last.

I heard a banging noise in the flat, but I ignored it, starting to feel slightly chilled, and light-headed. The room started to darken, as my body grew heavy, and my head tipped back against the bath. *Finally*.

The door crashed open, and that man, Marco, stood there, staring at me in horror.

"Oh for fuck's sake! Lenore, dammit, woman!" He approached me as my body succumbed to the blood loss, and I stopped seeing anything.

CHAPTER FIFTY-SIX
CASSIDY

DID I EXPECT TO find Sammy fast asleep in bed? Relaxed? Vulnerable? I'm an idiot. I was grabbed and slammed against the wall in seconds, his hand on my throat yet again.

"What the *fuck* are you up to, Cass?" He snarled quietly, glaring at me.

"I'm sorry," I gasped, pulling at his hands. "Please let go."

He did. I didn't expect it, and staggered before I caught my balance.

"What do you want?" He asked me quietly. I stared at the floor, wrapping my arms around me, because I'd stupidly avoided the clothes, and now felt too naked.

"I don't know."

He stared at me, a hard look in his eyes.

"Were you going to try and kill me?"

I looked up at him, stunned. I hadn't expected that question.

"What?"

He folded his arms, while I did my best to ignore the fact that he clearly also slept naked.

"Did you sneak in here, because you thought you could kill me in my sleep, Cass?"

I moved my arms, holding them out at my sides, reluctantly baring myself to him.

"With what weapon, Sammy?"

He snorted. "Maybe you concealed it *somewhere*."

I wrapped my arms back around me. "I just... can I sleep here?"

He snorted, glancing at his bed. "You wanting to get in my bed, love?"

"Seb destroyed mine." I watched him, to see how he'd react. He'd either tell me to sod off, or he'd give in. And if he gave in, would I even be allowed to sleep?

"Then get in his bed," he said finally, nodding his head at the door. *He was kicking me out.*

"What if..." I looked at the carpet again. "What if there's a way to earn it?" I asked, so quietly that I was sure he wouldn't hear me.

He chuckled. "What do you offer, love? I'm open to suggestions." Oh god. I chewed my lip, racking my brain. I couldn't suggest anything. He'd think I wanted to be with him, and... I was pretty sure that wasn't the case. Right?

"This was a mistake, I'm sorry. I'll use that empty room." I turned to leave, and he grabbed my arm.

"*Nobody* uses that room. You stay out of there." I stared down at his fingers, biting into my arm, adding more bruises. That was weird, but I couldn't focus on the empty room right now. I needed somewhere to stay.

"Then please. Tell me what I need to do, to stay here with you," I begged, blinking back tears as I officially hit rock bottom. If he said no, I had nowhere to go.

He glanced down at his cock, which had clearly been listening to our conversation, and now stood proudly to attention.

"Well... you could ride me, I guess." Oh god. I rubbed my hands over my face.

"Then you'll let me sleep here?"

He nodded. "In the bed with you?"

He smirked, and nodded again. "And you won't do anything to me while I sleep?"

He laughed, pulling me to the bed.

"Depends on how well you ride me, cowgirl."

He shoved me, making me fall forward onto the bed, then he walked around the other side, and laid down, his head on the pillows.

"Come here, Cass. I want you on my cock right fucking now." I blinked back tears, as I crawled across the bed to him. He reached out and helped me move up to straddle him.

He guided me over him, and then eased me down. I could feel his hard length sliding into me, thick and unyielding.

"Lucky you were so wet, love. Your body has been trying to tell you for days. You just needed to listen." He jerked me down as he bucked his hips up, and slammed the rest of him inside me, making me yelp.

He grinned. "You've got all of me inside you now, love."

He felt bigger than Seb. Of course, the position could have something to do with that.

"It hurts," I said quietly, and he nodded.

"That's okay, love. I can make that feel good too." Despite telling me to ride him, he used his arms and hips, to guide me, moving me up and down his cock, groaning with each hard landing. My hands were on his arms, holding on tight, because I couldn't focus on anything, except how it felt to keep getting impaled on him.

It was different from being with Seb, because although Sammy was also looking to get off, he didn't make threats, or demand that I don't speak. And yet, even with the free reign to speak, I didn't. I didn't say no. I didn't say stop. I didn't say I didn't want it. I just let him use me to get off. He stopped moving me for a moment, reaching into his drawer by the bed.

"Little late for a condom," I said quietly, and he laughed.

"We don't need those with you, love. You won't be with anyone else."

I glared at him. "But you bastards will!"

He shrugged, pulling something from the drawer, and not letting me see it.

A quiet buzzing noise started up, and he shot me a grin.

"Use this to get yourself off, while I fuck you. Best hurry before I come."

He handed me a small bullet vibrator, and pretty much shoved it and my hand in place, before he took hold of my hips again, and started slamming up into me. I came a few seconds before he did, the sounds muffled by his hand, which suddenly covered my mouth, as he rammed harder into me, and finished with a low groan. He was grinning as he pulled his hand away.

His hands both settled on my thighs, and he rubbed them slowly. I found myself smiling at him, before I realised what I was doing.

"Thanks, love. That'll help me sleep again, after you so rudely woke me up." I glared at him, trying to shove his hands away so I could move, and he laughed. "You're so easy to wind up. Come here."

He took my hands, and pulled me, so I fell against his chest.

"Kiss me goodnight, and I'll let you move."

"That wasn't the deal." He shrugged.

"I'm a bastard. Live with it." He raised his eyebrows, so I leaned down and pressed my lips against his, taking the opportunity to lift my hips, and let his softening cock slide free.

His hand latched on to the back of my head, and he turned a quick peck into a full-on tonguing session, while I tried to push away, only half serious, because his kisses alone could curl my toes.

He finally released me, and let me retreat just enough to stare at me.

"You've earned the opportunity to sleep beside me tonight, love."

"Go fuck yourself," I muttered, and he snorted.

"Such a delicate flower. Now go to sleep." He rolled, and released me, depositing me on the other side of the bed, before rolling away again.

I pulled the covers over me, and curled up on my side, facing away from him, with his cum oozing out of me, and fell asleep with tears on my face.

CHAPTER FIFTY-SEVEN
CASSIDY

WE WERE WOKEN BY Sammy's phone the next morning. I didn't move, but I felt him sit up.

"Marco? Christ, it's not even six yet. What's going on?"

I rolled over to look at him. Marco? The guy from the murder scene last night?

He glanced at me, and kept listening.

"Fuck me. How the hell did that happen?" I sat up, pulling the covers with me.

"Is it Lenore?" He waved his hand at me, presumably wanting me to shut up.

"You're staying with her?" He said into the phone, and I glared at him.

"Is she okay?" I asked urgently, and he glared right back, and angled away from me with the phone.

"Keep me posted. Yeah… thanks." He ended the call, and turned to glare at me once more.

"Next time you interrupt me on the phone, I'll gag you. Understood?" I frowned at him, surprisingly hurt, considering what had happened last night between us.

"You're such an asshole, you know?"

He shrugged, looking distracted.

"The call was about that Lenore chick. Apparently tried to kill herself in the shower."

I gasped, horrified at his words. "Will she live?"

He sighed, looking pretty shocked by this event himself.

"Uh… Marco rushed her to A&E, and they stabilised her. Had to transfuse her. It was close. She was apparently pretty thorough."

I covered my face with my hands. "My god. This is my fault."

He groaned. "Look, she was upset, and she did something stupid. Yes, we were all involved, but shit happens. We can't undo it. And Marco seems quite taken with her, since he's insisting on staying with her while she's unconscious."

"It should be me," I said quietly, sliding out of Sammy's bed, which I shouldn't have even been in. I shouldn't be anywhere. Why had I started to feel like I'd found a place in this world? I was out of my mind last night, obviously.

He stood up too. "Whatever the fuck you think you're planning, just stop."

I glared at him from the door.

"Why? What's the point? Whether you kill me now, or a week from now, I'm just hurting people. All this time, I blamed him, and you guys... but it's me... *I'm the monster*. Jesus... I'm the one I should have feared all along."

I ran from the room, and down the stairs, to the kitchen. I'd never seen it before, because I'd only run through it once, but never stopped. I grabbed the first knife I saw, and then I stared at it. Did I even have the courage to use it?

SEB

I DON'T KNOW WHAT the fucking racket was in there, but it woke me up. I heard running, and then Sammy opened my door, stark bollock naked. It was too early in the morning to be faced with his junk.

"Shit's hitting the fan, bruv. You might want to come and help." He kept moving and I sat up, cursed him, and grabbed some sweats, stepping into them as I got out of bed.

"Whatever the fuck this is, it had better be epic," I grumbled, storming from my room, and heading downstairs, because he definitely ran down them like his ass was on fire.

In the kitchen, I was surprised to see him standing still, hands out in front of him, like he was trying to calm someone down. *And there she fucking was.*

"What the fuck are you doing, love?" I asked, as Cass brandished a fucking knife at both of us, and didn't she look fucking hot doing that…

"Stay back. Just fucking stay BACK!" She screamed, with those delicious tears running down her face. I mean, I don't get off on tears specifically, not like my twisted brother, but I do like a woman in distress. Especially a naked one.

"Uh… I don't think you're the one calling the fucking shots here, love. Put the knife down, and fucking shut up. You're not getting out of here," I snapped, marching straight at her, ready to put a stop to this nonsense.

She backed up, letting out a desperate scream.

"If you're not careful, Seb, I'll kill you too. That's what I do. I'm a fucking killer!" She said, waving the knife. Her words threw me, what the hell was this?

"What the fuck is she on about? It's too fucking early for this shit," I snapped at my brother, because someone had better speak some fucking sense, before I lost it.

He shushed me, and stepped closer to Cass.

"Listen, love. You didn't make her do that, okay? She was a damaged young woman already."

Who the hell was he talking about? I gave him a moment to try and talk her down, before I took control, because I'd take her down, hard. She wouldn't get away with acting out like this. I thought we'd subdued her enough that this wouldn't happen now.

"She's dying because of me, Sammy. I'm evil. Just let me do this."

He stepped closer again. "Killing yourself isn't the answer, love. Besides, that's our job." He shot her a grin, and the knife lowered a little. Killing *herself*??

"You won't even do it. You keep saying it, but you don't."

I slammed a hand on the kitchen counter.

"Someone fill me in on what the fuck is happening here!"

Sammy glanced at me, looking worried. Actually worried. Was he getting attached to our little pet here? And for that matter... wasn't I? Fuck. *This wasn't the plan*.

"Lenore tried to commit suicide last night," he said quietly. That made me frown, because how the fuck did that come about? And, for that matter, how did we even know?

"Was Marco still there?" I asked him, casually moving closer to them both as I spoke. If she went nuts with that knife, I was sure as hell taking the hit, and not my brother. And then I'd gut her with it.

Sammy nodded. "Think he's getting attached. He's staying at the hospital with her."

Jesus Christ. *Why were we all suddenly growing vaginas?*

"What the fuck for? He did his job. Call him off."

Cass glared at me. "So you'd prefer that she wakes up alone, after what happened?"

I shrugged. "Not our problem. He was sent to stop her getting raped. As a courtesy, he probably cleaned up the murder. The rest of it isn't our job."

She waved that knife in my direction.

"You really don't have a soul, do you?"

Sammy cleared his throat. "Put the knife down, Cass. This isn't happening, do you hear?"

She looked at him, and I rushed her, slamming her into the tiled floor, knocking the knife from her hand as I did. My damn newfound vagina led me to cushion her head as we fell, so I didn't accidentally kill her. How the fuck had that suddenly become a concern for me? The plan had always been to kill her, when we'd finished with her.

She lay there looking panicked, and closed her eyes, my body pinning her to the floor.

"Do it, Seb. Please."

I glanced up briefly at Sammy, not moving, because I needed her to stay the fuck here for the moment, while I figured out what the fuck was happening. She lay beneath me, tense and silent.

"Uh... You want me to fuck you again?" I asked in the end, because she was, after all, naked. And doesn't that just fix everything?

Sammy dragged me away from her, and then pulled her to her feet, kicking the knife away as he did. Brave move with no shoes on, but I guessed he actually cared if she lived or died. *Interesting.*

CASSIDY

I SHOULD HAVE JUST killed myself while I had the chance. I stared from one brother to the other.

"Why won't you just let me die?" I asked finally, because honestly they both looked at a loss.

Sammy finally groaned. "Can we just have some fucking coffee, before we discuss this any further?" He shoved me onto one of the stools at the breakfast bar. "Stay."

While he made coffee, Seb just sat down and stared at me, like he had no idea what in hell was going on. I supposed it was a strange way for him to wake up, not knowing what had happened in Sammy's room. He glanced from naked Sammy to naked me. Mulled it over.

I shot him a glare. "Yes, I stayed with Sammy last night." He frowned a little, glancing at his brother, then looking at me again, his eyes travelling over me. I looked down, trying to see what he saw. Bruises. Around my hips. Were they from Sammy, or Seb? Both had pretty much tried to bury their fingers into my flesh when they screwed me.

"Yes, I'm sure some of those are from you. Well done, Seb. I hope you feel proud," I muttered, leaning my elbows on the counter, and resting my chin. I was exhausted. By everything. By fear, and worry, and the whole 'being a captive' situation.

They'd messed with my mind so much, that I didn't know if I even remembered who I'd been before this. Was there a time before I was taken? I couldn't picture my old life. It was gone.

And I realised something even more strange, as I sat there in the kitchen, with these two monsters. I didn't want my old life. I was more like the two of them, than anyone I'd ever met before. How hadn't I seen the evil inside me before?

"Right. Coffee. Here." Sammy slid a mug in front of me, and another in front of Seb, and then he leaned against the opposite counter, holding his own. He took a breath before he spoke.

"So... Harvey was a sick, stalking bastard, who was violating your life, Cass. He's dead. As he should be. Lenore seemed like a nice lady, but she was damaged goods, because of what happened to her a decade ago. She looks like she'll pull through, and I'm guessing she's going to find it hard to lose Marco now. He doesn't want to leave her side."

Seb groaned. "That's why we give orders, bruv. Keep them in line."

I glared at him. "She just lost everything. How about not being an asshole for five minutes?"

Sammy snorted. "I told him to stay put, and keep us posted. So there's no need for any big gestures here. We'll just carry on as we are."

I looked up from my coffee.

"So you're saying that you'll basically both keep abusing me, and I just have to put up with it?"

Seb smirked. "Abusing? You get off more often than we do. I think you're the one abusing us."

I opened my mouth to snap at him, and he shot me a glare, reminding me of his nastier side. Why did I keep forgetting the dynamic here? *They owned me*. I should just stay quiet. It had just never been my way, and if I was stuck here, I needed to find a way to deal with that.

"Abusing is a strong word, Cass. *You came to me last night*, remember? Offered to fuck me, so you could sleep in my bed," Sammy said, giving me one of those bastardly smiles that I fought to avoid returning.

"I have no fucking bed, remember? Dickhead here shredded it!" I pointed at Seb, who looked hurt for a second, before he laughed.

"Okay, yeah, that's on me. Although it's still your fault."

I looked from one to the other, sipping some of my coffee.

"Of course, there's another room, but Sammy wouldn't let me use it." They both suddenly looked morose. "That room isn't to be used."

The vibe they were both giving off, told me that the room had belonged to someone else. Maybe someone who no longer breathed. I didn't push it. I could use that info later, perhaps.

"So... what happens now?" I asked at last. "I mean, am I going to be confined to that trashed bedroom again? I feel like things have changed."

CHAPTER FIFTY-EIGHT
SAMMY (ONLY TO SEB, AND NOW, APPARENTLY, CASS)

I SWEAR, I KNEW exactly what she meant, but what did that mean for us? She was ours. She belonged to us. Did that mean she couldn't have some freedom in the house?

I stared at Seb, who just shrugged, and waited for me to make the decision. *Prick.* The only decisions he makes involve fucking or killing, and half the time he makes those ones on the fly anyway.

"That depends, Cass."

She gave me that little frown, the one that makes me want to do things to her. I'm not much for affection, or any of that shit, but she had started to matter to me. *A little.*

"On what? It's not like I can run, is it?" She shrugged those dainty shoulders, and that moved my eyes to her tits. They'd developed some bruising too, and I loved the different colours marring her pale skin. I couldn't wait to add more. Just for aesthetics, of course.

"On whether you're going to keep snatching knives, or whatever. You're still our captive. You'll still do what the fuck we tell you to. And now... we're pretty much going to fuck you, whenever the mood takes us. So... I guess... what more is there?"

She looked away. "Don't I get any rights at all?" Seb snorted, and I stared at my coffee, because I really didn't have an answer.

None of this had been planned, but now it had evolved into something neither of us had expected. She wasn't someone we'd just tire of and kill, not anymore. And she was evolving too, in a way we couldn't have hoped for.

"That's a no, then. You know, I'm a person too. Well... *I'm a person*, and you both aren't. You're bastards," she snapped, and Seb laughed.

"Hey, bastards are people too, love. I didn't know you could be so cruel."

She glared at her coffee, and her hand tightened around it.

"Cass... if you're planning anything other than drinking that coffee like the person you claim to be, there's going to be more trouble than you can cope with." I warned her. Jesus. Everything seemed to have shifted. She wasn't afraid anymore. *Not really.*

And I couldn't see us keeping her locked away anymore. I kind of liked having her around us. And we'd neglected so much shit, because we'd hidden ourselves away with her, to play... and maybe grown a little addicted...

Seb left the room, and I was left alone with Cass.

"We'll cook something for breakfast after I finish this," I finally said to her, because I was lost for words. I didn't feel like making threats, or demands. I didn't feel like putting that terrified conflict on her face.

I felt wrung out, after what had happened since we took her. We'd expected to play a little, break her, and then she'd disappear. She'd turned that shit on its head pretty fast. She didn't fall apart like we'd imagined. She seemed to grow stronger... and more than that... she seemed to adapt to life with us, no matter how much she pretended to resist.

"I can cook," she said, surprising me once more. I was still staring at her when Seb reappeared, having added a t-shirt to his ensemble. He passed clothes to both of us, and then sat down with his phone.

Cass looked stunned. "Th... these are for me?" She asked cautiously, blinking fast when Seb looked up from his screen.

"What, are you gonna cry about it?"

She flinched, like he'd slapped her, and then she stepped down from the stool, and dressed quickly in the sweats and t-shirt. He'd brought me a pair of my black jeans and a t-shirt too. I'd prefer to shower first, but I'm so fucking hungry. And not just for food.

CASSIDY

I DIDN'T UNDERSTAND WHY he'd given me clothes. Oddly, I didn't like this change from the norm I'd started to grow used to. Why did he do it? What did it mean? Was it a trap? Would wearing them making him angry?

I risked it, and put them on, because a layer between me and them was always a good thing, but I kept an eye on him the whole time, to see if he would fly into a rage, and tear them off me again. He didn't.

He looked up from his phone, but at his brother. Not me. He didn't look at me at all. Didn't I exist to him, when I covered up? And what the fuck kind of thought was that? It should be a good thing.

"Larkin just made his last payment, bruv. He's clear," he said, almost regretfully, and Sammy shrugged.

"Can't win them all. I'll update the logs later."

I watched them, listening to their business talk. They didn't seem to mind that I could hear. Was that a bad sign?

"However... *Garside is late*," Seb said, a dark grin crossing his face. Sammy snorted.

"Of course he is. Well... I believe that's strike three, right?"

Seb nodded. "We need to recheck his assets. See what we want to use."

I frowned. "What does that mean?" Seb shot me a sidelong glance.

"He's in the shit is what it means, love. Time to fuck with him."

I blinked. "Because he's late with a payment?"

He put the phone on the counter, and turned to face me.

"For the third time, he's late with a payment. He owes us twelve grand, love. Do you think we just let that slide?"

I chewed my lip. "So what... will you do?"

He shrugged, grinning easily.

"Enjoy it."

Sammy groaned. "His wife is off limits, bruv." He turned to start pulling things from the fridge.

Seb shrugged. "Pregnant isn't my kink, you know that. His daughter, though..."

I leapt at him, punching him in the face, and he staggered back, narrowly missing falling from his stool right onto his ass.

"What the fuck!" He snapped, shoving me back, as I tried to claw him.

"You sick bastard! You want to rape a kid now? What's the matter with you!" Sammy was suddenly holding me back, shushing me, and Seb was checking his face for bleeding.

"*Jesus*. She's a fucking psycho. And she calls *us* names," he muttered, checking his face in the reflective surface of the glass cupboard above the microwave.

"You can't do this again. Especially not to a child. Please," I begged them. I could survive their wicked treatment, somehow, but I couldn't let them do this. I wouldn't.

Sammy released me, and shoved me back onto my stool.

"Sit the fuck down, Cass. Nobody is talking about hurting a bloody child. First of all, she's in her twenties. And second of all, he means she has her own business. So far she's had nothing to do with her dad's debts, but she's our leverage, see?"

I took a breath, resting my hands on the counter. I felt a wave of guilt for attacking Seb like that.

"Oh god. I'm so sorry. I'm sorry, Seb."

He frowned as he sat back down.

"Huh?"

"I shouldn't have assumed that. Even you guys seem to have some lines you won't cross. I'm sorry."

He stared at his brother for a moment.

"*Wait*. You're apologising for misjudging me?"

I nodded. "Why is that so hard to believe?"

He rubbed at his jaw. "Apologising for what you thought, and *not* for trying to remove my face?"

I shrugged. "You can take that. I'm sure you've earned far worse from me."

He laughed, picking up his phone again.

"That's probably a fair point. Next time, though, I'll pull those pants down, and fuck you in the ass."

I gulped, and looked away from him. Suddenly I felt very much like their captive again. It was dizzying, the constant shifting inside my mind.

Sammy turned to look at me. "Cass, you wanna beat about ten of those eggs?" He pointed and I got up, taking on the task he'd given me, because believe it or not, I missed the simple things. I actually could cook pretty well, but it had been days since I'd had that chance.

He watched for a moment, then nodded, and turned back to the sink, where he was cleaning mushrooms and tomatoes.

We cooked together, and it almost felt normal. Natural. We made a fry up with toast, and bacon, to go with the scrambled eggs, and the fried tomatoes and mushrooms, and all sat at that breakfast bar to eat.

I kept glancing at them, waiting for something to happen. Surely this wasn't actually happening. Surely they weren't actually letting me eat with them. Like a person. Like an equal. And with clothes on.

They chatted among themselves, about various business arrangements, and debtors, and I just sat and absorbed it all. Most of it made sense, except for the part where they really seemed to relish it, when people couldn't pay.

"I can't believe people are dumb enough to borrow from you," I finally muttered, gulping when they both turned to look at me.

"Desperation is our bread and butter, Cass. When people get in so deep, that they can't find their way out, that's when they end up on our doorstep. When nobody else will help them out. And that's how we win. We lend them what they need, but they sign over pretty much anything of value to us when they borrow. Most of them don't even read the small print. So like you said. Dumb fuckers," Sammy said, shrugging one shoulder.

"Our interest rates are where we really crush them though," Seb added, almost proudly.

"You're despicable," I responded, pushing away my empty plate. My stomach felt pleasantly full, for the first time in a day or so. I liked the feeling. I got up and refilled our coffee mugs from the machine, because I needed more, and it felt strangely natural to do it.

CHAPTER FIFTY-NINE
SEB

SOMETHING HAD DEFINITELY CHANGED. Our pet, our captive, who we took just to mess with Harv, who became the person we most enjoyed playing with, and now fucking... she was pouring coffee. *For us.*

I watched her, as did my brother. When she picked up the coffee pot, we'd both actually tensed, expecting her to throw it over us. While I hadn't been disappointed that she didn't, because that shit would hurt like a bitch, at the same time, I missed her fire. Had we destroyed it at last?

"Making house now, princess?" I finally asked her, letting sarcasm add a little bite to my words. She shot me a glare.

"I just wanted more coffee, okay?"

I glanced at Sammy. "She just gonna do what she wants now? Is that what's happening here?"

He just shrugged, accepting the coffee from her.

"Oh my god... did you guys like 'make love', or something last night? I thought it was just a fuck!" I took the coffee, because it really was the least she could do. "I take sugar" I told her.

"Then I'm sure you know where the fuck it is. And for the record, *add a lot.* You need it," she shot back, and I laughed.

"Someone needs to add something to that sassy mouth of yours. I've got something right here," I commented lightly, and her cheeks coloured.

Sammy was watching her, his mind on other things.

"You worked in an office, right?" She nodded warily. He chewed his lip thoughtfully. "Might be a way you can make yourself useful... earn some... rewards..."

CASSIDY

WAS HE ACTUALLY SUGGESTING that I work for them in their criminal enterprise? What the actual fuck?

"Doing what?"

Seb smirked. "Yeah, I quite like the idea of bending her over the desk, while we're meeting with a client. It'd really distract them from the clauses in the contract, if I've got my cock buried deep inside her at the time."

I stared at him in horror. "I'm definitely vetoing that option."

He smirked at me. "It wasn't a suggestion, or an option, Cass. If that's what I want, that's what you'll do. And you'll love every fucking minute of it."

I shook my head vehemently. I could just about tolerate the fact that I'd let both of them inside me, but I wouldn't let them do it in front of others. No. *No way*.

"Isn't it cute when she thinks something is her choice?" Seb asked Sammy, and I flipped him off.

"I'll break those, if you keep doing that," he said, in that conversational tone that made it sound even more disturbing than it already was.

Sammy groaned. "Before you two escalate into some fucking almighty bullshit, can I finish what I was saying?"

Seb snorted, tapping away at his phone screen. Did I miss having a phone? Not really. I used to spend way too much time scrolling through social media, feeling envious of people I knew who were out there living their best lives, while I worked, and went home, and did fuck all else.

I'd always felt so inadequate. No, this felt better. I had no idea what anyone was up to anymore. It helped. Besides, what would I post now? *Feeling bored, might murder my captors later, idk?*

"I was thinking that we could use some help with some of the in-house stuff, you know, while we're being more... hands on..."

"Is that another euphemism for screwing me?" I asked warily, and he nearly spat his coffee everywhere.

"Sex on the brain, that one," Seb commented.

"Actually it was a euphemism for while we're out beating people up, or trashing their shit," he finally said. *Oh.* I could probably do that.

"What would it earn me?" I asked after a moment, because there had to be something in it for me, if they wanted me doing their work.

"I'll let you stab someone. Not us, though," Seb offered, and I grimaced.

"Do I have to work with him?" I asked Sammy, who laughed again.

"You'll be working FOR him. For me. And you'll do as you're told, and nothing else. You snoop, or mess with anything, and you'll be nursing broken fingers, got it?"

I frowned at Sammy. "Seriously?"

He grinned. "You're surprised? I thought you were getting to know us..."

"You're certainly pretty familiar with our cocks," Seb said, clearly trying to humiliate me. I smirked at him. Two can play that game.

"At least I have a better understanding now, of the differences between the two of you..."

He frowned. "What the fuck are you getting at?"

SAMMY

I COULD SEE THAT things were going to escalate, if I didn't shut it down.

"Seb, have Tyler bring Garside here. Let's have a little... chat."

Seb nodded, and strolled away to make the call, while Cass looked at me with those wide doe-like eyes.

"What?" I asked her, watching her chewing that lip. *I'm going to fucking take over in a minute.*

"You're bringing him here?" She asked nervously. I turned on the stool, to face her, because I was confused by her sudden fear.

"Is that a problem?" She wouldn't look at me. What the fuck?

"Cass, I asked you a question," I practically growled at her.

"Are... are you going to offer me to him? Like Seb did with Nev?" Oh. *Fuck*. Yeah, that's not happening again. I felt unexpectedly territorial at the thought. What the hell was that about?

"No, Cass, you're ours. We're not letting anyone else touch you. Got it?" She looked conflicted.

"So, what work *do* you want me to do?"

"Kinda thinking about getting you to suck my cock right now." She blinked at me.

"Oh."

"Is that a problem?" I asked again, because she looked almost shy. "Cass? Stop making me ask everything twice."

She ducked her head. "I... I don't like doing that." I snorted. *Like that mattered*.

"Get on your knees, love. Right now." I pointed, and she shot me a shocked glare. It was hot as fuck.

"But I just said-"

"I don't give a fuck what you said. I bet you even get wet, while I'm fucking your mouth." I pointed again, and added a glare.

She stood up, and looked around, before slowly dropping to her knees.

"You're such a bastard," she muttered, and I grinned. *There's my Cass*.

I didn't bother to make her undo my jeans for me. Her hands were shaking too much for that. I freed my hard cock, and stepped in front of her. Her eyes fixed on it, and I saw tears in them. Damn... they got me every time.

Stroking my hand over her hair, I waited until she met my eyes.

"I'll do all the work, love. Just do as I say. I promise you'll get off on it too."

She wiped at her eyes, and took a deep breath.

"Fine," she grumbled.

I leaned down, tilting her head up again, so I could get in her face.

"I wasn't going to wait for permission, Cass. Now open your mouth."

She actually did. *"Wider.* Like you said... you know my size now..." She obeyed again. It was beautiful.

"If you try biting me, Cass, I'll make you pay, do you understand?" She nodded, her eyes wide, and dripping with tears. Fuck me... *those fucking tears...* I wasn't going to last long with her looking like that.

Threading my fingers through her hair, I cupped the back of her head, and eased my cock in between her soft lips.

"Fuuuck..."

She shuddered, and I felt her try to swallow. *Yeah, that's good...*

I pushed in until I hit the back of her throat, and she flinched, pushing against my thighs with her hands. I released her only as she started to gag.

"See, love? All you have to do is take it." I tightened my grip on her head, and started fucking her mouth, tapping her throat as I did. Her choking sounds, and the tears pouring down her face were stunning. She'd never looked so beautiful.

As I pulled back, and let her breathe for a moment, listening to her gasps, I crouched, pushing her knees apart, before slipping my fingers inside the sweats she wore. She tried to pull away, but my fingers found what I was looking for. *What I knew I'd find.*

"I knew you'd get off on this. You're our perfect little slut, Cass. You do well with this, and I'll make you scream when you come." She blinked at me, wiping slobber from her face, while I sucked her taste from my fingers.

In a swift move, I stood back up, and aimed my cock back at her face. This time she just opened up, and let me in. I might have been a bit more ruthless as I fucked her mouth this time.

When I came, I held her tight against me, until I'd unloaded in her mouth, and then I pulled out.

"Don't you dare spit that out, Cass. *Swallow.*" She shot me a look filled with hatred, but did as I ordered.

"Fucking beautiful, love. Now pull your pants down, and bend over that stool."

CHAPTER SIXTY

CASSIDY

I FELT DIRTY, USED. It shouldn't have made me wet. What was wrong with me, that these awful things they did turned me on like that? Was it some Stockholm shit? I'd wanted to stop him... but then it stopped being so awful, and became something else.

Did I want to shower? Rid myself of his taste? Yes... but I also wanted to come. *Badly*. Because strangely, that vile act had made me desperate for an orgasm, and I'm clearly doomed, and going straight to hell.

"Cass, I won't tell you a second time." Fuck! I pushed down the sweats, and leaned over the padded stool, gripping it tightly with my hands. What was he about to do?

His hand came down hard on my ass, and I squeaked.

"What are-"

"Quiet," he snapped, taking time to spank each cheek in turn, several times, making sure not to leave an inch of flesh not stinging. Then he rested a hand on the small of my back, holding me still, while he slid two fingers inside me.

I was so wet that I could hear his fingers slipping in and out of me. It was mortifying, and yet... it was delicious. It felt so good that I found myself pushing back into his fingers, despite the hand on my back. That hand moved from there, to grip a handful of my hair, and Sammy pulled my head back, leaning close to my ear.

"How does that feel, slut? You can still taste my cum in your mouth, and now you're riding my fingers... still think you're not ours?" He nipped the soft flesh of my ear, and I yelped again.

"Stay exactly where you are, no matter what I do to you," he murmured, while I immediately felt a wave of panic. What was he planning now?

"I mean it, Cass. If you move, you don't get to come, and when Seb comes back, I'll make you suck him too." *Fuck.* I nodded, and his hand slipped away from my hair. He moved behind me, and his fingers slid out, and didn't go back in. Not in where I wanted them, anyway. One slick finger started probing at my asshole.

"No!" I gasped, my body flinching.

"Yes," Sammy said firmly, starting to slowly finger my ass with that thick finger. His other hand slipped between my thighs, and started to tease my clit, alternately dipping his fingers into my wet pussy. It was strange, and confusing, and amazing, all at once.

My ass stopped resisting a single finger, and so he pulled out, and then shoved two into me instead. My breaths were coming out in fierce gasps, as I bounced between enjoyment, and shock, and discomfort. This wasn't what I wanted, was it?

When my orgasm blasted through me, it was like nothing I'd felt before. My throat felt raw from the sound that poured out of my mouth, and I practically toppled off the stool, as my body reacted to his touch. I felt his lips touch the small of my back briefly, and then he pulled away from me, heading for the doorway.

"Don't try going anywhere, Cass. I'll always find you." He left the room, and I slowly slid off that stool and onto the floor, curling up into a confused, and yet sated, ball.

LENORE

I WOKE UP FEELING strange. I wasn't in my bed. That much was obvious, because the bed was a hospital bed, and there were machines beeping beside me. It took a few moments to remember everything that had happened, before I ended up here.

I glanced at my wrists, seeing the white bandages covering them. There was a man sleeping beside me, his head tilted down to his chest, ankles crossed, arms folded. He was dressed in dark clothes, and had dark hair. It wasn't Harvey. Of course it wasn't. Harvey was dead. *Because I'd stabbed him.*

I took a breath, and it caught in my throat, making me gasp for air. The machines started to beep faster, and the man suddenly lifted his head. It was the Italian guy from my flat. Marco?

"You're awake. Thank god for that," he said softly, sitting up properly. "How do you feel?"

I stared at him. Why was he here? What did it matter to him how I felt? I heard the machines beeping a little faster.

"Lenore? I'm a friend, it's okay." His voice was soothing, with the barest hint of an accent. It actually made me feel a little less panicked, and my breathing started to ease again, the machines slowing down their frantic beeping.

"Whose friend? I don't know you." My voice was croaky, and my mouth felt dry. He saw me looking around.

"What do you need?"

I glanced at the glass of water, and he first used the controls on the bed, to sit me up further. Rather than trying to hand me the glass, he lifted it for me.

"Small sips, I think that's what they said." He held the glass to my lips, and I took a few blissful sips, chasing away the dry feeling in my mouth.

"Thank you."

He nodded, setting the glass back down. He didn't sit back down, though, taking a moment to stretch his back out, before he stood beside the bed again. He reached for my hand, then stopped.

"I... uh... I didn't want to leave you," he said finally, and I found myself focusing on his voice, the soothing deep tone, and the way his lips moved when he spoke. After what had happened, I'd been reduced to this person who couldn't take in anything outside of the small details.

"I appreciate that. Someone must be missing you though, by now." I didn't want him to go. That shocked me, because I'm not used to needing anyone, but he'd come into my life just as I needed help, and he hadn't hurt me, or tried to take anything I didn't want to give. At least, not yet.

"Do you hate me?" He asked quietly, reaching for my hand again, leaving his right beside it, as he stopped himself again.

"Why would I hate you?" I asked him, staring at his hand beside mine.

He sighed heavily, drawing my eyes back to his face.

"I found you in the bath, blood everywhere, and I guess I thought you might be pissed at me, for making you stay. I just couldn't let you die, I'm sorry." He looked confused by his words, and his eyes darted away from mine.

"Why were you there?" I asked him, instead of thanking him, which I felt I wanted to do. Dying because of Harvey wasn't an option. He didn't deserve to have that much power over me. I knew it as soon as I woke up, and realised that I'd survived after all. And that had happened because of this man beside me. *Marco.*

He sighed, looking at our hands, finally taking the leap, and wrapping his around mine. He squeezed lightly, and I felt comfort from him, rather than wanting to retreat, as I might have done in the past.

"You work for the Bennetts." That detail had just popped into my head. He'd mentioned them, I was sure of it.

He nodded at me now, his hand tightening on mine a little.

"I don't want to lie to you. They had me monitoring that prick, Harvey. They cloned his phone, and saw that he was starting to pull that stalker shit on you."

I nodded. They'd sent me proof. Had they saved me from him? Or had they caused an attack that might never have happened otherwise?

"I didn't know he was capable of that stuff," I finally said, closing my eyes against the tears burning their way out. He let out a low growly groan, making me look at him again.

"He was a sick fucker, Lenore. I can't tell you how glad I am that they sent me to watch him. Even though I didn't get there in time to stop you defending yourself, I would have damn well made sure that he didn't hurt you. He wouldn't have survived either way." He finally met my eyes again, and his were full of emotion.

"I don't know you," I whispered, feeling safer in his presence than I had in more than a decade.

He smiled suddenly, and it was like the sun came out. "I'd like to change that if you'll let me, Lenore."

CHAPTER SIXTY-ONE
SEB

I DIDN'T KNOW WHAT Sammy was playing at, bringing Garside to our place, but I figured he wanted to set Cass on him. We could see it inside her, noticed it when she woke up after we took her. That darkness that lived within us both. She fought like fuck to keep it inside, but it was time to bring it out of her. She'd never leave us. I'd been pretty sure she'd never choose to stay, but... once she'd spilled blood for us, she'd truly have no choice.

I could tell Sammy had fucked her, the bastard. Done something to her, at least. She was a mess when I came back down from making calls. She finally staggered away, and headed upstairs, so I figured she'd gone to clean herself up.

Sammy had a real shit-eating grin on his face.

"You fucked her again?" He shook his head.

"You're gonna want to try that mouth of hers later, bruv. Fucking hell."

Bastard. I know I'd been the first to fuck her, but I also wanted to be first to fuck her mouth. It was selfish, I realised, but I'd wanted to be the one to watch her choke on my cock. The first one, at least.

"Stop sulking, bruv. She isn't going anywhere. Plenty of time to fuck all her holes," Sammy finally said, breaking the silence which had fallen after his last comment. I shrugged at him.

"Whatever. What are we doing when Garside gets here?"

Sammy shrugged, sipping the beer he'd grabbed from the fridge. *Good idea*. I got up to fetch one too. It might be early in the day, but that's the beauty of being fucking adults. We do what we want, when we want.

"I was thinking maybe you wanted Cass to spill her first blood?" I said, tossing the bottle cap, and taking a few gulps of cold beer.

Sammy stared at me. "I'm pretty sure she spilled Harvey's blood last time she saw him. Punched him in the face, as I recall."

I snorted, remembering the shocked look on the prick's face.

"Yeah... that was pretty priceless. I was thinking... uh... maybe she could have Nita's knife."

Sammy sucked in a shocked breath as he stared at me.

"Really?" He gulped some of his beer. "That's a big deal, bruv."

I shrugged like he was wrong, like it wasn't the hugest fucking deal for both of us.

"She'd have liked her." She would have. She had been the fiercest woman I'd ever known. A cross between Cass and Lenore, with a dragon's heart thrown in for good measure. We'd both loved her. We'd both lost her that day, and nothing had felt right since. Well, maybe until now.

"What makes you think she won't turn it on us, bruv?" Sammy asked, quite reasonably really, considering what we'd put Cass through since she joined us.

"Isn't that part of the fun, bruv? Finding out? I think she'd look sexy as fuck, trying to stab me." Sammy just shook his head at me, that look on his face that he sometimes gets, when he thinks I'm a lost cause.

"I might just let her, you know." I shrugged, sitting back with my beer, feeling a wave of excitement at the thought of her drawing blood. *My* blood. "I'd enjoy punishing her for trying, anyway."

CASSIDY

THEY WEREN'T KEEPING ME shut away anymore, so I took advantage of that fact. Helping myself to Seb's shower, and some of his clothes. If they weren't going to let me have my own, then theirs were fair game. It was bizarre to me that this newfound freedom didn't make me run for the door, but it wasn't as easy as that.

What did I have to run back to now? I probably had no job by now, and my landlord wouldn't tolerate many missed months of rent, before he ended up kicking me out. At least here I didn't have to worry about things like that.

I did have a few things at my place that I didn't want to lose, but maybe I could convince the brothers that I needed them here. They might even listen at this point, because it truly felt like things had shifted between us. I was more to them than just their captive now. I could feel it. And it didn't feel like the worst thing in the world anymore, being here.

I was worried about what they were planning, bringing this Garside guy here. Were they going to set him on me, like they tried with Nev? I know Sammy said that they wouldn't, but I couldn't trust that Seb wouldn't go rogue, and go against what he'd said.

What I could do, was to be more prepared... hence why I'd also stolen a pair of Seb's boxers to wear under the pants. I wasn't going to make it easy for them. Now I just had to figure out how to get a weapon from the kitchen, because for bad guys, they sure as hell didn't have weapons all over the place. But then... I'd only really looked at the bedrooms and kitchen so far, hadn't I?

After visiting my old room, because it was still a mess, I teased my freshly-washed hair back under control with the brush, and then I set out to explore other rooms, hoping to find something to use on the bastard, on any bastard who tried anything.

"Cass? Where have you disappeared off to?" I heard one of them shout, as I reached the bottom of the stairs. *Crap.* I thought I'd have more time than that.

I glanced at the other doors, before I headed for the kitchen.

"I was in the shower," I said, watching Seb take in my outfit, shaking his head slowly.

"Fucking hell, Cass. I'll have no clothes left at this rate." I shot him a cheeky smirk.

"So maybe you should think about letting me bring my own clothes here."

He and Sammy shared an amused look.

"Planning on moving in then, love?" Sammy asked, raising an eyebrow. It took the wind out of my sails, because I'd finally figured that I was never getting away, so I might as well accept it, and now it sounded like staying wasn't an option either.

"Damn you people. Will you make up your bloody minds? Either you're keeping me here, in which case, I need some of my own shit, or you're letting me go, or killing me, in which case, just fucking do it," I snapped, glaring at them both.

Laughter wasn't the reaction I'd expected, silly me, but that just reminded me of what a fool I was, and had always been. Of course they'd laugh. They didn't want *me*, they just wanted someone to play with, and discard, when they were done. I didn't matter to them, any more than I mattered to anyone else in the world.

"You're both real pricks, you know that?" I turned to march out of the room, but Seb stopped me.

"Wait, Cass. Come back here." I heaved a sigh, turning back to stare at him, folding my arms, as much to warm the chill inside, as it was in defiance.

"How about this?" He asked, revealing to me that one of his 'deals' was about to get offered to me.

I raised my eyebrows, waiting for the axe to fall.

"You help us scare the shit out of Garside, and we'll have someone fetch your stuff. How's that?" I frowned, looking from him to Sammy.

"Scare him how?"

Sammy facepalmed. "I knew she'd fixate on that part. Listen love, we're not going to offer you to him. You're ours to fuck, and play with, and nobody else's, but... you could... you know, have a stab at him, if you like..."

I took a step back from them.

"You people are fucking insane. Why would I want to do that?"

Seb stood up, and walked over to me, smirking when I backed up another step.

"Look, love. You're not that different from us. Don't pretend that you are. You like our darkness, because it speaks to yours. You like being forced to take our cocks, because that gets you off. And if that does, then I'm betting that messing with a lowlife piece of shit would too." I shook my head.

"You're wrong."

Sammy joined us, leaning against the kitchen wall.

"See, I don't think we are, Cass."

Seb smirked, holding out something. "Prove us wrong." I glanced at the item in his hands. A small, but deadly-looking, hunting knife. It had something etched into the blade. A name. *Nita*.

"Who's Nita?" I asked, and his lips drooped for a moment.

"Someone who isn't here anymore." I glanced at Sammy, and saw the same sadness reflected on his face. *Wait*. These guys could actually experience emotions? Apart from assholiness? It threw me. It almost made me feel something for them in return.

"The room that doesn't get used," I commented quietly, and Sammy nodded.

"It's hers. Even if she'll never sleep there again." I wanted to ask. I wanted to know everything, but it wasn't the right time. I heard a car outside.

"It's showtime, Cass. All we're asking, is that you let your inner demon loose, and maybe enjoy it a little. This guy is bad news. That daughter we mentioned? He abused her." I felt myself tensing up at Sammy's words, as I felt a wave of that rage that I'd always tried to bite back.

The rage that I hadn't truly felt since my early teens, when they'd decided I had behavioural problems. Picking fights at school, and verbally abusing the teachers, hadn't made me very popular back then. I just hadn't fit in anywhere. And kids can be cruel. We all know that. So yeah, I'd become an 'angry teen'.

Counselling. That had been their answer. Had it worked? Maybe. Mostly. Being an abandoned baby had left me with nobody to turn to, and my situation had been enough cause for other children to tease and bully me. Lashing out had been my release.

But I'd learned to bury it over the years. Smile and nod politely, when I wanted to scream at people. I'd almost fooled myself into believing I'd suppressed it for good. That I'd become a better person.

These two bastards had been encouraging that side of me back out again, almost training me to join them in their darkness. I hadn't realised that, as it was happening, because there had been so much fear in each of my interactions with them, that I hadn't recognised it. But there it was. The reason behind my 'fire' as they called it.

Maybe it was time to let someone feel the burn.

CHAPTER SIXTY-TWO
SAMMY

DID I THINK WE'D got through to her yet? No, not really. She was on the edge. Still holding in all that beautiful brutality. She'd stopped being afraid of us, or at least the kind of fear that she felt had changed, but I think she'd started to fear herself instead. Letting her loose on Garside would be a two-fer. Free her true nature from the cage she'd locked it in, and scare the shit out of the bastard at the same time. I couldn't wait to see how things unfolded.

Seb went to get the door, and Tyler walked in with a quaking Garside. Whatever he'd said on the way here had started things off right. He was already afraid. He had a cloth bag over his head.

While it had been essential, to make sure he didn't know where we were, it also added to the 'scaring the shit out of him' part of the game. *Perfect.* I glanced at Cass, who'd decided to lean against the wall by the doorway. I guessed she wanted to be where she could escape if she wanted to.

She had something to prove now though. If she joined in, it confirmed that she wanted to stay here with us. If she didn't, it meant that she still thought she was getting out. Either way, she was going nowhere, but it would be fucking fun to find out what she did next. I already knew I'd keep pushing her until she joined our side. Her coming to me last night told me exactly who she was inside.

Tyler shoved Garside into a chair in the middle of the kitchen, having snapped the tie on his hands, before dragging his arms around the back of the chair, and using a new tie on them. It was probably an odd place to do this, but it was a crucial part of Cass's 'training', to see what she'd do. And also, a tiled floor is pretty easy to clean, if things go wrong.

Seb pulled the hood from Garside's head, and his greying hair stayed standing up, as he blinked at the sudden light.

"How the devil are ya, *Mister Garside*?" Seb asked, leaning down to smirk at him. The man visibly shuddered, and pulled at the restraints on his wrists.

"Mr Bennett." He glanced at me, as I leaned against the breakfast bar, and nodded, although he gulped too. "Mr Bennett."

"You know why you're here, *Mister* Garside?" Seb asked, tucking his hands into his pockets. I watched Cass as she watched Seb. She looked nervous, conflicted, but intrigued. Good.

"Look, I know my payment is late, boys. I'm just having some issues getting what I'm owed from others. *Tomorrow*. I swear you'll get it tomorrow. You know I'm good for it." He already sounded desperate. It was exactly the way we liked them to be. I felt a familiar warm rush of power, watching his terror, the knowledge that he could well die here. Right now.

"How many times now, Eddie? How many times have you been late?" Seb asked, raising his eyebrows at the dickhead.

I could see the terror on the guy's face, as he stared back at Seb.

"I'm sorry. Honestly, I'm doing my best. It's been a tough few months. I mean, you know what the economy's like right now."

Seb snorted and glanced over at Cass, who chewed her lip nervously. She looked like she needed a push.

"How's that lovely daughter of yours, Eddie?" I asked, studying my fingernails, feigning disinterest, while staying very focused on Cass.

He swore under his breath. "Look, I get that you gave me a deadline, and I missed it. I get that. I know that I'm not doing great at paying you back. I swear I'm working on it."

I pushed away from the breakfast bar, and strode over to him, grabbing his tufty hair, and tilting his head back.

"That's not what I fucking asked, is it?"

Cass gasped behind me, and I grinned.

"See that lady over there?" I moved so he could see her. He looked at her then back at me.

"Yeah."

"She's the one you need to fear, mate. You think we're bad, you haven't seen her in action yet. I mean, I'm sure you're attached to your cock, yeah? Don't want it cooked, and fed to you?" Cass actually snorted at that. Seb had stepped away, laughing, and waved her over.

"Come here, love." She came to him, and stood beside him, that knife of Nita's in her hand, as she twirled it back and forth. Conflicted or not, she was fucking enchanting right now. I bit back a groan, as my cock twitched in my pants.

"You want to play, love?" Seb asked her, and she fixed her eyes on him.

"Now?" She whispered, slowly turning her gaze on the bound man.

"NO! Look, I'll get your money, I swear," Eddie Garside suddenly started babbling. Her fear was coming across as something far more sinister, and that worked in our favour. In more ways than one.

"How about just a finger or two?" I suggested, stepping back and gesturing to Eddie. Tyler had backed away, doing his best to keep his laughter under control.

Cass glanced at Eddie, and peered behind him at his tied hands.

"Which ones?" *Perfect.* That's our girl. I felt a wave of pride.

I leaned down to look at Eddie. "Got any favourites, mate, before I let her go? Might just be able to convince her to avoid them, if you're really lucky."

He was struggling against the plastic cable tie Tyler had used on him. He liked them because they cut into the skin so nicely. Sick bastard.

"*Please*. I just need a few more days. I'll find your money. I'll steal it, if I have to," he begged, and I groaned.

"Come on, man. We're business men. This is a business. And right now, you're hurting our business. Is that any way to treat our kindness? We helped you out, when nobody else would. Were we so wrong to trust you?" I laid the guilt on nice and thick, winking at Cass, as she stared at me with wide eyes.

He was breathing fast, looking from one of us to the other.

"If you kill me, you'll never get your money."

Seb snorted. "You think that's how this shit works? Your debt just passes to your ladies, mate. Your lovely wife, and that delicious daughter of yours. How's her business doing lately?"

Cass watched him carefully, because every time we mentioned his daughter, she stepped closer to that edge. We'd led her to believe he was an abusive bastard, just to push her buttons a little. We had to keep tugging at that rope, to see if we could nudge her past the line.

This whole situation was less about Garside's debt, and more about shaping Cass into what we wanted her to be. *What we knew she could be.*

Eddie was watching us, as we watched Cass. Finally, realising that she might be more dangerous than us, because hadn't we led him to believe that, he turned to her.

"Please. I'm doing my best. I don't want to hurt your business. And I really don't want this to hurt my daughter too. She's too important to me to bring this on her." Cass stared at him, forgetting her place in all of this, because for some reason, the daughter was her trigger.

"Does your daughter love you?" He blinked.

"What? Of course she does. What kind of... what is this?" He glanced back at me.

She frowned. "How can she love someone like you?" He looked downright gobsmacked. I figured if he started to make liars of us, I'd have to punch his lights out. No problem. His face was pissing me off enough that I probably would anyway.

"I love my daughter, and she loves me. She understands my situation. She knows I've made mistakes. We put all that behind us." His words actually fed into my lie. *Perfect.*

Cass leaned closer to him; Nita's knife suddenly close to his throat.

"People like you make me sick. You don't deserve to live. Why aren't you dead yet?" Eddie started to freak out, yelling at us to get her away from him, that she was crazy. Then he made his biggest mistake.

"Get this psycho bitch away from me! Don't let her touch me!" She frowned.

"Oh... you don't like being touched against your will? Wow... yeah, that must fucking suck!" She glared at him for a moment, almost faltering, and I shared a worried glance with Seb, as we both feared she'd back off.

Suddenly she moved, and the knife stabbed into his thigh. He let out a high shriek, and she stood there, blinking at him, horror on her face. Seb acted fast, grabbing her, and pulling her away, covering for her shock at her actions.

"That's enough, love. Leave him alive to pay!" I stared at the knife, and then shot Eddie a slow grin.

"You're lucky he stopped her there. Once she gets started... well, you're pretty much fucked."

"Oh my god, oh god... she stabbed me!" I nodded.

"And what did we learn from this little visit today, mate?"

"I'll find your money, I swear. *Tomorrow*. You'll have it tomorrow," he gasped.

"Maybe worth getting your next one in early, don't ya think, Eddie?" I suggested, and he nodded frantically.

"Yes! Yes, I promise! *Please*. Don't let her near me again."

Seb had dragged Cass from the room, so she couldn't let us down by showing her horror at what she'd done. This had gone better than I'd expected. Soon enough, word would spread that we had a new Nita. And then people would really start to shit their pants again.

I nodded at Tyler, who came over, and shook his head, staring at the knife, still embedded in Eddie's leg.

"I'm gonna need to go get my kit. The second I pull that out, we'll know if she caught an artery with it. If she did, he has seconds before he's dead," he said calmly, turning and heading outside.

"Fuck! What the hell did she do that for? Jesus, it hurts!" Eddie was still babbling like a fucking loser, while intermittently moaning with pain.

I leaned close, staring him right in the eye.

"That was the tip of the iceberg, mate. She's a loose cannon, and we're fed up with people fucking us around. Late payers are going to start getting visits from her, and I really hope she leaves enough alive to pay.

I can't promise that though, and to be honest, I think she's hot as fuck, covered in other people's blood. Now, I want your late payment, and next month's by tomorrow, or I'm sending her to you. And maybe I'll send her after your wife too."

Eddie groaned, sagging in the chair.

"Please... no..."

I nodded at Tyler again, as he returned with his medic kit. He'd sort this. I wanted to go find our girl.

CHAPTER SIXTY-THREE
CASSIDY

I CAN'T BELIEVE THAT I just stabbed that guy! I heard him talking about his poor daughter, and it pissed me off, because he has no right to talk about her, and even less right to not want to be touched. Like he gave her that choice!

Seb had dragged me away, as soon as I'd stabbed him, spouting some rubbish about stopping before I killed him. As if! Stabbing him like that had made me feel sick. The way it felt when the knife sank into his flesh, it made my legs give out, as Seb manoeuvred me into a room I'd never seen before. It was a lounge, but there was a bar at one end. A drink. *A drink would help.*

Instead, Seb turned me around, and kissed me hard.

"That was fucking magical, Cass," he said, when he pulled back. "He was shitting his pants."

"I didn't mean to! I was just so angry with him," I protested, trying to push Seb away, as he tried to kiss me again. He shot me a wicked grin.

"Baby gets a reward for her good behaviour."

I tried to back away. "Let me go home." He snorted.

"Yeah, not happening. You just proved that you want to stay with us, Cass." He led me to the bar, pouring three shots of something amber coloured, and handed one to me. *Thank god.* A quick burning taste of the drink was all I had time for, before he set it aside, lifted me up onto that bar, and pushed me back.

"Stay," he commanded, hooking his fingers into the sweatpants, and sliding them down my thighs, dropping them on the floor. I couldn't stop him, because he'd pushed me back onto my elbows, and the bar wasn't wide enough for me to try and push myself back up.

He snorted when he saw his boxers under the sweatpants. "Someone's got very light fingers," he commented, sliding those down too.

He pulled me to the edge of the bar, pushing my legs up over his shoulders, and then he used his fingers to part my pussy lips, breathing warm air onto me. I gasped, and tried to move, but nearly fell from the bar.

He smirked. "I told you to fucking stay, didn't I? I'm giving you your reward, dammit."

He trailed a finger through my wetness, and lifted it to show me.

"See? You're so fucking turned on right now. Is it from stabbing him, or knowing I'm about to tongue-fuck you?" I blinked at him, sucking in a shaky breath.

Instead of answering his question, I just said.

"Let me go."

He snorted again, lowering his mouth to me, his tongue flicking over my clit, before he began to slide it back and forth, making me flinch, and nearly fall from the bar again.

"Stop!" I gasped, and I realised, with a jolt of surprise, that I spoke the word only because I was afraid of falling from the bar. Not because I wanted him to stop going down on me. I'd officially lost my mind.

"Knew I'd find you two bastards getting it on without me," Sammy commented lightly, stepping past his brother, as his lips closed over my clit, and sucked lightly, wrenching a tormented squeak from me.

He grabbed his drink, and drained the glass, before he poured another. He moved around the other side of the bar, so he could get closer to me, and then he cupped the back of my head, and pulled me into a whiskey flavoured kiss, his tongue dipping into my mouth, as his brother's tongue dipped inside me, followed by two fingers. I gasped, and moaned, and Sammy trapped every sound with his kiss.

Sammy's hands, and then his mouth, started teasing at my nipples, with my t-shirt pushed up to my neck, and I felt his teeth pinching at them, while Seb's assault down below ramped up another notch.

His fingers were plunging hard and deep, and his lips joined his tongue, sucking at my clit, and I screamed as my orgasm rushed through me, and my arms gave out. I almost toppled from the bar, but Sammy had blocked my fall with his body, as he continued to suck at my nipples. Seb was laughing as he pulled back from tonguing me, and then a shout from the other room distracted both of them.

"Fuck," Sammy blurted, nodding at Seb to go check, while he helped me down from the bar, and back into my clothes. He didn't follow his brother, instead grabbing our two drinks, and leading me to the leather sofa, making me sit close to him.

"Did I kill him?" I asked now, because once my orgasm had released its hold on me, my first conscious thought had been about the man I'd stabbed.

Sammy shrugged. "I'm guessing the shout from Tyler was because he's bleeding out, which probably means the knife hit an artery. If they can stop the bleeding straight away, he may not die."

I gasped, hiding my face in my hands.

"I can't believe I did that. Did I really just kill someone?"

He shrugged, sitting back, and pulling me with him, so his arm was looped around my shoulders.

"Don't sweat it, love. It was your first. Next time, maybe go for the arms, or even the stomach. Avoid the big arteries, and they'll usually live. Of course, you can slash them in the face too. Leaves them with a nice reminder of their failure to honour their contract. It's also a nice warning to others not to fuck with us."

I pulled my hands away to glare at him.

"There are so many things wrong with what you just said. Your contracts are practically impossible for anyone to survive."

He shrugged again. "Not my problem. People need money, and if they're dumb enough to come to us, they know they're signing a deal with the devil. Honestly, I prefer to take their property. We can usually make much more from using or selling that anyway. Plus, of course, it's fun fucking them up too. Keeps it from getting boring."

I tried to move away from him.

"You're despicable. You're monsters. *Murderers*."

CHAPTER SIXTY-FOUR
SAMMY

I shot her a grin, as my arm tightened around her, and I grabbed her chin.

"You're one now too, love. Did you really think we couldn't see the real you? Hiding inside the little good girl shell. Doesn't it feel better to let that out, and just be you?"

She fell silent. "You're wrong. That's not who I am."

I pulled her closer, still keeping a tight grip on her chin.

"How did it feel, love? When you sliced into his skin with that knife? It felt good, right? Made you feel powerful. You were in charge. He was at your mercy. Not that you showed much. I was so proud of you, Cass. We both were."

She bit her lip, which had been trembling when I spoke.

"I'm... I didn't mean to do that. He hurt his daughter. He was a bad person." *Ah...*

"Yeah... about that... actually he's a great dad. Set her up in her business, very protective of her," I admitted, somewhat sheepishly.

She frowned, trying to pull away from my tight grip on her face.

"What?! Sammy, you're hurting me." I released her chin, taking her hand instead, lifting it to my lips. I kissed each of her fingers, sucking her index finger, while she sucked in a breath.

"Wait. You're distracting me." *She's a smart cookie.*

SEB

FUCK, SHE'D DONE A number on the poor bastard. An accidentally well-placed knife had caught his femoral artery, and once Tyler removed it, blood just started gushing out. We fought to stop the flow, tried to keep him alive, but... well, you know how it goes, he didn't make it.

I helped Tyler move the body onto plastic, and into the boot of the car, and then he called in some help to clean the kitchen up. *It was a fucking disaster*. Blood everywhere. I took a pic on my phone, because I could taunt Cass with that later, if she fell out of line at some point. I headed back to join my brother and Cass.

Truth be told, I was in awe of her. She had a long way to go, but I was enjoying each step along the path to our world, even though we had to forcibly push her down each one. She'd be one of us in no time. I just hoped she wouldn't stop saying 'no' and 'stop', when I fucked her. It was hot as hell.

I stood and watched her with Sammy, not announcing my presence, because they were having some deep and meaningful chat. She seemed to be protesting her dark side. *She could try*. I snorted, and they both looked at me.

Cassidy looked horrified, her already pale skin growing even paler, and that reminded me that I was probably covered in blood. I glanced down. Yep. *Soaked in it*. I looked at my hands, and saw that they were covered in dried blood too.

Sammy raised an eyebrow, and I shook my head at him.

"Bugger... guess we'll send his wife a copy of the contract then. She'll have to take it on. Give her twenty-four hours or so, just so she knows he's dead first," he said quietly.

Cassidy burst into tears. "Oh god, oh god. I killed him. I'm evil." Sammy hugged her against him, and I decided to approach. Blood-covered or not, I couldn't stay away.

I didn't sit down, because I actually quite liked that sofa, but I did grab one of her hands, and stuck it down my pants. She gasped, and tried to pull away, but I tightened my grip, because her touch made my cock twitch, and I wanted more.

"Listen, love, *I just watched a man die.* It was very upsetting. I could do with some comfort." She glanced up at me, her face tear-stained, and gorgeous.

"I killed him!" She gasped, and I nodded.

"Yeah, you did. It was so fucking sexy, love. So how about that comfort?"

She tried to pull her hand away, and I stopped her again.

"The only way I'm letting your hand go, is if you replace it with your lips, love." She blinked up at me, more tears appearing.

"No."

I glanced at Sammy, and nodded. "Yeah, you're right. Time for you to suck my cock." I pushed my pants down, allowing her to remove her hand, because I didn't need it right now.

Sammy pushed Cass forward in her seat.

"Go on, love. You don't want him traumatised after you killed that guy in front of him, do you?" She frowned, chewing her lip.

"I... um... no... I guess not..." I grabbed her hair and leaned down to kiss her, my tongue plunging into her mouth. She only paused for the briefest second, before she started to return it. *Excellent.*

I pulled back, and guided her face to my groin.

"Come on, love. Only you can make me feel better right now." Her hands grabbed my thighs, and she resisted for a few seconds.

"Cass," Sammy warned, and she sighed, running her tongue over her lips.

"I'm going to need a stiff drink after this," she said quietly, while we both snorted.

And then she lowered her face, her mouth enveloping my hard cock, and I groaned with relief.

"Oh god, yeah... Suck me, love." She started to slide her mouth along my cock, and her hand wrapped around the base.

It felt so fucking good, so I let her have control for the moment, enjoying each glide of her lips, the swirling of her tongue, but then I had to be the bastard I am. Cupping the back of her head, I started forcing her head down, making her take me deeper, wanting to hear her gag, and choke on me.

Her hands on my thighs started to push harder, once I filled her mouth, and held her down, blocking her throat for a few moments, before I let her take a breath. She pulled away from me.

"You're as much of a bastard as he is." She nodded at Sammy, and I shrugged.

"We're not done yet, love."

She took a long breath, and then I started jamming her down on my cock again, making sure to choke her with it, watching her eyes stream with tears, and enjoying her desperate gasps for breath, when I eased up.

Sammy groaned, and I could see he was desperate to join in, so I pulled free, and stood her up, shoving those damn clothes back down, and waiting for him to move. Once he'd taken her seat, I helped him guide her down, so he was seated deep inside her.

Her eyes widened, and she tried to move away, but he latched his arms around her, and held her, while I pulled her head back down to my cock. Once the angle was right, he could thrust up inside her, while I kept filling her mouth.

CHAPTER SIXTY-FIVE
LENORE

That Italian guy, who'd walked into my life right when I thought all was lost, and insisted on staying when I tried to give up... he might just be heaven sent. He'd stayed with me for as long as they'd allowed him to, after I'd finally woken up, but then they kicked him out.

Before he left, he insisted on programming his number into my phone, leaving me with strict instructions to call him if I needed anything. Even just to talk. *Marco.* There was something about him that drew me in. He didn't waste words, making his point concisely when he spoke, and saying a lot more with his facial expressions, and the way he held my hand.

Once the doctors had finished checking me over, and talked a lot about my mental state, because who tries to kill themselves? Only a crazy person, as far as they're concerned. Honestly, it's not an easy decision for anyone. It takes a lot to push a person there.

I was pushed to that limit, but of course, I couldn't explain that to them. How could I tell them that I'd murdered my best friend of ten years, because he'd started stalking me, and tried to rape me? They'd lock me up for sure.

And I had no idea where his body was. Marco had called an ambulance for me, when he found me in the shower. There had been no mention of a body in the kitchen when they came. No sign of a murder that they had spotted, otherwise there would be police, and I'd probably be cuffed to the bed, branded a murderer.

I was advised that I had to have mandatory counselling, and they talked at me about that, but I really didn't absorb any of it. I didn't know what the hell I was supposed to do with the rest of my life. How could I go back to any of it? I'd seen things, and done things, that I could never tell anyone about. And how do you spend time around anyone else, when you can't speak about the most significant moments of your life. *The horrors.*

When the doctor finally left me alone, I had a moment or two to myself, and then Marco peered around the door. He came back!

"Okay to come in, or do you want some time alone?" He asked, shooting me a small grin. I waved him in, because being alone didn't appeal to me right now, particularly if I could spend time with him. It felt strange to be this dependent on anyone, let alone a man, let alone a man I'd literally only just met, but I didn't want him away from me.

"They looking after you okay?" He asked, because I'd stayed silent. I nodded.

"They think I'm nuts, but I think some counselling is the most they'll insist on."

He shrugged, sitting down beside me, and reaching for my hand. I liked the fact that he kept doing that.

"I know it must be hard, not being able to tell anyone. And there isn't a trace of what happened left at your place."

I frowned at him. "How?"

He smirked, raising his shoulders slightly.

"Clean-up team did a good job. He's gone, and your place is immaculate. So the only thing you need to worry about is you. And getting better. I'd like to help if you'll let me."

I glanced at the water glass, and he refilled it from the jug, and passed it to me, standing beside me to take it away when I was done.

"Why?" I asked him finally. He stared at the glass in his hand.

"Seeing what he tried to do... I was so afraid that I wouldn't be able to reach him in time to stop him. I didn't want him to hurt you. I don't want to freak you out, but seeing you take him out the way you did... I guess it made me proud, even though I didn't know you. I want to."

I watched him set the glass aside, keeping his eyes away from mine, as if it hurt him to say that much, or even just made him feel vulnerable.

"I'd like that," I finally said, because it was true. He sat down, his smile lighting up his handsome face.

"And, you know... we can always use people like you... enforcing for the brothers."

I laughed. "Really? I can't imagine working for people like them."

He checked his phone, and pushed it back into his pocket again.

"They're not so bad. As long as you don't owe them money. Then they're complete assholes."

I actually giggled. "What's the pay like?" What the hell was I saying?

He snorted. "Bloody good. If you don't mind getting your hands dirty, now and then."

He reached for my hand again, so I let him take it, enjoying his warm skin against mine. Could I trust a man again? Maybe...

"Thank you." I squeezed his hand. "For saving me. For helping me. I know it's above and beyond what you were sent to do, but I'm very grateful."

He actually blushed. Just a little. *It was adorable.*

"I didn't want to have to touch you, when you couldn't agree to it, but you were bleeding out."

I nodded. "I understand. And I'm thanking you for that. For taking the decision out of my hands. Now, tell me more about this enforcer work..."

CASSIDY

I DON'T KNOW HOW the hell this happened. One minute he's bitching about how sad he feels for the dead guy, like somehow I should be comforting him, and the next, he's pushing me onto his brother, so they're both fucking me.

I kept pushing against his thighs, trying to escape their hold, but they were just too strong. Seb suddenly came, filling my mouth with his salty release, and forced me to swallow it, while Sammy continued thrusting up into me. His hands slipped up under my t-shirt, and played with my breasts, pinching and rolling my nipples, as Seb took hold of the t-shirt I still wore, and pulled it across my throat, using it to choke off my air, as his brother kept pounding into me.

Seb kept eye contact with me, watching me closely, and allowing air now and then. It was intense. It was *very wrong*, and intense, and somehow really getting me close. How could this kind of behaviour be turning me on?

How could we be doing this, less than an hour after I accidentally killed someone? And not the first someone. I blamed myself for Harvey's death. And Lenore's attempt to die. And even for Nev, who sacrificed himself, thinking that he could save me.

Maybe I really was just like them. Maybe this was exactly where I belonged after all. I screamed as another orgasm blasted through me, and watched the smile stretch across Seb's face. Maybe this really was home.

CHAPTER SIXTY-SIX
CASSIDY

As ever, when they finished with me, they pretty much just walked away, leaving me to clean up after their actions, and wondering why the hell I let them do those things to me. I felt dirty. But oddly, I felt free. *I felt wanted.* Was that all I'd needed all along?

They might immediately distance themselves after sex, but they cared. I could see it. In the little things they did. In the things they said. In the way Sammy looked after me when I was ill. Thinking back over the time I'd been with them, I could pick out moments with each of them, where they treated me like a person, rather than an object, and I think those moments are becoming more frequent.

Sammy went for a shower, and Seb took the car somewhere. They didn't even bother to warn me to stay. They were that certain that I wouldn't run, and they were right. Where would I go? Who would I go to? Who did I have, in this world, who might have cared for more than five minutes, that I hadn't turned up at any of the usual places?

I wandered to the kitchen, going to the sink and washing my face, gargling with some water, before I grabbed a coffee, and then started rummaging through the cupboards. They were surprisingly well stocked for a house in the middle of nowhere, owned by two mobsters, who pretty much seemed to look after themselves.

I found some chocolate digestives, and sat down with a handful, dunking them in my coffee, and enjoying the melty chocolate, as I ate the softened biscuits. I really had been left to my own devices. The peace was pleasant. Almost relaxing. My body ached, and I was sore in places I didn't normally have to worry about, so it was nice. A break.

I'd been surprised to find the kitchen spotless. Not a sign of any blood, or anything, that told the story of what had happened in here. *I'd killed a man in here.* Stabbed him in the leg, and somehow, accidentally sliced through an artery. How was I to know? I wasn't used to stabbing people!

Sammy reappeared, after about twenty minutes of peace and quiet, and I cautiously watched him, as he drifted into the room, stared at me for a moment, then grabbed a coffee, and the rest of the biscuits from the counter.

"Making yourself at home, love?" He asked, shooting me a small grin. He sat on the stool right beside mine, which, even a day ago, would have felt too close. Instead, his proximity didn't bother me, and the smell of his cologne, or the products he'd used, actually seemed to ease me even further. I sighed quietly, relishing the smell of him. I'd clearly lost my mind.

"Cass?" He was staring at me.

"What?" I frowned at him, watching him put down the pack of biscuits, and swivel on his stool to face me.

"Are you okay?" He asked, and I felt the frown return.

"You've never cared about that before," I whispered, afraid that I'd make him angry, but I was confused, because they really never usually asked that sort of question.

He shrugged. "I'm always in a better mood after a good fuck, Cass."

I groaned, looking away from him, feeling my cheeks burning.

"Jesus," I muttered.

Sammy stood up, swivelling my stool to face him, stepping up close, and tilting my face up, so he could look in my eyes.

"I'm asking, Cass. Are you okay? It was quite a morning."

I blinked, chewing at my lip. "I guess."

His fingers tightened on my chin. "Cass?" It was frustrating, really. Normally they didn't give a crap how I felt, and now, when my thoughts were all over the place, and I couldn't put them into words, he wanted to know.

"I don't know, Sammy. I... I guess I'm still absorbing what's happened."

He nodded.

"That's fine. Normal, I suppose. I just... we don't dwell on stuff like what happened today, right? We move on. We get on with things. Someone died. That's tough for them. But we're alive, and we keep on doing what we do. And you'll get better at these things. You'll learn where to stab, and where to avoid."

I tried to pull away from his hold.

"I'm not planning to do anything like that again!"

He was laughing, as he leaned over me, sliding his hands through my hair, and pulling my face up to his, drawing me to my feet.

"You'll do it again, Cass. Because it pleases us, and you like to please us, don't you, baby? You like making us happy. Making us proud. It's what fills that hole inside, the one you thought you had to live with."

I squeezed my eyes shut, as tears burned at them.

"Stop, Sammy. Please." He leaned close, pressing his lips to mine in a soft, gentle kiss.

"You know I'm right, Cass. You're one of us. You always were. You just needed a chance to let that side of you out. And with us, you'll have plenty of chances to let out your inner monster. And we'll stand proudly by, and watch, as you carve up this world, and leave a trail of blood... and then we'll throw you down, and fuck you in it."

"How can you be so gentle, and yet say something so barbaric, and evil?" I whispered, wondering why his words weren't terrifying me, sickening me.

His hands tightened in my hair, and his next kiss was more brutal, more possessive. His tongue thrust against mine, and I felt myself responding, pressing closer, holding on to him. It wasn't like it had been before. I'd been afraid, and resistant with them before, but now that I was learning about them, I was starting to realise that their forcefulness, and their brutality, were just a part of them. A necessary evil. So they liked to push me, and hurt me, and thought the word 'no' meant 'yes'... but did that make them bad people? We all have our quirks. We all have our personality traits, good and bad.

I'd been afraid before, but they'd never really hurt me, had they? They took what they wanted, regardless of whether I was willing or not, but they always gave me pleasure with it. So many women went unsatisfied in their sex lives, when they chose men who didn't seem to understand a woman's body. I'd been with men like that too. It was part of the reason why I'd stopped trying to find someone.

And now, whether I liked it or not... I had two men in my life, and they both seemed to understand my body, and my needs, far better than I did. Would I still resist them, and fight for control of my life, and my body? *Of course.* But, like Seb liked to say so often... wasn't that part of the fun?

A phone started buzzing, and Sammy pulled back to look at me.

"Right... before I decide to fuck your brains out again, Cass, we need to take this call."

I frowned at him, as he pulled the phone from his pocket, and accepted a video call.

"Yeah, bruv. We're here." He angled the phone, so I could see Seb's face grinning at us. What was going on?

"You wanna pass me off to Cass, and we'll sort this?" He asked, and Sammy shoved the phone at me.

"Yeah, I've got stuff to do. Cass, when you're done, you bring the phone back to me immediately, understood? I'll be in the office."

I stared at him dumbly. "I have no idea where that is." He smirked, as he headed out of the room.

"You'll have to hunt me down then, won't you?"

He disappeared, and I turned back to look at Seb, on the phone screen. He shot me a glare.

"Just so we're clear, love. I'm here to do something nice for you, so don't fuck us, yeah? When we're done, you don't make any calls, or send any messages, or mess with a fucking thing on that phone, right?"

I nodded. "What's going on?"

He raised his eyebrows. "Say it, Cass. Now." I sighed.

"Yes, *whatever.* I'll be good."

He smirked. "I'll punish you for that sass later, love. Right, take a look around. What do you want?"

He turned the phone, and suddenly I was looking at my bedroom. In my house. Oh god. My house. *He was there.*

I blinked back the tears that threatened to spill from my eyes, as I looked at my old life. The possessions which once seemed to mean so much. They didn't even look like they were mine now.

"Cass? I'm waiting." Typical of them to do this without me there, and to catch me unprepared.

"Is this my only chance?" I asked him, and I heard him laugh.

"Well, *I suppose*, technically, you have until your lease runs out. Anyway, come on, love... shall we start with your sexy undies? Where do you keep those? You can give us a little fashion show later."

I found myself smiling, as I directed him around my house, for the next forty minutes or so, pointing out various things that I didn't want to leave behind, and I watched him load those remnants of my life into bags he'd brought with him.

By the time we'd finished, I was crying, and felt worn out, torn apart along with my life. The realisation that I was never going back was sinking in at last.

"Cass?" Seb's face reappeared, once he'd zipped up the bags. "What are you going to do now?" I blinked, wiping at my face with my free hand.

"Sit and mourn my lost life?" I suggested grumpily. He chuckled.

"*No.* What happens when I end this call?"

Oh. Right. I shrugged. "I'm going to do some online gambling, run up some debts, make some long-distance calls, and then probably call the police."

He growled softly into the phone.

"Cass, your mouth is going to get you into serious trouble, and I think that's exactly what you're aiming for. Maybe someone needs a smacked ass, when I get home." I gulped. I'd pushed my luck far enough.

"No. No, I'm going straight to Sammy, I promise." He laughed, and ended the call, and for a moment, I just sat there staring at the screen. At the many possibilities in my hand. I could call for help. I could call someone, and tell them where I was being kept. No, I couldn't. I didn't know where I was.

I also didn't know any numbers without my own phone. I wondered where it had even ended up in the end. The screen suddenly darkened, and I realised that I'd wasted valuable minutes sitting there, when I should have gone straight to Sammy as instructed. But then, how would he know how long I'd sat here anyway?

I got up and headed for the hallway, starting to check each room for him.

CHAPTER SIXTY-SEVEN
SAMMY

*T*HAT LITTLE MINX. I knew she'd taken time to snoop through my phone, didn't I? Because Seb pinged me the second he rang off, and three minutes had passed, and she hadn't appeared.

I debated getting up, and finding her, but then I heard a door close, and then her footsteps approached the office. I looked up as the door slowly opened, and she peeked in.

"Oh! This is an office." She glanced around as she stepped in.

"Close the door, Cass." I watched as she did so, and then raised my eyebrows.

"Oh! Sorry. Here you go." She handed me the phone. It was warm. That made sense. She'd been carrying it in her hand, but then, was it warm because she'd been using it to betray me?

"Three minutes, Cass," I said sharply, as I set the phone on the desk beside me.

She was frowning as she kept looking around, taking in the small office.

"Huh?"

I stood up, leaning on the desk until she stopped pissing around, and looked at me.

"Three minutes," I said again, and she blinked at me with confusion.

"I don't understand," she said finally, chewing that lip again.

I pointed to the chair in front of my desk. "Sit." She sat, and folded her hands into her lap nervously. I ignored the way that made my cock twitch in my pants.

"*Three minutes.* That's how long ago my brother told me that he'd finished his call with you."

She gulped. Yeah, that's what I thought. We gave her an inch, and she took a fucking mile. I walked around the desk, and sat on the edge, facing her. She looked down at her hands.

"I didn't know where to find you. That's why it took a while," she finally said, and I knew that made some sense. She didn't know where the office was in the house. But there were only three doors to check. So she'd definitely wasted some time first.

"That doesn't take three minutes, Cass. What did you do while you had my phone?" I leaned over her, and rested my hands on the arms of her chair, while she tried to hunch down lower in the seat.

"I swear, Sammy. I was upset, that's all. Seb was at my house, and he was... *it was hard*... because it was my life, and now it's abandoned."

I felt a wave of something for her. I wasn't sure what it was, but her words made sense, and she'd clearly been crying, but still. She'd been under orders to come straight here, and she didn't. Would I be me if I didn't take advantage of that situation? The opportunity to play with my girl?

"Cass, you were under strict instructions to come straight here. *I trusted you*. I trusted that you'd do as I asked, and you didn't."

She finally looked at me, her eyes brimming with those delicious tears, and I bit back the groan that rose in my throat.

"So... I'm going to give you two options, because I'm such a nice guy. Both punishments. You can choose which you go for. If you don't choose, then I will. Understand?" She heaved a sigh, sitting taller in the seat, showing me some of that beautiful defiance that we'd seen glimpses of over the last few days.

"That's not fair. I didn't break your damn rule, Sammy. If you'd told me which fucking door you were behind, I'd have been here faster."

I laughed. I didn't mean to, but her sass... *I loved it*. I sat back against the edge of my desk.

"As I was saying, Cass. Two options. Option one, I bend you over this desk, and fuck you in the ass, right now, or-"

She gasped. "No! No, I'll take the other option. Please!" I stared at her, my smile slowly widening.

"Wow, Cass... that was brave. Choosing the other option, without even knowing what it is? I mean... it could be anything. It could be worse than the first option, which, by the way, is my preference."

She was shaking her head desperately.

"NO! Please. I'll do whatever the other thing is."

I smirked, because option one was still going to happen, and soon, but I had to finish up here before I could play.

"Fine. Option two is to go and clean up that fucking mess in your room. You have half an hour, and if it isn't fucking spotless, I'm going for option one anyway."

She frowned at me. "But-"

"Exactly. *Your butt*. Now get on with it. The clock is already ticking, love." I walked back around to sit in front of my laptop, and watched her run from the room, cursing me under her breath.

SEB

I DON'T KNOW HOW one woman has so much shit that she desperately needs to keep. Most of it was completely pointless. Like her little lacy panties. I mean, don't get me wrong, I'll take great pleasure in destroying every last fucking pair, when I fuck her, but yeah... they're pointless. She doesn't need them.

I dragged the bags up to her room, and shoved the door open. I was surprised to find her on her hands and knees, gathering up scraps of pillow stuffing, and other crap from my little redecorating session, and pushing them into the wastebin. She shot me a glare, while I fought the urge to fuck her while she was down there.

"Well, it's about fucking time, love," I said finally, dumping the first couple of black holdalls just inside the door.

She rose up on her knees, her hands on her hips.

"This is your fucking mess, you know."

I love that mouth of hers. I pointed to the first couple of bags of her shit.

"You're welcome, Cass."

I went back to the car for the other three fucking bags of her crap. Why I was the one lugging her shit around, I had no idea, but Sammy was doing the books, so it was up to me to fetch and carry for our fucking pet.

By the time I reached her room with the bags, she was already rummaging through the first two.

I dumped these bags further into the room, which looked almost as tidy as it had been before.

"That's the lot," I said, as I turned to leave.

"Seb?" I stopped, and Cass actually reached out and grabbed my arm, turning me around.

"What's up, love?" She'd never willingly touched me before, and I actually quite liked it.

"Thank you. For all of this. I... I appreciate it." She offered me a smile, and I tilted my head, wondering why that felt so good.

"Well... you know... you need some of this shit, I guess." I glanced at the bags, wondering where the hell she'd put it all.

"It means a lot to me, Seb. It almost makes me want to hug you." I quirked a brow at her.

"I don't do hugs, love. But you can give me a thank you kiss. I like those."

She groaned. "I just wanted to say thanks."

I took hold of her arm, before she could back away.

"Yes, love. And I'm accepting your thanks." I tugged her against me, and cupped the back of her head, as I brought her lips to mine, and kissed her. I started soft, so she'd think that's all it would be... and then I crushed her against me, as I took advantage of that little involuntary gasp, and stroked her tongue with mine. *Fuck me.* This was never going to get old.

When I released her, she staggered back a few steps, her fingers over her lips.

"I..."

"Yeah, baby, I know. I'll fuck you later. I'm starving right now." I headed out of the room, stopping only when she called me again.

"What now?"

She was back down by her bags again.

"Where should I put all of this stuff? I don't have furniture!"

I leaned back into her room, and shot her a sly grin.

"I guess you'll have to earn some fucking furniture then, love. After dinner. I have an idea."

She looked away, her cheeks pink.

"Actually, you know what, I can just keep it in these bags for now."

"Like hell. Tonight you're going to earn some furniture. *But you'll have to do something special.*"

CASSIDY

WHY DID THAT COMMENT fill me with such dread? It bugged me all the way through dinner, which was a yummy lasagne Sammy reheated for us.

It got worse, when I was ushered into that room with the bar, and handed a glass of that whiskey, or whatever the hell it was, and led to the sofa, to sit down, sandwiched between the two brothers. I felt so tiny and insignificant, trapped between the two of them this way.

Their broad shoulders pretty much penned me in, their firm thighs wedged against mine. It was too much. I tried to stand up, but they both stopped me.

"Where are you trying to sneak off to, Cass?" Sammy asked, pulling me back down to the seat. I could feel panic building inside. I didn't know what they were planning, and the longer I had to wait to find out, the more terrified I felt.

"Cass? Why do you look like you're about to bolt, love?" Seb asked, smirking at Sammy.

I reached for my drink, my hand trembling as I picked it up.

"You know you're both freaking me out, so stop playing innocent," I snapped, draining the glass of its contents, and then gasping because, that shit is strong.

They were laughing. "You think getting drunk will get you a reprieve, Cass?" Sammy asked, taking the glass away, and setting it aside.

"I'm... I don't want this," I said, pushing Sammy away from me. Seb snorted.

"Yeah, I think that's enough foreplay, love. Get your clothes off." I shot him a glare.

"*Go fuck yourself.*" He grinned at me, and I knew I was in trouble. The next moment, I was thrown over his shoulder, and he marched out of the room, while I struggled, and swore at him.

When we reached his room, he dropped me onto the bed, and pulled his t-shirt off.

"I said, get naked, Cass. *Now.*" I looked over at the door, planning to bolt, but Sammy stood there, arms folded, watching us.

"Please let me out of here. I'll just go to sleep. I won't be any trouble. I'll help in the office, like you said." I would say literally anything right now to escape. I had a feeling that I knew exactly what they were planning, and I wasn't ready. I didn't think I'd ever be ready.

Sammy stepped into the room, and closed the door.

"Cass, you're still wearing clothes. You have twenty seconds, before I forcibly remove them." He lifted his own t-shirt off, and tossed it aside, baring his disturbingly attractive body to me. It reminded me of his strength, and that I was too weak to fight either of them.

"Please. I don't want you to hurt me," I begged. They exchanged a look, then Seb crouched down in front of me.

"Cass, love. Doing as you're told is the best way to make sure you don't get hurt. Okay? Don't think. Just do as we say. I promise, it'll be worth it. Now, let me help you out of those clothes. Trust me." He was being way too nice. It pretty much ensured that I absolutely couldn't trust him at all.

"I can't," I whispered, but I let him lift my t-shirt off, and then stood up, when he directed me, so he could remove the sweatpants I wore, as well as the boxers I'd made sure to wear again.

When I stood before them both, naked once more, I wrapped my arms around myself, feeling more vulnerable than ever, feeling their eyes on me, creeping over my bare skin. Gooseflesh travelled over me, at the intensity of their focus on me, and the knowledge that I wouldn't get out of this room untouched.

"Cass? Remember, this can be good for you too. You don't have to be all tense, and nervous, and pretending you don't want us. Just let us show you how good it can be." Seb didn't waste any time, his lips hitting mine a mere second later, as he drew me against him, and plundered my mouth.

I resisted for a few seconds, more out of surprise than anything else, and then I let myself enjoy it, just for a moment, kissing him back. I'd closed my eyes, so I didn't see Sammy approach, but I could feel his hands sliding over my shoulders, followed by his lips, which trailed hot kisses, and nipped at my shoulders and neck.

They were both pressed tight against me, and I could feel how aroused they both were. Panic welled inside me again, and I pushed at Seb's chest, trying to escape this trapped feeling that kept trying to overwhelm me.

"Shhh Cass, relax..." Seb whispered, offering one last kiss, before he pulled my hands from his chest, and turned me into Sammy's waiting arms. Sammy took up where he left off, his kiss weakening my knees as it often did.

Seb ran his warm hands over my shoulders, and back, before easing them down to my ass, where he palmed my butt cheeks, and groaned. He started kissing his way down my spine, making me squirm, as those chills he always caused raced down my spine, chasing his lips.

He was suddenly crouching behind me, and his hands grasped my ass again, as he continued to kiss his way across one cheek, and then the other. Then I felt his teeth, biting down on the fleshy part of my ass, and I yelped, pulling away from Sammy, just as he started to laugh.

"Fuck, Cass. I love the sounds you make."

CHAPTER SIXTY-EIGHT
SEB

I SWEAR TO GOD, if I don't get my cock in that ass pretty soon, I'm going to be too far gone to try. We were trying to ease her into it. Why? Because, as much as we enjoy the protesting, and the fear, and the tears... we want this to be good. Because it's something we plan to do often. If we scare her too much this time, she'll freak out next time.

I backed away from Cass's fucking fine ass, and removed the rest of my clothes, making my way to the bedside drawer, where I grabbed a bottle of lube, and tossed it on the bed. I wanted to fucking enjoy this, and for that, I needed to prepare her.

If we didn't do this right, there would be no way I'd be fucking her tight ass, and filling it with my cum, and that's not a fucking option tonight. I've waited long enough, and I'm an impatient bastard.

I watched Sammy, as he turned and pushed Cass down onto my bed, stripping off, before he crawled over her, and started tonguing her again. I stood and watched, stroking my cock lightly, as he took some time to pleasure her, and make sure she's gagging for it. *For us.* Anal definitely worked much better when the recipient was willing and turned on, even I knew that.

Cass squealed as his head descended between her legs, and he started to tongue-fuck her. There was something almost magical about watching him with her. Maybe it's because we look so damn similar. It's almost like watching myself with her. Like an out of body experience. It's hot as fuck.

SAMMY

HER FUCKING TASTE. I couldn't get enough of it. And she can protest all she wants, but she was fucking soaked. It's all over my face. I went back to flicking her clit with my tongue, enjoying those tense jerky movements she made when I did.

Seb was standing aside and watching us, giving me time to work her up. The hornier she was, the less she'd fight him. And although he enjoys the fight, he also wants to get his end away, so he'd prefer her receptive. Her fingers tangled in my hair, as she squirmed against my mouth, and alternated moans and sudden gasps.

I was focused entirely on driving her fucking close, but not taking her over the edge. I wanted her desperate for us, and then we'd both be inside her at last. Where she would finally realise we, and only we, belonged.

I lifted my head to watch her for a moment, seeing a troubled frown cross her face when my attentions stopped. See, this is the trouble with her. She's still fighting her own needs and desires. The second we let her think, she went right back to deciding that we're evil, and she's damaged, or wrong, for wanting us. It was fucking frustrating as hell. I'm sure most women would have broken by now.

I used my fingers to start distracting that damn mind of hers again. Seb left the room, and she watched him leave, with something like regret on her face. Huh… maybe she was closer to giving in than we'd both realised. I started to tease her clit, my touch so light that it barely grazed her, wanting to frustrate her, and torment her, and pull her entirely out of her head.

Seb returned, sitting beside her, and lifting her shoulders, guiding a glass of whiskey to her lips.

"Drink up, love. Let's relax you a bit more. You want this, you just need to stop disappearing into that fucking head, or you'll miss out on all the fun." She willingly sipped the alcohol, obviously wanting out of her head as much as we did.

I let her swallow a few mouthfuls of the drink, before I thrust my fingers deep inside her, making her throw her head back, and almost drop the glass, spilling the last of the whiskey over Seb.

"Oh nice one, bruv!" He growled, then he looked at Cass slyly. "Here, love, you spilled some. Come lick it up." Her eyes fixed on him, and she took a shaky breath.

"Where... uh... where did it spill?"

He pointed at his lap, and I saw the conflict in her face.

"Sammy made me spill it. Let him lick it up."

I threw my head back laughing.

"Yeah, that's not our thing, love. Get on with it."

Seb nodded. "Yeah... my brother's mouth is going nowhere near my junk."

She sat up, blinking fast. "I don't want to do it."

He shrugged. "Wasn't a choice, Cass." He grabbed the back of her head, and pushed her face toward his cock. She shuddered, and *then she actually started to lick him.*

Fuck... I felt my own cock jerk in response. This little vixen just kept surprising us.

SEB

JESUS... IF SHE KEEPS doing that, I'm going to end up blowing my load in her face. Her tongue lapped at my cock, and when I pushed her, she sucked it deep into her mouth.

"Fuckkkk..." I groaned, and then Sammy must have started finger fucking her again, because her head suddenly came back up again, and she let out a low moan. I tossed the empty glass tumbler onto the carpet, hearing it land with a dull thud, then I took her face in my hands, and leaned close.

"Fuck me, Cass. I can't wait to hear what sounds you make, when I slide my cock deep into your ass. I think it's going to fucking destroy me."

Her eyes widened, and some of her senses seemed to return to her, as she pulled her face back.

"NO. I don't want that."

I smirked at Sammy. "Yes, you do, love. You just think you have to keep saying no. You ever even had a cock up there before?"

Her cheeks coloured a dark red. One of the best things about that pale fucking skin, was how we could see every dirty thought, or emotion, painted across her cheeks. She wanted us. I cupped her face, running a thumb over her lips, thankful that Sammy had stopped teasing her for a moment.

"Cass... I'm waiting for an answer. Tell me no other man has been there before." Instead of answering, she moved, and sucked my thumb into her mouth. Fucking hell! *What was she playing at?*

"I think she's avoiding answering you, bruv," Sammy said, laughing as he lowered his face to her pussy again. She gasped, and released my thumb.

"Cass! *I want to know right now.*" I gripped the back of her neck, and glared at her.

"N... No. I wouldn't let anyone... I don't want that," she whimpered, gasping and arching in my hold, as Sammy did something she really seemed to like.

"Don't let her come," I snapped at him, as I stood back up, and nodded at him. Sammy crawled back up her body, and started kissing her again.

CHAPTER SIXTY-NINE... DUDE

CASSIDY

IT WAS OVERWHELMING, AND terrifying. They were clearly planning to both be inside me at the same time, and Seb was going to do what he'd threatened several times. It was going to hurt. I knew it would, but I also knew that they would do it anyway.

I appreciated the fact that they'd actually been trying to relax me first, driving me into a heightened state of arousal, when they'd never hinted at any concern for my wellbeing before. Maybe they weren't so bad after all. Maybe I'd been misjudging them this whole time.

Sammy kissed me, pinning me down onto the bed, and then he rolled, bringing me with him, so I lay on top of him, his cock trapped between our stomachs, pressing deliciously against my clit. I stared into his eyes for a moment, my breathing speeding up again, because I knew they were really going to do this. They weren't going to stop. Even if I begged them to. He quirked his eyebrows at me.

"You gonna sit on my cock, or do I have to put you there, Cass?" His words actually made me giggle. *What's wrong with me that I can giggle right now?*

He was frowning. "You have ten seconds, love, or I'm taking over." I took a deep breath. I could do this. I pushed myself up, moving my legs, until I straddled his thighs, and then I looked at him again, suddenly feeling shy.

"You want a smacked ass, to go with the hard cocks we're about to fuck you with?" His words did things they shouldn't have. I felt my pussy clench, and my cheeks burned with embarrassment, and something more. *Arousal.* I closed my eyes. Was this a mistake?

A hand gripped the back of my neck and forced me forward, until my face pressed against Sammy's chest, and then I felt the sharp, biting sting of a hand across my ass. I yelped, and tried to sit up, but Sammy's arms wrapped tight around me, and my protests were ignored, as usual.

Seb didn't hold back, each slap against my skin sharp, and painful. I kept struggling against Sammy's hold, and soaked his chest with tears, as he rained down blow after blow, against my poor stinging butt cheeks.

"STOP please!" I screamed, sobbing harder, as I stopped struggling, and sagged in Sammy's arms. Seb placed his warm hands over my stinging cheeks, and I gasped as the burning intensified. Then I felt his lips, as he kissed my lower back, just above my ass. Then his lips came down on my hot, burning skin, and his fingers slipped inside me.

How the pain of that spanking suddenly became something beautiful, and delicious, as his attentions turned to caresses and kisses, I had no idea, but suddenly I was squirming in their hold again.

Seb's fingers stopped sliding in and out of me, and instead trailed my moisture over my other hole. The one I was so afraid of them using. I tensed for a brief moment, before his fingers plunged back inside me again, thrusting in again, soaking them in my moisture once more.

Sammy relaxed his hold on me, lifting my chin to look at me. His groan, at my tear-stained face, also sounded beautiful to me. I was starting to feel strange. Woozy. Out of my body, like I was floating on a pleasure cloud.

"Look at you, baby... so fucking gorgeous." Sammy sat me up, helping me guide myself down onto his hard cock, hissing with pleasure as he felt me take him deep inside me. Once he'd filled me with his cock, he pulled me down over him, so he could kiss me and, more importantly for him, so he could kiss my cheeks, and taste my salty tears. It didn't seem to bother me as much anymore.

Seb ran his hands over my stinging butt cheeks again, and the heat from his palms felt burning hot against them. I wriggled to escape his touch, and felt Sammy flinch beneath me, as he let out a surprised groan.

"Jesus, Cass... what are you doing to me?" He pulled my lips to his again, and started to kiss me, but he was gentle, teasing, sensual. I lost myself in the pleasure of his kiss, and his attention, so when I felt Seb's finger suddenly push at my asshole, it didn't feel as awful as I'd expected, although it made me jump.

He shushed me, and started to slide his finger in and out, just a little way, while Sammy intensified our kiss, distracting me once more. Seb's finger disappeared, then returned, pushing deeper, and making me clench down on Sammy, who groaned again, pulling back from our kiss.

"Bruv, she's fucking killing me here."

Seb laughed in response, and thrust his finger faster into me.

"She's gonna need some more prep, or I'll tear her ass up, bruv. You're just gonna have to man up, and keep going."

My heart stuttered in my chest, and I pushed against Sammy, to try and stop them. Even though I'd been floating with pleasure, the fear came back, and I remembered that I should be fighting them. Shouldn't I?

"Fuck. Cass, settle down." Seb pushed me back down onto Sammy, his lips by my ear.

"You want me to turn that ass even redder, love? I think I've got a belt around here somewhere."

I shivered at the thought, shaking my head frantically.

"Then settle the fuck down, and get ready to take me in your ass."

"But... but you said..." He chuckled, and returned that finger, probing deep, while his hand cupped my throat, easing me up from Sammy's chest. Sammy's fingers immediately started to caress my breasts, focusing on my nipples, which he stroked, and pinched, and rolled, while I started to moan, and writhe on his cock.

Seb moved away from me, barking at me to stay, and let Sammy continue to tease me, and I did. I didn't want him to stop. *It was exquisite torture*. He seemed to be watching Seb's movements, which I couldn't see without looking behind me, and I didn't look. I didn't want to know, because I'd tense up, and it'd hurt more.

I'm not as innocent as they think. I might not have done this before, but I've read books. Some of the books I used to buy from Harvey were the kind you read with one hand under the blankets. In fact, quite a lot of them were. Multiple men, alien men, vampires, you name it, I've read it. The one thing I knew from reading that stuff, was that tensing up was a bad move. It'd hurt more, and I really didn't want it to hurt.

Seb's hand returned to my throat, and his lips pressed close to my ear again.

"I can't wait to get my cock in this tight ass, love." He suddenly pressed something larger against me, and I gasped, fighting the urge to pull away. "Cass, relax... it's just my fingers, don't panic."

One finger slid into me, and then eased out, and two started to press inside. It felt wide, and uncomfortable, and I let out a shaky breath. It wasn't so bad. I could take it. Sammy did this to me, and it wasn't unpleasant. Of course, I wasn't impaled on another man's cock when he did.

"Feel my fingers deep in your ass, baby? You sucked them right in, like the little slut that you are." His words were doing more to me than even Sammy's touch right now. I felt myself clenching down on Sammy again, his answering groan telling Seb what was happening.

"What's getting you off, Cass? My fingers? His cock? His fingers? My words?" I trembled, biting my lip, because no answer would make things any less intense. None of it would stop. And, although I wouldn't admit it to myself, I really didn't want it to.

"Don't you dare come yet, love. If you do, I'm still going to fuck your ass, and Sammy's going to fuck that tight pussy. *Hard.*" I felt my breathing hitch in my throat, and my hips rolled in an involuntary motion.

"Fuck, Seb. She's getting off on the dirty talk... could she be more perfect?" Sammy asked, his fingers tightening on my nipples, pinching tightly, and staying there, like clamps flattening them in their grip.

"Our little slut likes to hear what we want to do to her, eh? I have no problem telling you every depraved detail of what I want to do to your body, Cass. I won't be happy until I've fucked every one of your holes, and left you trembling, and exhausted, covered in my cum, curled up in a ball like my well-used little whore," Seb whispered, and I felt another wave of that sinful pleasure.

And then Sammy rolled his fingers, twisting my nipples, while keeping that tight pinch on them, and I couldn't hold back. I felt my orgasm blasting through me, my back arching, as a scream tore out of me. Seb's fingers were jammed tight in my ass, and Sammy's cock twitched in response to my clenching muscles.

"FUCK! Jesus, Cass... you weren't supposed to come yet," Sammy gasped, breathing in heavy breaths, as he fought his own release.

Seb was chuckling at my ear.

"Oh Cass, our naughty baby... you're going to do that again... ten times harder, because we'll both be inside you."

I let Sammy lower me to his chest, and lay my burning cheek against his warm skin, my whole body trembling in the aftermath. I felt exhausted, shattered, and they hadn't even finished with me yet.

Seb started moving his fingers in and out of my ass again, and I didn't resist, or fight, even though it felt uncomfortable. Stretching, burning... strange, but not unpleasant, not really.

Sammy had slowed down his breathing, and fisted my hair, making me look at him.

"You little minx. You didn't even try to hold back, did you?" I blinked at him, my movements sluggish, and woozy. I licked my lips, my mouth feeling dry, and also like it wasn't even mine.

"That... was me... trying..." I finally whispered croakily, my eyes focusing on his lips, as they curved into a smile. He turned his head slightly, looking at Seb.

"She's thirsty," he said quietly, and Seb groaned. His fingers disappeared, and the pressure inside me eased for a blessed moment.

A glass of water was suddenly thrust at Sammy, who took it, and then Seb settled beside us again, his fingers teasing my ass once more.

Sammy carefully took a few sips of the water, and then he grinned at me. I didn't like the wicked look on his face. Instead of offering the glass, he dipped his index finger in, soaking it, and then he lifted it.

"Suck it, Cass." *Fucker*. I opened my mouth, letting his finger slide inside, because I wanted the water. I sucked at his finger, and relished the few droplets of water that I found, but I wanted more. When he dipped two fingers into the glass and held them up, I willingly sucked them into my mouth, leaning closer to him.

Seb moved behind me, and I felt him rubbing his hard cock against my ass. *It was time*. Now or never. I felt myself trembling again, but I didn't stop sucking on Sammy's fingers.

Sammy dumped the water glass on the bedside table, and pulled me down to him, so he could kiss me again. Seb pressed his cock against my asshole, and muttered something I didn't catch, but Sammy clearly did, or had been waiting for a signal, because he stopped kissing me, looking into my eyes. He grabbed my hands, and pushed them behind me, onto my butt cheeks.

"Spread your ass for Seb, baby. You want his hard cock inside you too, don't you?" I felt a tremor of wanton desire, and bit my lip, shaking my head vehemently. He laughed.

"I know, baby. Spread those cheeks." He guided my hands, pressing them apart, so we were both spreading my ass for Seb, then he winked at me. "Don't fight him, love. Push back into him. It'll feel so good, when you're stuffed with both of our cocks."

His words made me breathe faster. He and Seb had a way of saying the most graphic things, and somehow making my body respond to their words, as if they were terms of endearment, or sweet nothings.

Seb suddenly pressed forward, and I felt a burning, stretching sensation, as the head of his cock eased into my ass.

"No!" I gasped, trying to move my hands. Sammy held them down, held me pressed open for his brother.

"Exactly, Cass. We both know that's how you say yes." Seb eased further into me, making me feel every inch of his hard flesh, as he violated that part of me that I'd never offered. He kept one hand on his cock, guiding it in, while the other was suddenly sliding over my clit. The touch made me jerk, surprise and arousal making me flex back at Seb, allowing him to slide in another thick inch.

"Oh god... it's too much..." I suddenly whimpered, feeling uncomfortably full, knowing that Seb was still pressing in, so there was more to come. He felt so big inside me, that I kept praying he'd say that was it, but then he'd press further, and with the two of them inside me, I felt thoroughly pinned, and trapped, and owned by them. It was terrifying, and amazing at the same time.

Sammy pulled my hands away from my ass, now that Seb was inching his way into me, and pressed them against his chest. My fingers curled, and my nails bit into his flesh, making him hiss with pleasure.

"That's it, baby. If you're hurting, you dig those nails in, and share the pain with me. Fuck... yeah... come here." He pulled me back down to his mouth, while Seb moved over my back, his body suddenly pressing firmly against mine.

"There you go, Cass... you have both of our hard cocks deep inside you. How does it feel?"

Sammy let me speak, his eyes burning into mine.

"Big. *Too much*. Stop, please." He grinned widely, catching the look on my face, knowing that I only half meant those words. Now that they were both inside me, it felt bearable. Nice, even.

Seb leaned close, his lips at my ear, his cock angling inside me with his movement.

"Ready to get your ass fucked, love? Look at our little slut, bruv. Filled with both of us at once, and loving every second of it." He wrapped a hand around my throat again, and moved his hips, sliding his cock back, and then smoothly filling me again. It wrenched a choked gasp from me.

"Yeah, baby. Keep sucking that cock back into your ass. See, Cass... this is what you've wanted all along. Two big hard cocks, fucking you like the whore you are."

This time Sammy moved, rocking his hips up, and then Seb moved again, and they alternated thrusts, one moving, then the other, so that I felt like I was being pulled apart inside. If I thought my orgasm before had been the biggest yet, I had a feeling it was about to be outdone.

I could feel tingles running through me, and my body seemed to burn up from the inside out, and they just kept moving, their cocks sliding back and forth, in sync with each other. They were both groaning, and making the most animalistic sounds, as they increased force and speed, slamming into me with a roughness that I'd started to crave. It wasn't right. I shouldn't enjoy it. I shouldn't want them to keep doing it.

"Stop," I whispered, hearing Seb chuckle as he suddenly altered his pace, so he thrust at the same time as Sammy. It wrenched a garbled yell from me, as they were both suddenly pounding into me at the same damn time. It felt like they were trying to crush me between them, their powerful bodies crashing together with mine, their cocks ramming deep inside me.

Seb's hand tightened on my throat, making me gasp and choke for air, making my hands tense, my nails clawing at Sammy's chest.

"Fuck!" He hissed, bucking up harder into me.

It was intensively overwhelming, every movement, every sensation, every touch, every thrust. I felt like I'd burn up, with the heat filling my body, while every damn nerve seemed to be literally sparking.

"I can't... it's too much..." I gasped out, while they both completely ignored me, and kept fucking me. Someone's fingers crashed down on my clit, and I erupted, choking out a scream against Seb's grip on my throat, and then I felt first one, then the other, reach their own climax, grinding hard into me, to force their fucking cum deep inside me.

When Seb moved his hand, I slumped, draping myself over Sammy's hard, sweat-dampened chest, which rose and fell rapidly with his breaths. My heart was racing so fast, I felt like it might just explode, and coupled with the way the room had dimmed, and the spots that filled my vision, I was pretty sure I was dying. *What a way to go*.

Seb pulled out, his retreat a burning discomfort that I instantly forgot, because it all crashed down on me in that moment. I'd allowed him to fuck me in the ass. And worse than that, I'd let them both have me at the same time, in some depraved, carnal, lust-filled session... and I'd forgotten who they were.

My captors. Mobsters. Bastards. Evil. Monsters. Psychopaths. Murderers. Like me.

CHAPTER SEVENTY

CASSIDY

I PUSHED AWAY FROM Sammy, rolling onto the bed, and curling up into a ball, despair washing over me, tears running down my face, as I tried desperately to reconcile what had just happened with who I thought I was. Or had been.

Seb had disappeared to the bathroom, but returned, stopping by the bed.

"Oh, for fuck's sake."

Sammy rolled over beside me, wrapping his arm around me, and pulling me against his body, curling me into him. His lips caressed my shoulder.

"Shhh Cass... I'm so proud of you, baby. You were fucking amazing..."

Seb sat on the other side of me, moving to lay on his side facing me, tucking his fingers under my chin. I stared at him through a wall of tears, and thought I saw a smile. Not a cruel grin, or one of those smirks, but a real smile.

"Cass, love. The only thing you should be feeling right now is sore, and fucking elated. I know that felt like fucking heaven for you, just like it did for us. Any guilt you're feeling is unacceptable, so just pack that shit in. *Right now*."

I snorted, and felt Sammy chuckling against the back of my neck. I couldn't really hear him, but I could feel his body shaking against mine.

"He's got a way with words, eh?" He whispered to me.

It was strange though, because even though I felt wrong, and nasty, and depraved, for letting them, *of all people*, do that to me... in some ways, I felt free. Wanted. *Alive*.

Seb's words, as seemingly clumsy as they'd been, had taken root, sinking into my very soul. Maybe it hadn't been so wrong, what we just did. Maybe my attempts to stop it had been so feeble, because I'd really wanted that.

And if I'd wanted that, what the hell did I keep fighting them for? Was it just for their amusement at this point? Because didn't they enjoy it, when I fought, or cried, or begged them to stop? And how long had I been doing that purely because it pleased them?

And maybe that was why I knew this would work. The three of us. For how long, I had no idea. But I was actually starting to look forward to finding out.

EPILOGUE

CASS

When I woke up the next morning, I was alone in Seb's bed. They'd both stayed right beside me all night. Slept here, one or the other wrapped around me, as we rested after our experience together. It was the first time we'd had sex and stayed in bed together like that, sleeping beside each other, instead of me being discarded, or left feeling unwanted. It felt right. Normal.

I lay there in the bed, stretched, and felt everything – the delicious aching, the soreness deep inside. They'd been inside, and all over, every inch of me. *I was completely theirs.*

I slid out of the bed, and headed to the bathroom, using the facilities, and washing my hands. I leaned on the sink, and stared at the mirror.

For the first time, the person looking back at me looked happy. Genuinely happy. Carefree. Relaxed. At peace.

I wasn't sure if I was cut out for the violent side of their business, but I'd realised something last night, while they were playing with me, and inside me, making me scream with pleasure.

I was where I was supposed to be.

I'd come to realise that being captured by them had put me on the path I'd been made for. Harvey was nothing but the catalyst. The small, pathetic blip on the radar, which put me on the right course, and sent me to the men I was meant for. They'd seen it. That first day. It had taken me way longer. I'd spent so long fighting it, *fighting them,* that I'd forgotten to stop and understand what was actually happening. Had I ever felt so wanted? Needed?

Was it love? Probably not. Could it be something long lasting? I realised that I really hoped so.

"Cass? What the fuck are you doing in there? If you're not naked when you come back out, there's going to be trouble."

I grinned at my reflection. Strangely, *trouble sounded like fun*.

Glancing at Seb's robe on the back of the door, I slipped it on and tied the belt, and then I opened the door.

THE END

Check out the rest of the series over the page!

Also by Mia Fury on Amazon/KU

The Bennett Crime World series:
1. At Their Mercy – mybook.to/AtTheirMercy
2. Show No Mercy – mybook.to/ShowNoMercy
3. Cry For Mercy – mybook.to/CryForMercy
4. Worthy Of Mercy – mybook.to/WorthyOfMercy
5. Bleed For Mercy – mybook.to/BleedForMercy
6. Bringer of Mercy – mybook.to/BringerOfMercy
7. Stripped of Mercy – mybook.to/StrippedOfMercy

Hughes Stalker Duet:
1. Norton's Obsession – mybook.to/NortonsObsession
2. Nico's Mistake – mybook.to/NicosMistake

Bennett / Hughes Summer Crossover Novella:
Sun, Sex & No Mercy – mybook.to/SunSexNoMercy

Wolves of the Wiltshire Pack:
1. Asher – mybook.to/Asher_Wolves1
2. Derek – mybook.to/Derek_Wolves2
3. Jase – mybook.to/Jase_Wolves3

New very dark standalone:
Burning Depravity – mybook.to/BurningDepravity

Acknowledgements

I'D LIKE TO SAY a huge thank you to a number of people, for helping me get this book out of my head, and into your hands!

My husband, for suffering through distracted wife syndrome, while I put all of my time and effort into creating these bad boys, and their antics. He's the best support a woman could ask for, and I love him more every day.

I'd also like to thank my amazing alpha reader, Rachelle Anne Wright, for her valued thoughts and insights during the first read through, and overall assistance in shaping this book into its final version. In addition, I want to thank Lexie Talionis for her beta reading, and helpful advice, and thoughts, along the way.

Also, and in no lesser capacity, I want to thank my wonderful ARC team, Rachelle, Alexis Mayer, and Gloria Thomas. You all helped me find the confidence to let this book out there, for the hungry eyes of dark romance readers everywhere!

To my wonderful friend, and talented cover artist, Anya Kelleye, as always your beautiful work, and your steadying hand, were a godsend during this process (and with everything I write), thank you!

I hope that everyone loves the Bennetts as much as I do!

Printed in Great Britain
by Amazon